A SURPLUS OF SIRENS

A Trove Arbitrations Novel

AMANDA CREIGLOW

Waldron Lake Books

ONE

A Theft

You probably know a wizard. Or at least you've met one—or unknowingly heard the stories about one of them in college. Someone reckless who never seems to get what they deserve and never expects to. Fun at a distance. Not so fun up close. At least, not in the long run.

The wizard in my life is late to work. Again.

This shouldn't be a surprise, since he only took the job to keep an eye on me. He spends each day making sure I don't spill the magical beans until he can figure out a way to get into my head and erase everything he thinks I shouldn't know.

But still. Where's his commitment to the bit? Also, my phone is missing, and I'm pretty sure he stole it. So there's that.

At 9:45, an increase in conversation from the other side of the office lets me know Maxwell Jones, designated wizard of the Springfield mini-mini-metropolitan area, has arrived. It takes him another twenty minutes to make his rounds of way too much small talk for a Friday morning and come over to me, donut box in hand.

"Morning, Lizzie," he says to me, oozing boyish charm and opening the box to reveal the one remaining sugary confection.

I stifle the urge to tell him yet again that *no one calls me Lizzie.* Okay, not exactly true. My coworker Angela does, and she does tend to show up exactly at the wrong time. Which is why Max mostly only calls me Lizzie when we're at work, and he knows I can't respond that way without making Angela feel awkward. Angela's annoying, but she means well. Which is more than I can say for Max at anything below a surface level.

"All you have for me is a donut?" I ask. I do take it, though. No point in being wasteful.

"Ye of little faith," Max says. "I also have a surefire reelection strategy for Sharon. Came up with it last night."

My eyes flick over to Sharon's office door involuntarily. It's hard to detect when Sharon, mayor of Springfield and my boss, is worried about anything. But if she were, it would be about reelection next year. Sharon's great at being in power, but the kind of contrived shows required to stay there don't come naturally to her.

"Real plan, or just essentially mass mind control again?" I ask Max, keeping my voice down and looking around to make sure no one is in earshot. This kind of furtive glance has become way too common of a motion for me. Max doesn't mind "cleaning up" via a quick slight-of-brain when someone gets exposed to the supernatural, but I don't like him doing it.

"Please, the last one *wasn't* mind control."

"Mmmmm," I say around a bite of donut, skepticism emanating from my pores. "Wasn't it? Anyway, would you say this one is *closer* to mind control in concept? Or further away?"

Max rolls his eyes. "You have a strange way of responding to help," he says.

"You have a strange idea of help," I shoot at him, smiling despite myself. "You're in a good mood today. Got over your slump?"

Sheer exposure over the last six months lets me notice the uncomfortable expression that flits across Max's face when a conversation touches a subject he doesn't like. As usual, he covers with a sarcastic purse of his lips and a momentary widening of his eyes.

"Slumps are for superstitious athletes. I'm fine."

"You've been weird the last couple of days," I insist, not examining too closely why I feel the need to insist that *he* knows that *I* know he's lying. "You even almost got here on time yesterday. Don't try to claim *that's* normal."

Max shrugs and gives me a half smile. "Just because I don't get here at oh-dark-thirty…"

I roll my eyes. I don't get in *that* early—just a half hour sooner than I used to, earlier than most people do. And that's partially Max's fault. He selectively erased some memories from Mr. Thompson, my neighbor across the street. And while I've seen him enough times to know he's okay in the aftermath, I don't want to tempt fate by running into him most mornings the way I would if I went to work at my usual time. I was in a bunch of the memories he lost, after all. Not all, but some.

I'm looking for a way to redirect the conversation to Max's blatant phone thievery when fate, as it so often does, intervenes on my behalf. My phone, playing the cheerful rolling marimba chords that I have set for my sister Olivia, buzzes in the pocket of Max's perfectly tailored suit.

"It's been doing that," Max says, scooping the phone up gingerly with one hand, glancing at the display, tapping the answer button, and bringing it to his ear, all in one graceful motion.

"Hey, Olivia! How's things? Wrested control of the library away from the elder librarians yet?" he says into the phone.

I wince involuntarily. One disadvantage of Max worming his way into my workplace and life is that it gave him an excuse to introduce himself to people close to me. A wizard knows my sister's name. Not ideal.

A shade of worry passes over Max's face, and my heart drops.

"Let me pass you to your sister," he says, his voice gentle. Too gentle. It's hard not to like Olivia, with her bookish patience and careful assistance. Most people do, including Max. And it's because he likes her so much that his gentleness with her now makes me worry.

I take the phone. "Olivia?" I ask, like there's a chance I could be wrong.

"Hey, Beth," she says, her words clipped and bright like a soldier in a historical war movie with too-clean uniforms and not enough blood. "I'm just checking to see if you've heard from Mom in the last couple of days."

I immediately see what worried Max. Some people shut down when they're worried, or sad, or upset. Olivia does the opposite. You can often tell her stress level by the number of phases in her plan—*if* you can get her to describe it to you, which she's usually too busy to do. Her tone now is efficient, tightly controlled. It has an army of spreadsheets and phone numbers hiding in it.

"No, I haven't heard from her since… Tuesday? I think? Yeah, Tuesday."

"Okay," comes her clipped reply. "I haven't either, and she missed our check-in this morning. It's not like her." There's a brief pause, and it's not hard for me to imagine the look on my sister's face. Her features on the other side of the line are probably stiff against the fresh assault of worry she's decided not to accept. She treats worry like the characters in *Jurassic Park* treat the T-Rex—just don't move and it can't see you.

She carries on again after the pause, crisp and clean again as though nothing has happened. Which… I guess it hasn't. "Try not to worry about it. I'll get it figured out. Just let me know if you hear from her."

There's no such thing as resisting the flow of Olivia's river.

"Okay," I agree, unsure and already starting to panic.

"Perfect," she replies. "Love you."

Her *love you* was the most vulnerable she sounded in the conversation, but she hangs up without a goodbye too quickly for it to stick.

I don't waste time reassuring myself that Mom will be fine, whatever Olivia said. I don't hide from the truth. This is my fault. This is what I get. I should have seen this coming.

Six months ago, I learned the truth about magic. It's a thing, it exists, and there are human-looking people—like the one standing in front of me with powdered sugar on the side of his lip rendering his concerned expression a little comical—for whom magic is their birthright. They can see it without the aid of enchanted glasses like the ones I have in my bag, and they can feel it. When they learn magic, it's a matter of doing what comes most naturally to them. They get helpful hints and teaching from their masters, sure. But ultimately—ducks , water, etc.

When a human tries to do a spell, we have to struggle. I have to follow the directions in my secret trove of magic knowledge that isn't supposed to exist *perfectly*, or nothing will happen. It's like learning to dance not only without a sense of rhythm, but without ever having heard music or seen anyone else do the steps you're trying to do. All I have to go by are descriptions written in languages I don't speak, by centuries-dead men who lived all their magically extended lifespans steeped in the beat of the supernatural.

My father, when he was alive, had the hubris to try anyway. It's a testament to his stubbornness that he was somewhat successful. He even made the magic amulet that now protects me from Max's efforts to get into my head and do some erasing.

My mother paid the price for his pride with half her mind. A punishment intended for him ricocheted off a neighbor and hurt her instead, stealing all the sweetness in her past and future. She now walks around as half a person. She can enjoy the present moment, sure, but anything good disappears from her memories, and when she looks at the future, she finds no hope there. It took me a long time to figure that out—how to connect across that distance. It took eight years for me to find out what that strange distance even was.

And now? Like father, like daughter. Maybe there's a mundane explanation for my mother's disappearance, but I don't buy that. A supernatural friend of mine got a letter addressed to me this morning. That's never happened before. That *shouldn't* happen. The sick, sinking feeling in the pit of my stomach starts before I have the time to put the thoughts together in order. It's too much of a coincidence. Whatever is happening to my mother, it's on me.

Someone always pays when humans try to use what doesn't belong to them. But we don't get to choose who that someone will be.

I clutch the phone as though my sister is still on the line. Max asks me what's wrong, but I ignore him.

I need to call Faisal, my boyfriend of almost seven

years. He's in the UK right now for work, and I wish he weren't. But I don't want to do that here, where the crush of well-meaning coworkers will descend if I show too much weakness. Even the bathroom isn't safe from sympathetic spies.

"I need the day," I say instead, gathering up my things. I don't look at Sharon's door, but I don't need to.

"I'll tell Sharon I need you for a special project," Max says.

Do I love that Max uses his wizardly wiles on the mayor of a small town? No. No, I do not. But I'm not going to hassle him about it right now. Juggling the demands of the supernatural life with my normal one is tricky at best.

I have a feeling my mother and I will need all the help we can get.

TWO

A Call

I gather my coat close as I make my way out of the town hall building and trundle toward the parking lot. It's the coldest September the Northeast US has had. Ever. It's the coldest September a lot of places have had, if Twitter and the news are to be believed. It's kicked off another ongoing discussion of global warming and estimated sea rise timeline calculations, which always adds a great layer of panic to everyday life.

You know, before I had an actual, urgent emergency.

I climb into my dingy, beat-up white sedan, get it started, and crank up the heat. I didn't think through how uncomfortable this would be when I started heading out here—I just knew I needed to get out of the building. But the heating system in my car leaves a lot to be desired, and also makes the car smell a little bit like syrup, which I've heard isn't a good thing.

But I don't mind much right now. The cold helps center me, helps calm me down a little. I bring out my phone, preparing my patience to deal with the out-of-date hardware doing its best to run an OS version too rich for its electron-blood.

It probably shouldn't be a surprise that post-Max-kidnapping, it zips right along, opening up Faisal's contact card and dialing his UK SIM number at a remarkably improved pace. Max has a weird idea of help, but weird doesn't mean bad.

"Hey there," Faisal's rich, warm voice greets me, over a background of British-tinged banter. "We're just finishing up work and heading to the pub. You want to meet us there?"

I try to smile, so that he can hear it in my voice when I play along. "Sure, I'll just leave work and jump on a plane. See you there in eight hours. Order me fish and chips."

Faisal hesitates, telling me he hears the tension I was attempting to conceal. He puts the receiver to his chest and tells the people walking with him he'll catch up. Then he pulls the phone back up and asks, "What's wrong?"

"Mom's missing," I blurt out faster than I mean to.

"Says who?"

"Olivia. Mom missed their scheduled conversation, and no one has heard from her."

"Okay," Faisal says. I know without seeing that he's nodding his head, thinking things through. "If Olivia's on it, I'm sure she's calling all the right people. And you know your mom's memory issues. Chances are she's fine, and she just forgot about the meeting. If we have to worry about anything, it should be that Olivia will use it as an excuse to get your mom to move back up here, and she'll make us help."

I know Faisal can tell how worried I am, because he's saying things he'd never say to try to make me laugh. Faisal wouldn't complain about helping my mom move. Faisal would offer our help and then fend off my mock-complaints by promising me the customary pizza and beer my mom wouldn't remember to buy.

I've been thinking a lot about lying lately. I've been very careful during the last six months to never technically lie to Faisal. I just don't tell him the truth. I just don't say things like "Yeah, but I've been arbitrating supernatural conflicts, and now a requesting party apparently knows my name, so I think they've kidnapped my mother to get leverage over me." I don't say things like "I know what's causing mom's memory problems, and they wouldn't account for this."

It makes me feel better. It makes me feel like I'm not lying. But the difference is academic, an imagined difference. It shouldn't make me feel better, so feeling better is probably just another lie—one I tell myself.

And that means that in moments like this, when the omission feels too big and I hate myself for allowing it, I gear up to tell him the truth. I open my mouth and search for the words to say to broach the subject. Not everything —I don't have to tell him everything. Just enough to put us over the edge where I can't get by on omissions, and it'll force some point in the future where I have to outright lie, or I have to tell the truth. If I can force a choice between a real lie and the truth, I'll be strong enough to tell him the truth.

At least, I hope I will.

My heart pounds, and I feel trapped, and small, and terrified. I slink back from the cliff I should step over like the coward I am.

"Thanks," I say to Faisal, trying to make it sound genuine, like he's reassured me.

"All right," he says, the disappointment in his voice betraying his doubt. "Tell me when you find out more."

"Have fun tonight," I say instead of a promise I can't make. "Don't worry about this. I love you."

"I love you, too." He says the words like I just told him he doesn't, and he's insisting to the contrary. Faisal's not an idiot, and I'm not a good liar—not even by omission. He just hasn't given up yet on the idea that I might voluntarily tell him the things I've been holding back—hiding in the spaces he can feel in our conversations. A recently dead dad has given me a lot of leeway and him a lot of patience. But he'll give up eventually, and it'll be worse if he has to force the issue than if I'm able to come clean to him on my own.

When I hang up the phone, I feel worse rather than better. But for a different reason, so… progress?

Times like this, it's best to take a chapter out of Olivia's book and channel my anxiety into something productive. I dig in the pocket of my coat to find a very special pen, and fish a notebook out from my laptop bag.

The pen doesn't look like anything spectacular or magic. Even through my magic glasses, it just looks like a plain fountain pen. I have a feeling it's the ink that makes it extraordinary, but I have no way of telling.

I set pen to paper, think for a moment, and start writing.

Hey Wilbur. I need to move up our meeting to discuss the letter from after work to now. And move it to the Emporium. We need Gigi.

No sooner have I written the words than Max, apparently having finished his light not-really-but-definitely-mind-control activities, opens the car door and swings his tall swimmer's-build body into the seat next to me.

"Where are we going?" he asks.

And then he shuts up as my hand moves on the paper. The way it startles me and how I've been looking away from it gives away that it's not under my control.

Bad idea. Why? The handwriting on the page is as different from mine as night and day. It's conspicuously neat and even. The round parts of each letter are perfectly smooth and regular. In short, it's not at all the handwriting one would expect a troll to have. Which Wilbur probably likes—I think he enjoys surprising people.

"Oooh, I've heard of those pens. Where did you get it?" Max asks.

"Wilbur gave it to me. He doesn't trust phones. Says it's too easy for anyone online to use them for anything they want."

Max smiles. "So it's true, then? What they say about trolls and the internet?"

I roll my eyes and turn my attention back to the paper in front of me, even though I've made the same internet troll joke.

I don't trust her, either, I write. *But we need her. All hands on deck. My mom is missing, and I think it's related.*

People like to think of trolls as living under bridges and hassling people that cross them. And while Wilbur does technically live under a bridge—he says he likes it—as time goes by, the bridges he builds and charges people to cross have gotten more metaphorical. The only side effect is that if you don't pay him for his services, you'll be cursed to find it harder to connect again to whatever he connected you to.

Most commonly, Wilbur connects people to their own emotions as a street performer and artist. He also connects members of the supernatural community to me when they need me to settle their disputes as a neutral third party. I'm the only human currently eligible to do so, a job I accidentally picked up while getting myself out of the jam my father's death put me in six months ago. It's got to be good for Wilbur, having exclusive access to connect people to the

Arbiter. I wonder how much he charges them. I've never asked.

One tool Wilbur finds useful for making connections is the internet. As a side effect of his in-depth knowledge of the internet, he's not a huge fan of phones. He knows too much about what they can be used for. Hence the magic pen and paper routine.

The pen goes back up and circles *Bad idea.*

"I agree with the troll. We shouldn't trust the statue," Max says.

I fix him with an icy glare. "You're not coming."

Max reaches out, puts his hand over mine on the pen, and draws it down to circle where I wrote *All hands on deck.*

"They hate you," I tell him, and there's that passing expression he uses to mask feeling uncomfortable. I wonder, as I always do when I'm this focused on his face, how much of Max is natural, and how much of him is a result of the beautification spell that all wizards perform on themselves early on to make themselves more likable to us regular humans. Maybe one day I'll ask him, but that day isn't today. Today, as I always do, I'll just sit here feeling insufficient, instead.

My sandy-blonde hair is only a few shades darker than his, but his always looks artfully mussed whereas the waves in mine are neither pronounced enough to look intentional, or subtle enough to behave without a lot of effort on my part—effort I never spend. My dull brown eyes suffer in comparison to his flashing green ones, always alight with intelligence, mischief, or some combination thereof. My unremarkable features have served me well enough, but they're nothing next to his striking male-model angles and proportions. He looks sharp without looking delicate—a neat trick. And it *is* a trick.

"They don't know me," he says, his eyes almost as dull as mine for once.

"They don't have to," I point out.

The pen moves in my hand.

K, Wilbur writes through me. And for someone as well-versed in communication as he is, he must know how passive aggressive that looks.

"See, it's settled," Max says. "You're the Arbiter. Arbitrate. We're taking my car, though."

I go to argue, but Max is already sliding out the door and walking down the lot toward his low-slung, electric-blue sports car that proudly announces its owner is rich enough not to need to care about having good taste.

I notice him notice a blue jay hanging around nearby on a bike rack. I notice him not tell me about it. I've noticed him not tell me about the blue jay spying on me half a dozen times over the past few months. It's not new, but it's a gut punch every time all the same. Using a bird to spy for you is a wizard trick. And if even *I* know that, Max must. But keeping secrets, even important ones, from people you act friendly toward is also a wizard trick.

I could stand firm and insist I'm driving there in my car, but I don't. His heater works, and I'm already sick of the smell of syrup.

THREE

A Summons

Normally, I wouldn't bring Max around Gigi's bookstore café any more than I would knowingly bring him along to the bridge Wilbur lives under. Supernatural creatures aren't fond of wizards, and for good reason. Gigi once told me I should ask Max why I'll never meet a fae or a god. The genocide was implied. It was unsuccessful, though. I've met a god. So has Gigi. She just didn't realize it, which I think is how gods like it.

Because gods, it appears, have the good sense to be afraid of wizards, and they keep their heads down. More sense than I have, apparently.

Not that I trust Max, exactly. Max, who ate my father's eyes in front of me. Max, who gave me up for dead twice in one day. Max, who once described how he was going to kill me, like it would be a favor. A good death, he promised me. A peaceful one.

But he didn't *want* to kill me, and he doesn't, as far as I know, want me to die. Still, if it weren't for the amulet around my neck that protects me from any direct action I would interpret as harm, he wouldn't hesitate to force me to give him the trove of magical texts my father left me. And then, with zero qualms, he would wipe all knowledge of the supernatural world from my mind and give me the "gift" of a normal human life. That would mean re-extending the protection of the treaty between wizards and the supernatural community back over me, so I wouldn't just get pulled back in when someone approached me for an arbitration. But I'm sure he has a plan for that. At least, I would hope so. Again, I'm working on the assumption that he doesn't want me to die. Although I'm not sure how much I can trust that assumption if it comes down to a conflict between keeping me alive and getting his hands on my oh-so-valuable, oh-so-dangerous trove.

The thought bothers me when I settle on it for too long, and I try to reconcile what he wants to take from me and do to me with the friendly guy who fixes my phone—albeit without asking—and buys donuts for the office like he's trying to single-handedly keep the donut shop in business.

It helps to remember that he's got a pretty big motivator to do whatever it takes to get the trove from me. The ritual of longevity—the wizards' most valuable spell that extends their lifespan to five hundred years and stops the aging process in its tracks—is the big prize that old wizards hold over younger wizards' heads. No matter how much you learn or how powerful you are, there is nothing more valuable than more time. Based on what I've read about wizard society, if Max got his hands on my trove, he could leverage it to get someone to reveal the ritual of longevity to him. He'd get to be a full-fledged member of the wizard club, rather than just an apprentice trying to prove himself in my little backwater city.

I know what it is to want the ritual of longevity and not be sure what I'd be willing to do to get it. After all, I want it, too. The only difference is that he wants it to extend his own life and join wizard society in his own right. I want it to share with the world at large, and essentially destroy wizard society as it exists now. Tomato, tomahto. The inescapable fact is that we are each other's best chance of getting what we want, which both pulls us together and puts us at odds. Even if, like now, we don't much feel at odds.

"So you think your mom going missing is related to an arbitration?" he prompts, pulling me from my all-to-common ruminations.

"Maybe," I say. "I don't technically know. But the timing seems like too much of a coincidence."

I can see Max hold himself back from asking me more about how arbitrations normally go. That's the thing about wizards—they like finding out about things they're not supposed to know *almost* as much as they like deciding what other people are and aren't allowed to know. Since the supernatural community gained a human arbiter, he's been trying to get details about what that job entails and what I've learned doing it.

I don't tell him anything, mostly because I don't think my clients, if you can call them that, would approve of me sharing their business with a wizard. And maintaining their approval as much as possible is a great way to keep breathing.

That hasn't stopped Max from asking, though. Not until today. That break from his pattern is to spare me the frustration under the current circumstances, I know, but it still makes me feel a little more unsettled.

Driving anywhere in Springfield doesn't take very long. Our conversation and a couple more minutes of awkward silence get us to the Arts District, where the Emporium is.

On an early Friday afternoon, the place isn't busy, even as successful as it is.

There are plenty of reasons for the Emporium's success. The worn-in Art Deco aesthetic is one. The life-changingly delicious ice cream it serves is another. The charismatic nature of Gigi herself is a third. She told me once that she thought humans could sense that she tells the truth, and I think that's probably right.

Wilbur and Gigi are visible through the plate-glass storefront, each sipping beverages at a table together. Wilbur looks less friendly than he normally does, but they both look human to my eyes. All supernatural creatures do, to humans. And all magic looks like the kind of thing humans expect to see, the kind of thing that fits within our worldview. That's all thanks to a vast, far-reaching illusion that was part of the wizards' contribution to the treaty a thousand years ago—the one that regulated when supernatural creatures were allowed to kill humans, and established the current status quo. It's more impressive than anything else I've seen or heard of a wizard doing.

Anything, perhaps, except Gigi. As Max and I walk through the door, I flip down the thick-rimmed, seventies' style glasses I usually have perched on top of my head so that I can see her as she truly is. I try to do so regularly, so that I'm not lulled into thinking she's basically human. I've made mistakes when I've forgotten to account for her alien drives.

She's a woman made of living stone. When I'm close to her, like I am now, I can see that her skin is polished marble. She has diamond eyes and a smile sharper than the edge of a wizard's patience. She's the result of a spell a long-dead wizard cast long ago. He'd heard that riddle with the two gates and the two guardians, where one can only lie and one can only tell the truth. He decided to make one of his own. He remembered to make his guardians indestructible, so they couldn't be threatened into breaking the rules. He just forgot to include an off switch or a time limit. So the wizard and his gates are long gone, but Gigi remains—as does her lying sister, somewhere out there in the world. Gigi can't lie, and she can't die. She once went out of her way and endangered my life for the chance to ask a favor from the embodiment of death. I don't like to wonder what that favor was.

I flip up my glasses when she sees me, and the sparkle of her eyes and the width of her terrifying smile begin to grow. It's good for me to remind myself she isn't human. I just need to stop that reminder when she starts to scare me.

She stands, looking human to me again. The wizard's illusion blends what she is, how she wants to be seen and what I expect to see, so now I'm facing her olive skin, crimson hair, and inky black eyes. I'm only average height, so she towers over me. She's taller than Max, which I can't imagine he loves, considering how it lets her look down on him in the way she's doing now.

"Welcome," she says to Max. I try to unpack the layers there. Part threatening display, part question. Part expression of disdain, maybe?

Wilbur doesn't stand, which is good. In both his forms, human-appearing and natural troll, he towers over us, a few inches above even Gigi. Trolls are intimidating, illusion or no, even aware as I am that he no longer eats humans. *Not lately,* he told me, when I asked him that. Without my glasses, his black hair is wild, and his multicolored clothes are clean but worn and layered.

"My mom's missing," I say, pulling out a chair to sit down. Gigi puts one solid hand on my shoulder, signaling me to stop.

"Shall we go upstairs?" she asks, her eyes fixed on Max.

Max flares his eyes at her and gives her a sick, wicked smile that I hate seeing on his face, even when I put together what's causing it. "Let's," he says.

A big part of the treaty is that wizards want the supernatural community to stay secret from humanity at large. It was one of their conditions, and of course why they created the illusion. They enforce this treaty on a day-to-day basis by leaning on their reputation of past savagery and by generally being scary as all hell if you know enough. Max must maintain that, even if it's a bit of an act. I hope.

Beginning a conversation about contraband subjects in front of normal humans probably felt like a little test to Gigi, and Max's smile must look like a passing grade. She can try to intimidate him personally all she wants, but she knows better than to break rules in front of him. He could use those trespasses to get more powerful wizards to punish her.

With an elegant grace, Gigi strides toward a rounded, sweeping staircase that leads up to the second floor. It's got a sign across it that says "closed," which she removes when she reaches it. She extends one long arm out in an *after you* gesture and waits for us to pass.

I follow Max, feeling the reassuring bulk of Wilbur behind me. I haven't been upstairs at the Emporium before, and I'm not sure what I'm expecting, but I'm not surprised at what I find. There are more shelves and some locked cages with assorted artifacts behind glass or on pedestals, much like the ones that decorate the spaces between shelves downstairs. There are also some comfortable chairs and lower tables. Max and Wilbur head for a cluster of four chairs next to the industrial-looking antique windows. The glass is old enough that I can see warps and waves in the puddles of light cast on the floor.

"This is where I meet more discerning buyers, those with better-defined desires," Gigi says from closer beside me than I realized. I don't give her the satisfaction of seeing me startled at how quietly she narrowed the gap between us. "And I use it as overflow, of course, when things get too busy downstairs."

"Right," I say, my voice less forceful than I intend it to be. Then I head toward where Wilbur and Max are trying to intimidate each other with their eyes and sit down at the same time, which makes them look more ridiculous than anything.

I take the chair facing the bank of windows, settling into it as Gigi descends gracefully into hers. These chairs feel more suited to a nineties' municipal space than anything else, with wild patterning meant to camouflage stains, and thick arms that wrap around me like a wide hug. They reassure me more than I'd like to admit, even though I kind of want to ask Gigi why her decorating gusto ran out when she got to this room.

Gigi, for her part, looks about as dignified as a person can look sitting in such an inherently undignified seat. Wilbur looks wedged into his, and Max… Well, Max looks like a kid who has been called to the principal's office and is trying to look like a badass in the face of the consequences he knows are coming. But that's probably just the impression I get because I think I know him. To Gigi and Wilbur, with their existing views and knowledge of wizards, he's probably pulling the whole threatening badass thing off pretty well.

"So," Gigi says in a tone that would make it clear that we are in her domain, if her posture hadn't already gotten that across, "why, exactly, are you upending my day?"

I take a deep breath, trying to organize my thoughts without rattling myself again. I've told Max, and I've told

Wilbur, but saying it out loud as an announcement to this group feels so much bigger and more official, ringing in this cavernous room, drenched in the golden light of the afternoon.

"Wilbur got a letter for me, which I assume is calling me to an arbitration. That's very unusual—usually they just tell him they need me. At the same time, my mother has gone missing. I'm learning not to trust people who believe in coincidences. It seems like these two things are related, and if someone cares about the outcome of an arbitration enough to kidnap my mom to get leverage, then it's probably a pretty big deal. I could use some help. My amulet keeps me alive, which is great, but it does nothing to save her, and I'm in over my head."

Gigi tilts her head. "I believe coincidences happen. Are you saying you don't trust me?"

I raise an eyebrow and refuse to answer for long enough that she eventually continues.

"And you think I'd want to help you?" she asks in a light, breezy tone.

"I think you will," I say, my eyes locked onto her. "Will you?"

In the aftermath of finding magic six months ago, I came to talk to Gigi about her intentions toward me. Wilbur had revealed that she'd moved into town to be close to me, or more specifically, the trove he had reason to believe was hidden somewhere in town. She didn't give me firm answers—not really. But she essentially said that she expected for me to disrupt the balance of power in the magical world, and that she intended to be close enough to influence the fallout when I do.

So, you know, no pressure or anything.

Not that she can really say any of that with a wizard sitting mere feet from her. I see her eyes dart to Max as she recognizes that fact. Instead, she does what anyone unable to lie must inevitably become good at: She tells a portion of the truth and lets us believe that's all of it.

"You know, I think I will. I *do* get so bored. And this promises to be entertaining."

Sure, fine. Let's go with that. I make a conscious effort to loosen the muscles in my shoulders that are tighter than they should be. "Wilbur?" I prompt.

Without speaking, Wilbur retrieves a waxed-canvas envelope from somewhere within his layers and places it on the table. My name is written in a careful, elaborate script on the front. My full, actual name. Not *Arbiter* or *The Arbiter Elizabeth* or *The Unprotected Human*. Just Elizabeth Baker, clear as day.

"They won't like you bringing a wizard into it," Wilbur says in a tone that makes it clear to both me and Max that *he* doesn't like me bringing a wizard into it, either. I shrug with a forced casualness.

"If they know my name and who my mother is, they know about Max. Damage is done. Might as well use him."

I reach forward to take the envelope, my hands shaking a little. "Have you been paid?" I ask Wilbur.

"The sirens paid me," he says.

I don't put together at first why the word *sirens* shatters me. Not until Max asks a question, his voice tentative.

"Where does your mom live, Beth?"

"Florida," I breathe. "By the ocean."

Coincidences happen, my ass.

I don't feel my fingers as they fumble with the waxed-canvas envelope. The moisture protection makes more sense now, but it takes me a bit to locate the string to pull that lets me open it up.

Inside, I find a deep-green material that resembles paper, but has a different texture than I'm used to. It's not as smooth, not as well processed. Kelp, I imagine? The whole package smells like the ocean—saltwater and fish. But I'm picking up something else.

Decay. I'm picking up decay. I push that aside.

It's hard to read the writing at first, since the black ink doesn't contrast as much as it would on standard white paper. I have to squint my eyes to make it out. I read aloud, mostly to keep the three other people at the table from paying too much attention to each other. It makes me feel like a little kid reading in class, but that's a small price to pay for maintaining the peace.

Elizabeth Baker,

Your services as human arbiter are requested in an important matter. The tribunal will be held at the traditional meeting beach of the siren tribes at dawn on September 13. The Gate Guardian you have befriended knows the place.

Beneath that, there are two of what I can only assume must be signatures. They don't have printed names beneath them.

"I can't read the names on the signatures," I say.

With a flourish, Gigi stands and walks behind me. She leans over, bending from the waist with impeccable posture, towering over me and looking at the paper over my shoulder. I don't remember her being this straight and formal any of the times I've met her before. Max's presence has unsettled her more than I expected.

"Those are the names of the siren queens. One for the Atlantic tribe, and one for the Pacific tribe," Gigi says, her voice too loud in my ear, indicating which is which with one long finger.

"Shit," Max says in a loud, horrified whisper, pulling both my and Gigi's attention from the paper in front of us. His shoulders slump, and he rubs his face with his hands.

Gone is the tough-guy air he'd been trying so hard, and so successfully, to project.

"Men—so emotional," Gigi says to me casually as she raises back up, her back still ramrod straight. There's something in the way she's holding her face a little too still that makes me think Max's sudden shift in attitude has unnerved her. She addresses Max, her quiet words a coiled spring. "What is it, wizard?"

Max gets himself under control, but he doesn't quite make it back into his badass wizard persona. He looks between Gigi's patronizing stare and Wilbur's undisguised, slow-burning hatred before addressing me instead.

"One of my masters came by the other day. She wanted to make sure I had nothing to do with the Nymph of the North Wind dying."

The color can't drain from Gigi's stone face, but that's how the wizard's illusion shows me the terror of her realization. "A wind nymph is dead, and the siren tribes need an arbitration?" she says, putting pieces together in a way everyone at this table seems able to do but me.

I look at Wilbur. You don't usually have to pay him for questions, not unless it's under specific circumstances. And technically, my questioning glance isn't even a real question. He indulges me, though he doesn't take his eyes off Max. A violence hides in his tone that I've only heard there once before.

"Sirens hate wind nymphs. If a wind nymph is dead, and the siren tribes have a big enough disagreement that they need to seek arbitration between them, it seems like maybe a siren did it."

"Okay, I think I'm following. Not great, but I don't see why—"

"Wind nymphs are powerful. Extremely powerful," Gigi cuts me off as she walks back around the table and sinks down into the chair she abandoned earlier. "And they're—"

"Really fucking crazy," Max interjects, drawing an almost startled glare from Gigi.

"Not exactly individualists," she says in clipped tones. "They can't be. One wind isn't separate from another, really. They don't understand personal responsibility."

I'm beginning to catch on, but I wish I weren't.

"So if a siren murdered one of the wind nymphs, they wouldn't hold the individual responsible, they'd punish the entire tribe?"

I feel the weight of three sets of eyes on me.

"No," Gigi says. Her quiet, intense voice feels small in the cavernous room, even as ghosts of it bounce back off the metal bookshelves behind me. "They'd punish that tribe's whole ocean. They're wind. They're the sky. To them, the sirens are the waters they swim in."

"Whole ocean as in..." I say, my pulse pounding so hard in my own ears that I think I can hear it in my own voice, too.

"Atlantic or Pacific," Gigi says. "Which would you rather see boil?"

It's too big. It's too wrong. I decide small things. I settle petty arguments. I'm fine with that. I've gotten *good* at that.

"And if I don't decide? If I refuse?" The words don't feel like they're coming out of my mouth, but I know they are.

"The wind nymphs would destroy them both," Max says. There's horror in his voice and in his face. There's horror in Gigi's and Wilbur's faces, too, somewhere underneath their mutual distrust.

Hey, look at that. I found something they all agree on.

FOUR

An Old God

"I'm not taking *him* with us," Gigi says for the third and final time, her voice clipped and resolute. "I agreed to help you, and I will, but there are limits. It's understandable that I would bring *you* through the crossroads, and I could make a case for another human with a good reason. But I am *not* going to be the first person in almost eight hundred years to bring a *wizard* through the crossroads."

I don't blame her—much. The crossroads are one of the big advantages that supernatural creatures have over wizards, as far as I can tell. A pretty big advantage over normal humans as well, but they don't really think of it that way. Humans aren't a factor. We're livestock with occasional additional uses, not competition.

The crossroads are points dotting the globe that supernatural creatures can step to. Anytime, anywhere on the face of the Earth, a supernatural creature can take a step with intention and will find themselves at the closest crossroads in the direction they stepped, give or take. It's exact to an eight-sided compass, so each and every place on earth is in the catchment area for eight different crossroads.

Once they've reached the nearest crossroads, they have a choice to make. They can stop at that crossroads, meet with whoever or do whatever there, and then be able to return directly to the spot they left. Or they can continue walking the crossroads, but in so doing, they lose their original point of origin. They can travel the world in a series of steps, and they often they do, but they can only get to the closest crossroads to their intended destination. From there, they have to find more standard transportation.

Which is usually easier said than done. Humans don't tend to settle near crossroads. It's obviously not a fully intentional choice, but crossroads unnerve us, and we avoid them for reasons we can't put our fingers on. If you've ever been out hiking or exploring and came across an area that just made you feel wrong and suspicious of the trees around you, you were probably wandering somewhere near a crossroads.

Supernatural creatures tend not to settle near any crossroads, either. Plenty of things walk the crossroads, and not all of them are good. And while wizards can't *use* the crossroads, they have plotted their locations. And the eidetic memories wizards give themselves around the time they undertake their magical makeovers mean that they always have that map at their fingertips.

So crossroads tend to be in the middle of nowhere, both for the human world and for the supernatural world. Most supernatural creatures keep to their closest eight crossroads and spend time with others who share at least one of them. It's a much more efficient global transport system than air travel, but it does have its drawbacks.

Even though humans and wizards can't use a crossroads themselves, supernatural creatures can bring them along for the ride, which makes them very useful for my purposes. Usually I travel with Wilbur, since he's the one connecting me to requests for arbitration. We take his surprisingly nice car out to Springfield's nearest crossroads, park, and walk from there. Afterward, we often get burgers. Or sometimes, if I've put my foot in my mouth and said something that might have gotten me killed if I hadn't weaseled out of it, we get steak.

"Wilbur?" I ask. "Will you take Max through the crossroads? I'm sure he'll pay you."

I expect a begrudging yes, eventually. Maybe he'll posture, and maybe he'll command a high price. But Wilbur is the closest thing I've got to a real friend in the supernatural world, even if I wonder sometimes how much of that friendship is because of the payment he can command for connecting other people to me for arbitration.

"I'm not coming," he says instead.

"What?" I blurt out with an indignance that makes me feel foolish. Wilbur's face is colder than I've ever seen it. More set. His voice, though deep as ever, feels duller and less rich.

"I gave you the letter. I connected the sirens to you. I've done what I was paid to do."

He stands, and I'm struck by the sheer mass of him, too cowed by the visceral reaction to protest. My mouth opens and closes uselessly.

It's a natural instinct to think of supernatural creatures as essentially human with weird hobbies. Humans want to relate—to find commonality and build upon it. But that's a dangerous misapprehension to indulge. I'm reminded of that, now and again, when Wilbur does what he's paid for and then hangs me out to dry while I try to deal with the consequences. His drives aren't mine. He doesn't care that my mother is in danger. Does he even have a mother?

I'm always trying to force Wilbur to be something he's

not—not just to connect, but to *help*. I'm always pushing his boundaries. But as he walks to the staircase with a speed that gives away his true height, disguised as it may be to my human eyes, I can't fight for him to help me. I feel too betrayed to try fast enough to catch him. And then he's gone, and I feel unbalanced, more alone with the two people left than I felt without them.

"I can take a plane," Max says, drawing me back to the matter at hand. "I'd trust a plane more, anyway. Where are we going? Somewhere in Greece, I'm guessing. I love Greece. Beaches. Ancient history. Financial ruin and occasional unrest. All the ingredients for a memorable vacation."

Max has slid back into a familiar persona—light, friendly, and a little unpredictable. It's the Max I'm used to seeing, and I'm glad at least that I don't have to deal with him putting on his intimidating show anymore.

"Chios," Gigi says, her voice unreadable. "You won't make it before the arbitration. We'll meet you afterward in town. I'm sure you have a phone. You can text the Arbiter when you arrive, and we'll figure out if we have a use for you when you do."

Something snaps together as Gigi speaks.

"Gate guardian. Gigi. G.G.," I say.

Gigi's answering laugh could blister paint. It rings through the stacks, splintering and bouncing around the room in a way that reminds me of what her diamond eyes do to light.

"You really just got that?" she asks. "And to think the fate of the world is in your hands. It's a good thing you came to me. Wouldn't have a chance otherwise. Are you ready?"

I set aside the insult. "What, *now*? Don't we have plenty

of time before dawn tomorrow? Greece isn't that far ahead of us."

She rolls her eyes. "Maybe so, but I'm taking us now."

No, I'm not ready. Absolutely not. But I'd never be. I could try to fight Gigi on this, but I'm so far out of my depth, and my mother's life is at stake, and I've apparently already alienated Wilbur somehow. Or pushed him too hard, at least. Best to save my arguments for things that matter.

I think through what I have on me. Wilbur rarely likes to leave the supernatural community waiting, which seems unfair. Their longer lifespans give them all so much more time than I have, so why am *I* always the one inconvenienced? But at the same time, any single one of them could kill me, if they were willing to put in the time and planning to get around the protection of my amulet. So I keep a variety of objects with me at all times, in case I'm called away.

The list of things I always have on me includes my yellow leather jacket, complete with a lucky charm from a god of dubious intentions and a few enchantments worked in that, Max swore, hand on his heart, were definitely for my good. I wouldn't have let him enchant my jacket if I'd had any say, but he'd grabbed it from the back of my chair at work and taken it home with him over a weekend, the same way he'd done with my phone last night. I assume he put a tracking spell on it. Which, to be honest, I don't mind. It's a comfort to know, when Wilbur is carting me around the world, that if everything goes wrong, Max can find my body and bring it home. I don't think Wilbur would. I don't think he'd get why it's important. And today, at least, Max'll be able to catch up with us without too much trouble when he does eventually make it to Europe.

I stand, put my yellow jacket on, and lay my heavy

winter coat on the back of the nineties-leftover chair. I'll be cold for the first few steps while we're at higher latitudes, but we're heading to Chios, Greece. If there's one tiny little silver lining, it's that at least it will be warmer there.

"See you there," I say to Max. I nod to Gigi, and she picks up my hand. I keep my glasses off, but even so, her hand feels cold and firm. She raises her foot, and I prepare to step with her. My steps won't do anything the way hers will, but it makes me feel like I'm doing something.

Walking the crossroads doesn't really feel *like* anything. There's no magical tingle or jolt of energy. One moment you're in one place, and the next moment you're somewhere else. The difference in temperature, altitude, wind, the smell in the air—all of that hits you at once in a rush. It makes the journey overwhelming from a sensory point of view, but I've never been able to pinpoint anything that feels supernatural hiding in the experience.

The first step is familiar. It's an empty field. There was a casino here once, but it left without a trace after a few days. Magic, you know.

The second step is less familiar. Forest. It's a little warmer here than in Springfield, and it's holding onto the sweet scents of summer. There's a bit of pine in the air, but mostly it just smells clean. I'm used to a more artificial version of this smell in little paper pine trees hanging from rearview mirrors and in multi-wick candles in middle-class households.

Step three is a glorified sandbar, and I squint my eyes against the sudden glare of the sunlight reflected on the waves. The stench of rotting fish wraps around us, and I have barely enough time to notice a small collection of plastic along the shore of this tiny island before we leave it.

Step four is just as expansive, just as desolate. But dry,

dusty earth replaces the water, and I bake in the unob-structed heat of the sun overhead.

Step five lands us overlooking rolling hills covered in grapevines. It makes me feel like I'm on the set of a movie made for a much older woman. Either that, or the cover of a tourist brochure for a bus tour promising delightful tast-ings and evenings spent seeing ruins, all while gorgeous Italian men fawn over you.

With the last step, I'm standing in a sparse forest on the side of a hill, staring down at a sea of onion domes nestled in a valley floor.

I look to Gigi, pleading with my eyes for her to take another step. This can't be our destination. But she doesn't walk any farther. We've arrived.

"What a surprise," Gigi says. "Can't say I expected the Casino to be here."

My heart sinks.

I couldn't have been sure that the sprawling, city-sized building before me was the same essence as the one that had showed up at the crossroads near Springfield six months ago, just after my father's death. That one had been much smaller—it had only a single dome—and the styling was much more muted. There's the same set of stairs at the entrance, and the same red pennant flag by the front doors, although this time the breeze I can't feel must be blowing much stronger, because instead of flapping lazily on the post, the flag is straight out to the right. There are more colors on this one. Bands of blue and green and orange friezes are visible just below the onion domes, depicting scenes with figures doing everything from fighting to fucking to resting.

But it *feels* like the same building. I recognize it the way you recognize someone you once knew well but haven't seen in a long time after you see them walk and talk a little, the same familiar gestures and styles even if they've changed their appearance.

And then, as though I needed further confirmation, a tall, slender, Indian man walks out onto the landing in front of the grand entry doors.

He has an elegance to him that goes well beyond the clean lines of his tuxedo and the smooth, glowing complexion of his handsome face. He looks good. He looks healthy. And that's probably at least partially because of me.

You're welcome, Aloysius. So glad I could accidentally be of service.

Aloysius smiles as though he can read the thought. I'm compelled forward as much by an intense desire to talk to him building in my own chest as I am by Gigi beside me moving toward him. The loamy earth beneath us keeps our steps quiet, preventing anything from disturbing the peace of the evening.

The last time I saw the Casino, there were humans being escorted in by figures I could only see through my glasses. In the time I've thought of it since, I've decided they must have been some sort of extension of Aloysius's will, going out and pulling in humans through the crossroads to come gamble their souls in his casino. It's still too early for that, though—the sun is only just beginning to set, and it's plenty light. We've beat the rush.

He waits, not closing the distance as we walk toward him, and he doesn't speak until we're halfway up the staircase.

"How lucky to run into you, Elizabeth," he says, his accent through-and-through upper-class English. I'm pretty sure there's a lot of very intentional subtext loaded in that decision. And I'm sure it *is* a decision. He looks and

sounds the same whether I'm wearing my glasses or not—
no wizard illusions stick to him.

"What's a nice demon like you doing in a place like
this?" Gigi asks, without any trace of amusement in her
voice. She stops four steps down from the top of the staircase. I continue to the top. When I reach him, Aloysius
places a hand on my cheek fondly, and I feel very small,
and very mortal, and very warm.

Aloysius is not a demon. Aloysius is a god. And
whether or not I want to accept it, Aloysius is *my* god. He's
a god of gamblers, and I took a leap of faith accepting his
help six months ago, which without question saved my life.
In doing so, I also accepted his gold, jewel, and enamel
flower on my lapel, which links me to him and makes me
indebted to him in ways I don't fully understand—ways
I've been trying not to think about.

But what I do understand is that to him, gambling is
worship. That's what all the gambling in the Casino is
about. He doesn't take a cut. He doesn't steal any human
souls—just presides over their redistribution via games of
chance. Some humans leave with less soul than they had
when they came in, and some leave with more. It all evens
out in the end, and Aloysius feeds off their act of risking
the most valuable thing they have, disguised to them as
though they're just gambling with chips, or money, or
whatever implement makes sense to them.

But when I take a gamble, every time I go with Wilbur
to perform an arbitration and bet on my own abilities to
get out on the other side of it intact, Aloysius benefits from
that much more intentional act of worship. I think that's
what the pin is about. Maybe. I feel it more than think it.
But so much of magic is about intention. So taking
gambles and knowing that it is, in some way, an act of
worship to him, feels like it must mean more than all those

unknowing masses packed into his casino with their glazed eyes and desperate expressions.

"Did you come here on purpose?" I ask, my defiance laced with all the effectiveness of a rebellious teenager. It's embarrassing. *I'm* embarrassing.

Aloysius keeps his hand on my cheek and tilts his head to one side. "Not pleased to see me?"

"Answer my question," I say.

"Answer mine," he commands.

"I have kind of a lot going on right now, if you haven't noticed."

He holds my gaze. His eyes are deep and dark. Finally, after what feels like a longer time than it probably is, he drops his hand from my cheek.

"I hadn't," he says. "But I did sense something in the air. Chance is shifting quickly right now, more quickly than usual. You should be careful with yourself, Elizabeth."

I want to ask him what the fuck that means, and how exactly he perceives "the shifting of chance," but I think he would actually take the time to tell me. I think it would be a long conversation that would require going into the Casino, and that would make me feel more linked to him, more like I *belonged* to him. And I think that once I was in there and feeling that way, my mother's life hanging in the balance and the possible fate of the oceans would all matter less. I don't need that right now.

"I'm on an arbitration. There's…" I falter, feeling raw and transparent. "There's a lot at stake."

He nods slowly a few times, closing his eyes for a moment, and then he smiles like the sunrise. "I wish you the best of luck."

I'm not sure that did anything. I don't feel any different in a magical way, or so I think. But I feel reassured and less alone, and that's its own kind of magic. Then he turns to Gigi, finally acknowledging her.

"The closest town is up that direction." Aloysius nods his head back farther up the hill. "You should be able to rent a car from there. It will get you wherever you're going."

With that, Aloysius turns around and turns back toward his domain, only fixing me with an affectionate gaze in passing before he's gone.

When we're alone again, Gigi sighs.

"Don't humans know better than to make deals with demons? There's a song about it and everything. Violins were involved, I believe. There was even a crossroads."

I smile, trying to make the expression calm my roiling emotions from the outside in. "In the song, that was the devil," I say, walking past her toward the direction Aloysius indicated.

Following quickly, she calls after me, "Not sure I see the difference."

FIVE

A Drive

We don't speak as we climb the hill. Too much effort. But when we reach the top, we stop and take a second to catch our breaths.

Oh, okay, for *me* to catch my breath. Gigi, as she so often does, seems unbothered and possessed of perfect poise.

I look back down into the valley, at the massive complex springing up from the valley floor like a cluster of mushrooms.

"A lot bigger now, isn't it?" I ask Gigi, afraid of her response. I haven't been taking that big of gambles, have I? Is my worship somehow responsible for the bigger building? It doesn't feel proportionate.

"It's to be expected," Gigi answers. "Istanbul, Izmir, and Bursa are all in the catchment for this crossroads. The Casino is always as large as it needs to be."

That's a relief. I guess. Kind of. Knowing that Aloysius doesn't take a cut of the human souls gambled within the walls of the Casino makes me less upset about it, but it's still not something I want to enable. Not directly.

The little town at the top of the hill is sleepy and closed up for the season. It's more of a village, really, with a picturesque jumble of narrow streets and ancient stones. The light is waning as we walk around the place, searching for someone who will lend us a car.

Gigi, of course, speaks Greek. I, naturally, do not, which allows me a sort of objectivity as I observe her interactions with the people in the village.

I always forget how charming Gigi is to people who don't know better. She's warm, and funny, and instantly trustworthy. I'm so used to seeing her as I do—with the full knowledge of what lurks underneath the illusion and the things she's done to me in the past to suit her own purposes —that I forget how she is if you don't know her. All expressions of confusion or mistrust at two tourists asking for a car, when there's no way they could have gotten here without one, melt away into good will and helpfulness. We're directed to several different houses and end up drawing attention and speaking to no fewer than fourteen people, but eventually she secures us a bright-yellow hatchback, complete with a couple of blankets thrown in.

"Give him your credit card." The words in English jar me out of my ill-advised admiration.

"What?" I ask.

"He has a card reader at the café. He says he'll run it for your rental fee there."

I'm pretty sure the heads of the siren tribes, whoever they may be, have not authorized expenses. That seems a safe assumption, considering I'm not getting paid. Part of me wants to tell Gigi that, as the owner of a successful business, she has more spare cash than I do. But she's doing me a favor, and I don't want to test the boundaries of that favor too much, so I dig out my wallet.

I'm about to hand over the one I use for everyday

expenses, but I hesitate. I rarely travel; suddenly using my card in Greece seems like a great way to trigger a fraud alert. Instead, I pull out a card on a shared account that I know Faisal uses for personal expenses while he's travelling. He travels all the time—with any luck, that means the bank will be more accepting of the charge on this card.

My pulse races before I put together why this act makes me nervous. Faisal pays the bill on the account and rarely checks his statements, but there's a chance he might. There's a chance this will make him notice—will bring me to the breaking point and force me to tell the truth or lie. There's a chance handing this card over to Gigi will force me to break the careful dance my cowardly self has been engaging in these last six months.

Gigi snatches it out of my hand as I stare at it like an idiot who has never seen a credit card before. She hands it over to the waiting villager, who carries it off.

"How much am I paying for this?" I ask, trying not to think about what may or may not happen a month from now, if Faisal notices the bill is larger than it should be and investigates why. Gigi has gone back to charming what seems like half the village. She ignores me. She's clearly telling a story. I watch, letting my own worries melt away as I enjoy the villagers' reactions more than I probably would if I understood what Gigi is saying.

The man comes back, gives me my card, and gives Gigi the keys. I clamber into the car and wait for Gigi to extricate herself from the crowd with hugs and waves.

Finally, she slides into the driver's seat beside me.

"When was the last time you were in Greece?" I ask her.

She puts on a thoughtful expression as she turns the key, and the car does its best to come alive.

"Not long," she says. "The fifties, I think. Possibly the sixties."

And when was the first time you were in Greece? I want to ask, but don't. Best to save my questions and her patience for more relevant topics. I sit in silence as she maneuvers the car out onto the road and drives off into the gathering night.

Even in dimming light, the island has an impossible beauty to it. It feels ancient and alive and at peace—all at the same time. We must be driving down the east coast, because the sun is lighting the hilltops to our left rather than sinking into the ocean on our right.

Taking a long drive in rural, wooded surroundings into the oncoming night pulls me back into a memory, the same way it always does. I roll down my window, searching the air for any trace of the scent of pine, trying to strengthen the sweet memory. I think I might catch it for a second, but probably not.

Not long after Faisal and I met, we went away to a lakeside mountain cabin for a long weekend with some friends. We weren't yet dating, but we both knew we were headed that way and were carefully searching the other for hints we may be wrong, to keep from getting blindsided— that heady, terrifying Schroedinger's relationship that can only be achieved by two people young, inexperienced, and head-over-heels enough to be incapable of basic communication.

Jokes about how we were all definitely going to get murdered aside, we had all been looking forward to the weekend, but Faisal and I both had later classes than the others, so were driving up separate from the rest of them. Dusk fell as we neared the cabin, and we were driving down a pine-wrapped, twisty country road. I made some comment about whether we'd see many stars at the cabin.

I don't remember exactly what I said now. It made him laugh, though, and I shot him a glance. By way of explaining, he grabbed his iPod, plugged into the fake cassette tape in the stereo, and found a song called "Passenger Seat" by Death Cab for Cutie. He sang along to the lyrics, slipping into the comfortable, laid-back entertainer persona he still so often inhabits. The lyrics didn't all line up to the situation exactly, but enough of them did that I saw why he had laughed.

Faisal's not a good singer, but he's not a bad one either, and his voice is much lower than you'd think, looking at his somewhat spare frame. More than anything, I remember the strength of his voice and the way it filled the car, an octave below the singer in the recording.

And then there was a brief moment of terrible truth as both of us sweet, innocent babies realized that the lyrics of the song were going to swap from describing a drive to promising eternal love in the chorus. I remember blushing, expecting an awkward moment where Faisal would stop singing along. I frantically searched for something to say, blanking in the heat of the moment.

And then Faisal just leaned into the awkward moment. If anything, he sang louder. And I laughed in shared relief, seeing my laugh reflected in the smile on his wide mouth as he sang the words straight to me, with an earnestness hiding inside a joke, the way it so often does with him. Without ever saying it exactly, he pushed us out of plausible deniability territory. We didn't spend nearly as much time out on the lake that weekend as we had been planning to. We barely spent any time outside of the room we jointly claimed, to the surprise of none of our friends.

I love this memory, not least because knowing him as I do now, it's such a completely Faisal thing to do. There's a comfort in remembering, again and again, that one of the moments that made me fall for him is so representative of who he is. It makes me feel stable. It makes my life, and my life with him, feel stable.

How did I get so far from there? How do I get back there? I can't smell any pine through the open window anymore, and there's a chill in the air. I roll it back up and let myself consider my life now—mortal danger, the highest of stakes, and no one I really trust. Fantastic.

"Taking us to a hotel?" I ask Gigi as the car struggles to climb one of the many steep hills. She shakes her head.

"No. Safer to sleep in the car near the beach. We don't want to risk being late. Sirens don't really care about time, of course, but they like to find excuses to be angry. It gives them reasons to do what they do most naturally that other people will understand."

I don't ask what that is. I know a little about sirens from popular culture, and that tells me enough. I'll look up some of the translated info from the trove when we stop for the night, when reading on my phone won't risk making me carsick. There's a collection of papers that I've taken to calling *Wilhelm's Big Book of Monsters*—WBBOM—and I'm betting there's an entry for sirens in there.

We drive for an hour until the road dead ends into a little cove. It's too dark to see much, but I catch glints of moonlight on little ripples in the water, so I know it's out there. Gigi pulls us into a parking space.

"Right," she says. "Time for bed."

She gives me a smile I know is blunted significantly by the wizard's illusion and crawls into the back with dignity that shouldn't be possible. I consider scrambling back after her but think better of it. Instead, I lean back in my chair and start the process of pulling up the trove on my phone.

I mentioned to Wilbur once, in passing, that I planned to put a copy of the trove on my phone. It's perhaps the only time I've seen Wilbur sputter wordlessly. Instead, he set up some super-secure server somewhere that I access through my phone, punching in the numbers manually each time instead of saving the address. I do that now, then get out Wilbur's pen, and search the glove box of the rental car for a scrap of paper.

You? The pen moves in my hand to write, just as I get it against a Greek receipt.

It's me. I write. *Thanks.*

With that, my two-factor authentication is complete, and the trove loads up. At my urging, Wilbur set it up so that a little electronic payment goes from my newly established bitcoin wallet to his, automatically, every time the server loads. The last thing I need is to be troll-cursed into having a harder time connecting to the trove.

This whole rigmarole struck me as a bit much when Wilbur insisted on it. It feels a lot less over-the-top now that a wizard has had my phone in his possession overnight. I wait for Wilbur to write something back—anything to reassure me that we're all good and that little outburst at the Emporium was just a show for Max's benefit. But no words come, and eventually I give up waiting and turn my attention back to the task at hand.

WBBOM is in ancient German, and I need a few saved sites on the internet to translate it. I wince at the thought of how much data will cost while roaming in Europe, but I notice that my phone apparently still thinks it's in the States, connected to my usual network. *What?* Probably just a glitch. I load up a browser, head to my usual most helpful translation site, and watch as it loads blisteringly fast.

I stifle a laugh to avoid triggering a question from Gigi. *Max.* It's got to be something Max did to my phone last night. What other little upgrades did he give me?

Despite all that, Wilhelm doesn't tell me anything

useful about sirens—not anything that I didn't know already. They drown sailors, or other people close enough to the ocean to hear them sing their desires. It does seem like a very specific phrase—*sing their desires*—repeated a few times. It doesn't say anything else about music other than the word "sing," which seems like it could be significant. There are male sirens, though the queens have been in charge of the two tribes as far back as Wilhelm knows.

WBBOM also has an entry about nymphs, but it's not very detailed. They spent time with the Greek gods, when there were more gods and they weren't in hiding. They are the embodiment of nature, very connected to it, etcetera.

I start flipping through more quickly, looking at the sticky notes translating the names of the entries, all in my late father's messy handwriting. I'm searching for anything that I might come across in the next few days. Anything ocean-based, really. Anything to do with water. I'm just starting to decode an entry on "Ocean Glow" when I see something out the front window. Light gleaming on a figure out in the water.

The figure of a woman.

SIX

A Seduction

There aren't a lot of rules for the arbiter in arbitrations. The point isn't that we're supposed to be good, wise, impartial judges. The point is that we don't live long enough or know enough about the supernatural world to have biases. There's a kind of "from the mouths of babes" element at play.

But perhaps more than that, humans are disposable. Supernatural beings basically use arbitration as a way of flipping a coin to avoid armed conflict and the potential loss of precious immortal lives. And they find a coin flip with such high stakes is a lot less tense when they know that, if they don't get their way, they can always just destroy the coin in a satisfyingly brutal way after the fact to blow off some steam.

The other reason I suspect they use human arbiters, though no one has ever confirmed it for me, is because the more scheming among the supernatural community like to imagine that they'll be able to trickily influence us.

Like, say, for instance, by kidnapping my mother and holding her as leverage.

So there's no rule to stop me and a huge incentive to induce me to open the car door as quietly as I can to avoid waking Gigi, and head toward the water.

Even lit only by moonlight, the beach is beautiful. It's small pebbles rather than sand, but that only enhances the appeal. They seem all different shades of gray right now, and I can't help but wonder what they will look like when the sun rises. When the sun rises, and I have to figure out how to save the world. Because that's my thing now.

As I draw close to the edge of the water, the woman becomes clearer. She's about ten feet away from me, rising out of the water just above her navel. Her hair looks black, but that could just be because it's wet. It's hard to tell skin tone, but I think it's somewhere between Gigi's and mine. She's got the body type of a modern swimsuit model—thin but with generous hips and breasts, bare in the moonlight.

Jesus, it's a good thing I'm not really into women. Even so, I'm drawn to the perfection of her, and to the promise of her hungry gaze.

"Why don't you come for a swim?" she asks when I get close enough to hear, her voice traveling to me small and far over the water. God, it's a sweet voice. I get the feeling of hearing bells from a long distance away, straining to hear more.

"I'm good," I get out somehow, my voice cracking from disuse.

I'm an idiot. In a lot of ways, the illusion wizards created to hide supernatural beings from sight can be useful for humans. It may hide what the beings actually are, but it does give us more cues—facial expressions, body language—to their intentions than we would otherwise be able to glean from their alien faces. And the reinterpretation of magical harm into physical harm—spells into knives or bullets, as it were—lets us understand that there *is* danger without needing to understand or accept what that danger is.

But if there's one kind of creature that would appreciate looking more human than they are, and looking as they intend to, it would have to be sirens.

I slide my glasses down over my eyes, and my pulse keeps racing, but for a different reason.

Gone are her curves. She's slimmer, and her breasts are small, overshadowed by the three sets of gills beneath them that transition her skin from human to iridescent fish skin. Her heart-shaped face is more exaggerated now, with a chin that's just slightly too pointy. Her perfect, pert nose now seems lost—barely there. When she smiles, even at this distance and in this light, I can see her tiny, sharply pointed teeth. Squinting, I make out multiple rows of the needles. There must be hundreds.

That's more like it.

"You're a little early," I say, my confidence returned, filling the vacuum left by my departed attraction. "Why?"

"What a question," the voice comes. It's still a blessing to hear. It still draws me in, just as it did moments ago. "I bet you have a lot of questions I could answer. Why don't you let me answer them?"

The pull can't be strictly magic. I would consider that harm, and the amulet wouldn't let that through, the way it wouldn't let Max's mind mojo through. But I feel the pull nonetheless. I'm so caught in the glare of the strangeness of her that it takes me a second to remember what it is.

My mother. She might have my mother.

"Come here," I say. "I'll ask them."

I'll ask them, but I'm not mentioning my mother first. It might be she doesn't want to pull out the extortion card unless she thinks her tribe is losing. Or it might be the other tribe that has her. Either way, best keep it under cover for now.

"I'm not prepared for the air," the siren says. I don't trust myself to understand her facial expressions anymore, not with my glasses on, but I see her gills contract one after the other, shimmering in the moonlight. I wonder what that means.

I don't know enough about sirens to know whether needing to prepare herself for the air is a bullshit excuse or not. But I know enough about me to know I'm not going back to the car without finding out more. I take off the leather flats that were a much better fit for the day I thought I was going to have than the day I ended up having. I curse Gigi's impatience only a little when I remember I have no other clothes. I at least take off my yellow jacket and lay it beside my shoes. Does Aloysius still get the worship, I wonder, if I take a chance when I'm not wearing his charm? Is it enough that I'm close? Or maybe that I decided on my course of action when I had it on?

More questions, always more questions. But not the ones I need the answers to right now.

I consider stripping, but I don't. I feel exposed enough as it is.

Let me be clear: In no way would I *ever* walk into the water toward a siren if I didn't have my amulet. Absolutely not. I'm an idiot, but I'm not *that* much of an idiot. But with the amulet, there's a limit to what she can do. She can touch me, sure, but she can't force me underwater or drag me toward her. If she tries, she'll find her grip weak, unable to affect me. Same for trying to remove the amulet.

She can't do anything to me unless I decide to let her. And I'm not going to decide to let her—I'm almost sure.

The water is cold around my legs, and I feel the wrong-ness of wading in slacks—water seeping into the fabric and dragging me down. When I'm five feet from the siren, the ocean up to my mid-thighs, she begins to back away from me. She stops when she's submerged just over the top of her gills, where her fish skin gives way to human skin.

"Closer," she says, trying to pull me toward her with her voice. With my glasses on, I can see the threads reaching out toward me. And I see where they cease to exist, an inch from my skin, presumably blocked by my amulet.

But I move toward her anyway, stopping maybe three feet away. She must be taller than me, because I'm submerged as high up on my body as she is on hers, even though I'm not as far out.

"What have you come to tell me?" I ask, my voice sounding loud and clumsy after the nimbleness of hers.

"I've come to make you an offer," she says.

Oh, right. Bribes. Those are also a thing. They're usually pretty easy to turn down, since a lot of supernatural creatures don't seem at all in touch with what would appeal to a modern human. And I figure turning down bribes is a pretty good idea. Didn't work out great for Paris, after all.

I do, however, always let the supernatural creatures make their pitch. They tend to get very frustrated if I don't at least listen.

"What are you offering?" I ask. The siren smiles. That gesture, at least, seems to mean the same thing for sirens as it does for humans.

"Do you know what the gift of a siren is? Do you know what we do with our prey?"

I had guessed they just ate them, but that seems childish now. Although... those teeth. But that's not what she's talking about. I don't answer. She doesn't need me to.

"We get *knowledge*. We learn what they knew. Every

scrap of their lives becomes ours. And Arbiter, we have drowned *so* many wizards. So many spells, we have. Let me take you to the Seven Spires. All that the wizards keep from you could be yours."

I shouldn't take this seriously. Wizards are the boogeymen of the supernatural world. Most likely, she's exaggerating.

But even if it is a wild exaggeration, even if the sirens have only ever eaten *one* wizard, the knowledge would be incredible. One well-connected, *full* wizard…

What she's offering hits me, and I take in a sharp breath. The ritual of longevity. They have the ritual of longevity in this Seven Spires place. And here she is, casually offering it to me.

She smiles the smile of a fisherman reeling in a line.

"And for that I have to, what? Rule your way? Say the other tribe did it?" I ask.

I hate how clean and enticing her laugh is. I hate the authentic beauty of it.

"Oh, no. This isn't a bribe. This is a gift. You'll judge better if you know more—if you don't feel threatened by what the wizards would do. If you know you can be one of them."

She draws a foot or so closer to me, and I distinguish that her eyes aren't black—they're a deep, dark blue that human eyes just aren't issued in.

"It's all written down for you," she says. "I'll take you to it now. You can read all night."

Again, I see the strings of her words reaching toward me, stopping just short of my wet, white, button-up shirt.

If Gigi's right, my singular status as exempt from wizards' dubious "protection" makes me a kind of resource for the supernatural community. I'm the only chance they have to indulge some of their old traditions that aren't allowed by the treaty with the wizards. And since I'm a shared resource, a creature would think twice before killing me.

I lean on that too much, probably. But even so, I have to consider: What if she's telling the truth? I'm risking my life in the long run on the hope that I'll gain this knowledge, that I can eventually use it and share it with all the other humans who have been unfairly kept in the dark. Would going with her now really be so different from the decision I've already made?

No sooner do I think the question than I see, out behind the siren, a wide swath of the cove light up with a candy-apple-red light. It flashes five or six times, and my mouth drops open as my eyebrows draw together. But when the siren turns around to see what I'm gaping at, the flashing lights stop as suddenly as they started.

The siren turns back to me, questioning.

Interesting.

"Thank you for your offer, but I cannot accept," I say, trying to hide behind a measured, formal tone.

It doesn't work. She moves in closer. One foot from me. Six inches. I fight the urge to start back and flail toward shore. If there's one thing I've learned in the last six months, it's that you don't act like prey in front of anything with sharp teeth.

That horribly gorgeous laugh wraps around me again. When she speaks, her voice sounds deeper. Wider. Satisfied, somehow.

"I see. I see very well. You have a trove then, don't you? The wizards didn't find them all."

"I don't know what that is."

I'm not a very practiced liar, but most supernatural creatures, in my experience, aren't good at detecting lies from humans. They don't have the benefit of an illusion to interpret our expressions for them.

Then again, most supernatural creatures don't regularly consume the entirely of humans' lived experiences, so I'm probably way out of my league here.

If she detects my lie, and I think she does, she doesn't call me on it. Instead, she draws in closer still, until I can feel every minute movement of her body through the motion that it sends through the water to mine. Her face is maybe three inches from mine when she speaks, and I'm horribly aware of the closeness of her needle-sharp teeth to my neck.

"We had wings once. Did you know that? A long time ago. I remember flying. The unity of life on the breath of the wind with my sisters and brothers. It was brighter there. The cold was sweeter there."

The pupils in her eyes are wrong. Slitted sideways, only just barely. Subtle enough that you wouldn't notice unless you were up this close, and if you're up this close, it's already too late for you.

"What happened?" I ask.

"What stole them?" She draws out the O in stole with an alien ease.

"What stole them?" I breathe.

She looks away from me, letting out a harsh exhalation and raising her top lip in an expression I don't recognize or know how to interpret.

"What else? Wizards. A wizard. Just one. Back when they deserved the fear we still give them."

"Why?" I ask, as though wizards ever needed a reason to wreak havoc.

"We sunk his boat."

I can't help but imagine Max reacting to someone crashing his electric-blue monstrosity, and the thought warms me, bringing me a little closer back to the world I belong to.

"He must have really liked that boat," I say, my voice stronger.

"His apprentice was on board. Wizards *do* love their little apprentices. They matter more to them than anything in the world. The wizard decided he wanted to curse us to live almost all our lives in the water, to keep the boy's body company."

My momentary mirth drains out of me. Imagining the sirens dooming sailors has a certain charm to it, as long as none of the sailors ever have faces in any of your imaginings. But when I think of a wizard's apprentice, I don't think first of someone Max's age. I can't help but think of a child.

"Why did you do it?" I ask, my voice sounding even rougher than it already did in comparison to hers. By the way she suddenly comes back from her reminiscences fully into the here and now, I can tell she recognizes that I don't just mean the one wizard's boat. Her deep, dark-blue eyes lighten to a gorgeous shade of teal.

"Because, Arbiter, it's *fun*."

"It's not fun," I say, trying to make the words stand tall and firm in the face of the wrongness of her.

"Oh, but it *is*." She draws out the S just a little more than it should be. "It is the joy and the delight of destruction. There is nothing like it when it is deserved, and it is *always* deserved. For one reason or another, it is deserved."

Her eyes lighten further. They're closer to sky blue when she continues.

"I've heard about you, Arbiter. You have rage. Bubbling away just somewhere down there. You feed it little morsels to keep it quiet, so you don't have to think about it. But it grows. Rage *always* grows. And it's already pulling your strings. Here and there. Just enough to change the course of your life."

She leans in, closer still. Her lips are a few finger widths away from my ear, the sweetness of the music of her voice winding us together in an intimacy that I feel like I need to apologize to Faisal about.

She whispers again, her words barely anything but luscious breath. "Rage chains you—chains you to what gave it to you. But the joy of destruction sets you free. Free as flying. Have you ever danced with the body of a drowning man and made him like it?"

She holds like that, my heart pounding and her body still and close. Then she leans back, and I involuntarily take a gasping breath in with the freedom of the space between us. I breathe in decay.

"One day, if you keep reading that trove, maybe you'll learn how. When you figure it out..." She leans back farther from me, floating in the water now instead of standing. I can feel movement that tells me her legs—or tail, I guess?—must be not far from my left side. "*I hope you do*," she finishes.

I'm caught in her eyes, watching them deepen back to their midnight blue. When she speaks again, her tone is almost casual, forgiving. "I'll give you some of my blood when this is over. For when you figure it out. What do you think of that?"

I open my mouth, unsure what to say.

And then a tinny, orchestral version of "Call Me Maybe" erupts from my jacket on the beach and brings me back to my senses. Faisal's ringtone. Faisal is calling me.

"I have other things to think about," I say, stepping backward and turning around with quick, confident movements.

"Suit yourself," I hear behind me.

When I reach the shore, I'm alone again. I pull out my phone, now silent. I wait for it to ring again. I've just barely missed Faisal's calls enough times that if I don't answer, he always gives me one more try before assuming I'm actually busy.

When the phone buzzes, I catch it before it has a chance to make noise.

"Hey hotshot," I say, trying to sound casual, only a little out of breath.

"Hey, you," Faisal says. "Just wanted to let you know not to use the silver card. I got a fraud alert on it. Someone in Greece tried to spend hundreds of dollars at a café, apparently."

Oh, shit. The whole point of using that card was that it would be *less* likely to trigger a fraud alert. Well, half the point. The other part of the point was that it might force me to do what I've been needing to do for months.

But that was only a chance, not a certainty. And it was supposed to happen weeks from now. I'm not ready for it now. I can't, now.

I have to, now.

"Right. Okay. So…" I pause. Is it normal that I'm more scared now than I was a minute ago, with a mass-murdering predator practically wrapping herself around me?

A little longer. I just need a little bit longer.

But here's that line—that line between omission and active lies. I've been preparing myself to cross that line, I realize now. All that guilt-tripping myself I've been doing, telling myself that lies of omission aren't any worse than outright lies. I've been imagining the difference to make myself feel better, all so that when it came to this point, where I have to go just a little past that line, I'll be able to.

But I won't. I won't lie to Faisal. The line between just

leaving things out and knowingly giving him the wrong impression about something may be made up, but it's a made-up thing I believe in. I can't cross it. Not when I don't know how the tribunal tomorrow is going to turn out. I put on a light voice to force the words out. It's time to start telling the truth.

"So, funny story, but I'm actually in Greece right now. That was me, renting a car."

Long silence. I shiver in my wet clothes from a strong breeze.

"I talked to you four hours ago," Faisal says, his voice dry and even. "You said you were at work."

"I was at work," I reply, probably too quickly.

"That's not possible." There's no emotion in his voice. Faisal gets like that sometimes. For a while, I thought he could just set things aside for the time being. When I got to know him better, I realized he's not setting it aside, he's burying it so the person he's talking to doesn't see it. But he feels it all the same. More, maybe.

"It's complicated," I say. "I can explain it to you, but probably not over the phone. It's not a phone thing. I'll tell you when I get back."

Those would be the worst last words to leave him with. I see a vision of him, wondering forever what I meant, and I rush to fix my mistake.

"And if I don't get back, then ask Max. Max from work."

It hits me right after the words leave my mouth that saying I might not come back is not the soothing balm I was looking for.

"Beth, I need to know what's going on." It's distracting that Faisal's stern voice is also incredibly sexy, but not distracting enough to keep the panic from rising.

"It's complicated, and I can't explain right now. I

promise I will when I can. That's… that's the best answer I have for you right now."

"Beth—" he says.

And for the first time in the nearly seven years I've known him, I hang up on Faisal. When "Call Me Maybe" starts up again, I reject the call.

That was not the way to do this. I should have just lied. I'd have felt like shit for a moment, but at least I would have had the chance to explain everything in person where I could prove it was real.

I look back out at the ocean. Is it too late to take the siren up on her implicit offer of a quick, watery death? She said she could make me like it, after all.

SEVEN

An Attempt

Small stones and shells stick to the bottoms of my feet as I walk up the beach. The cool breeze of the night torments me all the way back to the car. When I get there, I open the passenger-side door, set my leather jacket and phone inside, and start stripping out of my wet clothes. I should have just gone in naked. The siren was naked, anyway. Why do I keep insisting on holding onto human social mores? No one else is playing by those rules, and it always just hurts me.

"Fun conversation?" Gigi's light, playful voice startles me.

"You were awake?" I blurt out like the accusation it is.

"*You* were awake?" Her voice sounds like she's mocking me, but I'm not sure why. I go back to struggling with my wet clothes, trying to force them to release me.

"I thought you said these people wouldn't kill me without good reason. I thought you said I was a resource."

I can only see the outline of Gigi's face, gobbling up the limited moonlight like it belongs to her. She's propped up on an arm, and I realize I've still got my glasses on. It hits me in a way it hasn't before how truly weird it feels to see a statue wearing clothes. Maybe it's because she's in a very typical statue-like pose at the moment. She looks more like she belongs in a museum than she usually does. All except the eyes. And the smile.

"I said 'of sorts,'" she just about purrs. "Anyway, you go wandering underwater with a siren, knowing full well what she is… anyone would agree that's on you."

Finally free of my clothes, I jump into the passenger seat and wrap the borrowed blanket around me, trying to get warm.

"Why would she kill me, though?" I ask Gigi. I try to make it sound like an afterthought, but it bothers me. It bothers me a lot. "Both tribes called me here."

"Good question," Gigi says, but I can tell from her voice she's already settled back into her sleeping position.

I set the question aside. Important, but unanswerable. Maybe the way she mentioned wizards not being worth the fear supernatural creatures give them anymore had something to do with it. Maybe the story about having been taken from the skies had something to do with it. I'll leave my subconscious to chew on her words. But there are other questions Gigi *can* help me with, so I try to get those answered so they don't bother me.

"What were those lights about?" I ask quickly, hoping to catch her before she falls asleep.

"What lights?" comes her lazy reply.

"The lights in the water? Behind the siren?"

There's a long pause before Gigi replies. "I wasn't watching that closely, I suppose. Don't know what they could be."

Okay, then. Gigi, for all she seems to collect information about the world just as she collects artifacts and books in the Emporium, doesn't know what those things are, either. Which tracks with the way they hid from the siren when she turned around to look.

"You knew they'd approach me if we got here early, didn't you? That's why you insisted we leave right away."

I can't tell if Gigi is feigning being half asleep or really there when she replies, "I thought they might. Sirens are predictable. You'll find out why. Did you learn anything useful?"

"Maybe," I say, more for me than for her. She doesn't reply.

I set that aside, too. I need to focus.

For six months, I've dedicated every moment of spare time to studying the trove. There's a *lot* there, and most of it is unreadable for reasons of language and script. But one spell that I've been practicing—trying to get right—would come in real handy about now.

It's a spoken spell, all of which my dad wrote off when he had the trove. All spells with spoken elements are in this strange, unknown language, and without recordings it's really impossible to nail the pronunciation of a language you've never heard.

But thanks to hanging around Max, I scored a recording of him doing a long spell—three whole minutes of this language being spoken. Things like that are the reason I don't mind keeping him around, and I may as well use it.

The two words in this particular spell are in the recording I have of Max. Not next to each other, but that's fine. I chopped the audio up on the computer and put them next to each other, and I have the soundbite of just those words stored on the Wilbur's special secret server along with the trove.

I place my wet clothes on my lap and play the sound-bite for myself a few times—*khule kreedagh* the trove has it written, which seems like an okay transcription. I set my phone on the dashboard and get my hands into the contortion the trove describes.

Now, it's time for Right Mind.

Every magical action has a state of Right Mind required to pull it off. For the one fire spell I know, for instance, Right Mind is righteous fury. For Max's mental magic, based on the look on his face, it's something like affection. Love, maybe. For the spell that removes the water from an object, Right Mind is "disgust, as one would feel for a goat."

That's the translation from the original Proto-German. I don't understand why one would feel disgust for a goat. As far as I can tell, it's not a commonly known cultural thing, either. The wizard who wrote the part of the trove this spell came from was probably just a weird guy. Wizards tend to be.

I focus on things that disgust me—mostly the images from an opening credits sequence for one season of *American Horror Story*, which I've found usually works the best—and say the words.

Nothing happens. That's normal. I rarely get a spell right the first time.

I try again. Nothing. Again. Nothing. I try eight more times, stopping after the fifth to listen to the soundbite of Max's voice again.

But no matter what I do, I can't get the magic to kick in.

If I were a wizard, it would have worked. I'd have been able to feel, in my body and bones, the sense of what about the spell was working and what wasn't. I'd have been able to let my body and mind focus around the feeling of magic and follow the sense of it. It would have been an exercise in trusting myself, instead of an exercise in frustration.

But I'm not a wizard, so eventually I sigh, climb out of the car, and hang my clothes up to dry naturally. Pants on one side mirror, shirt on the other, underwear lying on the hood. It'll probably work just fine, anyway.

That done, I settle back into the passenger seat and wrap the borrowed blanket tightly around me. I want to sleep, and I'm about to try, when I remember what I was doing before the siren so rudely interrupted me with attempted murder.

I shift in my blanket, getting my phone back out to where I can see it. The missed-call notification from Faisal sends a pang of guilt through me, but I push it aside. The Ocean Glow, apparently, is real. And it's hanging around, so I need to know about it.

Translation goes slowly. I'm tempted to send a message to Wilbur asking him to help and asking how much it would cost, but the memory of how brusque he was at the Emporium stops me. He performed our usual ritual to access the trove, sure. But normally he would chat a little more than that, and it bothers me that he didn't. I won't ask him anything else. I can't handle the rejection right now if he's still angry—not shaken as I am from the unexpected conversation with Faisal.

Besides, I *can* translate it. It'll just take me longer than it would take him. And it isn't that long of a passage.

The entry on "Ocean Glow" doesn't follow the same form as most of WBBOM. Rather than a page of accumulated knowledge, it's a paragraph outlining an anecdote. According to this, a wizard fell into the ocean and lights swirled around him. Though the man was a strong swimmer, he began to sink. He seemed unable to control his arms and legs, as though he were possessed. But when the other wizards hauled him back on board the ship, there were none of the usual signs of a spirit possessing him, and he was dead.

They performed an autopsy, which Wilhelm thankfully doesn't describe at length. But he does mention that, when all was said and done, they were left with a handful of goo that was not a part of the original man. The wizards performed experiments on this goo, which Wilhelm also thankfully doesn't go too far into, but he does say that when the wizards left the goo in a vat of seawater for long enough, it eventually lit up again in colors.

And there the account of what the wizards called Ocean Glow ends. No hint of what became of it. Wilhelm doesn't even name the wizards themselves. The whole thing has the feeling of a rumor that's been told too many times by too many opinionated mouths. I'm not sure whether to feel sorry for the glow or afraid of it. But I know that the lights jolted me away from what would have unknowingly been a terrible decision, so I owe it.

My phone startles me by vibrating and playing Olivia's rolling marimba ringtone when I've just about finished gleaning everything I'm going to get from WBBOM. I hesitate, staring at the picture of her that comes up. She's with her young daughters at a cookout that she threw. I hadn't really wanted to attend, since it was bound to be half full of her husband's old army buddies, but it turned out to be a surprisingly good time. It's one of my favorite memories of her—so deeply in her element, against what I would have thought. So happy. So grateful. So entirely unaware that her girls had *somehow* managed to sneak three dandelions and a tiny hors d'oevres fork into her voluminous blonde braid.

What the fuck am I going to say to Olivia? Unlike Faisal, I've never even considered telling her the truth. I can keep this—all of this—from her indefinitely. Or, at least, until I tell the rest of the world. I know I can. I know she'll be safer if I do. But I don't have the appetite to lie to her, either. Not heartsick and shaken as I already feel from my conversation with Faisal.

It's not fair to ignore Olivia's call with what's going on with Mom. But since when have I ever been fair to Olivia? I don't reject her call, but I let it ring out, staring at the picture and thinking of the oppressive heat of that day, and the chill of the condensation around the glass of slushy lemonade in my hand when I took the picture. She deserves better than me. I take so much more from her than I give. I risk her so much more than she would risk herself.

The ringing stops, and I take the change to disconnect from the trove server and put the phone in a cup holder so that I don't have to look at Olivia's face when she calls me a second time, giving me another chance not to hurt her. Then I wrap the blanket more tightly around me and do my best to sleep. It may be the last sleep I get in some time. It may be the last sleep I get ever. At least if it is, my last conversation with Olivia will be better than the last one I had with Faisal. That almost makes me feel less guilty for not taking her call.

But no sleep comes until I pull the phone out of the cupholder, and type in a quick text to Olivia. It's the least I owe her.

Sorry, can't answer, busy. Will call when I can. Don't worry, I'm fine.

I'm fine. God, I hope so.

EIGHT

A Hearing

I must succeed in falling asleep, because I wake to Gigi's voice.

"What?" I ask, voice full of sleep.

"I said we've come a long way for you to sleep through the meeting," she repeats.

I try to get my bearings. It's still mostly dark, the world bathed in a faint pink glow. But that tracks—we're meeting at dawn.

My bones are exhausted. My eyes are exhausted. I didn't go into the water over my head, but they're acting like I got saltwater in them. Traitors.

But at least I got some sleep. Given the jet lag—crossroads lag?—I'm surprised I got much of any.

I get out of the car, stretching my limbs. They object, not appreciating the position I slept in. It's colder out now than it was when I went for my little swim last night, but my clothes have made a solid attempt at getting dry. Almost halfway. That's something.

I dress, cursing my lack of magical talent with every motion, before I let myself look down toward the beach.

I look without my glasses on first. We didn't have the foresight to bring coffee with us, which I regret. I hope whatever I learned last night was worth not getting to pack properly.

I don't know what I expect, really. Maybe some kind of courtroom setup, minus the furniture? Scowling expressions? Weapons of some kind? Instead, I see something like two dozen naked women and men sitting in a loose, multi-layered circle on the beach. Well, almost naked. They all have wet pieces of cloth—towels, sarongs, etc.—draped across their bodies where their gills are. All except for the one figure closest to the water, sitting with a little more space around her.

I hear voices. Not English. Greek, I think? Maybe different from the Greek I heard Gigi and the people of the village speaking yesterday. But I'm probably making that up based on the assumption that they should be speaking ancient Greek and I know languages change over time. I don't know the language well enough to tell.

As I wander toward the group, I perceive more detail. They're on a layer of seaweed that's been woven together into something like a mat, holding them up from the stones and shells of the beach. And they're eating—feasting, really—from a spread of seafood in the middle. I don't know if the food is actually cooked, or if I'm just seeing it that way because of the wizard's illusion. Probably the latter. Not sure where they'd get a grill underwater.

They're also smiling. Their voices are friendly. I try to tell if it's fake or not—the wizard's illusion is good for helping me interpret things like that—and I think it's genuine. At least for most of them.

I can't tell the difference between the two tribes. They don't seem segregated. Most of them are attractive, although nothing remotely like the wizards I've seen. On the right side, I notice the woman I saw last night, but she doesn't look quite as enticing as she did then. I usually think of the wizard's illusion as changing people's clothing and trappings to align with how they're trying to appear, but I guess when you're naked, it affects your body. Her proportions are somewhere in between the swimsuit model I saw last night and what I know to be the proportions of her actual body underneath.

She's one of the queens. I don't know what cues I'm picking up, exactly, but it's clear from the way the sirens around her treat her. She sits between a girl who maybe looks a bit younger and a man who is quieter than most. I leap to the idea that they're a family unit, but I don't have any evidence for that. I don't have any evidence that sirens have families at all, except the girl reminds me of me in high school, forced by my family to attend a function that I don't want to, saving up sarcastic quips to use on the way home to make clear how little I enjoyed it.

There's more in there, though. She smiles when engaged, as the others do, but her smile seems sad to me. Her eyes do, at least.

I pick out who I think is in charge on the other side as I draw closer. It's another woman, also beautiful, but not in an exaggerated way. She's got that same black hair and dark eyes that I imagine must be that same blue as the eyes I watched color shift last night.

Directly across the circle from me, closest to the water, is one woman who sticks out like a sore thumb. A wind nymph, presumably. She's got strong Greek features and ringlets of dry hair. She sits straight, with a patient smile on her face, but anger flashes behind her eyes.

She looks solid to me. Not the way Gigi is—not stone. This woman looks like she *belongs* wherever she is. I have the unshakable feeling that I'm walking on her land—that the world is hers, and she's allowing me to be in it. She feels connected to everything in a way that makes me feel insubstantial.

She notices me first, nodding her head at me. And although I didn't see any of the sirens looking at her directly, her recognition of my presence triggers an immediate halt in conversation, and every head turns toward me.

And, because I already feel out of my league and I'm a glutton for punishment, I bring down my glasses.

My body doesn't care how many horrible, threatening creatures I've seen in the past six months. My body doesn't care that I have an amulet of protection, and I'm supposed to be here, and they've granted me a measure of power over them—in theory. Two dozen predators staring at me is always going to be two dozen predators staring at me, and the fight-or-flight response it triggers is automatic.

And mine is flight. Mine is always, *always* flight.

But I *have* gotten used to fighting that response, shoring up my legs and commanding them to keep striding forward before they decide to head for the hills.

I plaster on my best attempt at a solemn-but-friendly smile and keep my pace forward as steady as I can.

How many needle teeth are before me? How many gills? The estimation calms me down a little. Thousands of teeth. Hundreds of gills. No. 164? No. 144. A little math problem always works for this. Something else to focus on. I get my pulse under control. I can trust my legs a little more to do as they're told.

I note more details as I get closer. Their fins are split down the middle, but it doesn't look like a natural split. It looks surgical. I see scarring—knife wounds from mistakes during the process. The older-looking sirens have more of those wounds. For all the sirens' natural horror, their split tails—to allow them to walk on land, presumably—are the hardest to look at.

"So nice of you all to show up," I say. All those eyes. All those teeth. "How was the trip?" A thought occurs to me. "Can you use the crossroads?"

I thought it was a little bit of lightweight conversation, but the reaction to those words tells me I thought wrong. Even on those alien faces, annoyance and anger are clear. A few of them give the car, with Gigi leaning against it, a furtive glance.

Gigi is indestructible. She doesn't need my protection. But I still don't like the way they're looking at her. I shift my attention to the odd woman out, sitting across the circle.

"You're not a wind nymph," I say, noting the sirens' muted and quickly hidden reactions of surprise. I guess I wasn't supposed to know about the Nymph of the North Wind getting murdered.

The twisted tree of a woman with flowering branches of hair sways to the side, and I flip my glasses back up so that I have any hope of being able to gain anything from her expressions. Not that it helps much; the woman wears an inscrutable smile.

"No," she says, her voice warm and resonant, as if carried between us by the ground rather than by the air. "But I am a nymph, and kin enough. I'm here on their behalf, to represent their interests."

"They think they're above participating in this?" I ask, before I can recognize and feel proper shame and contrition for the pun. Luckily, no one else seems to notice.

"It's best for everyone they sent me," the tree nymph— dryad, I think they're called—says. "Since their promotion, my sisters are… unpredictable. Even for us, they can be difficult to communicate with."

I remember what Max said about them and nod slowly. I've gotten better at not showing my frustration at supernatural beings not fulfilling my expectations. Mostly. This one still feels a bit much, though. If they're the ones looking for judgment, the least they could do is show up.

"So," I say, holding myself up straight and strong, shoving back the idea that at least one of the people before me probably knows where my mother is, "what seems to be the trouble?"

I don't sit at the circle. I don't walk forward, expecting them to make room. I certainly don't eat any of the food. I'm different. I'm other. That's why I'm here.

There's a long pause—far longer than I'm comfortable with. I wonder if there are any human cultures on earth that would be comfortable with a pause that long, or if it's a result of immortality. What about wizards? Do any of them leave that much time waiting in expectation? If anything, Max seems to have the opposite inclination.

I don't let myself look impatient. I wait.

Finally, the queen I didn't meet last night speaks.

"The wind nymphs claim a siren has committed a crime. They claim a siren has killed the Nymph of the North Wind, and that he died himself in the act. But all of the Atlantic tribe are accounted for."

There is much less space before the next words—they slide in quickly, from the woman I met last night.

"As are all of the Pacific tribe. It seems the nymphs have mistaken a human or a wizard for one of us. I can't *imagine* how that happened." There's a barb in those words, aimed at the tree nymph. But that's not what sticks out to me about them most. I don't have to guess that they were inappropriate to say in the presence of a nymph. The expressions on the sirens' faces shout that at me through a bullhorn.

"There's no mistake," the dryad says, her voice barely louder but somehow uncomfortably resonant. "The dead murderer was a siren."

The Atlantic queen speaks next, her voice plaintive and pleading. "Then why not give the dead siren's body to us? We can identify it. We will have seen them before. That will simplify things."

I doubt it—if it *is* a siren, then half the people in this circle are already lying. No reason they wouldn't keep doing so. But it does seem odd, regardless. I study the dryad's face as she responds. Her anger, if you can call it that, is gone. It's replaced by something else. Sadness? Frustration, maybe?

"They will not do so. They know how much bodies matter to you, and they will not allow you to put him to rest. They also think that if he is returned to you, you will somehow bring him back alive." Frustration and confusion. The words are definitely a mixture of frustration and confusion, but not pointed at anyone on this beach. The dryad continues. "And they insist that the guilty party must take responsibility *voluntarily*."

It's a rare thing for supernatural creatures to be as confused by something another supernatural creature has done as I am. I'll take my wins where I can get them. No one sitting in front of me seems to think the wind nymphs are acting reasonably, and it scares them. Each and every one of them. I hurry to speak, as much to save them from sitting in that fear as anything else.

"Just so I'm clear, you want me to decide which tribe the wind nymphs should hold responsible for the death of the Nymph of the North Wind?"

Throughout the crowd, I see eyes casting down to the woven mat. Some close. Some faces twist in anger.

"That's correct," the dryad says, her resonant voice gentler than before. "Which do you choose, Arbiter?"

I blink. "What, *now?*"

My own surprise mirrors a few other faces in the crowd. Good to know I'm not the only one who was not expecting this to be a one-and-done decision, even if the crowd is a bit split.

"Yes," the dryad says, like she can't tell if I'm a little bit slow, or if she's the one that's missing something. "That is why you're here. To decide."

"Decide, yes. But I can't decide on nothing. I need more information."

The Atlantic queen speaks next, her voice with more music in it than I remembered being there the last time I heard it. Music and something else. Hope, maybe? "We've told you everything we know."

Something about the way she says it makes me certain she hasn't. It gives me a little boost of confidence that makes what I have to say next a little easier.

"I need more time," I say. Declaring, not asking. "If the wind nymphs want a faster decision, they can deliver the body to the sirens so that he can be identified. If not, then they can wait for my answer."

I see some wide eyes in the crowd. A few fleeting smiles, as well. The dryad regards me for another of those uncomfortably long moments.

"You're exactly who I heard you were, Arbiter," she says. She stands and strides through the center of the seafood spread. She doesn't look at her feet, but they find their places in between the piles of food with a steady, graceful certainty.

Through the wizards' illusion, she's almost a foot taller than me, but when she draws close, I have the impression she's much taller than that when she's all unwound and straightened. She gives me the feeling of being underneath a great, ancient oak.

I don't fight her as she picks up my hand any more than you would fight to stop the shaking of boughs in a strong breeze. She wraps her short, knobby fingers around my wrist.

"I can give you one day," she says. When she moves her fingers aside, I see twenty-four brown, bumpy marks, each about half an inch long. They give me the impression of bark hiding underneath my skin, but I don't know how accurate that is.

"I'll need more time than that," I say.

The dryad smiles and lets her fingers graze over my skin again. One more mark appears. I understand from the look on her face that this is all I'm going to get from her. I shift tactics.

"I need to see the wind nymphs. I need to talk to them."

The dryad drops my hand. "That's not possible."

"You speak to them."

She turns her head on its long, elegant neck and looks out over the beach. "I do. But I won't call them for you." The finality in those words leaves no room for argument.

I nod, my mind already racing. If she won't let me talk to the wind nymphs, I'll have to ask my questions here.

"When did it happen?" I ask the dryad.

"I don't know. Within the last week. The first I heard of it was three days ago."

"How did it happen?"

"I don't know."

"What was the weapon used?"

"I don't know."

I'm sensing a theme.

"Is there *anything* else you can tell me?" I let more

desperation seep into my voice than I mean to, but the dryad doesn't seem to hold that against me. There's an exhaustion in her features, but I don't think it's directed at me. And something else…

"I don't think so," she says.

Resignation. That's the other thing I can see in her features.

I don't have any more words to say. Sometimes supernatural creatures bring ceremony into arbitrations, but there isn't a set protocol. Times like these, I wish there were. No one's going to stop looking at me as long as I'm here. There's nothing I can do to get all those eyes and hidden teeth pointed away from me until I leave, so I turn and walk up the beach.

As soon as I take my first step, I hear the conversation between the sirens behind me resume in that same Greek that may or may not be ancient. But as I fight to keep my gait measured and casual, I spare some of my attention to listen to the tones of their voices.

It had seemed strange to me that they were in conflict and were sharing food together, talking across the circle to each other. But I can hear a desperate undercurrent to their exuberant and friendly chatter now, and I think I might understand it. One day may be all they have left. This may be the second-to-last time they see each other alive. And for immortals, that's got to hit different. That's got to hit harder.

And they're trusting me with it.

Poor, poor idiots.

NINE

An Unexpected Guest

I've been surprised enough times by supernatural creatures' good hearing that I say nothing to Gigi until we've gotten into the car and driven away from the beach for a solid two minutes. I even let Gigi break our silence, though that's admittedly more because I don't know what to say. I've got ideas—I'm just not sure I like them.

"So, who did it?" Gigi asks, only just audible over the sound of the car on the road and the wind through our open windows.

"No idea," I say. "But I'm sure that won't be the last I see of sirens. No one mentioned my mom. Not great leverage if you don't use it."

I shift my gaze away from the stupidly picturesque landscape toward Gigi, watching her crimson hair whip in the breeze.

"So you want to lie on beaches? Wait to be approached?" Gigi asks.

I can't tell what Gigi means by that, but I also don't care. If she wants me to know how she feels about something, she makes it obvious.

"Nope. How much of that did you hear?" I ask.

"All of it." She shoots the clipped words at me like bullets.

See? When she's insulted, she makes sure I know. "Including when I asked them about the crossroads, and they looked at you like you had something to do with it?" I ask conspiratorially. This has my intended effect of making Gigi laugh.

"Oh, did they?" she asks, amusement in her voice.

"Do you want to tell me what that's about?" I don't put any pressure on the words. I know it wouldn't do me any good. Gigi doesn't like being pressured into things, but she *does* like when she has something I want to know, and I come to her on metaphorical bended knee asking about it. Sometimes, like today, she even indulges my curiosity.

"No one is quite sure how they travel now. They must have some kind of crossroads equivalent, because they *do* get around, it's just that no one on land knows their methods. But five hundred years or so ago, they used to have a system of portals connecting all of their most-used and sensitive locations together."

I laugh to myself, seeing where this is heading. "And they don't use that portal system anymore?"

Gigi's smile could carve a new Mariana Trench. "*Undesirables* found a way in. They had to abandon the entire system. Poor things."

"Let me guess, one of these *undesirables* was you?" I ask. I let myself smile at her, though it's hard to shake off where I'm coming from and where I'm going.

"So they say. It's never been proven by anyone. Technically." She says it lightly. "But somehow, word got back to them that I had some of their stolen property, and they took that really hard. I have a bit of a reputation, so they were quick to blame me. But what can I say? I like showing up where I shouldn't be."

I try to carry a little bit of that lightness into what I say next. "Good, because we need to find a way to get to the wind nymphs and get them to give us a look at the body. And we'll bring a phone, so I can take a picture. That's at least something. And maybe we find out something that helps us in the process. A cause of death. A murder weapon. I don't know. Between the three of us, maybe we'll notice something."

Gigi takes her eyes off the road for a longer time than anyone not impervious to physical damage would dare. I try not to look at the road—I hear we're supposed to care about dominance or something—but I can't help it. The shoulder on our left cuts away way too close not to.

"Three of us?" Gigi asks.

"You, me, Max. We'll need Wilbur to connect us, but I'm not sure he'll stick around. Often, he doesn't. But we can all keep our eyes open. And we all have such different eyes."

"There's far too much *we* in that plan for my liking," Gigi says.

I shrug, eyes still fixed on the cliff I hope Gigi has some magical way of sensing that I don't know about.

"You live on this planet too, don't you?"

Gigi lets that sink in, and then finally, *finally* turns her eyes back to the road.

"What's the deal with wind nymphs, anyway?" I ask. "Max says they're crazy, sure, and I get that they have a more collectivist mindset than would make sense to a wizard. But even the other wood nymph seemed to think something's wrong with them. She mentioned they got 'promoted.' What is it that everyone knows about them but me?"

Gigi opens her mouth to answer and then closes it. She reaches down and rolls up her window and indicates with a glance that I should do the same. The squealing of the old windows and the worn-out little electric motor forcing them up cuts through the sound of the rushing air.

With the window up, the car feels more fragile somehow. But it's also much quieter.

"So. Gods. They're all gone. You at least remember that, I hope?"

I nod, since that seems to be the easiest way to tell this particular lie to someone who's so intimately comfortable with the truth. And Aloysius is the only god I know for sure is alive, so she might not be far off when she says things like this.

"But before the wizards made it their mission to eliminate the gods, nymphs of all kinds used to be close to the Olympian pantheon. They weren't as powerful as the gods were, exactly, but they knew them well. In some ways, with the gods gone, nymphs are the closest thing we have left, power-wise."

"And that's such a bad thing? The dryad I saw today didn't seem like someone to be afraid of," I prod.

Gigi's eyes widen, and she sighs.

"Dryads aren't. Most of the others aren't. Pretty easy to get along with most nymphs, as long as you aren't a human, really. There are some stories I could tell you…" Gigi trails off, shaking her head. "But the wind nymphs are different."

I stare at Gigi, at the mournful look on her face. Sometimes, Gigi looks much older to me through the wizard's illusion. It comes and goes, but every time it comes out, I'm enraptured. Gigi may never lie, but it's the only time I see her that I think her face is telling the truth.

"They didn't use to be wind nymphs. There were gods

for the winds, and nymphs were for breezes. But when the wizards killed the wind gods, they did what air does when it comes across a vacuum. They filled it."

I watch her jaw clench and unclench.

"And it wasn't a natural fit?" I ask.

A bitter half laugh sticks in Gigi's throat. "That's one way of putting it. They set themselves up in the place of gods and tied themselves to the whole sky of the world—a power that had been linked to gods, not merely to nymphs. They aren't *enough* for it. There are some rumors about things they did or didn't do to try to be enough for it, but I don't know if those are true. All I know is that every time someone thinks they can use wind nymphs to their benefit, it hasn't gone well for them."

I want to make a snide remark about whether she knows that from personal experience, but I don't. I don't want to reckon with the idea that there's something Gigi is afraid of—other than wizards en masse.

"And that thing you said yesterday about the seas boiling? Can they actually do that, or were you just giving us your trademark Gigi drama?"

Gigi takes the lifeline I've thrown her to climb out of that dark place. "Honestly, I told you what I am. You know my relationship with untruths. I should really be insulted you don't remember," she says with a sigh and all the drama I just accused her of. "But yes, they can do that. Not boiling because of temperature, mind you. They're *wind nymphs*. They have power over the atmosphere. And they'll pull the atmosphere—the nitrogen, mainly—that has dissolved into the ocean. And they'll keep doing it, as long as they need to. No nitrogen means no ammonium. No nitrates. No life. And an ocean without life..."

A cascade failure. It's too big. It's too big to be something I'm responsible for. "Do you think the wizards could kill them?" I ask. "If I fail?"

I'm expecting a resolute yes—plus something insulting about wizards and their bloodthirstiness. Gigi always seems eager to impress that vision of them upon me. But that's not what I get.

"I'm not sure how a siren did," she says instead.

I shake my head. "Right, yeah, that's a mystery. But the *wizards* could, yes?"

Gigi takes longer to answer than I wish she would. "A thousand years ago, absolutely."

I settle back into my seat and look out at the road ahead. I don't push Gigi to give me a more definitive answer. It's hard to say how much power someone has if they never have to use it. Maybe the wizards have as much power as they ever did. They all have perfect memories, after all. If they ever knew how to do something, they know how to do it now.

But wizards' power doesn't just come from spells or having access to the knowledge of how to do spells. Someone can know how to punch. They can understand the theory of it. There's a big difference between watching a lot of Bruce Lee movies and being a seasoned warrior. There's been no serious magical combat since the treaty a thousand years ago. How much practice could the wizards alive today really have gotten with those kinds of spells?

And that's all assuming those spells got passed down at all. From the way Max is terrified of his masters, and the general sense of paranoia that everyone reeks of when they talk about anything to do with wizards, it's easy to imagine plenty of the old guard took their favorite spells to their graves. I figure there have to be ways to find new spells—at least I hope there are—but I can't get anything out of Max about it. He always clams up or redirects the conversation whenever I try to find out anything more about the wizarding world.

Okay, so there's no wizard safety net. *Maybe*, if worse comes to worst, the wizards will step in and stop the wind nymphs from destroying the world. But I can't rely on it.

"They'd *have* to try to stop it, though, right?" I ask Gigi. "The treaty demands that all of you keep yourselves hidden. Destroying an ocean doesn't seem very hidden. Why aren't they stepping in already? Can't we just… get a message to them through Max or something?"

Gigi laughs like gravel. "They'd probably just roll it up under climate change the way the other nymphs do when they're angry at humans."

My eyebrows rise. "What?"

Gigi looks at me again. "You think nymphs are fine with what humans do to the earth? Of course not. But you're sort of killing it yourselves already. They just… help it along. A lot, sometimes."

I blink hard a few times. "I see," I say under my breath, thinking of the way that every time I hear about climate change it always seems to be coming much faster than earlier projected. But that's not my problem right now. I can't make that my problem. "What about the sea nymphs? Shouldn't they be doing something here?"

Gigi's getting toward the end of her patience with my questions and ignorance, and her tone shows it.

"They died with Poseidon. Some people claim he's still alive, but those are the same people who claim they've seen the Kraken and Nessie. That sort of thing. Everyone knows he called the nymphs to him, to the ruins of Atlantis, and made his last stand against the wizards there. And everyone knows the wizards won."

My eyes go wide. "Atlantis?" I ask, suddenly a decade or two younger.

Gigi rolls her eyes and smiles. "Yes, of course, Atlantis. What *do* they teach humans in those schools of yours?"

And with that, Gigi redirects her attention resolutely to the road ahead of us. I may ignore nonverbal cues from time to time, but I do notice them, and I let the conversation drop.

By the time we get back to the little village by the crossroads and the Casino, I've written to Wilbur via magic pen and gotten him to agree, however reluctantly, to summon the wind nymphs. We've even settled on payment, which is a Greek delicacy that I make him write in Greek, so I have something to show shop owners. His words, as much as I can tell through the unconventional medium, are a bit frustrated and overly formal. He tells me we have to do it at the top of Mount Olympus, and he'll see me there. When I ask him if there's really no other option, he just stops communicating. I'm used to Wilbur disappearing, but he doesn't usually do it when I'm asking him a direct question.

The village looks better in full light—more like a tourist brochure. I'd be shocked if it weren't on any, really. But as Gigi drives us way too fast around a corner of the narrow street, I see something I didn't see before.

There, towering six inches above the tallest villager, is a lanky Middle Eastern man, with too-big features that crowd his face and a stylish haircut that he's let grow out a little too long. He's got a folded garment bag slung over his shoulder, and his blue button-up shirt and jeans look like they're on their second day.

Here, in this tiny Greek village, is Faisal. And his face clouds when he sees me.

"Oh, look," Gigi says, half feigned amusement and half disdain. "It's your little human man."

She stops the car, and I'm not sure what to do about it. Get out, I guess. Go to Faisal. Talk to him. Explain. But he looks angry, and I don't know what to do with that. I've seen his anger so rarely that it makes him feel like a man I don't know. I'm not sure how to treat a man I don't know with the face of the man I love. The villagers he was talking to him seem to know what to do about it though—they beat a hasty retreat.

Gigi reaches over, opens my door for me, and unbuckles my seat belt. The actions set me into the automatic get-out-of-car sequence of movements, without me making a conscious choice.

I step toward Faisal, pulled like gravity. He's moving faster than I am, closing the distance between us. I feel like a prey animal in this scenario, pulled in by a predator's unbroken stare. My heart pounds, and the terror that fills me is achingly similar to how I felt when all those sirens with all those teeth were staring at me on the beach.

It's not *him* I'm scared of, some rational, disconnected voice in the back of my mind recognizes. I'm afraid of this *conversation*. I'm afraid of what that conversation inevitably will bring. I'm afraid of what I'm going to lose in an hour, a day, a week.

But the part of me that realizes that is losing ground to the mounting wave of cause and effect—the fight-or-flight reaction welling up in me as a response to impending pain.

"I checked," he says, his voice rough from lack of sleep. "Even if you left straight from the airport when we hung up, and even if there were a flight, you couldn't have gotten here."

I look for something to say to that, but everything is speeding up. Things I could say fly by me too fast for me to grab on to.

"Why did you lie to me?" he asks, and my heart breaks at the anger and hurt in his face.

"I didn't." The words rush out of me like a thoughtless reflex.

His face collapses in on itself. "Beth, you did."

"I didn't!" I insist more forcefully.

But I did. Not yesterday, not about what he thinks. But by omission. In a thousand tiny ways over the last six months. The accusations that hit the hardest are the ones you know are true but that you wish weren't. And that accusation, that *true* accusation, sparks anger in me alongside the fear. I'm losing that still-reasonable piece of my mind—the part of me that knows I'm not afraid of him, but afraid of losing him. The part of me that knows I'm not angry at his accusation, but rather angry at myself for making it true.

"I didn't!" I say it louder this time, as though the volume could stop his pace forward and make me feel less like a cornered animal. It doesn't.

"How?" he asks, his voice broken, his own anger slipping out. "You said you were at work—"

"Magic!"

I throw my hands up as the word I've been holding back for six months rips its way out of me. That dumb, hollow word. That horrible word that breaks Faisal.

Faisal and I met at a support group for people with mentally ill family members. His aunt, his only family other than his parents living in the U.S., developed schizophrenia later in life. The thought that it might happen to him, that it might happen to his parents, has taken up so much space in his head for such a long time. And I reassured him, over and over, that it would be fine.

He never seemed to worry it would happen to me, even though we believed at the time that my father had lost his mind. It always seemed odd that he worried so much about his own mind and never worried about mine.

But the way his face falls, the way his body collapses in on itself like a marionette with cut strings... He always worried. He just never told me.

"This is a stressful situation," he says. "With your mom missing. And after your dad…"

The words aren't for me. They're him making sense of things.

"I'm not crazy!" The words feel hollow. They sound hollow.

He steps toward me, hands up like he's approaching a frightened animal, a patronizing and pitying look on his face. My fear and anger roil up again, shoving back my reason—shoving back the part of me that can see the situation clearly and could navigate us through it.

"Let's just get you home," he says.

He thinks I'm so small. He thinks I'm broken. And how could he stay with someone who's broken? The part of my brain that makes sense, that knows why I'm afraid and angry, is gone. All that's left is the part of everyone that stands and screams at storms we can't outrun. That suicidal battlefield cry in the face of overwhelming odds.

"No!" I hear myself scream, like a trapped animal finding a new voice—one laced with poison and desperation. "I am not fucking crazy. That shit's in your blood, it's *not* in mine."

I see him absorb the blow. I see the poison sink into him.

What the fuck, Elizabeth?

The part that screams at storms, the part that lashes out in fear and defiance, fades. It's swept away by the tide of regret and empathetic pain at seeing Faisal wounded. I want to rush to him, to apologize. I want to undo everything and make it all better. Undo the last six months, if I have to. Whatever I have to do. Anything.

"Beth," he breathes, still walking toward me—always walking toward me. His hands are still up, palms facing me. He swallows, and I see him set aside my harsh words as just a wicked claw of the monster that's been hiding under our bed all these years, waiting to reach up, grab me, and pull me under.

"No. No, no, no." My vision blurs. I fucked it up. I fucked it all up.

Proof. I just need to find proof. That was all I ever needed to do. One of my hands reaches up to my glasses. I can fix this. I can fix all of this, if he'll just take them. I have to. I look back at Faisal's face, caught in the brokenness of his stare.

I watch as his heartbreak and worry give way to shock and blind panic. Arms have snaked around his chest from behind while he was focused on me and I was focused on him. A gorgeous face with flashing green eyes appears over his right shoulder. Max is all kindness, warmth, and affection as he kisses Faisal on his cheek.

Faisal's eyes roll back in his head, and he collapses.

TEN

A Flight

"What the fuck, Max?" I scream, stepping forward to take my boyfriend's limp body from his arms.

"What?" Max says, sunny but confused. "That looked like it was going badly. Figured you'd want another try at it."

Max doesn't fight me as I take Faisal from him. I'm not really strong enough to hold up his dead weight, and we sink in a controlled fall to the ground. I gather up the man I love, trying to straighten him out, trying to make his body lie the way it should. I must look like a pietà. I feel like one.

"What did you do to him?" My adrenaline is so high that it's hard to sort everything out. I'm feeling everything at once: guilt, anger, betrayal, *more* betrayal.

"I just knocked him out and erased the last couple of hours." There's wonder and confusion in Max's tone.

I want to scream at him and say a whole bunch of things that I know I can't take back. But I've done too much of that already. Instead, I take a moment to hold Faisal, look at his face, and breathe.

In, out. One, two. I count up to ten with my breaths,

and then start over. Two ten-counts. I begin to untangle things.

I shift my eyes away from Faisal's face, my emotions a little more under control. Max sits cross-legged on the street in front of me now. His worry looks genuine.

"Max," I say, keeping my voice even but unable to remove the edge from it. "Do not ever, *ever* mess with Faisal's head again."

He blinks. I can see the urge in him to explain. He opens and closes his mouth.

"You know I can't promise that," he says eventually.

I clench my jaw to stop myself from flying into a blind rage. I nod three or four times before I continue.

"Can you promise me you won't do it unless you've already gotten into mine?"

Max relaxes. "I can do that."

We sit in the de-escalation for a long moment. I unwind. I readjust Faisal so he lies more naturally in my lap. The cobblestones beneath me are damp—it must have rained since we were here last. Max's voice is sunnier, more himself when he speaks again.

"That *was* going really badly, though. You have to admit that."

I sigh, welcoming the familiarity of mild annoyance at Max.

"It was a bad moment," I allow. "It's been a weird twenty-four hours, and I responded really badly." That's an insufficient excuse, but Max doesn't call me on it. "We'd have talked it out," I say. At his disbelieving expression, I continue, "We would have. That's what people do."

I can see the words don't make sense to him, but before he can respond, Gigi's voice cuts through the moment. "If the three of you are finished, do get out of the street. I have to return the car. And people are watching, *wizard.*"

Gigi is hanging out the driver's-side door, unfazed as ever. I don't see the people she claims are watching, but whatever. She must see them peeking out somewhere, or she couldn't have said it.

"Would you give us a hand with him?" I ask. I don't think Max is weak, and I've been working out for just this kind of situation, but neither of us have Gigi's built-in supernatural strength.

She frowns. "No," she says.

"What?" I ask.

"No," she says again, looking down her nose at all three of us. "I don't like him."

I roll my eyes. I'd insist she explain herself, given that she doesn't even know Faisal, and I specifically haven't talked about him much to her, but I don't. There's no point in arguing with Gigi most of the time, about most things.

Max and I get Faisal up, sharing his weight between our shoulders, and I take back my earlier assumption that he isn't weak. I feel like I'm carrying most of the weight.

"You have a rental car?" I ask, and he nods. "That way."

The choices of rental car available on this small Greek island must have brought Max no end of pain. It's a decent vehicle, but not flashy. It's even—dare I say it?—plain white. Some European brand of wagon that I don't recognize. We lay Faisal across the back seat, and I lift him up as I climb in so that I can ride with his head in my lap.

"You're going to leave the front for Gigi?" Max asks, in the voice he uses when he's deciding not to sound put out.

I'm formulating an answer when Gigi slides into the front passenger seat. "Your card was charged back," she says as Max puts the car in gear and gets us underway. "You owe me."

"Oh, please," Max says. "I'm sure you can handle it.

You manage to prop up that bookstore. How *do* you make your money, anyway?"

I should referee, but I'm just glad Max is needling someone other than me for once. Although I have a very different assessment of the Emporium's relative success.

"Compound interest, mainly," Gigi shoots back in her most self-assured tones. "And how do you make *yours*?"

"Trade secret," Max answers.

I let their prickly conversation wash over me. I cradle Faisal's face, arranging his hair. I trust Max's competence, and he has no reason to lie, but I'm worried all the same. I shove it down when I realize the car has gone silent.

"Are you talking to me?" I ask.

Gigi answers. "The *wizard* wants to know what the hell you think you're doing, calling up the wind nymphs."

She says the word wizard like a slur, just as she did in the village. To her, it is.

"If you have any better ideas, let me know," I say. They must not, because they don't answer. When they speak again, it's the same chiding and poking of each other that doesn't involve me.

It takes less than half an hour to reach the main city of Chios. It's not a big town by any absolute standards, but it feels positively metropolitan compared to the tiny villages and clusters of houses that make up the rest of the island. After some quick googling, I find a hotel in our price range that's got okay reviews and direct Max to it. Max limits himself to four disparaging comments and helps me maneuver Faisal into a room and onto the bed. He leaves me in the room as I struggle to write a note for Faisal to read when he wakes up.

I'm not sure what to say, exactly. I don't know what Faisal will think when he wakes up. If Max only took a few hours of his memory, then he'll remember our phone conversation the night before, and will at least remember planning to come to Chios. His memory probably cuts out partway through the journey here. I do my best.

Faisal,

You're in Chios. I don't know if you remember arriving. You have a lot of questions, and I'll answer all of them. I'm happy I'll finally get to. But I'm on the clock, and I had to leave you here until you wake. Please, please, DON'T GO ANYWHERE until I get back. I don't know how long I'll be.

Elizabeth.

I don't know if that will work, but it's honest without sounding completely insane—I think—and that's the best I can hope for.

I go back outside to an argument—as expected. Back to the grind.

"You want to split us up right now?" Max is asking. "I just caught up with you."

"I'm *not* riding in that thing," Gigi says.

Max rolls his eyes. "Planes are better than they used to be. It's perfectly safe."

"Not with a wizard."

I look back and forth between them.

"You're scared," Max says, seeing an opening to get a little retribution for Gigi's constant complaints. "What can an indestructible woman possibly have to be afraid of?"

Gigi gives him a glare that would melt iron. "Falling is unpleasant. Plane crashes are reported. People notice when I don't have a scratch on me, and that's getting harder and harder to slip under the rug. Ask me how I know."

"I'm sure the crossroads will be faster, anyway," I note, not sure what I want the outcome of this conversation to be, but sure I don't want to let it boil over.

"They won't be," Max counters. "The closest crossroads to Mount Olympus is a long car ride over terrible terrain. The closest airport is fifteen minutes, tops, and the plane is ready to go."

Gigi takes my arm.

"Then you'll beat us there," she says, but I take my arm back before she can step.

A part of me is angry at both of them, for different reasons. I'm annoyed at Gigi for being stubborn—what else is new?—and annoyed at Max for, well, the obvious. But I've exhausted how much Gigi is willing to tell me about what she knows about the situation in private. I haven't gotten the chance with Max.

"I've never been on a private plane," I say instead. I feel about ten inches tall under Gigi's withering gaze, but I don't have to suffer long. She steps away into the north-northeast crossroads, not breaking eye contact until she's no longer there.

"It still shocks me more people don't notice that," Max says, glancing around to make sure no one has. He's already stepping back toward the rental car with a smug look on his face.

I search around for some kind of snide rejoinder, but I can't find one. Instead, I get in the car.

We don't talk about anything substantive until we're on the plane. It's a tiny plane by commercial standards—it probably would have looked hilariously undersized at a normal airport with normal-sized planes. But the Chios airport itself is tiny, so here it seems to scale.

We get buckled in.

"So, you have a jet?" I ask.

"It's a rental." He shrugs off the pretentious words and

looks around as if noticing it for the first time. "And a cheap one."

I laugh. Max and I have very different ideas of what the word "cheap" means. But then, wizards seem to amass vast material wealth the way other people amass collections of plastic grocery bags in the bottom of kitchen cabinets— almost by accident and occasionally useful, if in unnecessary volumes.

I look out the window during takeoff. I always do. But this time, I find my eyes drawn to the sea around the island rather than to the tiny cars and houses that look like toys. How many sirens are underneath? There were only two dozen on the beach. Did they bring more with them and leave them waiting in the sea? How would I know? Did they disperse as soon as their seafood feast was over, using whatever secret transport they have now? How many sirens even *are* there in the world?

"Okay, let's sort this out," Max says, pulling me out of my reverie when we've reached cruising altitude. We're alone in the tiny plane other than the pilot, which is a relief. I don't think the pilot can hear us, and it'll be good to know Max didn't have to invade the sanctity of other minds so that we can have a conversation.

"Sort what out?" I ask, though I doubt I'm going to like the answer.

"Summoning the nymphs is an idiotic idea. There's a threat to the world here. You're not qualified. I'll figure out a way to tell my masters what's going on without implicating you. They'll call in favors from some other wizards. We'll get this fixed."

I can't hold in a bark of a laugh. "Oh, you'll handle it, will you?"

"Yes," he says. "We will."

"Because the nymphs are on such friendly terms with

you? You'll just ask nicely, and they'll decide that actually it's fine? They don't need revenge after all?"

Max frowns. "They don't have to like us. They just have to fear us."

I shake my head. "If they were afraid of you enough for that to work, *you* wouldn't be afraid of them. And before you tell me you're not, let me remind you that there's a freak weather event going on right now, and no way do I believe it's not related to the Nymph of the North Wind dying. It's *way* too cold in the entire northern hemisphere, and wizards have done exactly nothing about it. If that isn't fear, what is?"

He doesn't respond to my points. Instead, he looks out the window. He's looking at the air around us like it's a threat. "Summoning them is a bad idea," he says, his voice less assertive this time.

"Why?" I ask, drawing his eyes back to me. "I've heard what Gigi had to say. They're crazy, etcetera, etcetera. What's your take?"

He takes a moment to decide how he's going to answer, which in itself is something uncommon for Max. "They think they're gods."

"And aren't they?" I ask. "That's what I don't get. They're tied to the winds somehow. They filled the vacuum left by the wind gods back when the wizards killed them. Why *aren't* they gods?"

Max shakes his head. "That's not... That's not how it works."

"So how *does* it work?"

I don't like to push Gigi. I don't mind pushing Max. I'm not sure why.

"Gods draw their power from worship. From people. They're not defined by people or defined by faith, but they do sort of... use them to give themselves power. When the winds were linked to gods, the gods used the power they harvested from people to control the winds. Nymphs pull their power from nature. When they linked themselves to the winds, it went the other way around. And that means they kind of weakened the winds. But they weakened all four of them equally, so that's fine. That's why it's been so cold in the northern hemisphere. The north wind doesn't have a nymph living off of it—harvesting it, weakening it. The other three can't fully compensate. Not without dying."

I absorb that without speaking, hoping he'll continue. After a moment, he does.

"They've always been kind of… off since they took over for the wind gods. They've got more power than they can handle. And there are some things about them that I haven't been told about, but that everyone seems to know but me. Right now, they're grieving and under stress, and I don't know if it's wise to mess with that. There's no rule against shooting the messenger in supernatural society. From what I've been able to find out on the wizard grapevine since Moira told me about it, every wizard is trying *not* to be the one to talk to them. Do you know how bad something has to be to make wizards shrink from an opportunity for notoriety? We give each other so few."

Moira. Max has never told me the name of either of his masters before, but Moira must be the name of the woman. I saw her once, while I was hiding in his living room, praying they didn't find me. I remember her spectacular, artificial beauty. I remember the way she kissed him like she was putting on a leash, and her smile at seeing how much it unraveled him. I remember how shaky he was after she and his male master left, puncturing the little balloon of airy invulnerability that carries him around. No wonder he's been off the last few days.

I listen to the hum of the engines for a bit, putting together my thoughts. This has to be the most pleasant flight I've ever been on, comfort-wise. It's probably gratitude, and the familiarity of human surroundings, that make me speak more candidly to Max than I should. Or maybe it's because I don't fully buy that slipping in Moira's name was an accident.

"The way people talk about wizards," I say, "I can't tell whether they're all powerful or barely hanging on, living on past reputation."

Max's face is hard set when he answers. "What's your best guess?"

I stare, up for a challenge, still mad at him for Faisal. "I know there are limits. I know I'm dumb if I assume what those limits are."

Max settles back. I passed the test, I guess. Or whatever it was.

"You don't think we should summon the nymphs, but even you have to admit the wizards won't take care of it. So how about gods?"

I've never mentioned Gigi's insinuation of genocide to Max. I've never wanted to see his face while discussing it. It's not that I think he'll be ashamed or sad about it—it's more that I don't want to see that he's not.

"There aren't any gods," he says, blank and plain. He doesn't look at me. He looks less like himself than I've ever seen him. There's always so much life in Max, for better or worse.

"Are you sure? Not even Poseidon? He'd come in real handy right now, don't you think?"

The blank expression on Max's face gives way to a harsh laugh. "Especially not Poseidon." His eyes dart to me as though he's surprised he said the words. It's good to know thinking about the death of the gods got to him—he gave away something he wasn't supposed to, and he knows it.

I lean forward. "Why especially not Poseidon?"

He looks up as though appealing to the gods his people killed. "He's dead, Beth. Just drop it."

"No, this is important. Why especially not Poseidon?'

We sit in a stalemate for a long moment.

"I need to know, Max. It could be important."

"It isn't."

"It could be. I need to know. I'm at summoning wind nymphs. We're down to bad ideas."

Max breaks first. "I don't know the details of the battle. But I know when it was over, Poseidon and the sea nymphs were all dead, and Poseidon's trident was left on Atlantis, full of the power he had when he died. It's still there. We check on it sometimes, and it hasn't moved. If Poseidon were alive, he wouldn't leave his power there. Gods don't forsake power. It's not in their nature."

"How do you know?" I ask, unable to keep a trace of bitterness out of my voice. "You've never met one." And hopefully, he never will.

He settles back in his absurdly comfortable private plane seat, looking a little defeated. "No god is going to leave his power outside his body where wizards can get at it. Believe that, Beth. Poseidon isn't going to come save us."

Max stares out the window for a bit, looking down at clouds. What would Poseidon think of airplanes? Is Max wondering that, too?

"If that's true, why hasn't a wizard taken it?" I ask. My voice is softer now, less desperate than it was before. I guess it doesn't matter so much, but I still want to know.

"God magic is in a different category from everything else. It functions differently. It's a different system. And it doesn't always mix with wizard magic. Sometimes it's fine.

Sometimes the interactions can be explosive. Doesn't matter as much when you're only dealing with small artifacts or simple spells, but the trident is a huge source of power. Any decent wizard would be taking his life into his hands by keeping it nearby. And it's a big enough source of power that trying to stash it somewhere won't work. It would just put a target on your back. So wizards leave it there. No one touches it."

Something's missing in this explanation. I can feel it. I give Max a chance to keep talking on his own, but he doesn't.

"They just leave it in Atlantis?" I prod.

He looks back out the window, and I wonder if we're wondering the same thing again.

"They just leave it in Atlantis," he confirms, clearly done talking.

I want to push him more, but I let it go. The expression on Max's face when I brought up gods might have been blank at the time, but I'm seeing the aftereffects in him now, in the way he seems more tired than he should be. At least, I hope I am.

This is more info on wizard anything than I've been able to get out of Max in the entire last six months. I can't help but think it has something to do with feeling guilty for what he did to Faisal. I feel dirty for pushing him and trading for that with Faisal's pain. Well, not pain. But I'm grateful all the same. Hopefully, it'll last. Hopefully, it's enough.

"So, summoning the nymphs it is," I say, but my attempt at brightness mostly fails.

Max opens his mouth to speak.

"Unless you have a better idea," I say quickly.

He doesn't.

ELEVEN

A Summoning

We take a helicopter to the top of Mount Olympus. Again, thanks to Max's overly sufficient resources. Technically speaking, the helicopter isn't allowed to *land* on Mount Olympus, just fly above it. But once we get in the air, it'll be a trivial trick for Max to get him to bend the rules for us. I don't know if he'll use money or magic, but either way, he'll get the job done.

It might be embarrassing how excited I am to ride in a helicopter for the first time, but I don't care. I can't play it cool. Too much stress, too much emotional upset, too high a chance I'm either going to get myself or billions of people killed.

When I texted Gigi with directions to meet us on the pad, she didn't want to, but it turns out it's a bit of a hike to the summit, and we're on a deadline. Plus, we have an animal with us. A goat. A female goat. And a group of people, most of whom don't even speak Greek, bringing a goat on a hike seems likely to get noticed.

We carry some other things with us, too. A handful of seeds. All the liquor from Max's rental jet's in-flight bar.

I don't know if they mark up the booze on a rental jet. Maybe? Max doesn't whine about it, but considering Wilbur was able to round up a live goat as his own contribution, it feels spiteful for him to force Max to pony up the liquor. Which makes me think that they probably *do* mark it up, and Wilbur knows this.

I spend most of the helicopter flight looking out the window at the earth below. It's so small from up here. Pride wells up in me. I spend a lot of time thinking about how unmatched humans are in the supernatural world— weighing the consequences of exposing the general public to what's been going on under their noses. If I achieve my goals and learn enough about things to reveal the existence of magic in a believable way to the world at large, I'm sure there will be bloodshed. I'm sure not everyone will like it. I'm sure there will be unintended side effects.

But I'm also sure that I am hovering above a mountain that was once considered the seat of the most powerful deities, and it's human technology that got me here. And wizards might not be really human, but they're built on a human base, and at least at one point, they conquered the world. We've got this. Maybe not at first. Maybe it'll be difficult. Maybe a lot of people will die. But we deserve a chance.

I glance at the inhuman occupants of the helicopter. I don't know if my thoughts are showing on my face. Gigi seems, as always, unfazed. But Wilbur?

I hadn't noticed Wilbur's expression as we got loaded up into the helicopter. There was too much to do, and I felt a bit rushed, trying to get off of the helicopter pad without the pilot asking any questions that would make Max mess with his mind. That was a little tricky since Gigi weighs a lot more than you would think from looking at her with the wizards' illusion intact. Getting off the ground was… interesting. The poor man seemed, in a word, *confused* by how his instruments were treating him.

But as I look at Wilbur now, I see that the clouded, furious expression he had at the Emporium yesterday has intensified. He doesn't meet my eyes when I look at him, but I'm sure he notices my gaze because his frown transforms to a scowl. He may or may not be doing the troll equivalent of scowling underneath, but the wizard's illusion tells me that's how he really feels.

I shift my gaze back out the window, my pride officially tamped down. Humans may be capable of miracles, but if I—a human—can't even figure out what's going on with my closest thing to a supernatural friend, we might need more than modern technological miracles to carry us through.

Wilbur doesn't address me when we land. He's not happy, but he goes about the motions of setting up for the summoning, nonetheless. He gives me the small basket of seeds, while Gigi holds on to the goat. He doesn't give Max any instructions, but when Wilbur heads to the end of the trail to put up some signage in Greek that I can't read, Max sets down his possibly expensive booze and heads over to the helicopter pilot. He gives him a kiss on the cheek and sends him on his way.

Seems excessive, but I'm not picking another fight right now.

The Big Freeze—as the news has been calling it—has had the lucky effect of scaring off most tourists, so I think Wilbur's sign should be sufficient. No human but me is in sight as Wilbur wordlessly adjusts us to our places in a rough triangle around the goat.

I almost forget to give Wilbur his payment, but as he moves me by my shoulders into position without meeting my eye, there's that little tugging thought of "I should give him something" that reminds me. I pull his honey and filo confection out of my pocket. Max and I got it from a roadside stall on the way to the helicopter pad. It's wrapped in cling film, and I feel like a kid at a bake sale, offering something so obviously homemade for his approval.

It's not actually an olive branch, but we're in the right place for that. And trolls are big fans of metaphor. So, as I offer him his payment, I have a hopeful expression on my face. Maybe that will be enough for him to forgive me for whatever I've done.

He pauses and clenches his jaw. He still doesn't look at me. I unwrap the cling film. With a quick puff of breath, he grabs the little treat with one hand and shoves it in his mouth. He still doesn't look at me. He's been paid but not won over.

Later. I'll have to figure that out later.

When we're all in position, Wilbur takes a deep breath in and out, and I feel we've crossed a threshold. He starts chanting something in Greek. I keep my mouth shut, but when Wilbur leaves a pregnant pause, Gigi and Max repeat the last phrase he said. Max's Greek isn't as easy and smooth as Gigi's, but he stumbles his way through it.

After maybe thirty seconds of that, Wilbur leads the goat to Max, who gets the clue and picks up the bottles. Still speaking Greek, with a steady, even tone, Wilbur gestures to the goat's back. Max empties the booze, bottle after bottle, onto the goat's back.

The goat, for her part, does not appreciate this, but Wilbur holds her tightly.

When Max's bottles are empty, Wilbur leads the goat to me, the grim and solemn constant of his chant in my ears. He gestures to the goat's head, and I sprinkle the seeds from the little basket onto the coarse tuft of hair between the goat's ears. I keep going until all the seeds are gone and

look at Wilbur's face expectantly. There's no acknowledg-
ment of me there. I try not to read that much into it. He's
got a job to do, after all.

The goat doesn't seem to mind my seeds as much as
Max's booze. She reaches up, trying to catch a few. I let
her. Might as well give her something nice. I notice many
of my seeds fall down off of her head—only a few get
stuck. I guess it's more about the action than the result.
Most of Max's booze has made it onto the ground.

Next, Wilbur leads the goat to Gigi. He doesn't motion
anything to her. They had the trip from the crossroads to
the helicopter pad to discuss whatever they wanted to do.
And maybe Wilbur isn't as annoyed at her as he is with
me? Whatever the case, Gigi doesn't hesitate. When
Wilbur pauses his chant, instead of answering him with a
repeated-back phrase, Gigi pulls out a knife I didn't know
she had sheathed in her sleeve. In one fluid, confident
motion, she slits the goat's throat.

As the goat struggles and bleats out its terror, I hear
nothing but its cries and some singing birds. The chill in
the air bites at me. I want to look away from the goat—
from its panicked eyes. I force myself to watch, hating my
part in this. Hating the hand that sprinkled the seeds onto
its head.

Wilbur pulls the struggling goat to the center of the
triangle. It fights his direction. It fights the coming dark of
death.

It loses.

I feel a little sick, ashamed of myself for it. We watch in
silence as the goat settles down. The birds have stopped
singing. After an eternity, the goat is still and silent.

Without speaking, Wilbur retrieves a matchbox from a
pocket of his worn-but-clean thrift shop clothes. His
stubby, clumsy fingers bend the delicate box getting a

match out. He lights the match, and the silence is so absolute that even ten feet away and outside, I can hear the sound of the match striking.

He drops the lit match on the alcohol-soaked body of the dead goat. Flame shoots up, faster and bigger than they should. Clouds of smoke—far, far too much smoke—billow up.

I look at Wilbur's face, hoping to get some sense of if the ritual is done and what we should expect now. Finally, he looks at me, spite and pain in his eyes. And then he steps into the crossroads and is gone.

I open my mouth to call out after him, useless as that call may be, but I feel the air pulled out of my lungs.

I look to Max, who has the same shocked expression as I do. And then the roiling motion of the smoke grabs my attention. Too much wind. Far too much wind.

In a matter of seconds, a hurricane-force gale besets the still day. My clothing whips and flaps. I have just enough presence of mind to take off my glasses and stuff them in an interior pocket before an unexpected shift in the wind blows me over.

I don't hit the ground. Another gust of wind catches me and throws me back the other way. My feet lift off the ground. Back and forth, farther and farther up, I'm pulled from the earth at the mercy of the sky.

TWELVE

A Question

The sickness I felt at the killing of the goat has a new cause now. I roll over and over, hit by gust after unexpected gust. I try to get my bearings, but the horizon becomes less and less helpful.

There are other figures rising up with me. Max! I reach for him, but I'm not in control of my motion. He reaches for me, but he doesn't look in control of himself either. It's pure luck that he grabs on to a handful of my jacket, and we have just enough of a hold to link arms.

We journey up and up together, wind stinging our faces. I cry out, the sound carried helplessly away. A vice has clamped on to my left ankle, and the odd sensation of feeling grasped so desperately, but without pain—the amulet wouldn't allow for pain—pulls me out of myself, out of terror of the moment.

Awash with sudden clarity, I look down and see Gigi, a firm set in her jaw and determination in her black eyes.

And then the sight of Gigi and the earth so, so far below her gets swallowed up in wispy white. A horrible chill sinks into my body. I shiver hard, but not hard enough to dislodge Gigi's hand.

Gigi's solid fingertips dig into my lower thigh, just above my knee. When we've cleared the cloud layer, I see her determined face again.

She wraps a cool, firm arm around my waist, anchoring me to her. Max, less dense than Gigi and only connected to me through our linked arms, flies out above us, mostly upside down.

Maybe I could try to get Gigi to wrap her other arm around his waist, but I don't try. I don't think either of them would like it. And besides, at least we aren't flying away from each other anymore, and our heads are vaguely near each other. I don't try to fight the wind to speak. I don't try to fight the wind for any reason at all. I may be foolhardy, but every now and then I know a futile cause when I see it.

We rise, battered together and propelling by shifting, raging winds. Up and up. Farther and farther. Further and further into a domain that can't support our lives. In the snatches between gusts, I feel the atmosphere around me grow less hospitable. Colder. Harder to breathe. And then, at last, impossible to breathe. Only the winds our captors provide us with offer oxygen. We struggle to keep ourselves calm, to keep ourselves alive.

Well, Max and I do. Gigi just looks bored and annoyed at me when she catches my eye. Funny how well she can communicate *look what you got us into* without saying a word.

I can't tell how long it's been; terror has a way of messing with time. But very gradually I become aware that we aren't rising anymore. The wild gusts back and forth even out to a steady current of warm, breathable air.

I keep as still as possible. Part of me wants to retrieve my glasses so I can look around and have some hope of seeing the wind nymphs. But though the glasses became hardier and more likely to stay on when my father enchanted them, I don't want to test their boundaries. Plus, the last time I saw my dad's notes on how he enchanted the glasses, the process looked challenging, so I don't want to risk losing them if I don't have to. Instead, I focus on keeping my body as still as possible, avoiding any movement that might catch the steady current of air in the wrong way and send us all hurtling uncertainly.

There's so much thin atmosphere. I read in a book, way back in high school, about how much thin atmosphere there is before our world becomes nothing. There's no solid line, like we think of borders. Just less, and less, and less.

As we wait for the nymphs to speak to us, my terror and horror gradually melt to gratitude. This is gorgeous. This is rare. This is an impossible moment I never would have had in my normal life. My mind wanders to NASA and the existence of space camp, and all those dreams of being an astronaut I never had and never expected would be fulfilled.

And then I hear a low, solid, languid feminine voice whispering in my ear with a slight Greek accent, and horror bathes my bones again.

"Well?" the voice says. "You called us?"

I swallow hard and resist the urge to shout. Somehow, shouting feels like it would be giving ground.

"We did. I am—"

A second lighter, higher-pitched voice cuts me off, in American English with a hint of California and more than a hint of excitement.

"Oh, we know who you are! We hear you, you know. We hear everything. *Just everything.* Do you want to hear a joke? I heard a good one the other day."

The first voice speaks again. "What do you want from us, Arbiter?"

I give it a beat, curious if the joke will come. But nothing does. I scan around myself for any trace of who's talking, but as expected, I see nothing.

"We need to see the body," I say, trying to keep my tone conversational, and maybe even succeeding. "Both bodies. And the murder weapon."

A third voice, this one all harsh edges and vocal fry with an accent I can't identify, answers me. It laughs before it speaks, though neither of the other two voices joins it. "You think there are two bodies, Arbiter?"

I look back and forth between Max and Gigi. Judging by the expressions on their faces, they're hearing at least the nymph's side of the conversation, even if they might not be able to hear my voice, but they seem as confused as I am about the third nymph's words.

"The nymph who died and the siren who killed her. Isn't that right?" I ask.

The third voice laughs. Again, she laughs alone. "And how many of us are there?" she asks.

I look at Max, who gives me a *hell if I know* look.

"Three?" I guess.

"And how many of us do you think there were before we were winds? When we were breezes?"

Neither Max's nor Gigi's faces give me a hint to the answer.

"More?" I ask, and the third voice laughs. This time, the second voice, high and thin and piercing, laughs with her. The third voice continues under the second voice's laughter.

"And how do you think we got that way?"

What do I know of Greek gods? What have I heard

about their deaths? What they do to one another upon each other's deaths?

My eyes widen. Max's eyes widen. Gigi's eyes roll.

"You ate them?" I ask, the words small and cracked.

The second and third voices laugh more at my reaction, but when the first voice speaks again, they grow silent.

"Oh, not like *that*," she says.

I open my mouth, hoping words will come, but the second voice speaks before I can.

"Do they not eat with their mouths like we do? I'm sure I've seen humans eat with their mouths. I'm sure I've seen it many times?"

At this, the third voice's laughter splits my skull. I can't think. The gulps of air from the slipstream around us aren't enough.

"And will you replace her?" Max's voice sounds almost as prominent as the nymphs' voices—not nearly as small and easily lost as mine. He must be pulling that magical ventriloquism trick I saw him use the day I met him. I'm grateful for the redirection, but I can't get the image of nymphs eating the dead body of their sister out of my head. It helps that I can't see what they look like, and I'm only working with stock images in my head. Thank God for that.

The third voice's laughter trails off, and while it's hard to be sure without seeing facial expressions, I have the distinct feeling Max has hit on an awkward topic.

"We will," the first voice says, not very convincingly.

"When?" Max insists.

The second voice pipes up, sounding like a whiny child. "It's so *complicated*. We can't just pick someone."

I think of the stories on the news about people in the south freezing in their poorly insulated trailers and houses, not meant for this kind of cold snap. "When?" I ask.

"When we find someone who *deserves* it," the third voice drips into my ears.

"Deserves it how? Good or bad?" Max shouts.

"Both," the first voice says, firmer this time. "It's a reward, but it's also a punishment. You wouldn't understand."

Max, Gigi, and I shoot each other annoyed looks that we probably shouldn't—just because we can't see them doesn't mean they can't see us, after all. The third voice laughs at us. The second voice joins in, high and chittering, like the time I visited a cousin's one-bedroom apartment with four birds in cages inside.

"Do you agree to be held by the ruling of this arbitration?" I scream into the laughter, losing the battle for control over my tone. I need to get us back on track.

My question stops the laughter. Hey, that's something. Screaming at bullies has never worked out for me before.

"If it's fair," the first voice answers. "But you understand what my sister means. When they killed the Nymph of the North Wind, it wasn't just one of us. Each of us is so many. They killed so many."

But if they ate her, then… aren't they in her now? Or is that only when they were alive? Yeah, I'm not asking that. I always figured the whole eating-family-members stuff was more symbolic than this. I'd say I'm on unsteady ground, but we left ground behind a while ago.

"Then will you help me make the ruling fair? Will you show me the body? Will you show me the weapon?"

No answer comes. I give it a few seconds. Ten. Twenty. Max, Gigi, and I look at each other. And then I see Gigi's eyes widen as she looks off into the distance. Max and I follow her gaze and see a small figure. It grows closer and closer, rolling and twisting bonelessly in the wind.

As it comes near, I can make out more detail. Pale skin.

Long, wavy black hair snapping in the wind as he moves. I see him as human, with my glasses in my pocket. But by the time he's an arm's length away, held up in the same slipstream as we are, I've managed to dig them out of my pocket and put them on without dropping them.

He has that same long tail I saw on the sirens on the beach, split and scarred. His features are sharper than they looked as a human, and he's close enough that I can just make out some of his needle-sharp rows of teeth. He has a short, curved knife in his left hand, decorated with Greek letters I can't identify. There's a desperation in his grasp that reminds me of a child clutching a blanket.

He's not a threat to me now. He's not a threat to anyone. His face is frozen, contorted in agony. He looks scared, and horrified, and sad. Is this how sirens die, locked in their final moment? Or is this because of how the nymph killed him?

"Do you have any idea why a siren would want to kill your sister?" I ask, the words coming from some automatic place in me that's watched too many police procedurals. The first voice answers me.

"Some sirens think we conspired with Poseidon and the wizard that cursed them. They think we agreed to cast them down into the sea, where the wizard's curse would change them." The words are even and measured, but they carry disgust within them all the same.

I stare at the man—the boy, really. He looks so much younger than almost any of the sirens I saw on the beach.

"And did you?" The wind carries the words away from my mouth before I can shove them the fuck back in.

I wait for the harsh rejoinder.

Instead, I feel myself start to fall.

THIRTEEN

A Fall

I look to Max and see my panic reflected in his face. I look to Gigi, but her face is only a mask of annoyance. By instinct, Max and I have flattened ourselves out, trying to get as much air resistance as we can without losing grasp on each other.

But Gigi, all aggravated smirks and rolling eyes, loosens her grasp from around my waist, folds her arms over her chest, and points her feet straight down toward the ground, speeding her fall.

I look away as she fades into the distance below us. She'll survive this. We won't.

Time feels weird and wrong. It must be passing slowly. Every breath is an age. Max pulls me into his side, tightening his grip. I've whipped around out of control and am lying facing up while he's facing down. I tighten my grip on Max in return and nod. I'm glad he's got a plan. I'm glad I brought him. All hands on deck.

He reaches out a hand below us, and I crane my neck to see what he's doing. He says a few words I can't hear, and a black stone about the size of a basketball shoots from his hand, racing down to earth significantly faster than we are.

Max curses. I still can't hear it, but I understand what he means.

Maybe it would have been a good idea to use the equal and opposite reaction of a spell to propel an object forward to slow our fall. But the problem with magic is that it can't be relied upon to listen to physics. The force to propel the stone from his hand was created from nothing—no kickback. Handy in a fight, to avoid being thrown around, but not so handy now.

Or is it?

I lean in toward Max's face, getting close enough to be sure he can hear me if I shout.

"Shoot up!" I say.

He gives me a confused look.

"Shoot! *Up*!" I shout again.

He doesn't seem to understand me, but he obeys anyway, maneuvering himself around so he can keep hold of me tightly while still being able to reach his hand out toward the little sky we have left above us. He aims up and a little to the left.

I don't watch his face as he says the spell I don't know again. I watch the end of his hand instead, so I can see the rock erupt from it, hurtling upwards with a rush of unaccountable force.

My trove of magic spells and information begins with a book by a wizard named Stuart. He chose his five easiest spells and put them right at the front so that humans would have something approachable to cut their teeth on, to believe that magic is real and achievable even for non-wizards who can't see or feel it. The first spell is creating a fire. The second spell is enchanting a key to open any lock.

The third is grabbing an object across the room and compelling it to fly to your hand.

I figured out the first spell in one day. The second spell took me a couple of weeks. The third spell I have been trying for months upon months, and I have begun to believe Stuart put it into his list of easy spells just to fuck with me. Wizards will be wizards.

I got the first part of it—forming a connection to the object and linking it to your hand—to work within three weeks. But I cannot for the life of me pull the object toward me. In hours after days after weeks of trying, the most I've ever been able to do to the object is move it the same amount that I move my arm.

But failure can sometimes have a purpose. I am really, *really* good at grabbing things.

I move my fingers into a position that feels as natural to them now as a handshake. I call up Right Mind for this part of the spell—a sense of desperate longing and despair. It's pretty easy to achieve.

My body jerks, wrenching as I make the connection. I cry out in pain. Max almost loses his grip. But I fight through it and hold the connection, robbing the little boulder of all its upward momentum to slow our fall, just a little. Just maybe, if we do it over and over, it'll be enough.

A mix of terror and joy on his face, Max shoots again, and I grab the projectile again. I want to swap over and use my right arm, but I stop myself. Given how painful this is, I'm guessing my left arm is going to be useless afterward. I can't count on Max to heal me when we hit the ground. I can't count on him to live. I need my right arm to work for whatever is coming next.

The second time is a little easier. We're just slightly slower, and I know the pain is coming. Tears fly out of the corners of my eyes. Max fires faster and faster. I catch each one. Pain screams through my body each time. I never get used to it. I force myself to keep doing it. My world—the wild, windy, loud, cold, horrific world—narrows to this one painful task. This one horrific mission. Sacrifice my arm. Stay alive.

I don't know how long it takes. A long time. Far, far too long of a time. I only know we must be closer to the ground when I hear Max's voice in my ear, fighting with the agony in my arm for my attention.

"Land on the jacket!" he tells me.

I can't acknowledge. There's not enough of me left outside of my task and the pain it causes me.

Another few thousand-year seconds go by, and then I hear Max's voice, closer to my ear so that he can speak more quietly. His lips brush against my lobe, forming a weird counterpoint to the pain in my arm.

"The knife was enchanted by a wizard," he says, his hurried voice surreally loud, not carried away by wind.

And then I feel him shove me away from him, propelling me out to the side, leading with my back.

FOURTEEN

An Admission

I hit the dirt hard, the pain in my arm upstaged by the wildly disorienting feeling of getting the wind knocked out of me. I struggle to find my breath, coughing and sputtering. The blue and white sky above me feels like a lie. It's a threat—a menace. I pull my thoughts together around that anger and it brings me back into myself.

I take stock. I hit the ground first on my jacket, but my back underneath it feels fine. My head hurts a little but not too badly. My arm is the worst. The rest of me seems… fine? Harsh, bitter laughter spills out of me, each sob of laughter strained and separate. I fell from the sky and I'm fine. Essentially. Alive, anyway.

And I am never, *ever* going to complain about Max borrowing anything I own to enchant it again.

Max.

I sit up, searching around for him. How far from the ground had we been when he shoved me away from him? Farther than it must have felt like. He's maybe twenty feet away from me.

He is not so lucky. He is not fine.

My glasses have stayed on my face through everything like a champ, so he looks the way he always does when I see him through them—like he's a high-resolution photo that's been pasted onto a completely different background and no effort has been taken to make him blend in.

I see the blood before I can tell where it's coming from. How did he land? How *hard* did he land? The ground between us is dry and mostly flat. I glance around, searching for help, but there's none nearby to offer me. In the distance, Mount Olympus looms farther than I would have thought, but we must have altered our angle of descent a decent amount. I guess we're lucky we didn't fall into water.

My legs feel strange and stiff, but they ultimately cooperate as I force them to scramble toward Max. I take stock of him.

He's conscious, barely. From what I can tell, he didn't land on his head, which is what matters. As long as he didn't bash his own brains out, he should be able to come back from this, I think. Just as soon as he can get the presence of mind to say the magic healing words that he won't share with me. But he's lost a lot of blood and he's losing consciousness.

"Max!" I scream at him, the sound of my own voice so weird without rushing wind to carry it away. He doesn't hear me. He's drifting off.

I need to find the wounds and stop the bleeding. If I can get him to the hospital and they can get enough blood back into him, he'll be able to heal himself when he wakes up. He just needs to not die in the meantime.

Just don't die, Max. Is that really so much to ask?

His legs are a mess. His left one, especially, has jagged bones breaking through the skin in multiple places. This is where the blood is coming from. How did it get all over him?

It's hard to take off his belt with my useless left arm, but I manage. It's even harder to get it around his upper thigh, just above his most profusely bleeding wound, but I do that, too. I cast around for a stick tighten it and find one. I think it might break as I twist it tight, dry as it is. Luckily, it doesn't. But twisting it requires both hands. Max's eyelids flutter as I scream in pain from forcing my left arm to participate.

I look at his wounds after I get the tourniquet as tight as I can manage. Belts are bad tourniquets, I remember hearing once. There's a risk you'll over tighten and cause more damage. But that's not an issue with Max, since he can heal whatever damage I do after the fact, so I'm fine with it. Just as long as it stops the tide of blood rushing from his body.

It does.

I rock back, letting relief wash through me. It's fine. We're fine. I didn't get us killed. Close, but not quite. Not this time.

I want to sit in that relief, but I can't let myself. Max needs to get somewhere that will look after him until he comes to his senses and can set everything to rights on his own. He hates hospitals—too much mental mojo cleanup afterwards—but too fucking bad, Max. You're taking what I can get you.

I stand up, glad the fall didn't hurt my legs, and look around. There should be a house, or a building, or something. I don't know what direction I'd search to find it, though.

My phone would know, but considering I fell from the sky, there's no way it's not broken.

Although…

I reach into my jacket pocket and pull out my phone. Not a scratch on it. Huh. Good jacket.

My first impulse is to call Gigi. She would have survived the crash, and she left her handbag sitting on the ground when we were taken, so there's a chance her phone is fine and she's found it again. She probably fell a lot straighter than we did.

But I know how Gigi feels about wizards. And I know how Gigi feels about opportunities. I need to get Max somewhere safe first.

I call up a map app, grateful again that Max's upgrades have fooled my phone into thinking I'm not roaming. GPS tells me I'm not too far from a road. I look back at Max. He's out. I stifle the urge to go back to him and tell him I'll be right back. He wouldn't hear me anyway.

What's the emergency number here? I try 911, 999, and 111 before giving up and googling. 112. I get through to someone who, *thank God*, speaks English.

The rest is easy but nerve-wracking. I describe to them where I am based on the map. I wait by the road—so, so long—for the ambulance to get here, and lead them back to where Max lies. I'm not sure if he's alive when the medical team gets to him, and I stop breathing until I see them check his pulse, and then start working on him as though he's alive, speaking rapid-fire Greek to one another and unpacking implements and preparing the stretcher. They give me the option to ride with him back to the hospital in the ambulance, but I refuse. I don't need Gigi to know what hospital Max is at, or that he's at a hospital at all. It'll be easiest not to worry that way.

A couple of the EMT-equivalents try to ask me questions about what happened, but I just say "what?" a lot and throw on a Southern accent for reasons that probably don't reflect well on me. They give it a good try, but I give them a lot of "I don't know whatchure sayin'. Talk English!" and that does the trick. They want me to go with them. They're insisting that I should. I probably look suspicious. But there aren't enough of them to fight with me and save the man's life, so they speak into the radio and yell at me to stay where I am.

Then they're gone, and me and my aching arm are alone.

I wait a few moments, trying to think of what this reminds me of. It comes to me—the time Max just about lost his mind in a graveyard, and I had to leave him there even though I'd told him I wouldn't. This isn't a direct parallel. The situation was very different. But it makes me feel good, anyway. I didn't abandon him this time.

I shake my head and let the memory roll off. I call Gigi, walking as quickly as I can toward a cluster of buildings to avoid whoever the people in the ambulance called on the radio.

"Well, fancy hearing from you," her voice comes to me as I slump against a wall. I can't get a handle on how she feels from the inflection. But that's normal, so I soldier on.

"You're fine, I presume?" I'm not as good at disguising my voice. The bitterness and jealousy come through.

"Always am." There's a weird, sad note in that. I push through.

"Me and Max got separated, and he won't answer his phone." Technically, both of those things are true. "I need to get back to Chios. Can you come get me?"

After some rough negotiation and talk of maps, carefully avoiding answering the question of how I survived (Magic, Gigi, obviously!) and whether I think Max is also alive (Magic, Gigi, obviously! I think! Probably!), we figure out it's easiest if I just take a cab to the nearest crossroads. Turns out where Max and I came down isn't too far away.

I'm able to pay for the cab with a credit card, and Gigi's waiting for me when I arrive. Without a word, she scoops her arm through mine and walks three steps.

And then we're back on Chios, standing looking at the Casino. It's still daytime. It feels like so much has happened, but it's only been three hours since I was last here, give or take, according to the disappearing brown bark marks on my wrist. And since it is day, there are no humans being walked into the Casino to bet their souls away.

How many had there been last night? I shudder and push away the thought.

We head back again to the village, and Gigi rents the same car as she did last time, though she doesn't pester me to pay for it this time. My injured arm and shaken disposition are good for something, I guess. It feels like we've come full circle when we're sitting there again, driving the same roads, headed again toward the hotel where we stashed Faisal.

And then Gigi rolls up her windows, and I do the same, so that we feel comfortable talking with less of a risk of spying wind nymphs.

"So," she says matter-of-factly, loud in the intimate space of the car, "you almost got yourself killed for nothing."

I shift in the seat, bringing up my feet to rest on the dash. I watch the landscape—trees and hillside and sparkling waters—go by outside my window for a minute.

"Not nothing," I say, when I judge I've left her waiting long enough that I have the slightest chance of having successfully annoyed her. "We found out a wizard was involved."

It was a mistake to have this conversation while driving. She stares at me with an intensity that makes me glad, as I so often am when Gigi is around, that I don't have my glasses on. And so long as her eyes are directed at me, they're not directed at the road.

"How so?" she asks.

"The knife was enchanted by a wizard," I say quickly this time, hoping she'll look back where we're heading. This game is getting old.

As if reading my mind, she looks back at the road.

"That's quite a coincidence," Gigi says.

"How so?" I ask.

And then she waits to continue, remaining silent for *just* as long as I did when I was trying to annoy her.

"How much has Max told you about his masters?" she asks.

I don't know how much Gigi knows about how I used Max's masters to solve the problems caused by my father's death six months ago. I don't know how much Gigi knows about them in general, or about how much they terrify Max.

"What about them?" I ask.

She fixes me with a mercifully short glance before continuing. "Wizards don't measure their lineages the way humans do. You never hear about wizard families. It's not really clear why, because wizards are good at keeping *some* secrets. My best guess has always been that magic wreaks havoc on the reproductive system, so they have to pull some disturbing magical shenanigans to make more little wizards."

I make a mental note to google my egg-freezing options when this is all over, presuming I survive. Gigi continues.

"So, wizards view their apprentices and their masters as their true families."

I wait a little longer, until Gigi's made it plain she's

expecting a little more audience participation.

"And how does wizard lineage relate to the current situation in which we find ourselves?" I ask, with just enough lip and sarcasm to make me feel all right with myself.

"Because I was around when the sirens fell from the skies, and the wizard who had his hand in it is in Max's family tree, as it were. He's a direct descendant, through his master. The male one. I know he has two. How sure are you that your little wizard is telling you everything he knows about sirens?"

Goddamn. Fucking. Wizards.

I lean my head back and groan.

"Yes, that's more or less what I thought, too," Gigi says.

I rearrange the situation in my head. "How do you know so much about wizards?"

Through mostly closed eyes, I sense more than see her shrug in my peripheral vision.

"It pays to stay informed of the things that can hurt you."

"And wizards can hurt you?" I ask.

A long pause follows, and I get the feeling it isn't for my benefit this time.

"They can make me suffer," she says in distinct but gentle words.

I let the conversation rest for a while. I'm not sure I want to hear about that. The air in the car is getting a bit stuffy, and the broken A/C and the underpowered ventilation system aren't doing much to stop it. I'd blame whoever the car belongs to, but it probably has more to do with my swam-in-slept-in-nearly-died-in clothes than it does with the car's failings. I want to roll down my window again and get some air moving, but we've got to finish the conversation first. Just for paranoia's sake.

"At least that means we have a lead," I say lightly—and a little too smugly for the circumstances.

"Oh, do we?"

"Yes," I say. "You won't like it, though."

I don't have to look at Gigi to know she's rolling her eyes. "When do I ever? What's the lead?"

"We go see Max's masters."

It is a thing of beauty to hear a woman as refined as Gigi snort. I treasure the opportunity. "Even if that were a good idea, which it obviously isn't, I don't know exactly where they are. Not since the seventies. Do you?"

I shake my head, my eyes idly picking one tree to follow in the world outside before jumping to another. "No, but I can find out."

Gigi breathes in and out slowly, as if reigning in her annoyance. Does Gigi have to breathe? She wouldn't die if she didn't. Does it bother her if she doesn't? Would she suffer?

"Have it your way. You find out where he is, and I'll take you to the nearest crossroads. But then I'm out. I'll go no closer."

I pull my feet back down off the dashboard and sit up in my seat. "Sounds good. You can take me right after we drop Faisal at home."

When I say his name, my heart gives a little jump. This time the conversation will go better. It has to. I'm not sure what I'll say, exactly, but it has to.

"Oh, I'm not taking Faisal through the crossroads."

I turn my head sharply to look at Gigi. "What? Why?"

"I told you, I don't like him."

She can't be serious. "Yes, you said that. But *why* don't you like him?"

Gigi pauses, and I resist the urge to fill the silence.

"I think he'll hold you back. He'll keep you from being

as effective as you could be for what I want you for. He'll give you too much of a reason not to go all the way, if all the way will put you at risk." There's no trace of emotion in Gigi's words, and she stares straight ahead.

"Wouldn't that be a good thing?" I ask, and Gigi shrugs.

"For you, personally. But I've never given you any reason to believe I care about you personally. I care about what you'll do. I care about helping you do it, so I can have a hand in how things play out afterwards. I think he'll hold you back."

Just when I think I'm starting to make headway with Gigi, our rocky—heh—relationship comes down around my ears. She doesn't *always* disappoint me, but she does just often enough that I can't rely on her.

"Besides," she continues, her voice returning to its usual conversational sharpness, "I told you—I'll bring a human other than you through the crossroads only if I have a good enough reason. You worrying about him isn't a good enough reason."

"Please, stop. You're making me feel too warm and fuzzy inside. I can't take it," I grumble.

"Some things are too important to trust to personal feelings," she says. And I know Gigi can't lie, but there's truth, and there's truth. And I think this may be the most honest thing she's ever said to me.

"Okay," I mutter, shaking my head as though I could shake off the funk our conversation is swiftly putting me in. "I guess I'm putting him on a plane."

I can tell from Gigi's voice that she has her sharp, wicked grin back on. "If you think that's a good idea, considering who you've angered recently…"

And then she rolls down her window, letting the wind back in, and ending the conversation.

FIFTEEN

An Intervention

Faisal isn't in his room when we get to the hotel. The note is still there, but he's gone. I open up the closet and look inside, feeling ridiculous.

"He isn't here," Gigi says from the doorway, her voice annoyingly chipper.

"I can see that," I say. "Would you mind asking the hotel staff if they saw where he went, or is that too close to helping him for you?"

Gigi obliges, but she takes her sweet time in passing the information to me in English, chatting with one of the housekeepers for a solid minute instead.

"He went to the beach," she throws over her shoulder at me casually.

"Which one?" I ask.

Gigi points a languid finger in a direction. She uses her left arm, even though it would have been more natural in her position to use her right. I try not to take that as a subtle dig at the injury I've tried, albeit badly, to hide. It probably isn't. I'm probably reading slights into her behavior from our conversation in the car that I shouldn't be.

That same sore left arm hurts with every step as I run toward the beach. I'm already exhausted—near-death will do that to you, even when you think you've started getting used to that sort of thing—but my mounting terror pushes me through it. I don't like the idea of Faisal so close to the ocean.

I search the beach. It's not warm enough for a crowd of sunbathers. I see only a few people in chairs and…

My heart drops.

Faisal.

In front of him stands a familiar naked woman with swimsuit-model proportions and a wicked smile. Her long, wet black hair spills over her back, and her feet—false feet, I know—have a layer of sand on them.

She doesn't have him in the water yet. There's that. But when she lays her hand on his chest, I scream.

It should have been his name. That would have made more sense. But the terrified animal noise I make does just as well at getting his attention.

And, of course, everyone else's.

The beach isn't big, and he's on the close end of it. It only takes seconds for me to reach Faisal and for the siren's smile to fade. I don't know what to say and talking just got me in trouble the last time I tried to do this. So instead, I awkwardly fumble my glasses off of my head and over his eyes. He adjusts them with his hands to make them lay right. Breathing heavily and still not sure what to say, I look at the siren, hoping that triggers him to do the same.

He makes a noise that can be roughly translated as *holy fucking shit* but less composed and stumbles backward. I can't see the siren's teeth as she scowls, but I know Faisal can. He nearly falls as he takes another step back.

"Looking for leverage?" I ask, trying for a deep, confident tone that I don't quite achieve.

The siren is already backing away back toward the water. She turns and starts walking forward, the illusion of her long, perfect legs strutting with a confidence that doesn't match her retreat.

"Just trying to even things out," she throws out over her shoulder, with that same horrifying musicality she showed at the other beach. "The Atlantic tribe has your mother. I figured I'd collect your lover. It would be… Well, it would be *fun*, wouldn't it?"

Collect. I hate the way she says that, especially with what she said earlier. I keep my eyes fixed on her as she retreats into the water. I don't breathe until her head dips beneath the surface, then my tense, rigid body slumps.

Faisal's hand is on my shoulder, cold and clammy. I pull in a sharp breath, my heart rate ramping up again.

"What did you expect me to see?" His words are steady, strong, and even. So much of the time, Faisal's voice flows around me, buoying me up, carrying our life along smoothly through any uncertainty or rough patches. But he's so tightly controlled now—stone instead of water.

"I…" I trail off, not sure what to say, the failure of our earlier attempted conversation that he doesn't remember oppressive in my memory.

"Beth," he tries again, so much tension in his tone it might be anger. "Tell me. What did you expect me to see?"

"Why?" I ask, still hesitant to say the words out loud, like that would be crossing some barrier.

"Because shared hallucinations are vanishingly rare." He all but breathes the words, and his hand on my shoulder trembles.

No, not anger. The tension there is fear. And the need

to alleviate that fear—to reassure him that no, he's not crazy—pushes away my own nerves.

"Freaky fish lady," I say almost casually. My lips are quirking up in the beginnings of a smile, but I'm not sure why. Tension rushes out of me, like the hard part is done, but the hard part is only just starting. "Gills. Scales. Mutilated tail. Oh, and teeth. Lots of teeth."

His jaw clenches as he breathes in and out. The trembling in his hand stops as he begins kneading my shoulder like a mix between giving me a comforting massage and reassuring himself that I'm still there—that he can still touch me.

"What happened?" Faisal asks, flicking his eyes down to my injured arm.

He looks better than when I last saw him. More rested, maybe, despite the shock he just suffered. Forced sleep will do that for you.

"What?" I ask.

"You're carrying your arm like you hurt it. And it's got... a tattoo?"

"I... hurt it," I repeat, not sure how to even begin explaining the timer the dryad put there.

He raises his eyebrows, waiting for me to continue. *Urging* me to tell him more of my own accord. We've crossed the boundary, and there are still waning traces of the rush of relief that I didn't fuck it up this time. But that relief is losing ground to a growing dread.

It's inevitable. I'm losing him. I held on as long as I could, but now that he knows, I'm going to lose him. I can try to push that aside all I want, try to pretend differently. But an aching cavern opens in my middle, and my mouth goes dry.

"We should talk," I choke out. The words have been stuck in my throat for six months—no wonder they don't want to come out. All the relief is gone now. All I want is to go back. Back to a week ago. Back to when we were in limbo, and I could keep things from rushing forward.

Faisal's expressive features scrunch up as he reads the mounting terror and grief in my face. He steps forward, wrapping his arm around my waist and pulling me closer to him, avoiding my wounded left arm.

"That would be good," he breathes with his trademark blend of gentle earnestness, only a trace of the manic confusion he's still working through underneath.

I let him kiss me, amazed he's taking this so well—so far. But I find fear in the desperation of his kiss and embrace, in the strength of his affection, just a little too hard and a little too tight. He's buried it to where I can only feel it. It's going to swallow me.

I'm stronger when he pulls back, but my hands are still shaking. His aren't anymore.

"Can I have those back?" I ask, nodding to the glasses on his eyes. Best he doesn't see Gigi through them.

Panic wells up over what's coming, the slow-motion train wreck on its way. Him taking in my new life and the choices I've made with it and the choice he should make in response. But we're in the here and now, and there are other things I can think about—easier things I can think about.

I scan around us, looking for a blue jay. I don't find one, but I do find a fairly similar-looking bird that's nearby and taking too much of an interest. I do my best not to give away that I notice it, but Faisal has noticed my attention shift.

"What is it?" he asks.

I shake my head and put on a distancing smile. "Let's go back to the room."

His eyes narrow as he follows my shift in focus, and he

wordlessly tables that discussion until we've dealt with whatever I feel we need to deal with.

"Okay," he says, finding my hand and striding back toward the hotel with me. I put on an unsteady smile, doing my best not to look at the bird as we walk. I also ignore Gigi as we pass her outside the hotel office, chatting up some hotel staff. She notices me in return but chooses not to engage, and I see Faisal take this in and file it away as another question to ask—another on top of how many?

The doorways to the rooms at the hotel aren't open to the outside on the wing where Faisal's room is, so it will be a little bit of time before the bird figures out which window is ours. I wish I could say I planned it that way, but it's just dumb luck.

When we enter the hallway, I pick up the pace. I don't run to the room, but I come close.

"What—" Faisal starts when we've got in the door, apparently believing that making it safely back to the room is the end of the issue I'm dealing with rather than the beginning. I silence him with a raised hand.

My eyes jerk to the window. No bird there yet. Good. I dig into the pocket of my jacket, searching for the tangled mess of threads I've been carrying around for the last five weeks. My fingers close around them, and I pull them out, heading over to the window and wincing as I use my left arm to pull the glasses down over my eyes.

And just as I realize that I'm going to have to either lose time to put the trap down and open the window with my good arm or try to get it open with my left, it opens. Faisal might not get the details of what I'm doing, but he saw my focus on the window and my one good hand occupied with something—albeit something he can't see. The man reads me well enough to tell I must want it open. Did he see me notice the bird, too? It's hard to say.

"Thanks," I say under my breath, and he gives me a tentative nod, expression wary but patient for now.

Time to set the trap. Through my glasses, the threads shine like spun gold. They don't have to be in any sort of order or positioning—I made sure of that when I was studying the twelve pages of the trove that covered its creation and enchantment. So I set it in a jumble on the dirty sill outside and withdraw my hand.

"Shut it," I say, already moving toward the little table and chairs by the TV. He does and joins me, coming to a rest sitting across from me. And all this before the bird caught up with us. We're a hell of a team. Always have been. Always would have been.

I take a deep breath, setting aside the easier save-the-world problem and picking back up the losing-the-man-I-love problem. It's not a comfortable transition. Faisal reaches forward and wraps his big hands and long fingers around mine. His eyes on me are gentle but intent. The kindness there should make this easier, but it just hurts.

"So, magic," I say, my pulse pounding distractingly. "Magic is"—and then the European blue jay equivalent, apparently much dumber and quicker to set off the trap than I ever anticipated, starts thumping its wings against the window—"something I'm going to tell you all about right after I kill this bird real quick."

SIXTEEN

An Ending

A lot of planning and forethought went into this moment. I had to notice the blue jay popping up way more often than it should and make an educated, albeit technically still unproven, guess at who sent it. I had to scour the trove to see if I could find the spell that he was using, and/or a spell that could counter it. Then I had to find some fibers with a *very* specific makeup, twist and knot and arrange them in a *very* specific way, and then set them on fire with a flame sparked from a kind of wood that does not grow anywhere in North America, while holding myself in a state of openness, transparency, and good will toward my fellow man.

And then, because that's a hell of a Right Mind to call up when responding to being spied upon by a malicious force, I had to do that eight more times until the spell actually worked. When it finally did, the ashes blew away to leave behind a magical trap to ensnare a spying spell and trace it back to its originating wizard. And then I had to carry that trap around, waiting for the right time to use it.

Lots of thought. Lots of planning. Lots of time. And

somehow, in that whole process, never once did I think through the fact that I would eventually be sitting here, holding an innocent bird that didn't ask for any of this and probably only got co-opted by the evil magician minutes ago, trying to get up the courage to kill it.

"Beth?" Faisal asks. He's probably trying to get me to look at him, but my eyes are fixed on the bird.

"You had that semester as an assistant in the bio lab, right? You got used to killing the lab rats?"

Faisal's face clouds with confusion for a moment before clearing into pity. "Yeah. You want me to kill the bird for you?"

I shake my head. "No, I have to do it. But just… how did you do it?"

He opens his mouth, and closes it again, and I can see his acceptance of the situation cracking—his worry that this is some kind of mental break seeping back in. The bird is docile in my hands, not freaking out at all the way it would be if there weren't a magical trap involved. That and the fact that it got caught at all when there was no visible trap should be proof, too. But this is a lot. I'm asking a lot.

Both my hands are occupied holding the bird, but I lean forward, tilting my head toward him and scrunching up my face to make the glasses move. "Take a look."

Tentatively, he reaches out and takes the glasses from me again. He takes the time to examine them now— judging the weight of them in his hands, looking closely at the arms and the lenses. Trying to gauge if there's any way it could be technology instead of magic? I guess that could be an easier sell.

But the glasses just look like glasses, and his expression sours with some private thought. He puts the glasses on and looks at the bird, this time presumably seeing the golden threads of my invisible trap. He lets out a long breath and just stares at the trap and the bird in my hands. There's more time now than there was on the beach. The bird is so small and fragile in my hands, and every second I hold onto it makes what I'm about to do harder. But he needs this time, and I let him take it.

"Can I touch the net?" he asks.

I purse my lips. "I'm not sure. The spell didn't say. Probably best not to risk it."

He nods slowly, his eyebrows raising. "Spell," he muses, turning the word over with his voice like he's examining a puzzle.

"Spell," I confirm around a nervous laugh.

His eyes meet mine for a long moment—longer than is comfortable. I can't read his face. Everything behind his eyes is locked down to me. I'm shut out. Then he swallows, and his eyes shift back to the bird. "You need to kill it?"

His voice is still gentle, but also businesslike.

"Yes," I say. "How did you do it?"

I didn't know Faisal well enough during his summer semester as a merciful lab rat executioner to have talked about it with him then, but knowing him as I do now, it couldn't have been easy for him. As unfair as it is to ask him what I need to do, I'm asking anyway.

I don't have to say any of these things to Faisal. He gets it. He blinks a few times and leans forward. He sets his hands just to the side of mine, clearly wanting to make contact but listening when I tell him he can't.

I sometimes think Faisal can't surprise me. I sometimes think I know him too well. But he sometimes does, like right now. "You're sure it has to be you?" he asks.

I frown. Faisal's never been one for wasted words, and he hates rehashing what's already been said. "I told you it does."

I don't understand the sadness I see in his face when I say that. But I don't have long to think about it before he continues, voice even with a certain chanting quality. "This is a bird."

My features scrunch a bit, but I repeat the words back to him. "This is a bird."

"Killing it will help humans." His words feel well practiced.

"Killing it will help humans," I repeat.

"So you can do it."

"So I can do it."

He leans his hands further away from mine, as though releasing them to do what they must. I snap the bird's neck in time with the gentle rhythm our call and response setup, without fulling meaning to.

I looked up *snapping bird necks* a while back, when I had first prepared the trap. Unfortunately, I didn't do it in incognito mode, so some of my ads have been... interesting since then. I wasn't prepared for how easy it was. I wasn't prepared for the bird not to struggle.

Faisal places his hands on mine, holding the now-still bird. His voice is stern, and even, and measured when he speaks next. "Is this the biggest thing you've ever killed?" he asks me. He doesn't mean roadkill.

I've thought through how I would introduce magic to Faisal. The conversation we started in the village by the crossroads wasn't how I saw it going, but neither is this. I thought I'd stick to the mechanics first. But he's asking the questions he actually wants answered.

And I hear those questions in his voice: *What happened six months ago? Why haven't you told me about it? What hurt you and how? Why haven't you told me about it?*

I tilt my hands out so that I'm no longer holding the dead bird, only his.

"No," I say. "I killed two people."

Faisal doesn't flinch. He very, very carefully doesn't let anything in his body react to my admission. My eyes flick up to his face.

"Not humans," I say. "There were humans I couldn't save, and if I were better, maybe they'd be alive. But I killed two…" I search for the word.

"Monsters?" Faisal provides, no doubt thinking of the siren he just saw. I must scowl more sternly than I think, because he raises an eyebrow.

"I try not to let myself think of them that way," I explain. "But sure, that's… maybe how I could put it right now."

Faisal nods.

I have never been enough of an idiot to play poker with Faisal. I've seen a few others make that mistake, and we once took a very nice vacation from it. Even as well as I know him, and as much as he doesn't try to hide his thoughts from me, his natural inclination is to lock things down.

So the relief I see flood through him is remarkable. The tension that's been coiled in him for months and months is more than I knew was there.

"You could tell something was going on," I say, like it's an excuse. His eyes widen and he lets out a half laugh.

"I thought…" He trails off. He shakes his head. "I didn't think *this*."

I want to ask him what he thought, but I'm afraid to, so I nudge at the edges of humor instead. Are we there yet? "You didn't think I'd found my father's secret spell books and gotten involved with real live magic? How was that not your first guess?"

He exhales sharply through his nose and gives me a sad smile. He's trying, but no, we're not there yet. I'm not going to mention that he thought I was losing my mind. It's too tender—too real to say out loud and give it life outside his private, terrified thoughts.

"Somehow that didn't occur to me." He looks down at the bird. No—at my hands.

"Somehow…" I trail off, looking at his hands holding mine. He gives them two quick little squeezes, and then just holds onto them tighter than he has been, his fingers warm and solid. I feel light in a way I haven't in a long time.

"And there are consequences to what happened, or…?"

I laugh, reveling in how connected I feel to him through his hold on my hands. This is all about to go to hell—in the next hour or day or week or month—but at least I finally get to feel honestly close to him again. It's one of those tension-releasing laughs that's louder than it should be because it just feels so fucking good to do it.

"Oh, yeah," I say to his patient, sad expression. "There are consequences. That's what I'm here for. That's why this bird has been watching me."

"That's what was up with the mermaid?"

Sometimes, when Faisal says something, I smile with just the right side of my mouth. I always feel self-conscious and affected when I do it, but I can't help it. It's a weird, automatic reflex that I've never understood.

"Siren," I correct, tamping down my uneven smile. The rest of my answer hits me with all the weight that just moments ago lifted off me and more. "She wanted to kidnap you to have leverage over me. There are other sirens who kidnapped my mom."

I see the realization filter through. "That's why you were so unconvinced Olivia was going to find her."

I set aside how hard I tried—and apparently failed—to not make that obvious on the phone the other day. "Yeah."

He sighs, and I can just about see the new thoughts and concepts fitting around in his head like Tetris blocks. Faisal has always been great at Tetris. He nods down to the dead bird still sitting in a net he can't see between our clasped hands.

"So you're a witch?" he asks, and the words strike me as weird coming out of his mouth.

"There's no such thing as witches," I say.

"Wizard, then?"

I give a short, involuntarily harsh bark of laughter. "No."

Faisal's lips twist up in a smile. "Oh, that's an insult, is it?"

I shrug. "It is to me. It is to most non-humans, too. Wizards are"—I search for the right words to describe our omnipresent genocidal hidden world order—"kind of dicks."

He laughs a little, though the laughter is weighed down by the seriousness of the situation. "How so?"

"They think they own the world. They decide what is and isn't allowed to happen. As a group, they've done a lot of pretty heinous things. They're also annoying as hell."

I'm still fucked. I still just fell out of the sky. I still have to go find and talk to a wizard who may be actively attempting to destroy the world by setting the wind nymphs on a collision course with the world's oceans, and it may or may not have anything to do with me. But God, it feels so good to tell this to Faisal.

Even if I wish with everything in me that it weren't happening.

Faisal, for his part, hasn't put all of it together yet. But he puts together something I don't expect. He laughs. "Your friend from work," he says. "Max?"

I roll my eyes. "Unfortunately, yes. Wouldn't call him

my friend, though. He wants to erase my memories and steal my spell books. He already erased some of yours."

Faisal keeps his easy smile on his face, but the hard-won jovial light goes out of his eyes.

"Did he?" he asks, like we're talking about an acquaintance's ill-advised vacation plans.

"Yeah." I buy into the fiction that Faisal is unbothered, if only because I can't deal with one more thing right now. "We were having an argument, you and me. Max isn't great with boundaries. I genuinely think he thought he was doing me a favor."

Faisal doesn't release my hands. He doesn't let any hint of displeasure cross his face. But I feel a chill in the air, and he feels cooler in a way that always scares me, even though I know it's involuntary.

"I can see why we would fight about this," he says. There isn't a trace of a threat, or anger, or accusation. Just the gentlest way that Faisal can see to broach the "*you've-been-keeping-a-really-fucking-big-secret-from-me-that-almost-got-me-killed*" topic. My face reddens.

"It's not a great conversation," I say, and the disappointment on Faisal's face just about breaks my heart.

"Why not?" he breathes.

I don't want him to ask me that. I don't want to have to spell it out for him. I had hoped that, somehow, he would put things together himself, later on, and wouldn't ask me in the moment. Where the fuck is Gigi? Why can't I count on her to at least interrupt me when I'm having a private, personal conversation?

"Because what I'm caught up in is fucked up and dangerous. And I can't get out of it, but you can."

The curtains on the window move in a spare breeze. Light, filtered by a tree branch outside the window, splays across the very nineties-looking bedspread. The man I love doesn't move. He looks into my eyes, and I have no idea what's going on back there. Not until he speaks.

"How so?" he asks. I've hurt him. There's just a tinge of that hurt in his voice, but it's enough. Oh, for fuck's sake, how am I still screwing this up even with a second chance?

"You can walk away. You're a smart man, and there's a smart option here."

Very rarely, Faisal reacts without thinking something through—he just goes on pure instinct and says what he wants to, and I can see him start to do that now.

"No," I say, before he can get words out. "Don't say things you think I want to hear right now, because I know you will. I know you'll say that you'll stay. But this isn't that kind of decision. You don't get to choose it right now, with no time to think. I don't want to hear it if it'll change later, and it *should* change later."

He closes his mouth. There's more hurt, this time written clearly on his face, but that was unavoidable. I can't bear to hear him spout reassurance that he might not mean tomorrow or next year when he fully understands the situation and has had time to make an informed, considered decision. I'd like to think that loving me is more important to him than life. That's a great sentiment for Valentine's Day cards. But at some point, the things we say to make ourselves feel good have to meet the world we actually live in.

He nods a few times slowly, stands up, and steps to the side of the table. He still doesn't let go of my hands, so I join him, wincing at the pain in my left arm despite his best efforts to be gentle. And then he pulls me into him again, the way he did on the beach, and kisses me. Slow, gentle, restrained—the way he does in the morning sometimes when I'm half awake and he's had some dream he won't tell me about.

"Well, since the thought police are telling me what I can and can't say at the moment, I guess I'll keep my mouth shut. Although there is something very serious I have to tell you."

He's teasing—lightly, gently, sweetly—but I feel a distance I hope I'm imagining.

"What is it?" I ask, aiming to match his tone and maybe even succeeding.

"Elizabeth Baker. Beautiful. Brilliant. Love of my life," he says, in a kind of melodramatic, overdone voice. He leans in and whispers in my ear, "You *really* need a shower."

SEVENTEEN

A Trade

I'm almost as relieved to be out of that conversation as I am to be under the showerhead, which was probably why Faisal sent me here. That, and I'm sure he needed the chance to think a little bit without me staring him down with six months' worth of expectations and worry on my face. The shower pressure is mediocre, but the water is hot. The salt and dust washes off me to reveal bruises from the fall already starting to form. There are more of them than I expected. It doesn't hurt as bad as it looks right now, but adrenaline probably plays some part in that.

That conversation could have gone worse. It *did* go worse, once. It ended as it should have, though there's a lot more he still has to know—a lot more I need to tell him.

I stand in the water for longer than strictly necessary and try not to think of what the tiny bottles of hotel shampoo and conditioner are probably going to do to my hair. It's possible, given my deadline and plan of action, that this is the last shower of my life.

I don't like to think like that. I haven't found it useful in the last six months—the period in my life when I've been in legitimate danger on a regular basis. I usually get out okay, and my magic amulet counts for a lot.

But this time feels different.

At least Faisal will know what killed me. Briefly. And when I'm gone, he won't mourn me for long. Max will see to that. He promised me that, and I think that promise is still good. I don't know how to think about it in the abstract, but looking at Faisal's face, with the fresh pang of knowing he's hurting and I'm the cause still hot in my heart, I don't begrudge Max saving Faisal from the consequences of my actions.

Jesus, I'm maudlin and defeatist in the shower.

I stay in as long as I can possibly justify, until I've proven conclusively that I'm just going to cycle through worst-case-scenarios if I stay any longer. Then I get out, dry off as best as I can, and wrap my hair up in a too-small hotel towel. A pile of Faisal's clothes have mysteriously appeared on top of the toilet lid without me noticing. Sneaky bastard.

I slip into a pair of jeans and a plaid flannel shirt. I've teased him more than once about this shirt—always in a way that he's correctly interpreted to mean I want him to keep wearing it. Faisal's slim for a man, but they're still a bit big. Boxers aren't my usual underwear choice, but at least they're clean. And traveling in Faisal's garment bag with the rest of his things has imbued them with a little of his scent—sandalwood and a few other earthy notes I can't identify but that I know of only as him.

It's heartbreaking and comforting in equal measure. I'm not sure if that's going to be a good thing for the day I have planned ahead of me, but I know for damn sure I'm not going to go out and buy a different change of clothes.

I'm still adjusting the belt from my original outfit to keep the jeans in place properly when I walk into the main body of the hotel room, so I don't see Gigi before I hear her voice.

"Elizabeth. Please tell your boy how ridiculous he looks."

My eyes snap up to the figures before me.

And, sorry Faisal, but I laugh.

I don't know where Faisal got a knife, but he's holding it like he knows how to use it. I know he doesn't, but I'd be convinced—as might anyone who also has no idea what they're doing. Gigi, for her part, has her arms crossed and an annoyed expression on her face.

"See?" she says to Faisal, like a sitcom character given poorly written lines. I can almost hear the laugh track. Nope, that's just me.

"I'm laughing at you," I lie to Gigi. "Just tell him you're invulnerable instead of being all huffy that he doesn't already know."

At the word "invulnerable"—and, I assume, Gigi and my casual tone—Faisal brings the knife down.

"Gigi, Faisal. Faisal, Gigi," I say. The intensity of the conversation Faisal and I had at the table right next to Gigi makes my attempt at a rote introduction feel out of place. But if Gigi notices, she doesn't say anything. In fact, she doesn't say anything about the introduction at all. She doesn't even look at Faisal.

"I have an idea for what we can do with him," she says, bland as dry pasta.

"Do with me?"

Gigi doesn't know Faisal well enough to hear the impotent threat there. I wince at him, almost entirely for Gigi's benefit.

"I might have gotten you into a little trouble. That

siren on the beach may leave you alone if I'm standing right there, but I need to go see a wizard about a bird, and you can't come with. And I pissed off some wind nymphs, so flying is probably a bad idea."

The more I talk practically about non-emotionally-loaded topics, the easier it becomes to dig myself away from thinking about losing Faisal to his own good sense. Now I just have to think about losing him to my enemies. That's *much* better.

"How about whatever way got you here faster than a plane? Use that to take me back to Springfield."

I sigh dramatically, this time one hundred percent for Gigi's benefit. "Because Gigi here has decided that in a day of everything going wrong with incredibly high stakes, she wants to make life more difficult."

Instead of pointing her annoyance at me directly, Gigi looks at the bird on the table. I'm not sure if she can see the trap still wound around it or not.

"We've talked about this. I'm not taking someone I don't know through the crossroads. It's a perfectly reasonable boundary that I'm going to enforce without any guilt, thank you."

And *that* is for Faisal's benefit. The idea of Gigi feeling guilty about deciding to do what works best for her own reasons is laughable, as is the idea anyone has ever needed to encourage her to set boundaries. I'm reasonably sure she knows that jargon because someone has explained very patiently that they're setting boundaries against *her*. Boundaries she most likely broke soon afterward.

"Besides," Gigi continues, "You just got me dropped from near-orbit, and I'm offering you an alternate option. I get that you're annoyed you have to stop lying to the boy, but you don't have to take it out on me."

Honestly, fuck Gigi. "What's your alternate option?" I ask.

Her bright smile sends anxiety shooting through me. "We can stash him at the Casino. Aloysius won't mind, will he?"

Still fuck Gigi, but she's not wrong.

"You're driving," I say, and she gives me her trademark sharp grin.

"I always do."

I explain as much as I can about Aloysius and who he is on the drive back to our favorite Greek village. At least this means we'll get to return the car, so there's that. No Greek families were inconvenienced in the making of this catastrophe.

I can't tell Faisal that Aloysius is a god in front of Gigi, so I explain that he's a friendly demon. We both sit in the back seat so that he can hear me better. I watch him, bright as always, draw lines between what I'm saying honestly and what I'm saying because Gigi's here, and he can tell I don't trust her. I hope he draws the lines in the right places. He probably doesn't. But he gives nothing other than a mild show of dissent that I'm leaving him in a demon's Casino of Lost Souls while I go figure things out.

When Aloysius has been discussed, I explain to him about everything else I can fit into the relatively short ride. He doesn't talk a lot—just lets me get things out as fast as I can. The words rush out of me, telling him about everything from the spells I've figured out—the ones Gigi knows about, at least—to the successful arbitrations I have under my belt that I don't mind Gigi hearing. When he's got enough context for anything to make sense, I tell him as much as I can about the current situation. By the time we reach the Casino, I've managed to download just about everything I don't mind Gigi overhearing from my brain to his.

He asks few questions—I think mostly because he doesn't want to push me into territory where I'd have to lie to him to avoid Gigi hearing something I don't want her to. But I can tell by the few he *does* ask that it's all sinking in. He doesn't, at any point, ask where Max is, and I don't volunteer it. We'll talk about that later. And hopefully that'll end in Faisal not feeling the need to get back at Max for his missing memories.

The one question he does ask that I can't answer comes when I explain—finally—how I hurt my arm. And it's not a question, at first.

"That seems a little extreme," he says. "Them dropping you like that, I mean."

I laugh a little, my rhythm ruined. "Right, I told you they're not all there upstairs."

He nods, slowly. "But still. They say they're going to go by the results of the arbitration if it's fair, and then they try to kill you?"

I don't split the hair that they just let me die, and that's different from killing me. He's right. Is he right?

"What do you know about what happened back then?" he asks Gigi, who seems annoyed to have to acknowledge that he exists.

"Not much," she says. "A wizard did it out of revenge. All very stock-standard. Although he did get Poseidon to help, which is a little less usual. And the sirens have always maintained that the wind nymphs—then the nymphs of the breezes—were in on it. No proof, though. Not that I know of."

Faisal turns back to me, a *this is significant, don't you think?* expression on his face.

"Thanks," I say, mulling it over. "I'll keep that in mind."

We've arrived at the village, and all conversation stops as we hold our breaths while Gigi navigates through the narrow streets. We return the car, and I'm relieved that Gigi's charm is still effective with the villagers.

The three of us head over the hill and start walking down into the valley with its sprawl of domes shining in the afternoon light. Even early as it is, there are a few figures coming up the steps. Flipping down my glasses, I see what I expect: an escort for every human, drawing them in to gamble their souls. Win or lose, it's a hell of a thing. I set the guilt of my own association with Aloysius aside. Faisal must sense my tension, because he takes my hand and gives it a squeeze.

Aloysius doesn't meet us on the stairs this time. It isn't until we're halfway across the entry landing to the large set of double doors that he appears from a more human-scale door-within-a-door on the left-hand side. His tuxedo is immaculate as ever, and if he's surprised to see us, he doesn't show it. I open my mouth to make introductions, but Aloysius beats me to it.

"Faisal," he says with a friendly air, stepping forward and taking Faisal's unoffered hand. "It is a pleasure to meet you."

He's not looking at me, but I feel the god's intrusive gaze as though I were standing in Faisal's skin, and I shudder. Faisal, for his part, has just a slight hint of looking like he's putting together a puzzle.

"You know me?" he asks, judging Aloysius's reaction to the question more than asking it out of curiosity.

"Of course," Aloysius says, with a strength and warmth in his voice that I've only heard there once before, when he revealed himself to me as a god and gave me his token for worship. "I don't, however, know why you've been brought here."

Aloysius turns to me. He doesn't ask the question directly, but the weight of his expectation lies on me.

"I seem to have ruffled some feathers. So to speak. Although I wouldn't be surprised if the wind nymphs *do* have feathers."

With that, Aloysius laughs. It's rich, and warm, and full. "They don't," he says. "You want me to keep him here as you sort things out? Away from the wizard and the sirens?"

I don't ask him which wizard he means—I wouldn't put it past him to already know somehow that I'm going to see a different wizard than usual. I'm too interested in trying to unravel the slight surprise in his tone. Disbelief, maybe?

"Should I not?" I ask, looking back and forth between him and the appropriately stone-faced Gigi, feeling suddenly like someone who doesn't get a joke that everyone else does. But as soon as I ask the question, Aloysius's concern and surprise have evaporated.

"Of course you should. Safest place for him."

Great. Just great. Suddenly I'm not so sure. There's no reason to believe Aloysius won't lie to me, but I press him anyway. I am, as far as I can tell, the goose that lays the golden egg for him. And I can't imagine he wants to piss me off by lying to my face and leaving me to find out about it later.

"Can you guarantee me he won't come to harm here?" I ask. Faisal seems to share my tension.

"I can," Aloysius says.

"And you won't cast him out? Or let anyone come here and take him?" My eyes narrow, but Aloysius's face remains opaque.

"I will allow no harm to come to him here, and I will not allow him to leave until you yourself come get him. He will not be allowed to gamble his soul, regardless of how good I may judge his chances to be. He will be as intact when you retrieve him as he is now. And when you come to retrieve him, you and I will speak. We'll have an overdue conversation."

The words hit me with a solidity that feels borderline physical. I look at Gigi and Faisal, trying to get a read on whether their experience of hearing those words was the same as mine. If it was, they don't betray it. But Aloysius's insistence that we'll have a "conversation" when I come to pick Faisal up makes this more of a trade and less of a favor, which feels like steadier ground.

I could ask what we'll talk about, but I don't want to in front of Gigi. Or in front of Faisal, to be honest. I have a feeling we're going to talk about what I am to Aloysius, and what he is to me—another inconvenient conversation I've been hoping to avoid for as long as possible. But I'm not allowed to get away with doing that today, apparently.

I take a step closer to Faisal. He looks small in front of this big place, burdened with such a conspicuously modern bag.

"Do you want to stay here?" I ask. He hasn't argued with me about coming along—at least not after I explained about my amulet and his lack thereof.

He shoots back an expression that clearly says *I'm not the one with the information to be making that decision, am I?* I shrug in answer to the question no one but us hears.

"I'll come get you when I'm done," I say, fighting to keep my thoughts from running down the paths of worst-case scenarios again.

I almost don't succeed until Faisal steps forward, and

for the third time since I saw him on the beach, kisses me like an attestation.

He'll have time to think in here. He'll have time to decide.

We don't say goodbye. I don't watch him disappear through the door-within-a-door and into the labyrinth. I turn on a heel and head toward the stairs, fleeing Faisal's eyes on my back. If I don't go now, I won't be able to.

EIGHTEEN

A Journey

When we reach the bottom of the stairs, Gigi gives me a minute to collect my thoughts. But this being Gigi, it isn't nearly long enough.

"If you're quite ready," she says, "we could perhaps save the world?"

I shoot her a wry look, comfortable in its familiarity. "You have a lot of faith in me all of a sudden."

Gigi smiles, seemingly as pleased as I am to return things to normal. "I have a lot of faith that implying it's possible means that *at least* you'll stop moping and try. As much as I love watching humans stare off into the distance and contemplate their life choices, I did think my day might entail something a little more exciting."

Her words are as acidic as ever, but I'm grateful for them all the same. Moping might be boring for her, but it'd be poison to me, and while Gigi may insist she doesn't care about me personally, pushing me onward and upward is a kindness.

I reach into my pocket and retrieve the tangled mess of golden, glimmering, invisible string. I slip on my glasses so I can see it, which is helpful. We left the dead bird back in the hotel—in a trash can, wrapped in toilet paper. We don't need it anymore.

I pull out a small weight on a hook that I've been carrying for just this moment. I hold the strings in one hand, hook the weight onto a few of them, set it swinging, and wait for its motion to stop.

As I'm waiting, I spare a quick glance at Gigi, and I will admit to a certain amount of gratification at the surprise written on her face. I don't know if it's surprise that I got a spell to work, or because she can't see the invisible strings holding up the swinging weight. But I'd like to think it's something remotely resembling being impressed. Even if that flies in the face of everything I know about Gigi, I'll take what I can get.

When the weight stops swinging, it's hanging a bit above where it should—indicating a direction.

I couldn't have been one hundred percent sure until this moment that it worked completely right. But a smile spreads slowly across my face. I did it. I found whoever it was that created the spell I used the trap to break. Max's master. One of them. Both of them? I'm guessing, but I think it's a good guess. There aren't many wizards in the world that would have a reason to know I exist.

A glance at Gigi tells me she's less enthusiastic about my success. I don't pretend I know Gigi well enough to decode her stone face and diamond eyes, but there's a lack of sharpness there in comparison to every other time I've looked at her like this. I interpret that lack of sharpness as fear. I hope I'm wrong.

"Do you have a plan for when you get there?" Gigi asks.

I shrug. "Not exactly. I have some thoughts." And it's

not a lie. I do have some thoughts; they just aren't very
good ones.

"I'll take you to the closest crossroads," she says, her
voice as close to uncertain as I've ever heard it. "From
there, you're on your own."

She's trying to put her usual fun, breezy tone into the
words, but she's not succeeding. I don't know how nervous
I should be that I'm breaking Gigi's usual air, even to the
point of her repeating information she's told me before,
which she doesn't usually do without insulting me and
implying that *obviously* I must have forgotten. Maybe I'm
just a little bit out of whack from the whole thing with
Faisal. Maybe I should give myself some patience and
accept that I'll be a little out of whack about that for a
while—or at least until he makes a decision, and I find out
if I'm going to lose the most valuable thing in my life.

Gigi takes my arm and looks in the direction the fishing
weight is pointing.

"This should be straightforward, at least," she says.
And then she steps into the crossroads.

I recognize the first step. It's the same way we came
here. It's still picturesque. We stay a little longer than we
did last time, and I get a better look at the vineyard around
us. But just as I'm starting to settle into the idea of
standing here, Gigi steps into the next crossroads. And the
next. And the next. Each few steps, we wait and watch the
fishing weight, to see if it's shifted direction, indicating
we've gone past who it's pointing to. For seven more steps,
it doesn't.

My sense of direction isn't good enough to know
exactly where we're heading. I do realize when we cross the
Atlantic, which doesn't surprise me. Max's masters showed
up within a few hours when I summoned them to Max's
house to clear up the jam I got into after my father's death.

It makes sense that they would be somewhere in North America, even if they probably have their own means of magically fast transportation that they just haven't yet taught Max.

When the fishing weight finally shifts and points a different direction, I think we must be somewhere in the Northeast US, based on the surrounding forest. I'd like to imagine that I've started getting the hang of recognizing regions for their foliage, but that probably isn't true. Gigi steps through a few more crossroads. Narrowing in. In the end, she returns to the original crossroads where we noticed the fishing weight shift to tell us we were getting close.

"End of the line, kiddo," Gigi says, with more affection than she usually has in her voice. Jesus, she really does think I'm about to die.

I pull out my phone to look at where we are. Outside Boston? That seems too normal for what I'm going to find. I guess it makes sense that wizards of any stature would set themselves up in a major city. After all, what is wealth in a small town? Max has a flashy car and a nice house, but it isn't really on the scale of showing off that I imagine most wizards enjoy.

I go to say something to Gigi. It could be the last words I say to her, considering what I'm doing. It could be the last words I say to anyone friendly. But Gigi's gone before I can find the words. As old as she is, it shouldn't surprise me that she has a strategy for dealing with potential goodbyes. And with what I know about Gigi, it shouldn't surprise me that her strategy for dealing with them is to avoid them. Sometimes I think we're not so different after all. Okay, rarely.

Oh well—I guess I didn't have anything worth saying to her, anyway. I set all the events of the last few hours behind me. I'm off to see the wizard. I check the marks on my arm that I've been avoiding counting. There are eighteen left. Plenty of time.

The map on my phone tells me that, luckily, I'm not too far from a road. Unfortunately, I find out on the way that the path as the crow flies crosses an impassable ravine. I have to reroute around it, and it's an hour and a half before I stumble, freezing, into civilization.

Luckily, civilization includes a combination 7-Eleven and Dunkin' Donuts. Just what the goddamned doctor ordered. I ask for a coffee through chattering teeth and make my way to a rack of T-shirts and jackets. No way am I leaving aside my leather jacket—not after what it just got me through—but it's also not nearly enough to deal with the untamed north wind this far from the equator.

The man behind the counter eyes me, presumably judging my lack of foresight as he makes my drink.

I offer him no explanation. What would I say, anyway? I just try on a heavy corduroy jacket with faux fur on the collar. It's not exactly stylish, but it'll do. Considering I'm in Faisal's castoffs, that ship has sailed. I shove my fishing weight on its invisible string in one of the pockets. It's a good pocket. I'll take it.

I could ask the man behind the counter about the train schedule, but luckily, I don't have to. He's slow making my coffee, but I don't mind. I need as much time in the warmth, bringing up my core body temperature, as I can get. If I were smart, I'd go to a doctor right about now. If I were smart, I wouldn't be going to see a psychopathic wizard with nothing but questions and accusations.

There's a thought. I search around the 7-Eleven's meager supply of random items and find a little notepad and a pen. The notepad is clearly intended for children, with pastel cartoon drawings of unicorns on each page. It's not the kind of thing that would get Max's masters to take me seriously, but I'm pretty sure I had little hope of that to begin with, so nothing lost there. I also grab a cheap ball-point pen and a bag of trail mix to add to my haul.

The thing about travel via the crossroads is that humans aren't really made for it. Teleportation seems great until you're catapulted halfway around the world with no buffer time to reorient yourself. And I've got an extra layer of confusion on top of it. I was in the supernatural world in Greece. There were monsters and wizards and ancient grudges breaking through to new mutiny.

And now, I'm standing at a train station outside of Boston, waiting on the platform with a collection of other people not working nine-to-fives. I probably look the strangest, with my jacket-on-jacket and the terrified expression I can't wipe off of my face despite my best efforts. I catch a few glances at me. There's pity in them, I think, but I also might just be imagining that.

The train is warm, at least, when it finally comes. And there are plenty of free seats so I can sit down and lean my head against the window. I don't know what to do with the lull in activity. I call Faisal to make sure he's all right, but his phone goes straight to voicemail. It doesn't shock me the Casino doesn't have cell reception, but it does annoy me more than it should. I try Max's phone, but it goes straight to voicemail, too. I guess it got wrecked when he fell from the sky, or the staff at the hospital turned it off. Also not shocking.

I take a deep breath in, steadying myself. I still haven't called Olivia back, and considering what's going on with mom, that probably makes me an asshole. I told her I would call her when I could, and what else am I going to do while sitting on a train headed toward self-inflicted doom and/or a day in Boston?

I pull up our text message conversation. Olivia hasn't texted again since I told her I would call when I could, which on its own isn't a great sign. I zone out, staring at the phone for a little while, trying to think of what to say. I can't tell her the truth, obviously. But I don't have an appetite for any more lying to the people I love. I can't tell her I'm not in danger. I can't tell her Mom isn't, either. I can't tell her she can help. None of this is going to be easy for her to take—her of all people. It would be kinder to lie.

I take a deep breath and tap the buttons to initiate the call quickly, before I can change my mind. It rings three times while I clench my jaw and stare at the wintry, miserable suburban landscape flying by the windows.

When Olivia answers, I hear her daughters babbling over each other in the background, melting my worried expression to a smile despite my best defenses.

"Have you heard from Mom?" Olivia's voice is tight, friendly, and strained.

"No," I say. "And you probably won't until tomorrow."

The cheerful sound of squabbling little girls fades as Olivia steps out of the room. I know her house well enough to imagine her path, based on the number of steps and the sound of the dryer as she passes it. She's in her bedroom, door closed firmly behind her when she answers, her voice cold and doomed as a melting glacier.

"And how do you know that?"

"Because I know who has her. It's related to some people Dad got involved with before he died. The stuff— the stuff I was going through six months ago that I never told you about."

Olivia didn't gently pester me the way Faisal has been doing, but chances are good she noticed, and he kept her at bay and told her he was working on it. Olivia has no qualms outsourcing active care, even if she's never seemed able to outsource worry.

"Are you in trouble?"

I didn't plan to laugh, but a couple sobs of laughter rip out of me, drawing a few stares from people around me. I get a hold of myself, but not before I've triggered Olivia's let's-get-going instincts.

"Faisal said you were in Greece. There are three daily flights, and I can get on one of them."

This was not the plan.

"I'm not in Greece. I'm in Boston. I've spoken to Faisal. It's fine—it's all fine."

"It's fantastic to hear that you can be fine and in trouble at the same time. I don't think I'd be able to do that." Olivia is seldom sarcastic, but she does an excellent job at it when given the opportunity.

"I mean, I'm handling things."

While I wait an age for Olivia to reply, I look at the faces of the people on the train around me. They're now studiously avoiding what they've correctly deduced is none of their fucking business.

"I want to tell you to call the police," she says flatly, "but you said you're in Boston, and this is to do with some people dad got involved with *somehow*, before he died. Are these people well connected?"

I'm not sure the assumption that the police in Boston are in bed with the mob is exactly current, but it is helpful. And who's to say that Max's masters aren't *connected*?

"The police won't be able to help with this."

Absolutely no one on this train is going to be able to meet my eyes all the way into the city, I can just tell.

"And I—"

"It would make it worse if you tried to get involved. I'm handling it. Faisal knows about it, and he's agreed that going to the police would be a bad idea, so this isn't just me catastrophizing things and not seeing the bigger picture."

"I'm sending Peter."

My eyes go wide in involuntary terror at the thought of my six-foot-four-inch, ex-ranger brother-in-law tasked with a holy mission from his wife stumbling headlong into the situation, likely with a gun in hand.

"Oh God, no, Peter would make things much worse. Olivia, I need you to trust me. I promise I'm handling it. I promise that if you could help, I would ask you to. I promise that I'm going to do the best I can."

I stare out the window. We're passing through a neighborhood filled with families and children, the way Springfield is filled with families and children. Like Olivia, and Peter, and their daughters. How many of these families are going to die if I don't fix things? I'm not going to promise Olivia that I'm going to bring Mom back safe. She can't ask me that.

"Okay," comes Olivia's voice, surprising me.

"What?"

Olivia's harried, half-hysterical laugh spills out, cheapened by the shitty phone microphone. "You're surprised I'm going to do what you're asking me to do?"

"Well, yeah. I mean, I wouldn't."

"No, you wouldn't. Which is data point five hundred and seventy-three that I'm older and wiser than you are." Her cheerful teasing should reassure me, but coming as it does in such unstable, uncertain circumstances, it just hurts the way a letter from home hurts a homesick kid at summer camp.

"I mean, thank you," I say, trying to figure out what to do with her about-face.

"What else am I supposed to do?" Olivia asks, thankfully having backed off the path to hysterical. "At least you're talking to me. Telling me about it. You wouldn't six months ago." The houses outside the window give way to a strip mall and some assorted run-down shops. "I trust you."

I blink furiously at the tears springing to my eyes, feeling betrayed by them. I stifle the urge to tell her she shouldn't.

"I'm not happy about it, but I trust you. I want to, and I do. You say the police can't help. You say Peter can't help. You've told Faisal, and he'd have called if…"

She doesn't finish the sentence, but I don't need her to. She remembers dad's days in the asylum and everything that came with them as well as I do.

"Thank you," I choke out.

"You could thank me by telling me more."

It's my turn to laugh semi-hysterically. "You wouldn't thank me if I did." I give up and let the tears fall. There are only a few of them. Relief can hit hard, but it never hits for long.

"We're going to talk when all this is over," Olivia says, with a stern certainty she was never capable of until she had kids.

"I love you, Olivia," I say.

There's the crash of something—probably ceramic—breaking in the background. A moment of silence, and then two little voices in unison say, "Moooooom?"

Olivia sighs. "I love you, too," she says, already moved on in her mind to the next mess that needs cleaning up. "Call me."

She's gone, but the conversation leaves me feeling more at ease in this space, in these mundane human surroundings. She made me fit again. I wish I had a way of telling her that.

The weight in my mind that my conversation with

Olivia removes lets me pull out the little notebook with the unicorn cartoons and Wilbur's pen. It's tricky to write with only one non-strained arm and no solid surface, but I manage.

I'm alive, I write, and then wait.

Nothing. The train pulls into a station. No one gets off, but about a dozen people join us. A group of high schoolers farther up are carrying on an animated conversation about a band they'd probably be glad I've never heard of. I return my attention to the notebook and try again.

Meeting went okay. But they dropped us. Know why they're so mad about being accused of helping the wizard put the sirens into the ocean?

I wait a little longer, staring at the nonsensical sentence and glad none of the passengers who got on the train at the last stop have sat close enough to read over my shoulder. But nothing pulls my hand to answer. Wilbur, it would seem, doesn't want to talk to me.

I don't get why. I wish I'd asked, but I also don't know when I could have. What would I have said?

Are you mad at me? I write. No response.

I've secured Olivia's trust, but I lost Wilbur's. You win one, you lose one. It's always a trade.

Twenty-five minutes until I get into Boston, my phone informs me. I pull out the weight and invisible string and confirm to myself that, yes, it's pointing into Boston. That's something, at least. The confirmation that I may be doing a dumb thing but at least I'm going to be able to do it at all is more comforting than it should be. I'm awash with unde-served self-satisfaction when I see a little girl—can't be more than six—looking at me with big, round, dark eyes.

She wasn't on the train when I had my suspicious conversation with Olivia, so her intense look can't have anything to do with that—even if she understood what she heard. I think for a second it must be my harried appearance. But then I realize how strange it must look to her to see a weight hanging from an invisible string and settling off-center.

"It's magic," I say, a smile growing on my face. My voice fights the muted clatter of the train but makes it through. The little girl's smile matches and exceeds my own, until she covers over it with her hands. Her caretaker, a middle-aged man consumed by his e-reader, doesn't notice our exchange.

There's no way of knowing if she thinks I mean the sleight-of-hand kind of magic or real magic—no way to know if she's been convinced yet that one is real and the other is not. But the glow on her face tells me I made her day, and the joy of that buoys me until we reach Boston.

I make the call to get off the train at Haymarket because the tilt of the weight tells me that Max's masters must be somewhere downtown if they're in Boston proper at all. And even that is an educated guess based on what little I know about the wizards that they must be.

After I disembark, I put on my glasses and follow the weight, walking down streets and shifting my gaze between the weight and the world around me. Back and forth, back and forth. It reminds me a little of when I first used my magic-finding lantern to find Gigi. Although, back then I'd been concerned about looking crazy, and carefully stepped into alleys and cast furtive glances. I was afraid someone might recognize me back in Springfield. Or maybe I was just afraid someone would think I'd lost my mind. But at this point, I'm too tired and worried and scared to care.

Just when my feet are beginning to tell me what a bad idea this has all been, I narrow in on the building. It's nondescript in context—brick, five stories tall, and wedged in between other similar buildings. It's unmarked other than the address on the front, and the massive wood-and-iron door on the front bears only a handle and a mail slot. No doorbell in sight. Through my glasses, it looks exactly the same as it does without them. I'm not sure why that surprises me. I guess I thought there was going to be some kind of a glow? An ominous magical fog? A dragon invisible to us puny humans?

I put my fishing weight away and walk a block over to a little corner park with a bench. I pull out my phone and save the location on my map app—oh, for a wizard's eidetic memory!—and feel my heart start to race. The focused action of following the weight had shoved my nerves down pretty effectively, but now that that part of the ordeal is over, I've got no defense, and they're hitting me hard.

It's just as well there's no doorbell. I wouldn't ring it, and I'm not going to knock. I'm sure they know I'm here—they must have some sort of warding or early warning system, considering even Max has something like that rigged up. As foolhardy as I may be, I'm not quite dumb enough to voluntarily enter the house of some wizards who probably hate me.

I do some quick googling and decide on a place to tell them to meet. Public is a must. Not too close to their house, but close enough that I can walk there without my feet killing me too much. And, on a whim, by the water. I choose a café, because I'm starving, too. The trail mix and coffee from the 7-Eleven wasn't nearly enough. If they don't show up to kill me, at least I'll get fed.

I pull out the notebook with the unicorn cartoons. I get a little pang of hurt and anger when I see the page that I wrote to Wilbur on, but I shove it down. And I also skip way forward in the notebook until I feel confident that there are no dents from that one-sided conversation on the paper.

How do I start this? I twirl the 7-Eleven ballpoint, cheap but functional, in my fingers. I've never even heard either of these people speak. I don't know which of them I'm addressing. I remember well what they look like—that would be hard to forget. They're both gorgeous, both terrifying. I know Moira's name from Max mentioning her earlier, but I have no idea what the man is called. I'm not sure if I'm hoping I'll see one or both of them, and I'm a little ashamed at the rush of attraction I feel at the thought. My body has no sense of propriety. It should really know better.

I roll my eyes at myself and move on. Whatever I write is going to be wrong. Best just write it anyway.

Hello,

You know who I am. I want to talk to you. Meet me at The Golden Narwhal in twenty minutes.

I barely catch myself in time to avoid writing "thank you" at the end. The letter is short, which is good—less to give away. I know that whichever one of them has been watching me through the bird is home—the weight on the invisible string tells me that much. Twenty minutes is short enough that hopefully they won't have time to lay any amulet-piercing traps.

I tear the note out, throw everything back into my pockets, and head for the nondescript townhouse. Then I toss the note in through the letter slot and head to the waterfront, my heavy breath throwing out frozen clouds in the cold air.

My better sense screams at me that this is a bad decision. But my better sense is a little late to the party. We're three bad decisions deep right now, and there are only fifteen dark marks on my skin left in which to make more.

NINETEEN

A Friendly Chat

I make it to The Golden Narwhal in eight minutes and am relieved to find it matches the pictures I found online. Seaside tourist kitsch abounds. It's empty enough that I get a table immediately, and I realize now how hungry I am. I glance at the appetizers just long enough to see that they have mozzarella sticks so that I can catch the waitress with an order for them before she leaves. She seems ever-so-slightly annoyed at this break in protocol for a ghost of a second before her tip-motivated unconditional customer service slips back into place.

I breathe in and out, trying to steady my nerves. The fingertips of my good hand find their way up to my amulet automatically, tucked away beneath my shirt.

Sometimes, when I worry I'm relying too much on my amulet, I like to think about a story Max once told me about how one wizard killed another even though he had an amulet like mine. The angry wizard threw a feast, *didn't* invite the wizard with the amulet, and then poisoned the food anyway and planned to be elsewhere on the night. A lot of people died, including the amulet wizard. The harmful intention was negated by being offset in time, as well as by going through several degrees of separation, since the angry wizard wasn't even the one to invite amulet wizard to the feast. I think about that story as a way to remind myself not to get too cocky. But I'm feeling a lot of things right now, and overconfidence isn't one of them.

My mozzarella sticks show up in five minutes—thanks be to every god the wizards didn't kill—and I dig in. I'm so distracted by how good the food tastes after traipsing around in the cold that I'm not even looking at the door every thirty seconds, so I'm surprised when a figure comes and sits down at the table across from me.

"I understand you're Elizabeth," she says, nearly surprising me enough to make me choke on a mozzarella stick.

I raise my eyes, readying them to see the Moira, the drop-dead gorgeous woman I saw six months ago in Max's living room, she of the shampoo-model hair and the gloriously feminine proportions.

Instead, I see an unfamiliar face. She's just as gorgeous as Moira—maybe even more so. But her beauty doesn't look as carefully maintained. Her hair is a riot of red curls, some tighter than others, cascading down over her shoulders. They give her a wild look, out of balance with her slight frame. A smattering of freckles dot her high cheekbones, drawing attention to her sky-blue eyes. I shudder involuntarily, reminded of the Pacific queen's eyes when she talked to me of drowning sailors.

The woman before me doesn't notice my reaction. She has a faraway look to her, which is only enhanced by the way she glances away from me and back. She doesn't seem to be able to focus on any one thing for more than a couple of seconds. I slowly chew the cheesy bite in my mouth and try to figure out what to say in response. A slight *tap tap tap* noise comes from the table, where she's gently rapping something in her hand against it.

Jesus, she looks almost as nervous to be here as I am.

I flip my glasses down, looking for the telltale photo-shopped-on-the-background look that wizards have when viewed through them. It's not there. The woman in front of me, improbable as it seems, is either human or one of the few supernatural creatures that look human through my glasses.

Her mouth opens when I flip the glasses on, like she's scared they're going to do something to her. I have an over-whelming feeling that I've accidentally cornered a fright-ened dog.

My mouth finally empty, I speak in a low, steady, nonthreatening voice. "I'm Elizabeth, yes."

Her eyes glance to three different places as she nods.

"And who are you?" I ask.

Her eyes light up for a bright moment. "I'm Phoebe," she says. I recognize a slight Midwestern tinge to her voice.

"Phoebe what?" I ask before I can stop myself. This isn't the point. I shouldn't be trying to find out too much about her. But the worry that she might be missing—that someone somewhere might be looking for her—stops me from doing anything else.

The brightness that she displayed when I asked her for her name fades. She clenches her jaw, and her eyes finally rest in one place for maybe five seconds. Her gorgeous features crumple in confusion. Then she blinks a couple times, looks me directly in the eyes, and plasters on a weak smile.

"I'm not sure," she says.

I let out a heavy breath. "How much do you know about all of this?" I ask, trying to hold on to the thread of the focus she's managed to weave together and extend to me.

"Plenty," she says. "I think. I know different things at different times."

I try not to let my pity show in my face. I try not to think too much about Sharon, and the number of times Max has pulled his mind-mojo on her. I try not to think about the people at the hospital he may be "cleaning up" as we speak. I've never seen anything like this in any of the people Max has messed with mentally. They all seem fine.

But then, there's no telling how many times this woman has been interfered with.

"You're beautiful," I say, letting the question in that observation slide into my intonation. I'm not sure she gets what I mean, not sure she has enough left in her to put that all together. But I want to know whether her beauty is what drew the wizards to her, or if the promise of it is what drew her to them.

"It was my choice," she says, offering the answer I want to know more, leaving aside the one about whether her appearance is natural or not.

I sit for a long moment, staring at her. She doesn't force any conversation. She doesn't seem uncomfortable in the heavy silence between us, the way most people would be with a stranger. I can't put a finger on why that bothers me so much at first, until I realize it's all part of the same base issue. She feels untethered.

I slide my plate of mozzarella sticks across the table toward her, and her face lights up like a kid on Christmas morning, revealing perfect, even white teeth.

"Oh, I love these," she says, picking the only remaining stick up with long, delicate fingers that remind me of Gigi's. They're nearly as pale. She takes a graceful bite.

What came first, the beauty or the servitude? Max's

masters sent her here. Asked her to come here? I don't know.

"Do a lot of wizards have people like you?" I ask, still making no progress directing the conversation the way it should go.

"I think so," Phoebe says between bites. "Most of them were alive when servants were more normal."

The mundane quality of her voice disorients me more. She's come a little more into her own, shedding a little bit of the scattered air she came in with.

"Servants are still normal for some rungs on the socioeconomic ladder," I say. My words feel weird. Do I normally talk like that?

Phoebe shrugs. "I don't know, maybe."

"But they mess with your head," I prod.

"There are pros and cons to the job. Just like any job." She says it brightly—casually. She can't know what she's saying. She doesn't know what's been done to her.

My heart breaks, and I can't hide the evidence of it on my face, but Phoebe doesn't notice. She finishes her mozzarella stick and slides back into that unfocused, scattered mode she was in when she first sat down.

"Phoebe?" I ask, when I've gathered my own self back together a little bit more.

She looks at me and fixes me with a smile. It's the exact same forced smile she gave me a minute ago—so exactly the same that it's eerie. It's not connected to me, or anything I say or do. The *tap tap tap* on the table draws my attention.

I look at her hand meaningfully. Most people would understand what I meant with that pointed glance. It would be communication. But Phoebe doesn't seem to.

"What's in your hand?" I ask after another ten seconds of silence—strained on my end and unconcerned on hers.

"Oh!" she says, and I'm relieved to find her thread of focus and engagement has returned. She opens her hand, letting the black, polished stone with gray, familiar-looking symbols etched into it sit on the tabletop.

"It's a communication device," she says. "In case you try to kill me or something." The words should be a joke, but the tone of her voice makes it clear they're not.

"And do you think I'm going to try to kill you?" I ask, my disbelief that I am actually saying that sentence obvious in my voice—though I can't say whether or not she would pick up on it.

She seems bewildered, and I'm overtaken with a wave of guilt for confusing her.

"I'm not," I say, and the words have the intended effect of calming her. "What are the names of the people you serve?" I ask, looking for any telltale signs of distress. I should want to push her—should want to get as much info out of her as remotely possible, whether she wants to give it to me or not. I'm relieved that she leaves the polished black stone on the table. I want to take it from her. I want to break the link they have with her as though it would break their hold over her. But I don't know, looking at her now, if they've left enough of her to survive in the world without them.

My mozzarella sticks, that I wolfed down too quickly and greedily, don't seem to be happy in their new home.

"Moira and Kristoff," she says, and I'm fortified by how easily the names come to her and her complete and utter lack of hesitation in telling me. If anything, she seems delighted that she knew an answer to my question, the way a child would be. "But Moira doesn't know I'm here. Moira doesn't know anything about you. Only Kristoff."

That tracks with the fact that Moira showed up asking Max if he'd been involved in the Nymph of the North

Wind's death. I'd thought maybe it was just an act. "And he trusts that you won't tell her?"

Phoebe laughs far too loudly and far too excitedly. My eyes dart around the restaurant, embarrassed to see the servers and the scattered other diners staring at us. Then she stops laughing, just as suddenly as she started.

"He won't let me know something I'm not allowed to tell," Phoebe says, with a well-executed wink and a conspiratorial air that feels too competent for her current state and doesn't make sense to me. "I never have to worry about anything like that at all."

I must be grimacing—I can feel it. But she doesn't respond to that.

"Okay, so Kristoff sent you here," I say. "Did he send you here with a message?"

I've lost Phoebe a little. She's back to giving unseen points of space fleeting glances. Untethered.

"He says he doesn't want you talking to Max anymore," she says, seemingly addressing an empty booth a row over.

A lump rises in my throat. "Do you know Max?"

She looks at me, her face again a picture of confusion. "I don't think so."

Would she know if she did? Would she remember? I don't want to believe Max has seen what's left of her and still does mental magic. But I don't know Max well enough to assume—not really. I know Max hates his masters. I know he was insistent, when I found out about them, that I shouldn't ever let them know who I was. Maybe Phoebe here is part of why. Maybe he has many other reasons why.

But I also know that Max didn't tell me who was controlling the blue jay, something he should have known.

I wince, unnoticed by what's left of the woman in front of me. I need to get back on topic.

"And did Kristoff do anything to make me not talk to Max anymore?" I ask.

At that, Phoebe's face lights up again.

"The sirens!" she says. "Yes, he did. And he'll fix it if you go away. He won't even kill you, he says. He'll let you live the rest of your life with the amulet, as long as you stay away from Max."

I open my mouth to ask her why Max having a work friend whose brain he can't erase is such a problem for Kristoff. But the memory of the broken jumble of bones and blood that Max was when I last saw him stops me.

Reasonably, I can recognize that this is good news. If Max's master is content to leave me alone as long as I leave Max alone, then he can't know about the trove. But I have a hard time feeling the silver lining, even if I can technically see it.

"My mom is missing. I think the Atlantic tribe has her. I can't just walk away from that. Will he save her?"

For the first time since sitting down, Phoebe is upset. Of all the fucked-up things she's said about herself and how she is, *this* is what gets her.

"I… I don't know," she says. I think for a moment that she might be upset about my mother being kidnapped, but I don't think that's it. She's failing. And she's upset about it —not afraid of what Kristoff would do. I don't see *fear* in her, per se. Just frustration and self-recrimination.

"Do you want to ask?" I prod, eyes glancing down to the stone on the table between us. I hate the words as they come out of my mouth. I hate what I'm encouraging her to do. But the words calm her down immediately like the flip of a switch. She scoops up the stone and closes her eyes.

The conversation between her and Kristoff—I assume —takes no more than thirty seconds. I see her lips move, but I hear no sounds. And I see her eyes moving underneath her eyelids, like she's in REM sleep. At last, she opens her eyes and sets the stone down at the table in front of her.

Her voice is lower when she speaks again, and I have the distinct impression of an addict who has just indulged their vice and has their peace of mind back—at least for a little bit.

"He says he'll see to it that your mother is returned to you," she says and adds, "Alive, even. The sirens being so ambitious wasn't something he saw coming, but he says he should have. They've never been a shy people."

I breathe in and out slowly, trying to decide whether the offer is genuine. And, for the first time in our conversation, Phoebe seems to correctly identify and react to my facial expression.

"I don't think it's a lie. I think he'll do what he promises. He wants to keep all of this quiet," she says.

I look at her, eyes sharp with suspicion. Possession is a possibility. It happens.

"It's still me," she says, moving her hand away from the stone on the table and holding up her palm to further demonstrate that she's not touching it. "It's all just me. I'm sure you're different sometimes, too. Don't judge."

I swallow the words I want to say to her. There's a sadness in her now. Enough of a sadness that I can tell she must recognize what's been done to her—what she's lost. I don't know if this is better, but I know it would be no mercy for her to dwell on it. And I don't know how long she'll be fully lucid and present.

"Why does he want to keep this quiet?" I ask, testing the waters but trying not to push.

"Moira doesn't know that Max is associating with humans to the degree he's associating with you. She's very fond of him. It would break her heart to think he might be getting knocked off course. Kristoff wants to save her from that."

I nod slowly, absorbing.

"I guess I should be grateful for that," I grate out, watching Phoebe's reaction carefully. She gives me a grim smile.

"Yes, you should be." Phoebe's brilliant blue eyes stay locked on mine while I try to decide how hard I can push —how much she can tell me without getting into trouble. "Ask," she says. "It's better if you know, even if you forget it later. Especially if you forget it later. It's good to have known."

She means more by those words than I have the frame of reference to understand, and it makes me feel like a kid talking to an adult. Such a disorienting reversal from just moments ago.

"I understand that apprentices are very important to wizards. I've been told as much."

"Yes."

"But Max and I aren't... Max and I are just friends. Work colleagues, even. He doesn't even join me for arbitrations. He was content to let me die six months ago. He's just... spying on me, really." *Content* might not be the right word, given the bottle of vodka he pulled out when he thought he was alone and thought it was inevitable, but that doesn't seem like an important thing to bring up right now.

"Max can't erase your brain. He can't control how you relate to one another. That means more, to a wizard, than you realize. It's more than wizards like to allow."

I lean back in the booth, unable to keep the Christ-you've-got-to-be-kidding-me expression off my face. Phoebe's posture relaxes as well, but it pulls her forward over the table, resting on one of her arms and letting a delicate hand disappear beneath her wild curls.

"Wizards have this kind of intense relationship with humanity. They know they're more like us than they are anything else. Some of them even have human parents, maybe. I've never gotten an answer on that. Well, not one that I've been allowed to remember, anyway. So if they let themselves—if they relate in a way that's real and that they can't just control and reset—they'd get too close to us. Try to help us. Make themselves vulnerable to us. And as powerful as wizards are, there aren't that many of them when you get down to it. The Salem witch trials, the inquisition… none of that involved any wizards. But they think about stuff like that a lot. And humans have nukes now. And humans could…"

Phoebe's voice drops, secretive now, as though everything she already said wasn't need-to-know. "Humans can do magic, kind of. If we get the spells, sometimes. Some of the spells, we would be able to execute. That's why I…"

She blinks, recentering, and continues. "That's how close humans and wizards are. That's why wizards never write anything down."

I try not to let my relief show that Phoebe, at least, doesn't appear to have any inkling I have a trove. I try to bury my guilt at the thought she might have suffered all this hoping to get what I was given for free. She continues.

"So wizards have to keep themselves and each other apart from humanity. They keep from getting too close, and being tempted, or letting their guard down. But they can't let any of each other get too far, either, or they'll go the other way. More than one wizard has gone the whole *rule humanity as a cruel god* route, and they don't want that either. Because if there's a crown, they'll all fight for it.

And nothing will be left. And it would be so ugly. Wizards don't like ugly."

I think of Poseidon's trident, sitting untouched in Atlantis, if Max is to be believed. That tracks, I guess. The bullshit stories about restraint and mutually assured destruction that wizards tell themselves and their servants are internally consistent, if that counts for anything.

"It's a careful balance. They police each other and keep themselves just close enough and just far enough away that we don't kill and torture all of them and they don't kill and dominate each other and all of us."

It's hard to read the emotions in Phoebe's words. I'm left with the impression of a teacher reading aloud from a textbook that she doesn't agree with, but that she's been compelled by a backward school board to teach verbatim.

"That all sounds very calculating," I say, trying to tease out a little more. Phoebe's eyes go out of focus somewhere behind me, spurring a moment of panic that I'm losing her back to the scattered frame of mind she had when she came in. But it's only momentary. She returns to me with more focus and intensity than she's shown so far, her sky-blue eyes glinting in the low light of the dingy restaurant.

"Maybe. Wizards can be calculating, sometimes. But if you *wanted*, I guess you could also think of them almost like a bad ex-boyfriend. They don't want to be with us—not really, not as equals. They wouldn't be *capable* of that. But they're also never going to leave us alone. They're obsessed with us. They want what they wish they could get from us but know they won't—to be a part of what we are and what we have. We're real life. We're the world. We built it all. That scares them, and they hate us for it. Everything they do, in one way or another, is about us. It's bad enough if you don't know about it. It's hell if you do."

Phoebe leans back, her back straight and her bearing

noble in a way that makes me wonder if she isn't older than she looks. Or maybe it's just training I don't want to think about.

"Max is the most important person in Kristoff's very long life. He's old, now—too old to try again with another apprentice. It's too hard and takes too long and too many favors to procure one. Max is his only chance at a legacy, and he's in a vulnerable stage right now, away from home but not yet matured into a full wizard. There's a chance he might go wrong, and not find the right balance, and have to be put down. Your amulet makes it impossible for Max to control your relationship and almost impossible to find the right distance. You probably think of yourself as harmless to Max, but to Kristoff, you're one of the scariest things he can think of. He doesn't have a lot of good tools for dealing with you without driving a wedge between him and Max and losing him anyway. Don't underestimate how important this is to Kristoff. Don't underestimate what he can or will do to resolve the situation. Take the deal."

I don't think of myself as harmless to Max. I remember again how he looked when I last saw him, broken and bloody and bleeding. I remember how he looked in the graveyard six months ago, desperate and screaming as I left him helpless, exhausted, and alone. I was never harmless to Max.

I judge the passion in Phoebe's face. It wasn't a mistake for Kristoff to send her here, knowing she might tell me more than the bare facts of the situation. This isn't a stolen confession. It's a sales pitch for his deal—or, at least, a more effective attempt at intimidation than Kristoff himself could ever have managed.

Phoebe was probably smarter than me once. She has a brash intelligence in her eyes, all the more precious for how fleeting I know it will be. She's definitely braver. I couldn't do what she did—I couldn't even call my sister until I ran out of excuses. I can't even tell secrets to the people who should know them, much less risk my mind and my life for them. I have to do better.

"Do I need to answer right now?" I ask, ashamed of myself for not having an answer already. A more morally upright person would know instantly how to respond. Someone with a clearly defined code would have no question.

Phoebe looks around us, her glances momentarily frightening me that I might lose her lucidity. But I don't, and she leans forward.

"Do you think you have another option?" she asks, a spark of daring in her expression. "After all that, and meeting me, do you think you can get away with saying no?"

I swallow hard, leaning forward slightly to meet her. I don't want to give her hope. Hope is dangerous for her.

"You're better off fixing this yourself, if you actually can. He'll keep his word in this, sure. But if you put yourself at his mercy, you'll regret it. And Max will still be around. I don't know if I know him, but I know he's a wizard. And wizards never let things lie."

I blink a few times and lean back. I'm ashamed of the relief that the choice has been, for all intents and purposes, removed from my shoulders. But that relief is replaced by a thread of doubt, tugging at me.

"A moment ago, you seemed really sure I should take the deal."

Phoebe nods. "You should. This is important to Kristoff. You don't know what he'd do."

My heart sinks. "But then you said I shouldn't."

Phoebe straightens, panic in her harsh, escalated

breathing. I'm losing her. I'm a fucking idiot. I'm pushing her away.

"Phoebe," I say, trying to keep the alarm out of my voice and failing. I reach out and grab her perfect wrist with my unremarkable human hand. "Phoebe, look at me. What do you know about sirens?"

She takes a few more harsh breaths.

"Sirens?" she asks as her eyes fight to leave mine and she forces them to stay put.

"Sirens. Anything you can tell me?"

"Not much," she says, calmer. She's come back to herself, though I don't know for long. She makes to take her wrist from me, but I make no move to let go. "I know they're fractious. I know they view death very differently than how we do. I know they're very angry at the wind nymphs for participating in the wizard's curse."

My pulse skyrockets. "So they *did* participate, then?" I ask.

Phoebe looks off into the distance, her glance darting between three points. A spike of fear runs through me. I thought I'd held on, I thought *she'd* held on, but it was a false spring in February. I'm losing her.

"I believe so," she says. "I think I heard that."

I speak quickly, trying to get everything out of her I can before I lose her again. She'd want me to try. "And what did they get out of it? Why are they so angry about it?"

"I don't know," Phoebe says, her voice beginning to take on the slightly singsong, unfocused tone it had when she first walked in.

"And who would know?" I ask with urgency.

"Kristoff," she says. "But he wouldn't tell you." She's slipping away.

"And who else?" I ask, my grip on her wrist tightening, pulling her eyes to me for one last focused second.

"Poseidon, maybe," she says. "If he's still alive."

And then her eyes go glassy. Shifting over toward the hostess station where the waitress and the hostess don't even pretend not to be staring at us. Her frown deepens into a slight pout, and then back to neutral.

"You're different again," I say, more to myself than to her. I release my hold on her wrist, but she doesn't move her arm away from its slightly unnatural position in the center of the table.

"I'm sure you're different sometimes, too. Don't judge." If she remembered saying those words the first time, it would be a joke. But her blue eyes are empty. It's an echo. She's just an echo.

"Would you like more mozzarella sticks?" I ask, the words sticking in my throat.

She doesn't notice the broken quality in my voice. Her face brightens. "I would love some."

The words hang in the air as I wait for her to remember that we're having a conversation, hoping that she'll speak again of her own accord. She doesn't.

"You can tell Kristoff when you get back that I'll be turning down his offer," I say. Her face clouds, but only for a moment before it defaults back to harried concern, her eyes darting around the room at unseen points of interest.

The restaurant is just down-market enough to have a checkout station at the front. I take advantage of this to get myself away from the table and away from Phoebe. I pay for my mozzarella sticks and tell the waitress that I can't stay, but that I'd like to pay for another order for Phoebe. I tip generously, partially because I feel sorry for her that Kristoff will probably clean up her memory after I'm gone, partially because I'm hoping that will keep them quiet, and partially because I'm feeling guilty for what happened to Phoebe, even though it had nothing to do with me and likely happened a long time ago. The logic of my guilt doesn't quite work out there, but I can't imagine the waitress minds.

There's a heaviness in my chest as I step out of the dimly lit restaurant and into the hazy autumn morning that feels like winter. I can pick out the ocean peeking through buildings. I stand on the sidewalk, trying to sort through what I should do or where I should go and how and why.

Poseidon. God of the sea. Just thinking of his name is almost intimidating enough to cut through the numbness that meeting Phoebe has left in me. Sure, I've met a god, and he didn't turn out to be so bad. But I don't even know Aloysius's true name, and I'm pretty sure I didn't learn about him in school.

Still, maybe Poseidon would help. Gods hate wizards. I hate wizards. Presumably, Poseidon would like for all living things in the oceans *not* to be destroyed. We're natural allies in this, really. So why does the thought of getting in touch with him terrify me?

I'm so consumed by this line of thought that I don't immediately register what's pinging against my danger reflexes, or why my eyes are fixed on a figure across the street heading away from me down toward the harborwalk. It's not until he risks a furtive glance back at me that I identify his features.

Siren. Atlantic tribe. Sat next to the queen. My legs are already in motion to chase him before my mind tells them to do so.

TWENTY

A Plan

If there's one thing the movies don't show you about chasing a mysterious, suspicious figure through a major city, it's the unwillingness of the traffic light gods to cooperate. Luckily, running on legs that may look normal but are actually two mangled halves of a lower fin must not be easy, because even with my left arm pulsing with pain with my every step, and the interference of three traffic lights, I'm able to keep him in sight for four blocks.

But as he disappears around a building and I realize how close we are to the water, my heart sinks. I struggle to propel myself forward with the same enthusiasm, but when I get to the waterfront, I'm greeted with nothing but a crowd of normal human strangers milling about. The sound of my heavy breath in my ears and my heavy heartbeat in my chest drown out their conversations.

My right arm reaches up to pull my glasses down over my eyes. I look around at the unknowing humans. No one looks like anything supernatural, although I see a group of girls looking at an area of the pathway along the water. One of them seems to be trying to convince her friends of something. She saw the siren, maybe. I watch the three of them—two skeptical, one earnest—head forward and examine the spot. They look over into the water. They see nothing.

I want to go tell her she's not crazy—that she shouldn't doubt what she saw. But I don't have a good explanation I can share, and I don't want to go sharing any truth around Moira and Kristoff's city. I don't know if I'll survive the target they've already placed on my back, and I certainly don't need another one.

But when the girls wander away from the spot where the siren must have disappeared, I replace them. I look into the murky water, hoping to see something—*anything* —there.

I shiver. My two coats aren't enough. Even with the run, I'm going to run out of warmth eventually.

And I'm already running out of options. I sit down on the boardwalk, hanging my feet over the edge, urging the siren to come back up to me. I think maybe I see his face somewhere down there, but I might be imagining it.

Why did he run? Was it the look on my face when I saw him, the remembrance that his tribe kidnapped my mother? Or was it more the instinct of a fish caught on land and suddenly very aware of his unsuitability for his current environment, the way I would get the hell out of the water at the slightest hint of something unfamiliar or unexpected brushing against my leg? Maybe it was just that he didn't want me to start asking questions within earshot of humans. I've got to imagine that of all creatures, sirens would have a more-than-healthy fear of wizards. And while I'm not with any group that signed the treaties, so I am technically not someone supernatural secrets need to be kept from, he would get in a hell of a lot of trouble if he were connected to me breaking the rules he *is* bound to.

But that's all speculation. I don't have any way of getting him to come back. I don't have a way of telling him I just want to talk. And maybe yell. And maybe ask a favor.

Snow starts falling. It shouldn't be, yet. It's too early. Damn dead nymph. But at least it empties out the boardwalk, and I find myself increasingly alone with the water and the cold.

And I am so very alone. Faisal is unreachable. Gigi made it very clear she won't enter Boston, so I'd have to get out to a crossroads if I had any chance of her helping me again. Wilbur's angry at me for unknown reasons. Max is either dead or wounded, and possibly angry at me for getting him in such a state. What does that leave, other than a sister I can't turn to without risking her safety… again?

It's better this way. I'm already getting my mother killed, probably. Extinguishing what little life my father's mistakes left her with. If I'm going to go full Karen and speak to the ocean's manager, the least I can do is not take anyone else down with me.

I spare a glance around to make sure no one is watching before I take off a sock and shoe and roll up one leg of Faisal's jeans. I need this siren to help me, and I'm sure he's still got to be around here. Maybe I can go to him? How cold can it really be?

Really fucking cold, it turns out. I jerk my foot back from the surface of the water almost immediately after I make contact. But as I do, I notice something.

Shivering and struggling to get my socks back on, I peer into the inky, dirty water.

Lights. Lights in the deep. What WBBOM called the "Ocean Glow." The same lights I saw in Chios, only this time they're green rather than red. It's harder to see them in the daylight, and I contort myself trying to get closer.

Flashing green lights, both just under the surface and farther down.

I blink and look around again, as though someone else seeing what I was seeing would make any difference. I take my glasses off and put them on again, but there's no difference.

I open my mouth, though I don't know what I'm going to say. I don't have time to figure it out before I notice a change in the lights.

Rather than just twinkling, flashing on and off like a massive, surreal string of Christmas lights, the lights form a pattern.

Arrows. They're forming into arrows. They remind me of one of those arcade signs that create the illusion of movement by some of them blinking on and off at specific times. They aren't in anything so clear or orderly as a grid, but the motion is clear: They're pointing me out toward the harbor. They're pointing me out to sea.

I stand, the cold lifting out of my bones just a little. Do I trust mysterious lights in the water? Should I?

Mysterious lights in the water have never abandoned me. They've never admitted they eat people. They've never told me they're going to kill me. Mysterious lights in the water, in fact, seemed intent on warning me against getting myself killed when I was in Chios. As far as allies go, mysterious lights in the water no one seems to know anything about are probably the best I've got right now.

And mysterious light in the water once successfully killed a full-fledged wizard. That's role-model material right there.

Not that I'm getting *into* the water. I'm an idiot, but the microsecond the flesh of my foot touched the water was all the convincing I needed that it was the dumbest idea I've ever had.

So, no. I need to default to the second dumbest idea I've ever had.

No one is around. That should help me. There's a dock a couple blocks over that's separated from public access by a metal gate with bars extending out over the water. But that gate is only kept shut with a lock. And what kind of second-rate, knock-off, dollar-store wizard would I be if I didn't have a key that opens all locks?

I don't allow myself a self-satisfied grin as I walk toward the gate. If anyone sees me, it needs to look like I'm not doing anything I shouldn't. I don't know how well that'll hold up if someone stops to think about why someone wearing a 7-Eleven jacket, poorly fitted jeans, and a thick-rimmed pair of seventies-style glasses on her head is walking onto a dock with boats worth—just guessing— three times as much as my house.

I don't know how well I would have gotten away with it if someone had been around to see me, but luckily no one is. Or at least no one yells "Stop! Thief!" as I slide my skeleton key into the dock gate. There are nine boats at this dock, and I eliminate three targets immediately because they're sailboats. I need something with a throttle, a wheel, and nothing more complicated than that. I eliminate three more for just being too goddamn big. I intend to return this boat. Hopefully. Maybe. If I can. But if I can't, I'd rather piss off people with fewer resources with which to hunt me down.

That leaves four candidates. I choose the one called *Why Knot?* because honestly… why not?

I attempt to move with easy, practiced motions, which isn't easy when you haven't practiced them. But again, there are no cries as I get all the ropes—which I'm sure there's a better term for—disconnected from the dock and stowed away. Then I head for the engine, and I hope to God that a key made to work on all locks also works on engines.

The key slides in. The key turns. The engine comes to life. I finally let out my breath.

I've driven three boats in my life, all much smaller than this and all on various vacations. Not stolen, of course. It occurs to me for the first time as I manage to get the boat away from the dock and heading toward open water that maybe I should have looked into renting a boat. But the bark lines under my wrist are disappearing too quickly, my bank balance is less than healthy, and I don't even know where I would begin or if they even rent boats to foolhardy tourists in the middle of the deepest fall cold snap in decades.

Those all seem like perfectly acceptable excuses.

I wait for a coast guard boat to come out of nowhere and pull up beside me with pointed questions, but it doesn't happen. I have nothing but the sound of the engine, the horrible sharp cold of the air, the smell of salt, and the wide green bands of arrows directing me onward as I thread myself down the channel, under the bridge, and away from land.

Would anyone have noticed if I checked the fuel levels on different boats before choosing which one to steal? Probably. But when I figure out how to check, I find that I got a lucky with an almost-full tank in this one. The knowledge reassures me enough to open the throttle all the way and head farther and farther away from land.

It takes time. A long, long time. When the wide green arrows get less enthusiastic and eventually die down, another full mark has disappeared from my arm. Fourteen left.

I kill the engine and drift. I look back toward land. I pull out my phone and check my GPS. I'm out past cell service and I don't have the map loaded, but my little blue dot is out bobbing in the gray.

It would be quiet if it weren't for the wind. I gather my coat close around me and huddle down into the cockpit further. I want to go inside. I'm sure there's some kind of heater in there. But if the siren was watching and is willing to come talk to me now that we're away from any prying eyes, I want to make sure I'm here to greet him. Plus, going inside feels like more of a transgression than stealing the boat somehow. That's breaking and entering. What I'm doing so far is just temporarily relocating. Much better.

In the dead time while I float untethered, I look at some of the things I have on hand. Unsurprisingly, there's fishing gear and scuba gear, and even a couple of sea kayaks, which feels like a little much.

"What are you doing?"

The deep, slightly Greek-accented male voice spins me around. He's naked, which I guess shouldn't be a surprise. He was shown as clothed to me on land, but he was trying to fit in there, so the wizards' illusion would do that for him. My hand goes to bring my glasses down to preserve his theoretical modesty, but I hesitate. I need to be able to see his facial features as interpreted by the wizards' illusion. I know what sirens look like, anyway. I'm already familiar with the deep rows of sharp teeth and mutilated fins.

I put on a smile I don't feel, but I try to make look real. "Waiting for you. I thought you might be more comfortable talking out here."

Nothing greets my words but the lapping of small waves against the side of the boat and the whistle of the wind making its way around the craft's varied edges and instruments. I open my mouth to say something clever and charming, but what comes out sounds like a recrimination.

"You have my mother, after all."

I watch his face carefully, looking for signs of guilt. I see them. Guilt and shame.

"The Pacific tribe would have taken her if we didn't," he says reluctantly. And then, like he can't stop himself, he adds on words I'm sure he didn't mean to say. "And she was so *easy* to take. We told her we had her memories, and she slid right under the surface."

My breath catches in my chest. I clench my jaw and feel tension in my muscles as they cry out for me to do something—anything—to this man. Instead, I take three calming breaths before I respond.

"Did you kill her?" I ask.

"No."

Relief, albeit muted, flows through me. I hadn't let myself think she'd been killed—and it wouldn't make sense for her to have been killed if the tribes were looking for leverage. But it was good to have it confirmed. Assuming that the siren in front of me isn't lying.

"So you can take people underwater without killing them? You said she went under the surface."

The siren's face tightens. "She'll be all right as long as the Atlantic is. That's all I can tell you."

We stand, bodies tense and unprotected from the wind, for a long time.

"Aren't you cold?" I ask. The possibility of a bawdy joke occurs to me, but I don't indulge it.

"No," he says. "Did you only want to ask me about your mother?"

"No." I turn over how to word this in my head. It'll go down like a lead balloon when I get to a certain point, I'm fairly sure. Best just to dive in. "I want to talk to Poseidon. I want you to facilitate that."

The siren doesn't react. He very, *very* carefully doesn't react.

"Poseidon is dead," he says.

I nod with a mockery of thoughtfulness on my face. "Oh, right. Forgot about that. It must be mighty fun playing with his trident, then."

The siren looks away quickly at the mention of the trident, like he's afraid we're going to be overheard. "We do not have his trident."

I incline my chin in a show of nonexistent confidence. "The Pacific tribe has it, then?"

He fixes me with a caught glare. "No," he grates out.

"Why not? If he's so dead."

The siren breathes in and out, resets his shoulders, and again toes the party line, although with a good deal less of a show of conviction. "Poseidon is dead."

We understand one another.

"If you won't take me to him, I want your help in getting him to come to me."

The siren laughs. "If he were alive, you think that would be a good idea?"

I can't help but feel offended. He's so superior, so mocking.

"What else am I supposed to do? You have an idea? You think your species is the only one that dies if the oceans do?"

The siren looks out over the water. "But if it's the Pacific…"

"Oh, come on. I don't know how they'd limit it, practically speaking. But even if they do, this is extinction-level-event stuff. And yeah, maybe the wizards will figure out how to fix it. But look at how cold it is, and they haven't done anything about *that*. A thousand years ago, sure, there was a lot they could do. But now? Killing three wind nymphs? Or stopping a spell that spans half the planet? Do you want to bet the lives of all living things that they can still do something remotely similar? Or do you want to bet all living things on the nymphs suddenly being reasonable? From what I've heard, they'll probably be glad if everything but them died off. They'd get a chance to restore nature without anyone sentient messing it up."

The siren winces. "And what do you think Poseidon could do about it? If he were alive?"

I slump against the wheel, slack with lack of direction. "I don't know. But the Greek pantheon was closest to the nymphs, everyone says. Always hanging around Olympus together. And he might know a little bit about the god-like power that's driven them out of their minds. And I also think their anger has something to do with what happened way back when you got… *rehomed*, which he also might know something about."

The anger in the siren's eyes—the hurt, the agony—is brief. But it's so pronounced that it's easy to catch.

"I'm sorry," I say, and I mean it. "It's hard to quantify what you've lost and gained when I've never had either."

More waves. More wind.

"It's not what we lost," the siren says at last. "Not really. It's that we changed."

He speaks the words with a weight I don't understand.

"All things change," I say, but he shakes his head like an adult who has just heard a child ask if all dogs are boys and all cats are girls.

"Good things *shouldn't*." There's a brutal danger to the smile he gives me. A chill that has nothing to do with the ungoverned north wind wanders down my spine.

"Do you want to drown me?" I ask, keeping my eyes from darting to the inky water off the side of the boat.

"Yes," he answers, without a trace of malice or apology.

"Why?"

"Because I like what you are, and I'd give you the gift of never becoming anything else. We draw worthy humans into the water with promises of what they want. We give them what they need."

I swallow hard. "So drowning people is, what? An act of charity?"

The siren breathes in and out slowly. Does he enjoy doing that, given how rare it is for him? "We get something out of it, too. We get your memories. From what I've heard of you, Arbiter, those are memories worth keeping. I could keep them for you. You'll only lose them eventually, if you keep them to yourself."

That is, by far, the weirdest compliment I've ever received. I don't know how to respond to it, so I don't. "If you won't bring me to Poseidon, that's fine. Just bring me his trident. He strikes me as the kind of guy who doesn't like people messing with his stuff. When he comes to me to discuss, we can have a conversation about the end of the world and what he should do about it. You can use your super-secret water crossroads to do it, I assume. I won't tell anyone. Scout's honor."

The siren laughs, harsh and bright, but there's fear hiding in that laughter. "I'm not touching the trident. No siren is touching the trident. If the oceans don't boil, we still have to live in them."

I sigh, looking around the boat like something's going to jump out with an answer. And, as my eyes rest of the scuba gear, something sort of does.

"That wasn't a 'no' on the water crossroads. If I bring

my own air, would you take me to it and then bring me back here?"

When the siren doesn't immediately respond with a flaw in my plan, I find it myself. "Except I'd probably freeze to death." I cast around for another idea.

"Not necessarily," the siren says. "You could survive the journey to the trident, I believe. And once you were holding the trident, it would keep you warm. It has a lot of power. It wouldn't let a bearer die, if it trapped one."

The way he says that the trident has a lot of power makes me think there's something about it he's not telling me. Probably a whole lot of somethings. But if I press him on telling me about the trident, I can't press him to take me to it. It feels like it's an either/or. And when it comes to choosing between looking and leaping, I know where I stand. Just looking at something never solved anything.

My eyes lock onto the siren. "So you'll do it?"

The siren looks away, out over the glorious unbroken expanse of the ocean. When he looks back at me, he seems nervous in a new way. "I'll take you to Atlantis. I'll help you find the trident. I will not transport you when you have it. From there you are on your own."

Never one to skip a gift-horse mouth inspection, I blurt out, "But what if I run out of air before Poseidon shows up?"

The siren smirks. "Then you'll just have to breathe the air in Atlantis."

TWENTY-ONE

A Descent

My college roommate of four years was very into scuba diving, and not much interested in anything else. Over summer break one year, I took a scuba course to exist as a person to her. After the classes, I went on a couple of dives and really enjoyed them. But there was always too much to do, and Springfield isn't exactly close to the ocean, so I never went again.

As I struggle to sort out the pieces and how they all connect to each other, I wish I remembered more about that class. I wish I'd gone diving again. I wish, not for the first time, that I were just more prepared. In general. For everything.

But I remember enough of the basics to get the gear assembled and mostly guess what I think is the right amount of weight to put on my weight belt, and I'm fairly confident that I know which controls do what on my buoyancy vest.

I do not want to bring my phone with me into the water. I do not want to bring my leather jacket into the water. But there's really no choice on either account, unless

I want to leave physical evidence linking me to the theft of this very expensive boat, which I don't. I tuck my phone, glasses, and keys away in the zippered inner pocket of my jacket, hoping whatever protection spells Max put on it have something to say about water.

With my arm still wrenched, it hurts like hell to get my gear on. The siren winces in sympathy but doesn't offer to help. He's looking at me like he's not sure about something. I'd think it was because he doesn't think I have long to live, but that wouldn't bother him. I don't press him on it. I guess it doesn't need to matter.

"Okay," I say when my ensemble is assembled, fins and all. "Let's do this."

With a dancer's grace, the siren bends at the waist and disappears into the water. A second later, he comes bobbing back up to the surface.

"Come in," he says. "I can get you what you need to save everything. To save your mother. To save Faisal. I'll take you to it."

How the hell does he know about Faisal? And, while I'm asking questions, how the hell did he know about my mother's memories? I almost comment on his sudden reversal and the faith he's putting in my shitty plan, but I don't. He's just luring me into the water with what I want most. He probably can't help himself.

I shuffle my way to the very edge of the swim step. Then I take my giant stride out into the water as far as I can go.

The freezing water disorients me. The pain in my left arm as it pinwheels wildly in panic vies with the bite of the cold to drive my breathing faster and more desperate. I'd just filled the tank on my back from the compressor on board, but if I keep sucking it down like this, it won't last long.

I come bobbing back up, buoyancy vest full to keep me from sinking immediately, aided by my kicking feet. But I must have gotten the weight wrong, because even with my full vest, I start sinking.

Panic—this time from a fun new source!—shoots through me. But when I feel a hand grasp around my wrist, holding me up out of the deeps, I begin to steady.

The siren looks more comfortable here in the dim light just under the surface of the water. He should be more terrifying, not less, knowing what I know. But all the same, the sight of him and his flowing hair expanding out around his head like a halo calms me.

My breath through the regulator is so loud in my ears. I'm overwhelmed, oppressed by it as I watch the siren reach with his other hand to a flat scar on the side of his fin, just where his hip would be if he were a human. He parts the skin and reaches inside, and the sickening realization that he has a self-inflicted pocket of skin underneath hits me hard.

His hand reemerges with something thin in it—maybe an inch or two long. I kick my feet so I can get a closer view as he manipulates it in his fingers with practiced ease, leveraging it against his fingers to apply pressure to the middle with his thumb. Just as he breaks it, I realize what it is: a small bone.

And then the light is gone. I blink my eyes, trying to adjust. My ears go haywire, painfully popping at the too-sudden change. The pressure around me is so much greater, and I have a sudden overwhelming memory of when I got myself trapped in a glass box in Max's living room six months ago. That same claustrophobic terror, the mind-numbing panic.

I suck in air from my regulator hard, over and over, centering myself around that one movement. I should be more careful with my air. I shouldn't be using this much. But that mechanical, overwhelmingly loud action is the only thing that pulls me back out of the glass box and into the here and now.

And where I am is a bit farther below the water's surface, where there is less light and more pressure. My eyes start to adjust, and I can see a dim light from above. Not too far down, then. Not so far down that it'll crush me. The cold bites at me. My legs are numb. I can make out the shape of the siren, still holding my wrist, still keeping me from sinking to the bottom where I won't ever be seen again.

So *that's* how the sirens travel underneath the water, now that they can't use their portals or the crossroads anymore.

I can't make out the siren's facial expressions—he's just an outline and a mess of floating hair. But he seems able enough to gauge mine to mark when I've calmed down enough to move on. Or maybe he's just noticed that the wild movements of my arms and legs have finally settled down.

As I scan around me, I notice another, much larger void in the light. A great hulking darkness lurks off to the right, in the direction that the siren starts pulling me toward.

I start kicking my legs to assist and blink my eyes as we get closer, willing them to adjust to the low light faster. I'd assumed Atlantis must be an island—that it would be somewhere on the bottom of the ocean—but it's suspended here, floating untethered.

As we draw closer, I make sense out of the dark shape. A forest of white anemones, their tendrils responding in unison to the gentle current like a whimsical chorus line, cover a wide, gently sloping plane.

I start as it hits me: a ship. I'm seeing a ship. An old steam ship floating upside down, with its great hull bared upward toward the surface like a dead fish, and the great big stacks for steam jutting down below. As we get closer, I read the careful Art Deco lettering, upside down along what would be the top of the hull, black tinged with gold: *The Atlantis.*

I pause my journey toward it, letting the siren pull me forward without my assistance. My mind is so blunted by the terror and sensory overload and cold of the last five minutes that it takes me a good thirty seconds to realize what's going on.

My glasses. I don't have my glasses on. This is the wizards' illusion taking the supernatural and repackaging it as a compromise between what is and what I would expect in a world without magic. Disappointment fills me, and I make a mental note that when we get inside, if there really is air trapped in there, then I will get my glasses out and put them on. I'll never forgive myself if I come all this way and don't see Atlantis as it truly is.

The siren pulls us under the hull to where the deck would be and maneuvers us through to a circular hatch. It's sitting wide open, but I can't see within it. The siren goes first, letting free my wrist so that he can use his hands to climb up out of the water.

I see nothing but a void. The meager light filtering through the ocean above doesn't reach into the hull of the ship. Some instinctive part of me screams not to continue. There may be air in there, but who knows what else? It's a trap. That darkness is a trap. Monsters live in a dark that absolute.

But I have no choice. I can't stay here. I can't go back. So I go forward, plunging myself upward into the open air trapped below the decks of the illusory ship.

The darkness is complete around me as I emerge out of the water. The lip—or ledge—that I'm trying to pull myself onto is thicker than I would expect. Probably because it isn't metal and wood, but likely something else. I try to get my body up out of the water, but it's difficult with only one usable arm. I end up needing to use my wrenched left arm to make it to a position where I'm lying on my side, tank out to one side. I see stars from the pain as I lie in the darkness.

The siren doesn't rush me. I lie for a long minute until the stars begin to clear. Cautiously, I pull out my regulator and breathe in the stale, salty air. It smells disgusting, though I can't place the smell exactly. There's something of dead fish mixed up in there, but it's buried in other distasteful scents I don't recognize. But after five breaths holding my regulator ready and waiting, it does appear that the air is at least giving me the oxygen I need.

I'm not ditching my air apparatus—no way I'd do that. But I figure it'll be easier to walk around inside if I leave my flippers here by the entrance.

"Will you lead me back here?" I ask the siren. My voice echoes in the enclosed space, accompanied by the sound of dripping in the distance.

"Yes," he replies. Part of me is hoping he'll change his mind and agree to bring me back to my stolen boat. But that hope isn't based in anything real.

"Give me a second to get situated," I say. I take off my gear so that I can get out of my soaked 7-Eleven jacket. I keep my leather jacket on, but I open it up and root around inside until I find two things: my glasses and my cell phone. I take off my goggles and get the glasses on underneath, tightening it down so that it'll keep the glasses on but won't let water in. With the way this thing is designed, I think it might actually work.

Then I attempt, hope against hope, to turn on my phone.

The light forces me to blink and look away.

Nice going with the spells, Max. I keep my eyes closed, opening them in bursts to adjust to the new light level without going completely blind. By the time the phone lock screen deactivates, my eyes have adjusted enough that I can see the screen to swipe up and activate the flashlight.

I take the opportunity to look around me. Though the glasses, it doesn't look anything like the inside of a ship. Stone walls, carved out and fitted tightly together, make up the hallway we find ourselves in. The siren, now looking again like his true self, seems a natural fit here. I note the way the split halves of his fins bend around the vestigial bones of his bird legs. There are creases there that look worn, but it doesn't look natural. I'm reminded a little of those running blade prosthetics.

Intricate carvings cover the stones around us. Some of them are vaguely geometric and patterned, but most of them remind me more of hieroglyphs. I could spend hours and days and years staring at them, trying to make sense of them.

If I weren't so goddamn cold.

My shivers outweigh my wonder, and I close up my leather jacket and get back into my gear—with one less weight around my belt to make it easier to get to the surface, if and when I need to.

"Do you know the way?" I ask the siren when I'm finally ready to move. But by the time I've finished the words, he's already moving forward at a pace I'd find annoying if I weren't so cold and so desperate to get warm.

I follow along behind him, feeling sorry for the weird motion of his legs at every step, wondering if it hurts for him to walk this way. Maybe it doesn't anymore. It must have when he was first learning to do it. It couldn't not have. Most of my attention as we walk through hallways and climb stairs is occupied solely in keeping myself moving forward despite the cold and the unforgiving pace. We pass endless hallways full of carvings and climb curling staircases with carvings on the smooth, round walls.

Archeologists should get a chance at this. How many brilliant people would love to spend their lives unraveling the mysteries of this lost tribe, this lost nation? How many papers, how much of an obsession? What would they learn about them? What would they teach us? How is it fair they haven't had the chance?

Maybe it's the cold-induced delirium, but I imagine a world where kids dress up as Atlanteans for school plays, and fourth graders do school projects on Atlantean hieroglyphs. From what I've heard about the original myths of Atlantis, the Atlanteans themselves were humans. And human history belongs to us. It's not right that it's been stolen from us. It's not right that we've been disconnected from this nation of ourselves.

The righteous indignation helps keep me from falling —keeps me warm enough to get me into a large, cavernous stone room. The light from my phone flashlight doesn't reach up to the ceiling, so I can't say how big it is. I work the leather of my jacket up so that I can check my wrist: thirteen marks left. We must have spent an hour walking. It felt like so much longer than that.

"Is this it?" I ask, mostly to hear my own voice in the dark space. I don't expect an answer from the siren, and I don't get one. I just get an echo of my own words that tells me this space is huge—as big as the great cathedrals I visited in Europe during a summer trip that Faisal and I took with Olivia and her family a few years back.

The siren steps aside and motions forward with one

arm. I can't see the trident yet, but this is as close as he's willing to get to it. Not for the first time, I wonder if this is a really dumb idea. I check back over my options—or rather, my *lack* of options. I don't see any good ideas hiding there. Is it too late to turn back? Is it too late to change my mind?

As I'm thinking, I let my phone drop to my side. Without the beam pointing forward, I see another source of light in the room—a dim blue-green glow emanating from something resting maybe forty feet away.

I step forward, awkward under the weight of my gear and struggling to keep my breathing regular as excited gasps at what I see in front of me work themselves out anyway.

As I grow closer, keeping the light from my phone directed only at the ground directly in front of me, I see the glow of the trident more clearly. It's smaller than I would have imagined—only maybe four feet long. It looks like metal, though which metal, I can't identify. A light brass? A yellowed silver? It has intricate symbols all over it, though they look raised up rather than carved in. They probably help with grip, although I can't imagine Poseidon needing help with that. The symbols themselves don't look like wizard symbols—not regular or geometric enough for that. They don't look like the Greek lettering I've seen over the past day. They also don't look like the hieroglyphs on the Atlantean walls around me. They look more like purposeful scribbles—like someone was writing very quickly in a language I don't speak. In that way, they remind me a little bit of some of the older pages in the trove, inked in a foreign language I've never seen by a casual hand, writing quickly.

My steps slow in reverence as I approach the trident. It's lying on its side, almost haphazardly. All my instincts scream that I should run from this, the way I'd run from nuclear waste or a venomous snake. But the numbness of my legs and the conviction that the cold will kill me more surely than the power in the trident pushes me past it.

I turn the light on my phone off and tuck it away in the waterproof pouch in my jacket. I don't need the light of it now that I have the trident. Then I reach down and pick the trident up in my right hand.

As I do, I cry out in shock at the sudden warmth that shoots through my body. Breathing heavily, I nearly fall to the ground, awkwardly burdened and off-balance from the weight of the tank on my back.

I feel everything. I feel the water—the ocean. I feel the steady, destructive strength of salt and the anger of the riptide. I feel a vastness that I can't fit my mind around. That vastness rips open my chest and pours into me. I feel warm and true and powerful. *The joy of destruction*, the Pacific queen had said. I feel the joy of destruction. I feel the glory in decay, in claiming and rearranging what was and using it to feed myself. It feels right. I feel right. The trident buzzes up my arm with power and gives me pins and needles all over my body.

Too much. It's too fucking much. I fall first to my knees and then down onto my ass, the heavy ringing of my tank as it hits the stone floor dancing with the clatter from the trident falling, both sounds echoing back from the dark and distant walls of the hall.

I take deep, shuddering breaths, waves of shivers running through me one after another after another. I claw at my face, freeing myself from my mask and the glasses as the cold pours back into me. I bury my face in my hands as the tears come. The salt in them—the way it belongs here when I do not—feels like a betrayal.

Panic washes through me unchecked until it has run its course, and I'm able to pull my face from my hands.

The Atlantic king, again in his disarming guise of a human man, sits a spare few feet from me. I look askance at him and the unacceptably calm look on his face.

"Your amulet is protecting you. It won't let the trident change you. I thought it might."

"You didn't know?" I choke out, my voice weak and harsh. "And you let me pick it up?"

The siren's face is beautiful here in the dim light—here where he belongs. He's strength and joy and danger. Too beautiful to be angry at, however much I want to be at his calm and almost smug expression. "If you let it change you, you might truly have the power to do something about the wind nymphs."

Another shudder rips through me. "No," I say, the memory of the trident heavy in me. I understand, now, why the wizards left this here—why none of them want it for themselves and none of them want any of the others to have it, either. There's power in it, sure, but what it offers is more than death. The thing that the trident created out of me would not be me. Not in any way that truly matters.

"I *am* going to do something about the wind nymphs."

The siren's strong features are cold and still. I reach out, wild-eyed, grabbing one perfect, muscled arm across the dead space between us. "I *am*. I have more to fight for than you do. I'm *going* to fix it."

The siren stares impassively—unimpressed. "You won't let the trident change you, yet can't wield it as you are."

I clench my jaw and release his arm. "I can. And I will do something about the wind nymphs. *Believe me.*"

I reach down and take hold of the trident again, letting the warmth and the power rush back into me—back through me. I know what it is now. I know what it wants from me and what I won't give it. I won't be its god. And I won't let its power—the crush and the pull—consume me. I won't let it force me to serve it the way it wants me to. I've already pledged myself to one god, and Aloysius doesn't strike me as the kind of man who shares.

My wrecked left arm, the pain muted from the power and the strength rushing through me, reaches up to clutch at Aloysius's flower pin on my lapel. The sharp edges of the jeweled petals cut into my flesh, that small point of pain giving me something real—something that is *my choice* —to fight back with. This trident is mine to use, and I will use it.

I don't know how long it takes before I can open my eyes and stand. When I do, there's a new steadiness to my legs. The pain in my arm and my hand and the ocean's chill in my bones are there—but somewhere in the distance, unimportant. I fix the now-standing siren with an appraising gaze. His calm is gone, as it should be.

"I believe you," he says.

He's mine to command, as he should be. *No.* That thought isn't mine, and I push back on it. But the way the siren is looking at me now, I know I've gained his help. His fear, certainly. His respect, maybe. I ask him what I couldn't before. "How did you know about Faisal when you were luring me down into the water? How did you know about my mother's memories when you were luring her?"

The siren takes a step back, unsteady. What does he see when he looks at me? "I sang her desires," he says. "It's the power we've always had. When I'm enticing you, I know what will do it."

I nod slowly, thinking of the night I met the Pacific queen, and her promise of all the knowledge I could ever want—of what was kept from me. I scoop up my glasses and the mask and fit them over my eyes again, my left arm easier to command than it had been. Then I take a step toward the still-unsteady siren, his eyes full of terror, gleaming in the close, bright glow of the trident.

"Will you lead me out?" I say, more statement than question.

He does. He moves faster going out than he moved on our way in. He wants away from me, I recognize in some rational, unimportant part of my mind. But though he's walking faster, I have a less difficult time keeping up with him. It's easy now. It's all so easy.

When we reach the portal that brought us in, I slide into my flippers with a new grace and position my regulator in my mouth, barely feeling the pain of using my left hand over the new strength and power of my body.

The siren doesn't wait for me. He glides into the water and through the exit portal with a swiftness that only comes from giving in to a fear long resisted. I could stay here, if I wanted. I could wait in Atlantis for Poseidon to come take responsibility for his domain. But the trident is mine to command, and when I have it in the water, I'm certain I can command it to carry me away. I want to speak with Poseidon on solid ground, not here where he has the hometown advantage.

I step forward to fall into the water.

As I fall, time slows down, and I notice three things at nearly the same time.

Carved wizard symbols that I hadn't noticed on the way in, glowing like red-hot embers all around the exit portal.

A swift increase in the buzzing sensation from the trident in my hand.

A color shift in the trident's glow from blue-green to bright gold.

Goddamn fucking wizards. I put the pieces together in

the slowed-down world. They rigged the entrances to Atlantis with spells that would react to the trident to keep it from being removed. As I pass through the portal with the wizard markings around it, my grip on the trident firm and desperate, the world explodes around me in a rush of white water and a sharp, metallic clang.

TWENTY-TWO

A Transformation

I breathe in saltwater, choking and writhing. The water around me is gold, gold, gold, then blue-green. Something is wrong with me. Something is wrong with my back.

It doesn't have the heavy weight of the tank on it. The tank has been wrenched away from me. I need to breathe. I barely keep myself from pulling in more saltwater.

Oh God, I'm going to die. One gamble too many. One choice too foolhardy. And my mother, with no reason for them to keep her alive, is going to die. And Faisal will be trapped in the Casino. Aloysius won't release him if I don't come to get him. I was a fool to bet that I would live to collect him.

How many people will die because I wasn't strong enough? Because I wasn't smart enough? Because I thought myself too clever by half and dove in deep without recognizing the consequences? Because I let Kristoff manipulate me into going to the trident, where he knew I would die, amulet or no?

How many…

How many will die…

All I know is guilt and desperation and the feel of the trident, so strong but so insufficient in my hand.

Until the feeling of lips on mine. Soft, strong lips, pulling out the saltwater and pushing in air. My eyes widen, taking in the siren's sharp face and sharp teeth as the oxygen fills my lungs. It's all so hazy, so distant. I feel a need to breathe out, but a large strong hand clamps down on my mouth, and I hold the air in.

My eyes track down the siren's body in the blue-green glow of the trident. I'm drawn by the harsh, strange motion of his abdomen. There, I see his gills heaving, pumping water through wildly. Even on a face so alien as his, I recognize signs of stress.

I fight the contraction of my muscles as they tell me to breathe out, tell me I've got to rid my lungs of stale air so I can take more. It's not enough. My vision goes hazy around the edges again. The siren's lips hit mine. He takes the air from my lungs into his, and for one interminable moment, I'm afraid he won't return it. But he does, and I take it in.

The breath back in my lungs gives me a glimmer of hard-won lucidity. It's still not enough. He's still straining, and I'm still dying. Can we get to the surface like this? Why isn't he dragging me upward?

I'm not quite at my limit—though I'm close—when the siren gives me my third lifesaving breath. When the air is fully back in my lungs again, there's a stabbing sensation at my abdomen, not painful, but strange. I cast my eyes down toward it.

The siren has a knife—just like the knife the murderer of the Nymph of the North Wind had. I didn't see him get it out. He's trying to cut me just below my bra line. My jacket and Faisal's shirt are already open. But he can't puncture me with the knife. He can't hurt me. Not with my amulet.

Horror, fear, and anger well up in me. My grip around the trident tightens and thrills me. Yes. I will destroy him. Yes. He will deserve this. I can do it. It's my right to do it.

But the air in my lungs is out of oxygen. I need to breathe out. With another desperate motion, the siren again pushes his lips to mine.

The air he gives me doesn't feel like as much as before. I feel the exhaustion in his body, pressed to mine and connected through air and lips. He can't do this much longer. He can't do this again.

He's trying to cut me. He's trying to save me. I should let him. If I live, then I live. If I die, he'll keep my memories. He'll remember what I tried to be. He'll remember the nobility of my failure, and how far from enough it was.

In a non-hazy moment before the oxygen runs out again, I nod. I decide. He's not doing me harm. I reclassify his actions for the benefit of my amulet. This is help. The knife is helping.

Pain shoots through me at the feeling of his knife rending through muscle, hitting against my ribs. I can no longer hold in the precious little air we've shared. It escapes me, rushing out in a cloud of wasted bubbles, mixing with the red cloud of blood around us, purple in the glow of the trident.

Another cut. Another. Deep, deep slices. Four, five, six.

And then no more pain. No more of anything. The trident begins to slip from my hand, and I grip it tighter, afraid of the cold that will rush into my bones if I let it go. I've known that dying cold. I won't have it again.

The siren's strong hand grabs my chin. There's no red around us anymore. Just the glow of the trident and no more bubbles. I must have no blood left. That must be why I'm not bleeding. No more blood.

Something stirs in my mind. Not right. That can't be right. There'd be no thoughts if there were no blood. I blink my eyes open, not knowing when it was they'd closed.

The siren is speaking to me, mouthing words I can't hear. I move the fingers on my pained left hand to my abdomen, trying to find the wounds—trying to find the blood that should be there.

Instead, I find folds of skin and sensitive flaps of flesh.

My eyes fly wide.

"Breathe!" I can't hear him any better, but I read his lips better now, knowing what he must be saying.

I search for the mechanism—for the muscles to send water through my gills. They come when I call for them, new instinct rising up to greet my new self.

I pump wave upon wave of water and relief through my gills. Each time I fight the instinct to pull saltwater into my human lungs, it grows softer—weaker—easier to manage. The haze around my mind starts to clear.

Without the sound of my breath in the respirator, the ocean is a different place. It's a calmer place. It's a lonelier place. It's a wider place. I look around at the smooth stone surface of Atlantis above me, illuminated in the gentle glow of the trident.

The siren's face, awash with what I think might be relief, hovers a few feet away from me. I don't recognize his expressions well in this form. I think maybe I see fear as he reaches into the flap of split, scarred skin on his hip. He puts away the knife he used to cut me open and give me gills. His hand lingers in the space there, until he pulls out a new, thin bone, this one maybe three inches long.

Panic surges through me. He'll leave me alone. He saved me because he believes I'll help with the wind nymphs, but that isn't enough to counter his fear of what I hold. He's going to leave me, and I'll be all alone in the vast expanse of sea. I can't stand it. The fear overwhelms me. I shove it down just enough to get into Right Mind—a sense of desperate longing and despair—and contort the fingers on my left hand into shape. Using one of the few spells I know—the only spell I can reliably call upon to work right every time, I grab ahold of him across the distance between us, hoping that magical connection is enough that he will take me along with him when he transports himself away.

It is. It does.

The pressure around me is less intense, the change making my ears pop. Much more light filters through. We're so close to the surface that I can even see rays of light coming down through the crystal-clear water. The siren looks at me with an expression on his face that I can't interpret, and then he swims down and away from me. Down toward a rambling collection of domes made from lashed-together bones that cling to the cliffs and peaks of an undersea mountain range, light shining out from within them like a macabre chandelier of immense proportion.

TWENTY-THREE

A Mother

One of my flippers came off in the blast when I went through the hatch leaving Atlantis, so swimming to the closest dome is a little awkward. I'm sure I could figure out how to get the trident to carry me, but I don't think I have enough time. The siren that unwillingly brought me here disappears quickly. Probably going to warn someone about me. Probably going to ask his wife what to do.

If I'm going to find my mom, I'm going to need to do it fast, before they come up with a plan for what to do with me. Maybe that plan wouldn't be so bad. It's hard to tell. I may have convinced the Atlantic king that I'm going to help them, but that was before I hitched a ride back to his home village without permission while holding an artifact that terrifies him.

Even with only one flipper, I make it to the closest dome in a couple of minutes. I can see as I draw near that they're not quite a regular geometric pattern—not exactly as neat and tiny as the kind of triangle-based domes humans make. But they're not just bones piled up on top of each other, either. They're lashed together with what looks like seaweed.

Up close, the bones are more distinct, and I wish I didn't have my glasses on. There's flesh hanging off of the newest ones. They shore up these buildings over time with fresh kills. I'm guessing that must be something to do with the magic.

And they *are* magic. I can tell for certain as I get close enough to peer through the surface and peek inside. I see a couple of sirens, sitting in a rock pool in the middle of the floor, chatting away cheerfully, clearly not underwater. They've created pockets of air, despite all the gaps. Like a magical bone-powered forcefield. An orb suspended in the exact center of the dome lights the room. For a glowing magic orb, it seems a little underwhelming. I'd say it was just an LED light fixture, if I didn't think electricity was probably a no-go in this environment. I guess there are some things about magic that were way more impressive a couple hundred years ago than they are now.

The gaps between the bones are almost large enough for me to shimmy through, but not quite. There has to be some kind of entrance. It would be easiest to use the closest bone crossbeams to pull myself around the dome, looking for it, but no way in hell am I going to touch those things. Just looking at them close up makes me feel a little nauseated, and I don't want to add swimming through my own vomit—and possibly breathing it in through my gills—to the pile of shit that makes up this supremely shitty day.

The entrance turns out to be on the opposite side of the dome from where I originally approached it. It's an unnervingly beautiful shape—a long slender archway that's slightly pointed at the top. If it weren't built from dead people, I might give them points for artistry.

Supernatural creatures and wizards have very different

kinds of magic, so I think it's unlikely to clash with the god-magic in the trident the way the wizard booby trap on Atlantis did. Even so, I keep a careful eye on the trident as I pass through the threshold, looking for any telltale golden shift in the hue of its glow.

When I step into the open air of the dome, three sensations hit me almost at once.

First is the effect of gravity as I'm released from the weightlessness of being underwater. I should have expected it, and I guess some part of me did. But I was a little distracted, hoping the thing in my hands wouldn't explode, so I stumble a bit and almost fall down because of my weight belt when I'm in all the way.

Second is the horrific stench of a decaying human body. As soon as I find myself steady on my feet, I'm doubled over, failing to hold in my nausea, puking all over the smooth stone floor. I've never smelled something that foul. Being close to Max when he ate my father's eyes was close, but even that was at a distance and outdoors. Here, the stench enfolds me, like it's putting as much pressure on me as the deep water outside.

Third is the stream of angry Greek words hurled at me by the sirens whose home I just invaded. They'll have to wait.

I try to steady my reaction to the smell in here. It's horrific, but you can get used to a lot of horrific things if you don't run away from them. I *want* to run away, but I stand my ground against it.

I don't get used to it. Not really. But after probably a full minute of hunching over the floor, trying to get used to the concept of breathing through my lungs again, I get to the point where I can think about things other than the smell around me, and the horror and disgust it evokes.

When I do, I realize that the voices have stopped. And

when I straighten, painfully pushing my hair away from my face with my left hand, I see why.

The three sirens have positioned themselves as far as they can get from me in their rock pool. All three are staring at the trident in my hand.

I don't know a lot about siren facial expressions without the aid of the wizard's illusion, but the slack- jawed, frozen cast reads as shock, horror, and fear.

I swallow, trying to ignore the rancid taste in my mouth.

"English?" I ask. My voice is all kinds of messed up from the retching and the saltwater. The word is rough and weak. It doesn't get any of the sirens to look away from the trident to look at me, but I know they hear me because one of the sirens nods.

"You should not have this," another siren, one of the two women, says with a Greek accent so thick I can barely understand it. It feels ridiculous and wrong that her voice should be so musical and beautiful in such horrific surroundings.

"I'll take that under advisement," I say. "I'm the Arbiter. Where is my mother?"

It's a shot in the dark that they'll know who I am, and they'll know their tribe took my mother, and they'll know where she's being held. But I only saw something like a few hundred domes from higher up, so this is basically a tiny town. And if there's one thing I know, it's that everyone knows everything in a small town.

So I'm not surprised when the third siren, never taking her gaze from the trident, reaches out a trembling limb, pointing one elegant finger. Her English is much clearer and easier to understand than the other siren's, but it's infused with a kind of husky terror that sends a jolt of unreasonable guilt through me.

"The highest nest on the other side of the mountain," she says.

"Thank you," I say. And for the first time, one of the sirens, the woman who first spoke, breaks her gaze on the trident to look at me. Species barrier be damned, I know spite and hate when I see it. My "thank you" feels insufficient—insulting. Even though they're the ones who took my mother.

But I know they don't see it that way.

I turn and head back through the archway. When I'm out of the air, I fight down a surge of panic—a deep terror that I'm drowning. What is waterboarding, again? Is this what it feels like? But I have muscle memory to rely on now, and my gills start working. Eventually, my dumb human brain gets the message that we're fine, and I start my awkward swim off in the direction the siren had indicated.

As I go, I keep a lookout for any signs that I'm being watched. I see none. I'm exhausted by the time I get to the top of the ridge and pass over to the other side. There are more domes—nests, I guess—on this side. At a guess I'd say a hundred and fifty, though it's hard to be sure. I draw an imaginary line in my head extending from the siren in the first nest, and it matches up with what looks like the highest nest on this side. So far, so good.

I head for the nest, digging deep for reserves of energy I hope I have. But there's no second wind—just a weariness that settles into my bones.

This nest is small—maybe twelve feet across, at a guess. I swim around it to the side that faces down the mountain and find another archway there, much like the nest I first visited but a little wider. I get close to the threshold and look in, hesitating both out of fear of what I'll see and because I'm not looking forward to the way I know it will probably smell.

What I see surprises me mostly in how human it feels. There's that same light orb hanging in the middle, and it looks even more like something I would pick up from Ikea —only without the cord—shining on these contents. There's a little desk with a chair by it, metal and rusted. I can't help but imagine it was salvaged from the captain's office in a sunken ship. It has that kind of tradesman's-office look to it. Across from it, there's an old claw-foot bathtub.

And inside the bathtub is my mother.

Relief washes through me as I step forward. The stench in this dome is as potent as in the other, but not important to me anymore. I stumble a little over my remaining flipper and in the sudden feeling of weight, but I make it to the bathtub, coughing up seawater and finding my breath.

She's not breathing. Oh God, why is she not breathing? They weren't going to kill her, he said. They hadn't killed her.

Did they do it just now? Was this punishment for bringing the trident here? Why did I do it? Why couldn't I have just stayed there alone as was the plan? Why was I so afraid of being alone?

Through sobs of pain and terror, I reach into the bathtub to my mother's neck, searching against hope for a pulse. I can't tell where my fingers are supposed to go. I bring my hand to my own neck to find mine, and then search again, informed by where I found it on myself.

I feel it, just one little flick of movement beneath her skin. I can't tell at first if I imagined it. I keep feeling for another heartbeat, moving my finger around a little when it doesn't come.

Thirty seconds or so later, I feel another. This time I keep my hand still, in exactly the same place. I should have done that before. Another pulse. I count. One one-thousand, two one-thousand...

Eight seconds. It's eight seconds between heartbeats. I lean back, not sure if I'm feeling horror, relief, or some mix of the two. Reaching down, I lift up her sensible polo to check for gills, but I find none. She's still human. More human than I am now.

A musical, feminine voice speaks from behind me. "She's all right." I whip my head around so fast it just about wrenches my neck. Nice going, Elizabeth. All you need is a wrenched neck to go with your wrenched arm.

There in the archway, just on this side of the water, is a siren. It takes me a moment of parsing her features to match her up with the leader of the Atlantic tribe that I met on the beach less than a day ago. The heaviness of how much I've jammed into that short amount of a time settles down hard on me.

"Her heartbeat is slow." I say like a question. Her face is unreadable as she steps toward my mother, looking down at her in the bathtub.

The siren nods and steps forward, looking ridiculous walking on her split-fin legs. Her face is unreadable as she moves toward my mother, still looking into the bathtub. I need to be able to read her face, so I reach up to pull off my mask and glasses, registering the distant pain in my arm as muted by the trident. With the glasses off, she looks like a woman again. A sad woman. A regretful woman.

The room around me transforms, too. It makes me feel like I'm in a movie about deep sea exploration—or maybe space exploration. It's a geodesic dome with aluminum struts and matte, dark-gray panels in between. The entry archway turns into a hatch like I'd expect to see on a submarine.

"She's in stasis," the woman says. "She's all right. We didn't do to her what my husband needed to do to you."

Normally, stressed and overwhelmed, I'd say something snarky. But the look on the woman's face stops me.

"I wasn't aware you could do either of those things," I say instead, continuing to study her face, hoping it'll tell me something about why she feels the way she does.

"We haven't been able to for long. Only the last few hundred years. It took… time for us to learn what our new bodies can do, to find the edges of our new magic. There were centuries when we couldn't speak to one another without surfacing, before we learned how to build our nests."

The queen navigates around me, leaving a wide berth around the trident, though she's not as intimidated by it as the others have been. She kneels down and touches my mother's face, moving aside an errant wet strand of hair.

"Why do you take us alive?" I ask. "Not my mother, I mean. I understand why you took her. But why take any of us that way?"

The queen lets out a long sigh, using her lungs to their fullest extent. "It seemed a kindness. My husband told you, I believe, why we usually bring humans under the water?"

That's an interesting way of saying "murder."

"Yes, he did. You… preserve them." I do my best not to let what I think of that outlook on life bleed into my words. I think I succeed.

"We do. Those who are worthy of it. But there are so many humans who aren't. So many humans who are drowning up there in their lives. We give them a chance to be something better. To become something worth preserving. As difficult as the transition is, often they adjust. They improve. With talk, often. Many times, we find they simply needed a new perspective. And then we can preserve them."

I swallow hard, my disguised feelings slipping a little. How must it be to be dragged down here to nests like these? To be drenched in that stench with nowhere to escape? A "difficult transition" is putting it lightly. I'm amazed any of them "improve." And those who do, those who make peace with their new place in life and succeed in doing as they're asked, are summarily killed. They can't be warned. I can't imagine the sirens would warn them.

Or maybe they do. Maybe the reason the queen thinks any of them improve is because that's what the humans tell them when they learn what their only escape is. Their memories would be preserved, sure, but how well could the alien mind of a siren interpret them?

I clench my teeth, trying to put away my anger so that the queen of the Atlantic tribe doesn't see it. She seems too distracted looking at my mother's face to notice. "You said 'seemed.' Do you not think it's a kindness anymore?" I ask.

A jolt of bitterness mars the woman's fine features before they fade back to sadness. "It's still kindness," she says, looking around the room with a thousand-yard stare of remembrance that I recognize all too well. "But I wish we hadn't done it."

There's something about her face that's setting off alarm bells. What is it? I search for a moment, until it just about slaps me. She looks just like that sad, lonely siren boy I saw in the sky.

"He was your family," I say. "The siren that killed the Nymph of the North Wind. He was your family, and this was his room."

Mild surprise greets my words. "My son," she says, after a moment. "He was my son."

We look at each other, neither of us commenting on the things we could say about it. That I've discovered the truth I was engaged to discover. That she could threaten me with her custody of my mother, should I try to take that truth back to the nymphs. That I could threaten her with the trident if she did, though I would have no idea what to do with it. Where does that get us? A stalemate full of acrimony?

"Why lie?" I ask instead. "Why try to hide it? And why do you think what you're doing to humans is to blame?"

The flash of rage on the Atlantic queen's face tells me more about her than anything the Pacific queen told me on the beach last night said about her. But that rage melts to confusion and frustration.

"Because he wouldn't have done it. It doesn't make any sense. He was born underwater—one of the youngest of us. He had no need for revenge against the nymphs."

"And the human connection?"

Her face scrunches up, trying to find a way to explain to the dumb human. "Humans change. They're influenceable. Sirens are not. We are what we are from when we're young to when we die. If we die. But Aleko spent so much time with the humans we kept. They... infected him, somehow. They made him changeable. And someone used that weakness to make him do this thing. I know it."

She looks around the room, and the human elements I noticed when I first looked through the archway take on a new meaning. When she speaks again, there's pain in her musical voice. "It made him weak. It made him someone's tool." She looks at me. "I was hoping you would find out whose. He did the act, I admit that. But it wasn't his fault. He isn't to blame."

I fight the urge to roll my eyes or threaten her uselessly

with the trident. I try to keep my voice level when I respond. "Why not tell me this to begin with?"

She looks back at my mother, and I try to find if there's a threat hiding in that action. "Because you might not have discovered it. And if you hadn't, then you certainly wouldn't have found who was pulling the strings."

Pulling the strings? Sounds like Kristoff. The knife was enchanted by a wizard, and Phoebe admitted to Kristoff's involvement. How like a wizard to risk a potential planetary collapse to take care of a petty personal problem.

There's a glimmer of hope in that. If Kristoff started all this, he must have a way to fix it, right? I just don't know if I can trust that, or if I'd like how many people would die in his version of a "fix."

But I'm not going to tell her that I'm the target—the cause of this—not an innocent bystander pulled in to help. At least, I'm not going to tell her that while she has my mother. Maybe with the trident, I could get my mother out of here and bring her back to civilization. But even if I did, I wouldn't have the first idea of how to start getting her out of stasis.

"Is there anything else you haven't told me?" I fix the Atlantic queen with my best intimidating glare, made more effective by the glow of the trident. She seems unfazed. Unchanging. Unchangeable.

She shakes her head. "No, that's all of it. He seemed more human lately. He did this thing we don't understand. He's spoken to no one that we know of outside of our tribe, and no one in our tribe would convince him to do this act."

Her face leaves no room to question such a grand statement, however much I may want to. I look down at my mother, running through my lack of options again.

"I'll leave you the space of ten minutes alone with her,"

the woman says, "since it may be your last chance. After that, come to the top of the ridge. My husband will take you wherever you tell him you need to go. We cannot let you stay here with the trident."

With that, she stands and strides toward the door. The awkwardness of her siren walk doesn't seep through the wizard's illusion at all. She looks strong, graceful, and true. I look back down at my mother—so small and vulnerable here. Her mind already mangled, her life hanging by a thin wire. I stay looking at my mother for a few seconds after the queen gets to the door, giving her a chance to clear the room and swim away.

And then I stand, my motions quick and desperate, and survey the room. Ten minutes. I've got ten minutes to search this room for anything I can find to pin this on Kristoff and kill two birds with one stone.

What? The man likes using birds so much, why not let the nymphs turn him into one? I'm sure they'd love to get a wizard up where they could play with him.

TWENTY-FOUR

A Tower

There's not much in Aleko's room in the way of personal effects. Sirens don't exactly wear clothes, so there's no wardrobe. There are also no bathroom facilities, which I'm not going to think about too much. Some questions lie firmly outside the realm of my curiosity. The tub has to be a bed, basically, so that he can sleep in the air with his gills underwater. Which raises an interesting question about whether my own gills will be a problem for me when I get back on land. I'm already getting weird twinges from them, just standing in the air, even humid as it is. It's almost like an itch. Just annoying so far, but will it get worse? I set that question aside.

The desk is mostly bare. I find a fancy fountain pen—likely stolen from land—and some of that seaweed paper like my invitation was written on. If it weren't a waste of time, I'd go back down the road of wondering about how they got the paper dried out when their space is so humid, but there's no time for that. Not that it stops me from wondering why they don't just steal paper as well, since they're stealing pens. Maybe this stuff does better with the high humidity down here? Not sure. Wasting time. Get it together, Elizabeth.

In a drawer, I find some thin sheets of wax, a candle, and a lighter. A way to waterproof paper for journeys between nests, I guess? It's a clever little system, to be honest. There are also some envelopes, almost identical to the one that my summons came in, with wax already applied.

Then I find the first thing that doesn't in some way match the letter I was given: some sealing wax and a little dish of etched stones and signet rings to make impressions. It must have been Aleko's own quirk. That delivers a pang of sadness. There was a time when Olivia was in college when she got kind of into sealing wax and signets. She used to write me letters and seal the envelopes. I still have them in a box in the closet of my home office. I didn't appreciate them nearly as much as I should have as a young teenager, but I find them charming now.

Where are Aleko's letters? I look in the bottom drawer of the three-drawer desk and don't find them. Instead, I find a knife. A knife very much like the one his father used to cut me open, and very much like the wizard-enchanted knife he had been found with—that he probably still has clutched in his grasp in the skies.

Hand shaking, I pick it up to look at it more closely. It's curved and intricate. Detailed and valuable. The siren who gave me my gills kept his knife in his skin-flap pocket. I got the feeling he always kept it with him—that it was something all sirens had and prized.

But the knife that Aleko used to kill the nymph is in the sky with his body, accounted for. Would he really have two? Or was that knife not his? I sit staring at the knife for a long minute. I play with the idea of taking it with me. Would it be evidence? Do I *need* evidence? Would the nymphs grant my word any more credence if I brought a siren knife with me than if I didn't?

I spare a glance toward the entry arch, not that it would make any difference. If I'm being watched, they could be watching me from anywhere around the nest. Not big on privacy, these people. I guess I shouldn't be surprised, considering the nudity. Or maybe that's not a fair comparison.

I try fitting the knife into the pocket of my jacket. It works, though it's a little bulky. I slide it out and set it on the desk, delaying the decision of whether or not I'll take it. What does it really mean, if he doesn't have two knives, and his is here?

It would mean another siren is involved. The Atlantic queen seemed pretty sure of herself that none of her tribe would do this. But with the way sirens can travel throughout the ocean, what if it were someone in the other tribe he was spending time with? Did that just not happen?

And, if so, why did none of the Pacific tribe call out his conspicuous absence on the beach? The rest of the royal families were all there.

They weren't telling me things, either. I let myself get irrationally angry at that for just a moment before pushing the thought away.

Ten minutes. I have ten minutes. My eyes scan the room, looking for anything I'm missing. Nothing. But the second drawer is bothering me. Something about the bowl of tools to make indentations in the wax seals…

The drawer opens with a satisfying office-like noise. I pull out the little Corelle bowl, white with a familiar blue-line pattern around the edge, and look at the contents. He had amassed his own little-mermaid-style collection of things from the surface. I can't imagine sirens like walking around up there too much, considering how awkward their walking is, but Aleko must have visited pawn shops and gone searching. The decorative stones with deep patterns etched in them make more sense. I could see him making them—indulging his habit. I smile as I use my good hand to rifle through them.

My smile fades when I come across an oblong black rock, a little smaller than the rest, with familiar symbols of wizard-magic carved into them. It's the same as the communication rock Phoebe had. Similar, at least, if not identical. The main symbol on the flat face is a different one. I maybe wouldn't have noticed if I hadn't spent the last six months poring over the trove.

I draw my hand back from the bowl like it's poisonous to the touch and clench my jaw. How many of my ten minutes are left? How long before the sirens come looking for me?

I know what I want to do: I want to pick up the stone and give Kristoff the piece of my mind he avoided getting by sending Phoebe out to greet me instead. The problem is, the stone seems to be some kind of mind-to-mind communication, so "giving him a piece of my mind" might turn out to be a little more literal than I would like.

My amulet protects me from injuries borne of harmful intention. I often wonder just where the boundaries of that lie. It can be tricked by chain-linking cause and effect so that the harmful intention is separated from the action. I could ingest poison intended for me and it wouldn't affect me. Max can throw all his mind-mojo at me, and unless I think of it as something nonharmful, it won't hurt me.

But this? What about this?

I push the little bowl of stones and signets away from me, unable to take my eyes off them. I shouldn't do the thing I want to do. It's too big a risk.

But then again, what else am I going to do? I think

there's another siren involved. Okay. So what? Have them take me to the Pacific siren town, if they even have one? Ask the Pacific queen to make good on her offer to show me all of the sirens' shared knowledge?

A thrill runs through my body, and I sit up a little straighter in the chair. The Pacific queen said sirens received and preserved memories of the people they killed. Preserved how? Preserved where? In the "Seven Spires" place that she mentioned?

My heart starts beating faster as I remember the conversation on the beach. The promise of preserved spells, just there for the taking. It had been a threat, then— a lure.

But I could go there now. I would just need to look. If I could pull it off, I could get what I truly want. I could be powerful. I could get the ritual of longevity and share it with everyone. I could take the wizards' power and expose them—overthrow them.

The glow of the trident intensifies, drawing my gaze to it and away from the bowl. It feels like it's responding to me—responding to my desire or ambition.

I take a deep breath in and out. It feels good to get carried away with that while holding the trident in my hand. It feels a little *too* good. I scrape up every last shred of my willpower and push those thoughts away. It's enticing, and I'll get there if I can. I'll figure out a way to do this after I've saved the planet from ocean-originating ecological destruction.

It's hard, but I manage to come back from the edge. Looking at the brown bark bars on my wrist helps. But imposing that much restraint is exhausting, and when the thought comes up that it really wouldn't be *that* much of a risk to just see if I can chat with Kristoff about his whole fucking-over-the-world plan, I don't have enough willpower left to stop it. My hand shoots forward with a will of its own, plunging into the bowl and wrapping my fingers around the smooth black rock.

I blink, trying to make sense of what my eyes are seeing. At first, I think that I'm having some kind of weird reaction with the glasses—that they've slid down and half-covered my eyes or something. Because I see the room through the wizard's illusion, with all its undersea-exploration glory. But it's overlaid with the vision of a siren's nest made of lashed bones.

I reach my hand with the stone in it up to feel and make sure that my glasses are still up on my head. They are. I look closer at the nest version, trying to focus on it exclusively. It comes into focus. But as I try to look around to get a better grasp of what I'm seeing, I find that my vision doesn't change. It's as if a display is affixed to my eyes and moves with me.

The disconnect, along with the sudden return of the stench of decay, almost makes me feel sick again, but I'm able to shove it down. Not like there's a lot left in my stomach anyway—I left my mozzarella sticks back in the random Atlantic nest I'd barged in on and terrified.

My view shifts without me turning my head. Actually, it shifts in the opposite direction in which I turned my head before, which is further disorienting. It lets me get a better look at the nest. It looks different than the one I'm in in a couple of ways. It's less of a dome and more of a cylindrical room. It's also much lighter. The nest I'm seeing must be closer to the surface. The floor, instead of being stone, is a flat lattice of bones, with several openings just large enough for a human—or siren, rather—to slide down between them and rest their arms on the struts.

With a harsh breath in, I realize that I'm seeing the world as though I'm situated in just such a fashion. And though I know I'm fully in the air right now, if I close my eyes and focus on my body, I can detect the now-familiar feel of pumping saltwater through my gills.

"Aleko?" comes a tinkling, feminine word from within me. It's followed by a string of hopeful, breathless Greek, like sparkling water falling over a cliff edge.

I want to respond to these words in my head, but I can't for a moment. I'm too busy trying to put the pieces together. There's a long pause before the voice continues, transformed to mourning bells.

"You're not Aleko."

I find my voice. "No, I'm not. I know you, though. I've heard you before."

There's a long pause. My nest-vision looks down at someone else's hand, perfect and feminine, but too slender to be human. It holds another smooth black stone matching the one in my real hand. It has that same symbol that's on mine—the one that's different from the symbol that was on Phoebe's. These are a matched set, maybe? Psychic walkie-talkies tuned to the same frequency?

My not-vision rests on the stone as if deciding whether to discard it. I want to try to convince her not to, but I stop myself. It has to be her choice to talk to me, or I won't get anything. Sirens won't be influenced. Or, at least, that's how they see themselves.

"You're the Arbiter," the bell-voice says, softer than before.

"I am," I respond. "And you're the Pacific queen's daughter."

The hand that's not mine closes around the stone, like the girl is making a decision.

"I am Zosime," the voice says with new determination.

Fantastic. She's angry. Anger means she's going to help me. I've just got to resist the urge to push too far too fast.

Do I need to get her to agree to testify? Would the nymphs need her confirmation to consider my ruling of "a wizard did it" to be "fair"? Would they take my word for it? At least I can get her to confirm it for me. Maybe if she doesn't agree to testify, they can look at this conversation in my mind, somehow.

"Who gave you this stone?" I ask, and then I remember that the knife was enchanted. "And the knife?"

"My mother."

My heart drops. "Your mother?"

"Yes." She says the solitary word with an overriding sense of horror and despair.

I swallow hard. What was it the Pacific queen had said? "The joy of destruction"? How do you fight the joy of destruction?

"Why?" I ask, fearing the answer.

Zosime takes a deep breath, and I wonder if it's as much for effect as anything else. She's breathing under-water as well, after all. "It's her way. It's what she is. Revenge, I guess. Against the nymphs and against wizards. She killed the wizard that made us what we are now—that changed us from what we were when she was a girl. But it's not enough for her. It's never enough. She thinks the wizards are weak, and if something challenges them, they won't be able to stop it, and they will be revealed for what they are. The world the wizards want will fall."

"She thinks the emperor has no clothes and wants everyone to see it," I say. She might be right.

"The wizards have an emperor?" Zosime asks with a hint of delight or curiosity, maybe, though it's weighed down with grief.

"Never mind," I say. "Do you know where your mother got the stone and the knife?"

My vision tilts. Zosime must be tilting her head in consideration.

"I don't know," she says. "It seems very strange. It seems like wizard magic. But she would never ask a wizard for help. I don't understand."

I think I do. Kristoff wanted me away from Max, but didn't want Max to know he'd done it, and he had to figure out a way to kill me through my amulet. He's been spying on me through the bird enough that he knows about the arbitrations, so he engineered one deadly enough that he didn't believe I'd survive it. Maybe he's been doing it for a while, amping up his efforts bit by bit until they got here, extreme enough that I'm finally catching on. He knew about the bad blood between the sirens and the nymphs because, well, everyone seems to. But as an heir to the wizard who originally made the deal with the wind nymphs and Poseidon, he'd know more about what happened and how he could manipulate the situation than most. And he'd know which siren held the biggest grudge and would be most willing to throw everything into chaos in order to get revenge.

Oh, how the Pacific queen must have laughed after Kristoff approached her. How she must have reveled in the thought of using his own plan against him. He must have given her the knife—given her the knowledge needed to send someone to kill the Nymph of the North Wind. I don't know where the communication stones come into it. Kristoff wouldn't offer—Kristoff wouldn't care which siren did the deed as long as it caused a problem big enough to trap me and get me to do something dumb enough to kill myself. The Pacific queen must have asked.

"So she gave you the knife and the stone and told you... what?" I say it gently.

"She said that Aleko was weak. That he was influenceable. Something to do with the Atlantic tribe taking humans as pets. She said that if I spoke with him and got to know him, that I could convince him to do this thing. He's always liked me."

"And it worked," I say. "Do you wish it hadn't?"

I feel mean for asking, but I need to.

"I changed him," she says, her voice dripping with regret. "I made him do what he never would, and now that's all he'll ever be." And then her voice shifts from regret to tightly controlled rage. "And my mother changed me. She made me do what I wouldn't have done. And now that's what I am. It's wrong. It's the worst thing one siren can do to another—to change them. And my *mother* did it to me."

I search for a response that can possibly comfort her, something to make it better, but a sudden vibration of the floor underneath me stops me. An image of the glass of water from *Jurassic Park* jumps into my head. After a second, it happens again, but more intense this time.

There are no dinosaurs underwater. But there are other things. My gaze shifts to the trident in my hand, loosening my focus on Zosime's tower so that I can see both worlds.

"You have the trident?" Zosime shrieks. The image of the tower of bones disappears completely, and I'm alone.

The earth beneath me shakes again.

TWENTY-FIVE

A Messenger

Something's coming. Something big. And chances are, it's coming for me. I tuck the communication stone into one of my zip-up interior jacket pockets as quickly as I can and shift the trident into my right hand.

I need to get away from Mom. Something big enough to shake the earth around me can't be gentle enough not to disturb the small magical bubble that's keeping her alive, albeit in stasis. I don't want to leave her. I have to fight the feeling that this is the last time I'll ever see her in order to force myself to the exit arch, settle my glasses and mask over my eyes, and swim out into the open water.

Up. I've got to go up and away. Just get as far from this as possible. My one fin does as much work as it can, but it's an awkward, difficult struggle. Adrenaline finally shows up and gives me a second wind.

I swim up and over, toward the other side of the mountain, for a solid thirty painful seconds. I don't look at the thing that's coming for me. It terrifies me, and I'm already scared enough. I'm already giving the swim everything I have.

Until I realize what I've got to do: swim toward it. Because even if I keep it from destroying the nest my mother is in, I can tell by the great big shadow in my peripheral vision that it's well within the village now.

Still kicking, still fighting my way up, I let my head turn in the direction of the thing. The sight of it stops my gills from pumping for a long moment before I remember and restart.

Giant squid. No. More than that. Bigger than that. It has a name. I know it. Gigi said that the same people who said they had seen Poseidon said that they saw the Kraken.

Kraken. Poseidon released the fucking KRAKEN after me.

…I may have slightly underestimated how annoyed he would be that I took his trident.

The scale is hard to understand. Its tentacles roll down either side of the mountain ridge with alarming grace and reach. It shrinks the mountain in my view. I can't contend with the idea of something that massive. It makes all the bone nests—many of which it destroys without apparent thought with the determined crawl of its tentacles—look like toys.

And I have barely made any headway up. My effort, my struggle, is nothing compared to the sheer scale of this thing. In less than thirty seconds, my mother and her little bubble of air will be nothing but a broken pile of debris sliding down the side of the mountain into the endless abyss of the ocean.

I shift direction and swim directly toward the kraken, terror and desperation propelling me forward.

Everything in me screams at me to flee—to ignore that I have the amulet. Get out. Get safe. Save myself. But the last time I listened to that dumb, dumb instinct toward self-preservation, it almost got me killed. It's not in charge of me. I shove it aside.

When the kraken reaches out a massive, endless tentacle to pluck me from the water and pull me back with it, I feel terror and relief in equal measure. If it's reaching toward me to grab me and pull me back toward it, there's no way it has crushed my mother. It won't. She's safe. As safe from immediate threat as she can be right now.

There's no way to read the expression on a kraken's face. I'm not sure it even has one. There are eyes somewhere on its body, but I can't see them from this angle. All the same, I read malice in the tentacle that comes in close and wraps around me.

Then the kraken stops. It just… stops for a long moment, motionless in the water. Why?

If I could figure out how to laugh underwater, I would. My shoulders shake, which is the next best thing. The amulet is stopping it from crushing me, and it doesn't understand why. All that power—the massive master of the ocean, brutal and unquestionable. And here I am, just a puny human holding a shiny stick, and it can't crush me. It pulls me toward it, and I let myself go, not struggling to get out of the grip of the tentacles that are loose enough that I easily could. If it pulls me toward it, it pulls me farther away from the nest my mother is in. That's something. The least I can do is swallow down my fear in the face of the profound to save her life.

I don't fight the tentacles as they pull me closer to the weird oblong shape I take for the monster's head. I don't fight them as they draw me around in front of one deep, dark, glossy eye about three feet across. For a long moment, the world stops. I know nothing but the churning of seawater through my gills, and the dim, hazy filtered light from the surface, tantalizingly close but a world away.

Okay, Mr. Kraken, I think uselessly. *Take me out of here. I have what you must be after. Take me away from this village of bones and back to see who sent you.*

Eventually, with an unnerving slowness, the kraken shifts. It turns around and begins back the way it came, pulling itself along the top of the mountain ridge one massive tentacle-length after another. Looking at what I can see of its limbs before they disappear into the depths, the thing moves slowly. But the rush of water past me as it pulls me along reminds me of putting my hand out the window when barreling down the highway at full speed.

Maybe this is working. It's not going deeper. Speaking to Poseidon was my original plan, and since I can't exactly get the Pacific queen to testify so I can pin this thing on Kristoff, it may again be my best option. I almost have time to feel pleased with myself before the tentacle wrapped around me shifts, covering my gills.

With my only way to breathe now covered, my body fights to take in air. I wriggle, trying to get back to the way it was holding me before. But the more I struggle in the tentacle's grasp, the more it fights to regain its hold over me. I can't breathe. I just need to breathe. I stop trying to readjust and start trying to get free.

And then I am. I'm free in the water, swiftly getting left behind by the kraken's tremendous momentum. I churn wave after wave of water through my gills, my relief warring with terror. I eye its tentacles as the thing slows. It's something like a football-field-length away from me now, putting me just in the far reach of the ends of its grasp.

Maybe if I pull the trident down so it's across my gills, it will keep whatever tentacle reaches out to grab me from covering over the space I need to breathe. Seems like my best option, so I start maneuvering it into place.

I've barely started moving it when I'm struck to my

bones with cold. My muscles convulse painfully. I look to my hand, trying to figure out what's happened. My numb fingers are empty. The trident is gone. I search for the blue-green glow in the hazy water and see it, pulled away by a tentacle with unexpected speed.

One spell. One reliable spell. I reach out my right hand, form the gesture, and get into Right Mind. Longing. Despair.

Pain shoots through my remaining good arm as I'm jerked forward, but along with the pain comes the harsh warmth and intrusive strength of contact with the trident. Oh, thank God. My magical hold is enough contact to link me with the trident. It works.

I can't tell if the kraken realizes it's pulling me along behind it as it continues its way along the mountain range. But it doesn't matter—I can't risk something interrupting this connection. I let my body warm up as I prepare for what I have to do.

The first thing is easy. It takes a lot of muscle—enough muscle that I'm glad I've been working out lately—but it's doable. I pull my outstretched arm in, so that I can reach forward with my left hand, gaining maybe two feet of distance.

This is going to hurt. The anticipation of that pain makes it hard to get into Right Mind to grab again with my wounded left arm. But I've done this a thousand times. More than a thousand times.

I succeed. My screams make no sound underwater. My vision blurs into white as I let go with my right arm and pull myself forward with my weak, destroyed left arm. The pain is too much. My gesture falters, and the cold rushes in as I lose my grip.

As fast as I can, I reach out my right arm, shift my

magical hold on the trident to my right hand, and let myself hang by it for a few long seconds.

Three feet closer. All that effort brought me about three feet closer. And the trident was probably fifty away by the time I managed to get my initial hold. I grit my teeth. Nothing to do but to do it. I need to get to the trident so that I can hold it, physically, with my hand again. It's the only chance I have to ride to Poseidon without losing my grip somewhere along the way.

I repeat the process again and again. I can't pull in any with my left arm, but that's all right. All the ground I can make comes from bringing my right arm in close to me, and I can snatch it with my left just long enough to move my right arm out to grab it at full extension.

I climb this magical rope one arm-length at a time. The pain in my left arm makes me lose my grip again twice, and the second time I lose a few hard-won feet. But at last, I'm close enough to latch onto the trident physically, closing my fingers around the shaft. I let myself hang, pulled along. If I never have to climb an invisible rope with a wounded arm again, it'll still be too soon. But the buzz of the power of the trident in my hand reassures me as much as it terrifies me. That's probably not a good thing. I close my eyes.

I shouldn't get too full of myself, but to be honest, I'm a goddamned superhero. And every single time I've gone to the gym in the last six months was absolutely worth it. I'm going to skip fewer days when I make it back home.

Assuming, you know, that I survive.

My lips curl up in a grim smile at the thought. Oh, I'll survive.

Through my closed eyes, I sense a change in the light. When I open my eyes and my blurry vision clears, my blood runs cold.

There's a series of red Xs, lit up the way the arrows were in Boston Harbor. Traveling as fast as I am, I have just enough time to see each one before I'm past it.

A warning. The lights in the water are warning me. And they're brighter than I'd think. But then, that's because it's darker than it was. We're still traveling along the mountain, but now the kraken has angled us slightly down.

Slowly but surely, the kraken is pulling us into the depths. If I keep hold of the trident, the pressure will crush me. If I let go, I'll freeze.

TWENTY-SIX

An Extinction

I'm out of my depth. Okay, literally, sure. But figuratively, too. I'm weak, I'm wounded, and one way or another, I'm dying. And my adrenaline surge is starting to wear off.

A not-so-small part of me wants to give up. I did the best I could. I did more than the best I could, more than once. But if I do that now, people I love die and/or are trapped forever at the mercy of supernatural creatures.

Okay, so, what do we do when we don't have the power to win?

We borrow someone else's. And I have the power of a god of the ocean in my grasp. And hey, would you look at that? We just so happen to be in the ocean.

Deep down in the ocean. The light is fading. Second by second, I can see less and less of what's around me. The dim blue-green light from the trident does a little to illuminate my immediate area, but not nearly enough. Maybe it doesn't matter. Maybe it wouldn't change anything either way, but I would sure feel a lot better if I could see what was going on.

No sooner than I think it, the area around me—the trident and about twenty feet of the kraken's tentacle—is bathed in a soft white-gold light. It's so instantaneous that I blink my eyes, trying to get used to it. That's handy.

The illumination around me pulses, momentarily becoming brighter and then settling back to the same comfortable level. I start.

Thanks? I think.

Another pulse. Huh. Okay. I guess I should have known the mysterious lights in the water were telepathic in some way. I think of the way they lit up in Boston Harbor the instant I made contact. They can read minds, but the person has to be in the water first. Maybe.

The world around me turns bright apple-green for a fraction of a second before settling back to white-gold.

Okay, that wasn't really a question—I was just thinking things through. But I guess I don't mind answers.

And then—I shit you not—a little green circle with a smiley face, like the Microsoft Word version of an emoji, lights up green in the water in front of me for a split second. My shoulders shake in a manic laugh I can't properly execute underwater.

Okay, I don't suppose you can help me with this whole imminent death situation? I think in clearer words.

Unfortunately, I get a red sad face.

Just me and the trident, then. The pressure around me increases as the light grows dimmer. My gills don't like it. I have a feeling they'll fail first. I don't have long.

Magic is about intention. So much of it hinges on *what* you intend to do, and *why* you intend to do it. The wards around my house, for instance, are almost entirely about intention. If someone wants to do what I would perceive as harm to me, the rightful owner of the building, they won't be able to come in. My amulet is also all about intention.

If someone intends to cause harm to me, that harmful act can't hurt me. Though, as discussed, there are some pretty fucking inconvenient workarounds (see: my current situation). Right Mind is an element of pretty much every spell and enchantment, and the one bit of god-magic that I've previously encountered—the flower on my lapel—also works on intention.

So, good news! I probably don't have to speak Greek or say any kind of incantation to get this trident to work. By the way I feel the intense power of it in my hands, I know that it will respond to me.

A green smiley face lights up for a split second in front of my eyes.

Thanks, peanut gallery.

Another momentary green smiley face.

The growing pressure in my gills informs me I need to hurry the fuck up. Stop thinking. Start doing.

Okay, Poseidon. God of the ocean. The ocean is water. How much do I want to bet this thing can control water?

The world around me flashes that bright apple-green color three times in quick succession.

Great. I focus. I think of freezing water. I intend to freeze just a little bit of water. The buzzy, chaotic power of the trident surges in my hands. Icicles form on each of the prongs. Relief fills me, right up until the moment that they break off and I have to contort my body wildly to keep the sharp ice shards from hitting me as they are carried along by the rushing flow of water around me.

My gills ache. But I can change states of matter of water. This is going to work.

The way the kraken is carrying us, casually letting the tentacle hang and drift in the water behind it, the tip of the trident sometimes comes into contact with it. It's a little hard to predict, and it doesn't happen often, but it happens. With the light of the… mysterious lights, I can make out a decent amount of tentacle. As I think my plan through, a little more of the tentacle illuminates, although that illumination seems almost hesitant. Not sure what that means.

The ache in my gills becomes more desperate. Is it my imagination or have we changed angle, shifting toward the deeps? I watch, waiting for my opportunity. When it comes, I think of water vapor and then hold the entire image of the kraken, especially the part I can see, in my head.

A boiling red cloud appears where the tentacle was. Relief gives way to pain as some of it hits me, burning my jeans and some of the flesh of my legs. I scream soundlessly.

A new tentacle wraps around me, as tightly as it is able through my amulet. I can't breathe.

Wriggling out, I think pointedly of my need to see the whole of the kraken, down to the tips of its tentacles. When I've gotten clear of the tentacle that shot out at me, the world around me lights up, dazzling.

The sheer size of this thing almost makes me lose my nerve. I'd assumed it had eight tentacles, but there are so many more, and they go so much further than I had thought. Some are larger, longer, reaching out to the unfathomable depths below.

But I'm losing time, and as far as I can tell, no part of the kraken itself is directly beneath me. I stretch out the trident, bringing it as close to the kraken's flesh as I can. I hold water vapor, the whole of the kraken I can see, the whole mind-melting mass of it, in my mind. And I add desire. I add intention—the joy of destruction.

The ocean around me broils. Hundreds of thousands

of blood-red bubbles cloud my view. Some of it hits me, and it's all I can do not to shriek in pain again.

And then it's over. Other than the dim blue-green glow of the trident, the water around me is dark. Completely dark. I'm drifting, far from the sirens' village. Far, far from the surface. Far from everyone and everything I know.

TWENTY-SEVEN

A Possession

I float. Maybe I sink. I don't know where I end and the water begins, because there is no line. I used the trident. It's a part of me now. As much as the water of my body is a part of the water of the ocean. The difference was a story, and that story would be over, except that the story still needs.

I need, I need, I need. I need not to be alone. I need my people. And as I need them, the trident needs them.

I see sky above me, warped and warping. I hear birdsong. I see the outline of a bridge—the bent, refracting lines familiar. I'm water—I'm the water of the stream underneath Skyline Bridge. Wilbur is up there. He must be. I call out, my voice burbling and bent by the motion of my waters over smooth rocks. He's too far away. It's no good. Pain. It hurts. My gills hurt.

And then I'm still—contained. The world around me is bathed in a deep, dark amber. It's contorted, but in a more regular way. Max is here, but he isn't looking at me. He's staring out one oval window. I recognize the lines of his rental jet. I recognize the lines of worry on his face.

"Max!" I cry out.

He's startled. He must have heard me. He looks around, hope lighting his eyes. But the sound of the engines is too loud. I can't cut through it, even as I shout his name and beg him to look at me. Could he even see me in all this amber? What am I, whiskey?

I hurt more. It's getting worse by the second. Max's hand reaches out toward me. I can't move as he grabs me, bringing me toward his lips. Oh God, he's going to drink me!

I'm warping freely again. It's like I was when I was a stream but with more regular, repeating patterns. I can only make out the rough silhouette of a figure against a wash of blue, green, and orange.

It still hurts. I still can't breathe. But the momentum— the increasing magnitude of the pressure and the pain— has stopped.

Those shades of blue, that shade of green, that shade of orange… I know those colors. I saw them a day ago. I saw them on the outside of the Casino.

I was reaching for my people, and I see the colors of the Casino.

"Faisal?" I say, and the rough outline of the figure jerks in response. "Faisal, it's me."

There's a wash of movement, of disorientation. Faisal's face fills my field of vision, and though he's still shifting and warping, it's just clear enough that I can feel certain it *is* him.

"Beth?" he asks. "Are you okay?"

Faisal's laugh—more familiar to me than breathing— ricochets off the tile of the courtyard around him. "You're asking if *I'm* all right?"

I try to laugh, but I can't. "I know *I'm* not."

It's supposed to be a joke, but he doesn't seem to

think it's funny. "I'm fine," he says, sounding resigned and bitter in a way I don't understand. "How are you doing this? You were in the water in the fountain. I've got you in my hands now. I can hear you and sort of see your face."

Can he see what I've done to myself since I last saw him?

"It's the trident. I got Poseidon's trident."

"You *what?*" He doesn't sound nearly impressed enough. More worried than anything.

"I used it to kill the kraken."

I can't see him well enough to make out the intricacies of his face, but his eyebrows move enough that I can tell they're drawing together.

"You killed the *kraken?*" Theeeeere's the awe and wonder I was looking for.

"Killed it real dead. But I think I'm sinking now. There were these lights, and then an explosion. I made the explosion. I made it so it can hurt me. Everything I do just hurts me. I don't think I can be trusted with an amulet."

I'm rambling, but it just feels so good to talk to him, even if I know I must be scaring him by the sound of his voice answering me, his words lined up like the long rope of a machine-gun magazine.

"Okay, Beth, if you're sinking, you shouldn't keep talking to me for too long. Even just a few seconds makes a difference. You must be running out of air. Ask the lights for help. You can trust them, and they can hear your thoughts. They'll help you. You need to focus on where you are. Get out of it alive and come get me. I'm okay, but I need you to come get me as soon as you're done fixing what you can. The *moment* you're done. And don't use the trident like this again. It's not safe to let it in your head. I've been talking to people and reading everything I can find, and Beth, that thing is dangerous. Be careful with it. I love you. Come back to me."

I'm not running out of air, but I can't tell him that, because my vision of the world he's in shatters.

He dropped me! He let me splash back into the fountain! But the falling sensation from Faisal's hands matches the sinking sensation of my body in the water, and it calls me back into myself—back into the pain and the pressure that has begun increasing again.

It's so much darker now. How long was I sinking while my mind reached out with the trident, looking for comfort? I struggle in the direction I think is up. I'm that shot from the trailer of every horror movie with drowning in it. The one where the camera pulls back and shows how tiny I am in the vast expanse of the ocean—how little ground I'm gaining, and how far I have to go. I'm not running out of air, but it doesn't matter. The panic and exhaustion and pain from the pressure around me, horrible even despite the help of the trident, is too much. I'm trying to swim up, but I'm not enough.

My hands fumble with the buckle of the weight belt. I get it free. But it's not enough.

The trident. I need to command the trident. I reach up with it in my hand, intending to go upward. Intending to fly. Intending movement—something! But it doesn't work, and my thoughts—my intentions—are shattering.

The lights. Faisal said to trust the lights, but I don't see them. I don't see anything but shades of dark and darker.

Are you still here?

Tiny glints of green light up around me, like fireflies that are so few and far in between that you're not sure what you're seeing.

Help. I need your help.

Nothing answers. I'm going to die here. Maybe I can

reach out again to Faisal, but why? So he can watch me die?

My breathing isn't right. Something's stopping my gills, stopping the water from flowing through them. I feel around them with my left hand, bleeding again from the wound I made with the flower in Atlantis.

Something is covering my hands. Goo? Slime, maybe? I pull it closer to my face and see a few tiny flickers of green in the goo before it washes away.

Panic gives me a moment of clarity and strength. The lights are made of goo, and it's trying to get in. It's trying to force itself in through my gills, but the amulet won't let it. My hands wipe at my face. More goo—against my lips, trying to go up my nose. The entry for Ocean Glow said that the goo was inside the dead wizard. He fell in the water, he couldn't control his arms and legs as though he were possessed, and when they pulled him out, he had goo inside him.

Not this. Goddamn it, not this. I don't want to. I just don't want to. I've been possessed before and though that was a spirit, it's still too close—too horrifyingly familiar. My tears are indistinguishable from the saltwater around me. Even I can't hear my screams.

I loosen the muscles in my body. I stop my kicking, my useless uncoordinated struggling.

The lights are not harm. I reclassify them for the benefit of the amulet. It's not harm. It's allowed.

My body tenses again, this time in a searing pain. It's like when my gills were made—when the knife split open my skin my blood spilled out and clouded around me. But now it feels like that pain, that cloud of dysfunction, is pouring into me. I clamp a hand over my mouth and nose. I can't take it through there.

Just come in through the gills. That's all I can take.

The pain spreads through me from my gills, reaching out through my limbs and to the very tips of my fingers. My vision goes white again.

The pain takes on ebbs and flows. It throbs. I give myself over to the motion of the pain, riding it like a surfer rides waves. Until the tide goes out, and I'm less aware of the pain in my limbs than I am of them moving.

I'm swimming in long, perfect, efficient strokes. Exhaustion, defeat—none of it matters to the skillful movement of my muscles. I'm carried along like a passenger in my own body. I don't need to think about swimming. I just need to think about the cool, sweet water running through my gills.

Panic is easy to find underwater, but it isn't as easy to lose. I can't count my breaths the way I normally would. And while the world around me is lightening slowly, the lingering dark is still oppressive. I can't pick out things to focus on, to ground myself.

I do the next best thing: I think about where I'm going.

I could go back to the village, with its nest of bones. My mother was there. But no sooner has the thought occurred to me than I feel my head shake sharply, side to side.

Thanks, peanut gallery, but I wasn't actually talking to you. You just keep your focus on the swimming, and I'll keep my focus on the planning. Let's stay in our lanes.

Snark. The snark has returned to me. I must be feeling better. The pressure is letting up. I almost don't feel it anymore. I must be thinking slowly—each thought takes an age.

Sorry for my manners. It's a stressful situation. You understand.

It's hard to tell if I give myself a little shrug, swimming as I am, but I think I detect one. And then my head nods, and I'm sure I did. I let myself swim longer, losing myself in the feeling. The little conversation worked. The lack of pain worked. I relax. Even as my body moves, I take some time to rest.

I rest until I feel ready to ask the question I'm afraid to.

Am I going to survive this?

My head tilts to one side.

This possession, I mean. Not the situation. I know you can't know that.

My head nods sharply.

I close my eyes for a long moment in gratitude and then open them again. It's appreciably lighter now. I'm safe, whatever that means.

I can't go back to the village. I don't think anyone's back there, anyway. They must have all cracked bones and fled. But I need to know what happened with the deal, when the nymphs and Poseidon and the wizard sent the sirens into the ocean. I think the answer to how to fix this mess has to be in there. And that information is in the Seven Spires. Do you know where the Seven Spires is?

My limbs stop pushing me upward at full speed. My legs keep kicking just enough to keep me from sinking down. Treading water, I guess. My head gives three quick, enthusiastic nods.

And I can get there, if I figure out how to make the trident do it. I couldn't figure it out before, but I was having a moment. There must be a way.

That wasn't really a question, and my head doesn't nod. But my right arm, holding the trident, swivels in its socket like a compass needle finding true north.

All right, team. Let's figure this out.

TWENTY-EIGHT

A Sacrifice

Now that I'm out of immediate danger, the answer to how to use the trident to move seems simple—embarrassingly simple. The trident controls the sea. Controls water. I don't need to try and move *myself*, I need to use the water to move me. I've got to sort of connect with it through the trident—to *feel* it, the shape of it, the mass of it.

The depth of the ocean, and the horrible crush of it dropping down to infinity below me, would make me lose my mind if I let it. I pull back from that edge, focusing mostly on just the water in the few hundred feet around me.

When I'm able to detect the movement of fish and other creatures darting through my delineated space, I know it's working. I can even, if I focus on the very fine details, feel tiny grains of not-water, scattered in schools throughout the space.

Is that you? Some of you that's not in me?

The answering nod is so slight I barely feel it.

Are you one thing? Or many things?

I feel myself shrug.

Okay, badly worded. Are you one thing in many parts?

My head shakes.

So you're many, many little parts working together as part of one swarm?

My head shakes again.

Neither? How are you neither?

My lips twist into a grotesque frown, sending a spike of panic through me. Controlling my arms and legs is one thing, but controlling my face is another. It's too invasive.

Please don't do that.

My head nods tentatively.

But thank you for helping me. For saving my life.

A little gratitude never hurts. I get a one-shoulder shrug in response, and I think I know what it means—that they know what would come would be fatal to them and they're acting in their own best interest. That's fine. I'm grateful all the same.

When I've got my big circle of awareness drawn, I draw a smaller one to control. This one, only four feet around me, will be what I move. It'll be what I intend to move, anyway. Hopefully that works.

Hopefully that works?

This time, the shrug is anything but subtle.

Okay, okay. You're just here for the navigation. I get it.

I center my mind—my intention—around movement and around the smaller, closer sphere. I hold on to the awareness in the bigger sphere, and it's through that awareness more even than any feeling of motion that I know I'm moving.

It's slow at first as I find my feet, so to speak. But as I get used to the strange, contrary motion of moving and observing my movement while keeping a mental eye out for obstacles and hazards, I'm able to pick up the pace.

It's like riding a strange, powerful, unruly bike. That's made out of water and goes, at top speed, faster than I even know how to quantify. I lose perspective the faster I go. I don't have the willpower to try to figure it out and keep my awareness sharp enough to avoid any obstacles at the same time.

Monotony is a hard enemy to fight. Exhaustion, too. The lights kept exhaustion from taking me down while I was swimming, but they have no help for me with this kind of mental exercise. How long have I been awake now? How much physical exertion? And with the two bubbles around me, I feel safe. Sort of. At least during those times when I *don't* feel a terrifyingly large creature in my larger awareness bubble.

Conscious thought—conscious intention—fades. Attempts to track time fade. I enter a state of flow, giving up what I am and what I will be. All I am is the power of the trident. The crash of the waves. The churn and the rebirth. The overarching order of constant chaos. I am holy and unquestionable. I have the right of dominion. I have the right of decision. I am the natural apex of the world that fuels me. The world that makes me. The world that belongs to me.

And when I am this—when I am everything—nothing hurts in my body anymore. Everything is sparks and seafoam. Nothing matters much, either. The goals I had feel like shadows. I move forward not because of will, but because I am a current in chaos.

And then, something changes. My left arm flies out in front of me with a *Stop!* motion. A contrary voice in me. A contrary feeling to me. I come back to myself. I find a name for myself. I find a name for love and for fear and for pain. I push back my sense of oneness—my sense of dominion. Not mine, not mine, not mine. Not my right, not my right, not my right.

My left hand reaches back up to clutch my flower pin from Aloysius. I don't grip it so hard as to break the skin this time, but it gives me a point to hold on to that feels real. With that fixed point of sensation in my hand comes the pain of the ache in my left arm, muted though it is by the trident. The memory of falling—the memory of clinging to Max and fighting together.

With that pain comes other pains. My burned legs. My father's death. My mother's loss. Faisal's movement away from me.

I work on slowing my bubble with my new will and restored identity. It's not quick or easy—I've got a lot of momentum. I feel our destination, the Seven Spires, in my outer bubble way before I'm ready for it.

I can't stop in time, so I deflect up and overshoot it by a bit, then double back at a more considered pace.

The Seven Spires is aptly named. A round central body of the building, maybe the equivalent of one of the bigger office buildings I've ever seen, evolves into seven circular spires jutting up at uneven angles and uneven lengths. Even if it weren't made with human remains, I'd hardly call it pretty.

Entrance, I think, the single, concrete, bounded word coming more difficult than it did the last time I "spoke" to the lights. I blink my eyes against the effort of narrowing in my consciousness, but it helps. I try again, contracting my sense of self in more.

Do you know where the entrance is?

My trident arm swivels, showing me the way to go. I follow it around, circling the building until I see the archway of bones.

Okay. Giant siren library. Presumably full of books? I hope? My heart sinks. I didn't think this through. Why do I never fucking think things through?

You don't speak Greek, by any chance, do you?

For the first time, there's no answer. All my limbs and appendages float free in the water. I let myself sink, with no air in my lungs to keep myself buoyed up.

The lights in my body don't answer me before I'm standing upright on one of the smooth stones in front of the entrance. They remind me of flagstones. Did the sirens make them this way to imitate humans? It's not like any of them are walking in.

All right, not speak. Read?

Still no answer, unless you count a slight tremble in my left hand. But I don't know if that's them or me.

Are you really going to play dumb and pretend you can't help me out here? I don't speak Greek. All of this is for nothing if I can't find what I need.

The words I choose might be harsher than I would ordinarily use in this circumstance. There's still a trace of command in it—of the right of dominion. I push that back.

Please, I think, trying to put myself back into place. *Please help me, if you can, or tell me if you can't.*

A long pause. But then, finally, my head gives one decisive, solemn nod. But then my left hand raises up painfully again as if to say *wait.*

I do. I wait until the pain—the same horrible, invasive pain as earlier, but more intense—shoots through me, starting in my gills and spreading out.

It's longer, this time. It's so much longer. My thoughts spin out, disassociating over years and days. Faisal. Where is Faisal? Why isn't Faisal here now?

I fight the desire to dull the pain with power—with

oneness and divine right. I hold the tingle of the trident at bay. I don't need it. I don't call for it. But it's there—it tells me. It's here—just here.

When the pain transforms from a constant stream to just throbs, there's not enough left of me to ride it. It washes over me. The grimace on my features is painful in its rigidity, but I can't change it.

The world around me begins to dim. Something is wrong.

Something—not me—flutters in my abdomen once. Twice. I'm not breathing. I need to breathe. I search for the right muscles, and panic surges through me as I can't find them. The not-me twinge works again. It feels in the wrong place. Everything feels in the wrong place. Everything is too much, too full.

One leg kicks, out of my control, too fast and too far. If I weren't in the water, I'd have fallen over. Then the other. Then the first.

The lights walk me toward the entrance. I still can't find the right muscle for my gills.

I'm at the entrance arch. It's wide and graceful like the others, at least two stories tall. The ripples of the surface tension across the arch are beautiful. Beautiful, but dim. The air is so close. The wretched, breathable air.

My right foot raises, poised to carry me across the threshold, and hesitates. With my own will, I bring it forward and down onto the smooth stone inside the Seven Spires.

I don't fall. I almost do, but some weird joint coordination between my own reflexes and the possessing beings inside me keep it from happening.

Coughing and sputtering, I want to stop. The smell isn't as bad as I was expecting, and my lungs have been breathing air long enough that they've got this covered and want a second to really get some oxygen in me. But the guest in my body keeps urging me onward—forward. My head jerks around, taking in signs written in Greek.

There's nothing to do but cooperate, though something in me resents that. I should be in control. I should be the power. I fight that impulse and give it up—give up the decisions to my guests.

The things don't know quite how my body works on land as well as I do, so I add a little coordination to their intention. They want me to run—that much is clear. So run I do. The glow from the trident isn't enough to see much of the bone walls and the contents of rooms beyond arched doorways, but I can make out scrolls shoved into cubbyholes and on shelves.

We reach a staircase, and my revulsion at it—at the way the steps are formed of more tightly lashed, uneven bones—is the only thing that feels truly mine. I don't want to walk on them with my bare feet. It feels cruel and wrong. But the influence of the trident tells me it's my right, and the guests in my body tell me it's my need, so I do. I keep walking over the lashed-together bone floors of separate floors and run through different rooms full of scrolls and some objects.

We've been on our way for maybe three minutes straight when I notice a strange sensation under my gills. The muscles in my neck fight me, but I force my head down to look, slowing my stride just slightly.

Goo seeps out from my gills in long trails.

I snap my head up in horrified understanding and quicken my stride. I pay attention to the little motions—the little indications of direction coming from unexpected the muscle jerks.

Is it my imagination, or are they getting weaker? My head stops longer, paying more attention to the signs over archways, to rooms full of racks of scrolls. The motion that points me toward the rack second to the left is so weak. I hover my hand over each labeled rack, and just barely detect where to stop.

Five scrolls on this shelf. I pick up one and feel a twinge in my wrist as though to toss it away. I do. I grab the second. Same twinge, same toss. I pick up the third and my grip tightens, just slightly.

Under my own power and intention, I run to the closest bone wall that borders the outside ocean. There are gaps here just as there were with the Atlantic sirens' village of nests. When I get to the wall, I cast aside the precious scroll and the trident, letting them hit the floor. I gasp at the shock of cold when the trident leaves my hands, but don't let it slow me down.

With both hands, I begin scooping away the goop under my gills, glistening in the glow of the trident. I shove it through the gap between bones into the water, scraping it off my hands and then going back to my gills for more.

More and more keeps coming. I think, now, that it might be moving. That might just be hope. But I keep going until there's none left, scrape at my raw, sensitive skin as I might.

Out here, in the air, I can feel the tears running down my cheeks. It's so cold. The trident would fix that, but I leave it where I flung it on the ground. I squint into the darkness of the water. The fingertips of my left hand gently scrape the surface tension.

I don't think they're dead. The wizards that did the autopsy were able to get the lights even in that body to blink again. I have to hope. One or millions? Why couldn't it answer?

In the darkness outside, I think I see tiny specks of

green, drifting on breezes they're too weak to fight. At least, I hope I do.

I turn away from the wall when the last of the specks of green disappear.

Now I'm alone.

TWENTY-NINE

A Reunion

I sit down cross-legged on the floor of bones, a few feet away from the trident. I let myself feel the pain in my legs and arms. I let myself feel the pain from the cut in my hand that I gave myself on Aloysius's pin. It feels good. It feels right. It helps me feel human. It makes me feel like Elizabeth.

I'm cold, now. A shiver runs through me. But I don't want to pick up the trident again until I've bolstered my sense of self. I pick up the scroll, sending a mental apology to Olivia for what I'm about to do before I fold it in half and tuck it away neatly into my magically waterproof inner jacket pocket. I can't understand a word of it, but my treasure is secure. The smaller of my goals in coming here has been achieved. I should feel more accomplished. But I just feel tired and sorry for whatever happened to the little lights—my friends and sometime-possessors.

I breathe the stale air in and out. I detect the decay, and it's not pleasant, but it's not overpowering. I sit there on the bone floor for a long, long time, just being myself. Thinking like a human. Breathing like a human. Wanting like a human. I put my head in my hands, rubbing the tears from my eyes.

I would sit here forever, I think, if the blue-green glow from the trident doesn't catch my attention. Something's wrong about it. Something's changing about it. My eyes fly wide. It's turning to gold.

Wizard magic. The trident must be interacting with wizard magic. But I'm not doing anything. Kristoff? Is Kristoff here somehow?

Heart pounding and breath coming in jagged gasps, I grab up the trident, backing myself into a corner and holding it like a weapon. The shock of the trident's power coursing through me hits my adrenaline, catapulting me into greater awareness.

No one is here. Nothing moves in the room. My eyes dart to the sea through the bones of the wall. My heart sinks at what a see through the little, irregular, macabre windows.

The net looks familiar—almost looks like the trap I made for the bird not so long ago in such a better place. The strands are thick and knotted rather than twisted and haphazard, but they're the same shining, spun gold.

I swallow hard, remembering my judgment of the bird when it rushed so quickly into my trap. I thought I was so much smarter, and it horrifies me now to find that I'm not.

Careful to keep the trident from getting too close to the exterior walls, I head back the way I came. Maybe I can make it. Maybe the net hasn't drawn in all the way over the spires yet. Maybe if I get to the entrance, I can get out of here. But fear more than hope spurs me forward, aided by an ugly anger from the trident that someone would dare to think they could trap me—me, who they should fear.

All hope dies when I reach the arch and see a patient

figure standing in front of the entrance, framed in front of an opening by two edges of the shimmering spun-gold net.

The Pacific queen. I still don't know her name. I don't care to know it.

I take off my mask, feeling foolish, and push my glasses back up on my head so I can see her in a more recognizable form and judge her intentions better. Around me, the oppressive feeling of death lifts. Dust replaces decay. Smooth walls of ancient millwork and paneling replace the lattices of bones. The stone beneath me becomes a well-worn carpet, mostly burgundy with little red fleur-de-lis flourishes. It feels comfortable and calm. I don't think the wizard's illusion would get something so wrong, but maybe that's how the Seven Spires feels to sirens.

I step forward, trying to keep my stride confident as I approach the naked woman, who looks so much like she did at the hearing. I expect wrath or mirth on her face, but she greets me instead with a sly smile, just a hint of tentative hope hiding somewhere in it.

The trident begins shifting from blue-green to gold about five feet from the door, and I stop. That's about as close as I wanted to get to her, anyway.

"When Kristoff said you'd probably end up here, I didn't believe him," the siren says, her voice far too calm and conversational. "I said there was no reason for him to give me this net. No reason for me to ensure the place was unguarded and unoccupied and then lie in wait. But when I sang your desire on the beach that night, I knew he was right. I suppose he must know wizards better than I do."

"I'm not a wizard," I say quickly, as if by impulse.

"A wizard would come here," she says with a teasing smile.

"I had a reason to come here." I resist the urge to place

my hand over my jacket pocket, over where the scroll is safely tucked away.

The siren just holds that same smile on her face, perfectly balanced on the tip of teasing malice out of affection. "A reason, Arbiter, or an excuse?"

Blood rushes to my cheeks. I keep my eyes fixed on the siren rather than let my head turn toward where the ritual of longevity must be—tantalizingly close and yet unreachable. I shepherd the conversation back onto steadier ground. More useful ground. "Why kill me? Why go along with that part of his plan? It doesn't suit your purposes."

The siren shrugs, the modern gesture looking so at odds with her naked body, already at odds with the academic surroundings. "I wasn't going to. But then you talked to my daughter, and you learned things you weren't supposed to find out."

A touch of anger was in that. Good. She has something she cares about. If she cares about something, I can make her suffer. She deserves it. And I deserve to make her. I force my grip on the trident to relax. I'm holding it too tightly. It's getting into me.

"Is what she says true? You really just want to burn everything down? You really mean all that?"

She looks behind her, out into the ocean. The wizard's illusion is struggling with that one—refusing to show me the water out there, and unable to show me the net but needing to portray that I'm trapped. What I see is a thick set of oak doors, almost closed, and beyond them the forbidding dark of a moonless night.

The siren shudders like she's seeing what I am. And, in a way, she might be. "Why shouldn't I?" Her voice is soft and hurt, but somehow not vulnerable. "I'm not what I was."

I clench my jaw. "So that's it? Someone changed you

and you just can't get over it, so you're taking the rest of the world down with you?"

"I'm taking *his kind* down with me." She still doesn't look at me, still stares out into what I see as the dark, her perfect body twisted into an elegant pose worthy of a still life. God, the whole thing reminds me of a painting.

"For changing you? But isn't that just what you did to your daughter? She hates you for it."

At that, the siren's face snaps back to me, and I feel the predator underneath her pleasing expression, even if I can't see it. "I didn't change her. She can't be changed, whatever little favor she may have done me." Her expression softens, shocking me. "She's perfect. She always will be."

The Pacific queen doesn't hate me, that hits me at once. For her teasing earlier, I'm not what she hates. And she's looking at me—who knows her more than I should, who knows her through actions others aren't privy to—like she's asking me to agree with her approval of her daughter.

The wizard's illusion is a lie. I can think I'm understanding these people by reading the momentary expressions on their faces, but I don't. "So why are you talking to me? You've got the net. I can't get out of it. Even if I left the trident here, I'm sure I couldn't. You've won. Why gloat?"

Her expression is still soft, but the whisper of hope I thought I saw in her when I first came down here reappears.

"Because I don't want you to die like *this*. You're worth preserving, Arbiter. I've heard that you killed the kraken. That's true, isn't it? And you wield the trident without letting it take you." It's not my imagination—there's real warmth there. She steps toward me. Like it did when I met her in Chios, the movement sends my pulse sky-high, but the source of the threat she poses is harder to pin down now. "Let me drown you. Let me take you and keep you. I will build your bones into my *own* nest, Arbiter. Into the walls of my *own very room.*"

Barely a foot away, the siren stops, reading the tensing in my pose and reacting with a confused expression. "I promise," she says, with an earnestness that disarms and bewilders me.

Then she reaches a hand toward me, and my bewilderment disappears in a wave of disgust that she could dare to threaten me. The disgust makes me want to drop the trident—it isn't me. It can't be me. But the disgust also keeps me safe from considering her offer. And if the choice is between death by starving while surrounded by books I can't read, or death that is quick and enjoyable and preserved forever, the choice might be closer than it should be.

"I don't want my bones to rest near where you sleep," I say, my voice tight and dripping with displeasure. The words hit her with the force that I hoped they would, as great an insult to her as I guessed they might be. She stumbles back, losing her impossible elegance for a moment.

"Then die forgotten. Die into nothing."

She slides out the doors with marine grace and quickness. The trident clatters to the floor as I dive after her, trying to throw myself through the doors in time. But the doors aren't really doors, and they snap shut faster than wood ever could.

I'm left leaning against the smooth illusory surface, trapped like Kristoff's bird, waiting for the hands of time and inevitability to snap my neck.

THIRTY

A Failure

Four lines. I've got four lines left on my arm. I push despair away. I've been trapped in tighter spaces before, and with fewer tools.

Tools! Valuables! If Gigi stole from them way back, they must have something here worth stealing. I flip my glasses back down and head back into the depths of the Seven Spires. I'm looking for knives—anything. It's a long shot that a blade can cut the net, but I've got to try something. I've got to keep moving forward so I don't give up.

The trident would help me not give up, but I don't retrieve it as I step by it. The way it's twisting me is too much—too far. It can't get through my amulet to wholesale change me, sure, but what about a thousand little choices? A thousand little influences that are helpful to accept, one at a time, and that I don't think of as harm, just this little bit, just this moment. It'll win in the end.

And the pain helps. The chill of the stone underneath me helps. It makes me angry, and I need that anger. And the light from my phone's flashlight, once I leave the glow of the trident behind. The battery, impossibly, is still at

90%. I whisper a thanks to Max, wishing he were here with a ferocity that surprises me.

Most rooms I come across are full of scrolls. Shelves upon shelves upon shelves of scrolls. Plenty of them are labeled, which would be nice if I could read the labels. But all I need to do for now is identify if a room holds written information or artifacts, and that's fast enough to do.

Adrenaline and I didn't use to know each other very well, but over the past six months, we've built an increasingly close relationship. And it comes through for me as I go room to room, moving between them in a sort of half jog.

The first artifact room I come across is jewelry, and it breaks my stride just long enough to wonder if this is the sort of thing Gigi stole. But I don't have time to waste with it, even if I can't help but take a few steps into the room to get a closer look at some of the things on the shelves.

The shelves themselves don't do the jewelry justice. They look very much like they came from a commercial ship and would have stored gear at some point—all sheet metal and thick, chipping enamel paint. I guess the bone-based racks that store the scrolls just won't cut it for such fine things as jewelry.

There's not much organization to the jewelry that's arranged in piles on them, but they glint and glitter and shine in multicolor, taking in the light from my phone and throwing it back at me in a glorious display of transformed hues.

But it won't help me, and I can't say for sure it wouldn't weigh me down.

There's a spell in the trove that I think would help me here, a spell that appears to be able to enchant a bag to hold an infinite amount of material without adding weight, but the enchantment has been well above my abilities thus far. It's a bunch of different timed gestures and multiple incantations and it calls for a few ingredients and materials I don't know how to translate from the Spanish-ish-looking language it's in. Still, I sure do come across some pretty things in the process of almost getting myself killed. I should really look into that further.

With difficulty, I pull myself away from the jewelry room and get back to searching. More scrolls. More scrolls. Room after room after room of scrolls. I come across a few other artifact rooms, two more jewelry rooms, a random object room that doesn't appear to have anything interesting but does feature an unusually large number of pens (as any junk drawer must), and a room of unique fine clothing that I imagine probably looked a lot better before a dip in saltwater and centuries piled in moldy heaps.

If there's one thing I've learned about sirens in the last day, it's that they must not have a very good sense of smell.

Finally, just when my new friend Adrenaline is starting to give in to my old friend Exhaustion, I find it: an artifact room full of weapons.

I grab the first sharp-looking knife I can find—a great curved conquistador-looking blade that seems to have held up better than some of the others.

I hurry back toward the entranceway, slowing as I pass where the trident lies on the floor, as if in reverence. When I'm past it, I move up to the net quickly, feeling the strangely heavy fibers. They're warm, I realize, now that I'm not distracted by the novelty of seeing them there. Very warm. And the more I try to force against the net, the warmer it gets. It doesn't *hurt*—it can't hurt me—but it's noticeable.

I'm not sure what that means, but it doesn't matter for my purposes. I take a step back and ready the long, curved blade, swinging it into the net with all the force my broken, exhausted body can muster. A thrill of victory runs through me as I feel only limited resistance to the blade. It's working. It worked.

But the searing pain of heat in my hand forces me to throw the sword away. And when I look down, I see that the blade didn't sheer through the net with ease—it was the other way around. Red hot shards of antique blade lie on the floor. I dropped the blade as soon as I felt heat, but my hand still screams with pain—red and swollen from the burns.

Kristoff, you stubborn, overachieving bastard. All this because you're afraid a puny little human is a bad influence on your pseudo-son? He hates you, anyway. He hated you before he met me. Maybe he won't go soft on humans the way you're fearing with me gone, but you're going to lose him in the end. I know you will.

But that doesn't matter. I'm right, and Kristoff won't win, but I'll be long dead before he finds that out.

Right hand burned from the sword, left hand cut from the pin, I'm not spoiled for choice for which one to use to try to raise up the net. Maybe I can slip under it? I go with my left hand, although it's the one that's wrenched worse. I'm too weak to lift very hard, but I don't think it matters. It's not gravity holding the net down, keeping it from budging even an inch.

It's magic. I'm fighting fucking magic. Why did I think I could do this?

A thought sparks. *I* have magic. I have the trident. That's got to be something. But when I pick it up, I'm already losing hope. I get it as close as I can to the net before it starts shifting to gold, and I try to connect to the water outside of it.

Nothing. Nada. Zilch. I don't know if it's because I'm not touching any water with the trident, or if it's something to do with the bad interaction between this spell and god magic, but it's not working. I give one last effort, reaching out to connect across the distance, pouring some of the same desperation that I had in the wake of the kraken's death.

But that worked because I was the water, and water calls to water. I'm not the water anymore—I'm not in it and surrounded by it. I'm just a person again, and a person may contain water, but a person can't *be* water. Not if I'm not touching it. The certainty strikes me, too solid to be my own invention.

Inevitability settles on me with an irresistible weight as I head back down the entranceway and away from the door. I want away from the water, away from the ocean. I stop a good fifteen feet from the entrance, sitting down heavily on the floor, feeling the unforgiving contact of my broken body on the hard stone, and laying the trident aside. The floor is cool—cold. My burned right hand enjoys the feeling. I pour my attention—the scattered, frustrated, hopeless chains of thought—into appreciating the relief of that feeling. I build up a shred of hope around the tiny spark of good luck that this relief represents. Into the firmness and cold of it. Into the way it vibrates under my hand.

My eyes snap open. Left hand shaking, I set it down beside my right and feel the floor beneath me with it, too, afraid that the feeling was a mirage. But it's there—just a tinge of vibration in both my palms.

A smile spreads across my face.

Gigi stole artifacts from the sirens because she could, because she was able to get in through the portal system. Sirens used to travel with portals. Watery portals. And they might have closed the system off, but it feels like maybe—just maybe—there's still one here.

THIRTY-ONE

A Connection

It doesn't take me long, relatively speaking, to find the portal room. All I have to do is drop down and feel the floor and move in the direction of increasing vibration. Finally, I reach an area that's been walled off with big square stones. When I place my ear to the cracks between the stones, I hear it: a faint sound of rushing water in the room beyond.

The walls make me proud, remembering the glint in Gigi's eye and her mischievous air when she told me she found her way into the sirens' secret, sacred place. Gigi may not care about me personally. Okay, whatever. But that doesn't mean I can't like her. Just a little. Just for who she is.

My smile fades. A door would defeat the purpose of this wall, and it's not like I can push it down.

I need help. I just do. But I know how to reach it.

I lean my back against the wall enclosing the portal room and slide down to sit against it. It's going to be hard to write with my burned hand. Wilbur is also mad at me, for reasons I don't know or understand, but that's not

something I can do anything about. And it won't stop him
from helping me when I'm in mortal danger.

Probably. I hope.

I pull out the notebook with the unicorns on it, and
Wilbur's solid, antique-looking magic pen. Turns out to
have been a very, very lucky break that whatever Max did
to my jacket made the pockets so effectively waterproof. I
hold the pen close to my phone so that I can check the ink
level in the light.

Ink level looks good. This should work.

What to write? I purse my lips for a second, and then
begin scribbling. My handwriting is worse than usual, but
all things considered, I'm pretty sure he'll cut me a break
on that.

*I need you. I'm caught in a wizard trap, and I need Max's help
to get out of it.*

I keep the pen poised over the paper, waiting for a
reply. None comes.

I know you're mad, but we can't talk about it if I'm dead.

The longest it's ever taken Wilbur to respond to one of
these messages was thirty seconds. However this interacts
with him, it must be mental rather than physical, because
it's never taken him long enough to respond to dig out his
own pen and piece of paper. This gap—this long, long gap
—must be intentional.

I'm sorry? I write at last.

And then, after another minute of no response, I cross
out the question mark. And then I wince as my hand
tightens around the pen, ignorant of my self-inflicted
wounds, moving mechanically to lay down a few words in
Wilbur's uniform writing.

Why don't you call him?

My laughter, real and warm and genuine, rings
through the hall, disappearing into the bones.

I'm in the Seven Spires.

It's possible Wilbur hasn't heard of the Seven Spires, but I'm guessing he has. My hand jerks down a line.

How?

I hesitate. Knowing Wilbur, he's probably not asking for a play-by-play, and my hand hurts too much to write one, anyway. He's always more curious about mechanisms than plot.

Gills. I write.

There's a long pause, and I'm just about to write *Hello?* when the pen starts moving again.

Is he alive?

A pang of something like guilt shoots through me, but I did what I could for Max at the time.

I think so, I write. *His phone number is—*

I don't get to write the number before my hand is moving down another line and changing to Wilbur's handwriting.

I know it. What message?

I take a deep breath, bracing for the possibility that pulling the connection stone out of my pocket will connect me to someone. Zosime, maybe. It might not be bad to talk to her. Maybe she's angry enough at her mother to come help me. But still, I'm relieved when touching the stone has no effect.

I squint at the largest symbol on the communication stone—the one in the middle that I noticed was different from the one that Phoebe had. It's tricky to copy it down exactly onto the paper using Wilbur's magic pen and with my burned hand, but I've gotten pretty used to paying attention to the finer details of magical symbols lately. When I've got it copied over, I write *Connection Stone* after it. And then, on the next line, I continue *He'll know what it means.*

You know, hopefully. Really hopefully. My hand jerks down another line and continues in Wilbur's handwriting.

I'll tell him.

I go to relax against the stone, thinking that when I get home, I should do something nice for Wilbur to heal our strained friendship, as soon as I figure out why that friendship is strained.

The thought seems to come out of nowhere, and when I realize why I feel mildly compelled to give something to Wilbur, a jolt of fear like you get when you almost get out of a car before putting it in park runs through me.

And the price? I write, shoving aside the idea that Wilbur didn't prompt me because he didn't want me to pay him. That he wanted for my nonpayment to make it harder for me to reach Max in the future. I nearly just did by accident what Kristoff is willing to risk destroying the world to accomplish.

My hand moves again without my telling it to, but instead of moving down to write on the next line, it instead moves up to earlier in the conversation. Deliberately, it circles the word "Gills" that I'd written earlier. My eyes widen, and my eyebrows knit together.

What? I write, back down at the bottom of our conversation.

The hand goes back up to the word "Gills." It underlines the word three times.

If the world were a fairer place, it would mean that he wanted me to go to the seafood market, grab some fish, and bring him the gills. But I don't think it does.

I think it means *my* gills.

I sink my head into my left hand, making my arm yell at me. I clench my jaw. If it were harder to get to Max, I'd have a hell of a time healing from all of the things I've put my body through in the last twenty-four hours, even if I survived.

I write *Accepted* on the piece of paper, overlapping one of the cartoon unicorn's horns. A pit opens in my stomach at the thought of how I'll need to surrender the gills to him, and what he's likely to do with them.

Does that cover a message to Gigi, too?

There's only a couple of seconds' pause before Wilbur responds.

Yes.

I think for a long second, and then smile despite everything.

Tell her I'm following in her footsteps.

Unnecessarily cryptic. Important, but frustratingly vague. Absolutely perfect for Gigi.

My hand goes down underneath that line, to the last space left on the page, right over the illustrations of frolicking unicorns. It writes down a single, decisive check mark, and then surrenders back to my own control.

And then I have the feeling of being alone again, trapped and afraid, but hopeful. I go to the entrance and get the trident, bringing it back to the wall that closes off the portals.

I wrap my fingers around the communication stone, close my eyes, and wait.

THIRTY-TWO

A Choice

It takes a long time—or it feels like it does, anyway—before I become aware of the abrasive hum of airplane engines, most recently heard during my momentary foray as a glass of whiskey. I smile.

"You've got your eyes closed," I say.

"So do you," I hear Max's voice. "Didn't know who I'd be talking with. How did you get this?"

I open my eyes, just as Max does, and I do my best to reconcile my double vision of underwater bone castle and modern private jet. It is, without question, a weird combination.

"Jesus fucking Christ, Elizabeth Baker, what did you do?"

I start to respond with a defense of what I'm doing in the Seven Spires, but then I realize that is probably not what he's hassling me about. Despite myself, I let out a little laugh. Hearing another human—kind of—voice has done wonders for my mood, angry at me or not.

"What?" I ask, picking up the trident and holding it up

so it fills more of my field of vision. "You don't like my new favorite toy?"

"That thing's dangerous," Max says, giving his best impression of someone much better at handing out admonishments than he is.

"Yeah, I've figured that out. But you *told* me about it. What did you think was going to happen?"

"I didn't think you were *that* much of an idiot."

"You should know by now that I absolutely am."

There's a tense half second where I think Max might yell at me, but instead, a long rip of unconstrained laughter and relief flows out of him, matched by the one that flows out of me. When we've both gotten it out of our systems, I speak again.

"So you made it out okay, then?"

My vision of the airplane goes up and down, and it takes me longer than it should to realize he must be nodding.

"Yeah, I'm fine. Last time I kissed that many European women one after another, it was a *much* better day, though."

I smile. "I don't need details, thanks."

"Are those bones?"

I look around me, giving him a better look.

"Yup. Sirens' favorite building material. Turns out they're real creepy. I can't tell you how much I regret having a mermaid on my binder in elementary school."

"Hey," Max says, straightening in his seat, "own it. You were unknowingly super metal for a little kid. I don't get it, though. Wilbur said you needed help, but if you have the trident and you're underwater…"

My eyes involuntarily shift up, as though I could see through all the layers of bones and tons upon tons of seawater and all the way to Boston where I imagine

Kristoff must be sitting, twirling a mustache he doesn't have. "Yeah, turns out your dad doesn't like me much."

There's a short, strained silence.

"He's not my dad," Max says, his voice low and tense.

"Not sure he knows that. I'm a bad influence, apparently. And he has a very proactive approach to eliminating bad influences in your life." Body weary and aching, I stand up and face the wall to the portals as I talk, so that he can see it. "So it's only fair you help me knock down this wall so I can escape. Since this is all about you."

There's another silence, longer this time, and I think he's deciding what spell to tell me to do to get through the wall. But when he speaks again, I find I was wrong.

"Does Moira know?" His voice is barely audible over the hum of the engines.

"No, he doesn't want her to. He put this whole thing in motion behind her back, as far as I can tell."

Max leans back in his chair, slumping with relief. "That's good."

"Yeah, I'm pretty lucky," I say, trapped in a castle of bones at the bottom of the ocean by an evil wizard.

"You really are," he says.

I resist the urge to look at the flower pin on my lapel. "No, I'm serious. I'm lucky, I know."

Max heaves a great sigh. "So you want to knock down that wall, huh?" he asks, sounding almost as grateful for the subject change as I am.

"That would be nice," I say. I don't sound terrified and desperate anymore, though the situation hasn't changed. Sometimes company can be its own kind of magic. "I was thinking maybe you could show me how to do that boulder-throwing thing you did when we were falling."

I'm already reading my hand like an actor in a bad made-for-TV fantasy movie, knowing I'm going to do something impressive but not knowing what it's going to look like after the fact.

"Probably easier to just grab one and compel it toward your hand. That's a really easy one. And you know the first half already."

My optimism wanes. "I've been trying to do that for months. I can't."

"That's what I'm here for," Max says, and the vision of the plane around me shifts in such a way that I know he's standing up. "So, you've got the grab," he demonstrates by grabbing on to a glass sitting on the table a few feet away.

I can tell it's worked by the small motions of the glass on the tabletop in sync with the small motions of his hands as he keeps himself planted on the slightly unsteady floor of the plane. I can also tell because as he goes through the motions, there's a building feeling of energy and a force like gravity that affects his hand, pulling it into the right shape. When he grasps it, it feels like it's clicking into place —it feels the way a heavy, solid, well-hung office door sounds when it slams shut.

"And then you…" He moves his hand in a gesture that looks very familiar from the many, many times I've tried it and failed. But this time, unlike when I do it, it has that gravity again, and a sense of building energy. The glass flies to his hand in a way that reminds me of magnets.

Jesus, he doesn't even have to try. It all just slots into place and clicks together for him. I have to tamp down an unflattering vein of jealousy. That becomes easier to do when something occurs to me, and anger takes the place of jealousy.

"Hold up, you could do this the whole time?"

"Of course I could. It's one of the most common spells."

"So you could have done this when we were falling, and you didn't?"

There's a slight pause. I wish I could see Max's face. "I was throwing."

"Throwing was faster than catching. You could have thrown two in the time you threw one, caught one yourself and had me catch one, and the whole thing would have been a *lot* easier."

Max shrugs. "Yeah, but it looked like catching *really* hurt. Besides I thought you were doing fine. Turns out I was wrong, and I paid for it. So."

I shake my head and go through the familiar motions of readying myself to try and fail to call something to my hand. "Maxwell Jones, when I get out of here, you better watch out," I say, and then I grab one of the stones and feel my hand trapped by its connection to the unmovable object. Then I attempt to call it back to my hand. As always, I fail.

Max's voice is bright in my ears, loud and reflected off the hard surfaces of his private rental jet. "Oh, I see what's going wrong. That's easy."

I go to reply with something snarky but stop myself. There's an edge to his voice.

"That's good," I say, a little unsteady.

When Max replies, the edge in his voice has grown. "Say, Lizzie, where exactly is 'here'?"

I clench my jaw. Does he feel it when I do that? Considering I felt his sense for magic through the connection, it seems likely. "Why do you want to know?" I ask.

Max shakes his head, as if clearing something away. I've seen him do it from the outside before, but it feels different from the inside. Subtler, somehow. When he talks again, his voice is lighter.

"Not for any bad reason. For a good one. There's...

there's supposed to be this place called the Seven Spires, where sirens keep all their knowledge. No one knows where it is."

I roll my eyes. "No one but you, if you're tracking my jacket like I assume you are."

In the hesitation that follows, I focus on the feeling of my body, looking for another set of input. It's there. Max is clenching and unclenching his fists, deciding whether to take the bait and confirm or deny the tracking spell he has on my jacket. He decides against both.

"You get what that means, right?" he asks hopefully.

"They've killed wizards and taken their memories, so the ritual of longevity is probably here, somewhere, yes. But it's all in Greek. I can't read the signs."

A face that isn't mine smiles. "My Greek isn't great, but I can read signs. I've *seen* a dictionary." He starts talking faster. "I'll make you a deal. I'll show you how to call one of the stones to your hand, if you walk us around after and we look for where they keep the spells. If we don't get the ritual, we'll probably at least get something good."

I raise an eyebrow. He can't see it, but I'm guessing he's focusing enough to feel it. "And you'll share those with me? Whatever spells we find?" Sure, I'll try and stuff as much as I can in my pockets, but he'll be able to see more than I can fit.

He hesitates. "I'm giving you one already."

"Okay, so you get one free that you don't share. The rest of them, we both get. And the free one *can't* be the ritual of longevity. We find that, we both get it." Will he hold to this deal if we make it? Would he really?

Max sighs. "Not like you could do them, anyway."

That stings. I shake it off. "Then no harm in scribbling them down when you get them translated and giving me something to add to my trove. If you get your way, it won't matter in the end."

Max and I don't mention our incompatible goals very often, which is another way of saying that I don't like to dwell on the horrible thing he wants to do to me. But when we do, it always sours the air a little. At least the air in the Seven Spires is already pretty foul.

"Deal," he says. "Okay, grab one of the stones again."

I do as he instructs, and he does the same, aiming at another glass on the table of his jet, this one filled with an amber liquid that looks to be made of expensive bad ideas —like I was not so long ago. I'm able to feel his hand pull into place as he does. I mirror his hand with my own, lining up my vision with his so that our hands overlap. I make tiny, tiny changes to the way I hold my hand so that they're indistinguishable.

"Okay," he says, "Right Mind for this part is a feeling of uncompromising command."

That wasn't the exact wording the trove had used, but close enough. "I can manage that," I say, feeling genuinely competent for the first time in a while.

"Just make sure to drop the spell before it hits your hand. It'll come at you fast."

I nod. "Got it."

My heart pounds as I get into Right Mind. Authority. Control. Unquestionable power. It feels different this time. Most of that is probably from Max doing the spell on his plane. But still, it feels good.

And then a two-foot by two-foot block of solid stone is hurtling toward me like a fastball. I drop the contortion of my hand and throw myself awkwardly to the side. It catches my arm. That'll be a bruise tomorrow, if I can't get Max to fix it first.

"Beth, are you okay?" Max's voice comes to me lying

on the ground. He sounds worried, which is idiotic considering he knows for a fact that I'm fine through our connection.

"Never better. Except for all the wounds and mortal peril," I say, stronger than I feel. I pick the trident back up, which helps with the pain a lot. I hope Max doesn't feel the pull of it. I need the pain relief and cold relief right now more than I need the relief from its influence. I thank God for the warmth that it sends through my bones.

Well, I should thank Poseidon. But fuck that guy. I'm glad I killed his terrifying pet.

"Then go look!" Max says, with the endearing glee of a kid on Christmas morning, though I can tell he's trying to shove it down.

"Keep your pants on," I say, and it's a testament to how focused Max is on what we're about to see though the wall that I don't get something lewd back.

The stones are as wide as they are thick, and I have to basically crawl through the wall to be able to get a decent view. The room beyond is more or less as I expected: a large space with a collection of whirlpools.

The vision of the airplane shifts as Max sits down hard in a chair.

"Portals," he says. "They use portals. Of course."

"Nah," I say, already wiggling out awkwardly from the wall. "They used to, but not anymore. Hence the fact that it's walled in. They had a pest problem."

Max shifts away from the portal room to our next task with an ease that makes it obvious that he's sitting in a comfy chair safely in the sky and not fighting a ridiculous collection of injuries at the bottom of the ocean. But I let it drive me forward rather than make me bitter. He wasn't lying: His Greek is pretty rough. He may have access to a mental dictionary, but it's not one that's well-thumbed. But some understanding of the signs is better than none.

Unfortunately, there's no single, central spell room. A word that Max swears means magic—probably—appears on a collection of signs. But nothing that means wizard shows up in any of the places we look. When we get to one room that he said he had a good feeling about, but it turns out to be a small collection of how sirens have come to believe dragon magic works, I can tell he's getting frustrated. I look at my arm. One mark.

"We've got a few hours left. We'll find it."

I shouldn't give this an hour. I have an inkling of what I might do at the arbitration, but to be sure, I need Gigi's help translating the scroll, and who knows where exactly the portal will dump me out.

But the draw of the possibility that the ritual of longevity is here is strong. We keep searching. We find a variety of rooms with a variety of information about magic. But when none of them pan out, he becomes well and truly frustrated, and his frustration is calling to my exhaustion like two best friends that bring out the worst in each other.

"Wait!" Max says as I round a corner. "Go back and look at that sign again."

I do, staring at a Greek sign. It's meaningless to me, but whatever it says pulls Max up onto his feet and into the air. He's jumping. He's actually jumping.

"Wanna clue me in?" I ask, my heartbeat already rising in empathetic excitement.

"Wizard magic is in the third spire," he says, when he catches his breath. "We haven't found it because none of it's down here. We have to go up into one of the spires. But it's there. It's all together there."

My feet are moving before I consciously process the information. "Any idea which one is the third spire?"

"No clue," he says around a smile. "But we're going to figure it out."

I don't point out the issue with that: Chances are decent that I won't be able to bring the trident with me up into the spires due to the likely proximity of the net. Without it, I'll be cold and defenseless. But his enthusiasm is irresistible, and mine is, too.

I thought this was going to take years. Decades, maybe —if I survived. I thought it was going to be a slog that might get me killed. And here we are, six months in, and it might come true. And whatever Max may promise is fine, but when we get to the scroll he's most excited about, I'm folding that sucker up and taking it with me.

This has been a hell of a day, but it's worth it. It's worth it if we win.

I head up the stairs with as much vigor as I can muster. It isn't much, but I do my best. But as I climb the third flight, I begin to slow, and my already racing heart goes into overdrive. My skin feels clammy, and I can hear my own breath so much louder than I should be able to. I come to stop in the middle of the stairs, my feet uneven on the brittle bound bones.

"What is it?" Max nearly screams at me, manic. "Keep going!"

"It's darker," I say. "The light that was getting through to us isn't making it down here anymore."

"No, it's just…" Max starts. I see him doing the same math I have been. It was already mostly dark. It wasn't like the light was ever shining through the gaps in the bones. But if I look out one side of the bones and do my best to look out through the other side of the building, there's a clear difference of ambient light in the ocean outside.

"What are you doing?" Max says, his voice lowering as I shift direction.

"Poseidon wants his stick back," I say.

Max greets the words with a harsh laugh. "Poseidon is dead. They're all dead. Get back up there and find my spells, Elizabeth."

I shake my head, nearly stumbling on the uneven stairs. "It's him, or it's something he sent. It's not worth it. I'm not dying for this."

Sorry, Aloysius. Sometimes I gotta not *do the dumb thing.*

A breaking of bones and the unmistakable sound of crashing water somewhere in the distance tells me that I'm making the smart choice by running away.

"You have the trident!" Max screams at me. "You have an amulet! You'll be fine! You have to go get the spells! Elizabeth, turn around!" His voice is hoarse and breaking from emphasis. I go to throw the connection stone away from me, where it would disappear between bones, but catch myself in the last moment and shove it in my pocket.

I nearly fall three times before I make it back to the steady flat stone of the main floor. By the time I do, I can hear water crashing into the Seven Spires from more than one place. I shake my head, trying to clear the panic without giving in to the pull of the trident. Whatever is doing this is huge. Whatever is doing this apparently doesn't care about the heat that Kristoff's net is putting out. That's all I need to know.

When I make it to the hallway that leads to the portal room, the sight of a growing, crashing wave of water greets me from the other end.

Moving water has more power than people think. Even shallow, slow-moving water can knock you off your feet and drown you whether you respect it or not. I don't have time to be knocked off my feet. I don't have time to fight the approaching water before whatever is out there breaks enough bones to bring the net down on top of me, where it can't help but set off an explosion in the trident. I take off in a sprint, heading toward the missing block in the wall.

I make it maybe ten seconds before the water, diving into the hole with awkward abandon.

Seconds. I only have seconds. I reach back out, contorting my hand and mind to grab hold of the stone I pulled out earlier. I do my best to judge the angle and tilt my wrist and adjust my fingers the way Max told me.

I command the rock to come to me.

It slides back into place, walling me in and wedging tightly with the stones around it. It's slightly out of line with the smooth face of the rocks around me, but that's fine. It'll do. I hope. And when the streams of water from the pressure outside spray me but don't drench me, I know it's enough.

Right. Portal. Best get out of here quick before my temporary shelter gets overrun. I could use the trident, but I won't. If I use it, it'll take me. I won't be strong enough to fight it off.

The portals aren't even labeled. That makes no fucking sense. Sirens don't have wizards' eidetic memories. If they did, they wouldn't go through all the trouble of this place. They have to remember things. And they used this system regularly as a species. There has to be something that indicates which portal goes where, but all I see are some seemingly random lines winding around them all, traced in gold.

Something explodes in the distance—or maybe not so far of a distance. The sound of the explosion sounds familiar, like the metallic ring I heard and felt at Atlantis. God power and wizard magic not mixing.

Or maybe not. Maybe I'm making that up, giving my

greatest fears the benefit of the doubt when I shouldn't. Maybe it's just a giant, ancient building being destroyed over my head.

Focus, Elizabeth. The lines. The lines mean something. I walk around, trying to get a different angle—trying to see them from a different light.

Another familiar crash. This time I feel it, and I'm certain it's the same metallic clang from Atlantis. But I pay it no mind. It doesn't fucking matter.

The lines are a map. They're a world map, oddly distorted to make room for the portals and completely out of scale, but a map, nonetheless. And there's only one portal near Greece.

I line up a running start. The thing is ten feet in diameter, and I think I need to come down in the middle of it, not the edges. The middle looks different to me than the edges. I can't slip. I have one chance at this.

Another crash, this one so close it almost feels like it's in the room with me. The glow from the trident begins shifting to gold. The Seven Spires are broken. The net is closing in. The spray of the water through the stones soaks me.

I run on wounded, unsteady legs. I don't falter. I don't fall. I reach the portal edge and launch myself forward into the center, tightening my grip around the trident against the growing buzz of violent power it's sending through my hand.

And then the world is a mess of bubbles and movement. The golden glow of the trident is gone, replaced by the familiar, comforting blue-green. I'm disoriented, going end over end over end. But my gills remember what they're supposed to do, and the enchanted seawater of the portal is sweet and cold and pure. I feel drunk on the goodness of it.

I give myself over to the bliss of the portal and let go of my tight hold on time.

When the world has order to it again, there's a grip on my arm and the smell of salt and the sound of seagulls in the air. When I open my eyes, they're met with Gigi's diamonds. On reflex, I pull from her grasp, crashing into the couple of feet of surf beneath me.

Getting to my feet is tricky, but I don't mind. There's a movement of air—a breeze. It's freedom and joy and life.

I put away my glasses, impressed they've stayed on through all that. I should really believe the magic texts that I'm risking my life to hold on to when they say things like "when you enchant these glasses, they'll stay on." But I've subjected myself to enough of the glasses' abuse today. When I look back at Gigi, I'm grateful to see just a tall, statuesque, olive-skinned woman with soaked clothing, messy red hair, and a relieved smile on her face.

"Fancy meeting you here," I croak.

Gigi purses her lips. "You called, I came." She says that like it's at all a guaranteed thing. "Of course, if I'd have known you had *that* thing, I probably wouldn't have."

I follow her gaze to the trident, which is gleaming in the moonlight. It's a crime that it's been locked away in Atlantis. Truly.

"Well, I'm glad you didn't know then," I say as sunnily as I feel. "Because I need your help translating something."

THIRTY-THREE

An Arbitration

The portal let me out on the next beach over from the meeting beach, it turns out. Gigi takes me in our same underpowered rented car to a little seaside café tucked away nearby. The sight of the overweight, middle-aged server and the cheap plastic chairs and tablecloth may be the most beautiful thing I've ever seen. The server, for his part, does not appear to think the same of my trident. The glow isn't noticeable under all the electric lights, but he's still looking at it like he doesn't trust it. I wonder what Gigi told him to get him to open for us in the middle of the night. Whatever it was, I'm glad she did. I'm glad she guessed that I'd be starving, now that I'm finally away from the smell of decay.

"They thought it was very clever of them," Gigi says with a smug smile. "Putting the portal there, close enough to the meeting beach that they could reach it easily, but not by the beach itself. Like no one would figure out it was there. Like no one was watching them."

"I'm glad you were here," I say. "I figured you would be."

Gigi shrugs. "Everyone has to be somewhere. And I really thought you were going to miss your appointment. You cut it close. We've only got a couple of hours. I was starting to think of what I'd have to say and do if you didn't show up."

The marks on my arm confirm it. A couple of hours out of the water? My gills are already starting to itch. But french fries arrive, and I gobble them down. And Gigi lets me sleep in the back of the rental car, a sopping-wet towel draped across my gills, while she translates the scroll. She lets me sleep as long as she can.

And then Gigi's waking me up with the dawn spilling over the mountains behind us, and the meeting beach full of beautiful, brutal naked bodies.

"You were right. The wizard promised the nymphs of the breezes Poseidon's trident, if they went along with his plan and pushed the sirens into the sea. He promised Poseidon the sirens would be his servants if he held them there long enough for the spell to take effect. He had no way of keeping either promise, so he broke them both. Everyone believes wizards can do what they say, just because they've done so many terrible things. You'd think we'd learn."

She has a thousand-yard stare on her face that I don't see there often. I regard it for a while, trying to shake off the déjà vu from the last time I was here. "I didn't tell you I thought that's what he promised them."

She looks back at me, her face almost soft in the dawn light. "No, but you wouldn't still have the trident if you didn't think you needed it. You wouldn't keep it. You wouldn't give up what it would ask of you. Give me some credit, Elizabeth. I do know you a little."

It strikes me in the moment that when Gigi and I were talking yesterday as we drove through the hills, she didn't say she doesn't care about me personally. She technically only said she'd never given me any reason to believe she did. The distinction seems important until I gather up the trident again, and it pushes everything gentle in me aside.

I walk toward the crowd gathered on the beach, my bare feet crunching into shells and rocks.

Even without the glasses on, it's easy to tell the wind nymphs and sirens apart. The sirens are naked, as they do so like to be. The wind nymphs, on the other hand, are wearing exactly the kind of flowing, draped dresses I would expect from a real live figure from Greek mythology. The dresses are a pure, cloud-white that would never survive long contact with the living would and its messy edges. Their features are striking—thick black curls and cheekbones for days. Prominent noses. There are differences between them, but they're slight. The wind nymphs are more of each other than they are of themselves.

"Right," I say when I get close, in a voice that hopefully sounds stronger from the outside. "The gang's all here."

One of the nymphs gives me an unexpectedly modern smirk.

"Yes, you are a fan of *levity*, I do remember." The third voice. That was the third nymph voice I heard in the sky. Snide and mocking—I remember her.

"I'm a fan of getting to the point, as I think you all should be, too. It's been a hell of a day, and I don't appreciate it. But that's not the fault of anyone here."

The wind nymph in the middle raises an eyebrow. She's taller than the others. I know before she speaks that hers is going to be the first voice we heard. "Surely it is the fault of *some* people here."

I give her a wide smile that matches what I'm sure are my wild eyes. "No. No one here. Neither tribe."

The middle nymph goes to talk, but I cut her off.

"They were the bullet. You know guns, right? That's not too modern for you?"

"Oh!" says the wind nymph on the left, the second voice I heard yesterday in the sky. "We know *all* about guns."

I give her a smile that's warmer than she deserves. "Then you know it's not the bullet's fault when it gets fired."

I've been thinking a lot about lying lately—about the way a lie shared can pull people together just the same as a lie believed can pull them apart. "Conspiracy" literally means to breathe together. And what's more intimate than breath?

I address the wind nymphs. "Centuries ago, Poseidon lied to the sirens. Maybe he didn't like you, or maybe he was just covering his own ass and giving the sirens someone else to hate so they made less trouble for him down there. I don't know. But he told them that the wizard who cursed them with their transformation made a deal with you somehow, to cast them down out of the air, so that Poseidon's waves could trap them underwater and his curse could take effect."

The side of the center wind nymph's mouth curls up in the hint of a smile. She knows that I know I'm lying. She must. She'll breathe together with me. This is going to work.

I hold up the trident and note how the other two wind nymphs' eyes fix on it, greedy as all hell. The middle wind nymph holds my gaze. I continue.

"But Poseidon is dead, so we can't punish him. The closest I can come to giving you vengeance for your sister's death is to give you the greatest part of the power of the man who caused it."

The smile on the wind nymph's face when she reaches out to take the trident from me could dry out the flooded Seven Spires.

"The god, you mean," she says, as she holds it in her hands. "The creature or creatures who this belongs to, who truly wield and accept it, are not men or women or nymphs. They are gods."

I am, in so many ways, thankful for the wizard's illusion. But I'm thankful for it now mostly because it allows me to see the relief on the wind nymph's face. I can detect a tension—a pain, maybe—in the other nymph's faces, now that it's been relieved in hers.

I don't know whether the wizard knew why the wind nymphs agreed to his bargain. He knew the trident was powerful, and assumed, as men like that do, that everyone was as power hungry as him.

And maybe, at the time, he was right. Maybe they just wanted the power, or they wanted to play the Olympian politics and gain something from Poseidon for its return. But the wind nymphs, struggling as they have been lately, standing in the place of the gods that have died but without the nature to fill that role, no longer *desire* the trident. They need it to become the kind of being who can handle the power they stole—the vacuum they're trying to fill.

I want to cry, not in the least because when the trident leaves my hand for hers, it feels final. I feel lighter and more human. The trident was a curse for me—trying to turn me from what I am to what I don't want to be. For them, it will be a saving grace. A cure, even.

I read the right of dominion in the wind nymph's eyes as she looks at me, in the smallness of my relief. Have I misread things? It all seemed so certain before, when I had the trident. I believed everyone would listen to me. How could they not? But now my voice is so weak.

"You really expect us not to punish anyone? After our sister's death? Knowing what her loss was to us?"

I told myself I wouldn't want to do this when the trident left my hand. I told myself the trident gave me the anger. But I feel it, again, now, a part of me.

"No, I think you owe one person here a punishment and a reward. A bullet must still be dealt with, after the fact."

The wind nymph's eyebrow rises. "A punishment and a reward?"

She recognizes her own phrase from yesterday—the one she applied to the being they would choose to replace their fallen sister.

"Zosime of the Pacific tribe played a role in the loss of your sister. For that, she should be punished, even though it was not her idea. But to do so, she gave up herself—she gave up what she was for the sake of her family. That is worthy of a wind nymph, isn't it? If anything is?"

Zosime stumbles forward, lacking a siren's usual poise. She stares at me in shock. I give her as much of an apologetic look as the situation and my exhausted face can manage. But if Zosime seems merely out of sorts, her mother is furious.

"This isn't true! She isn't at fault! If any siren should be punished, it should be me."

The wind nymph catches something in my expression —some small part of the lust for vengeance that I never wanted to own but was always mine. It makes her smile. I hate that it makes her smile. "Oh," she says to the Pacific queen, the grace of her movement speaking to the crashing of waves, "I think it is."

The wizards' illusion has limits. It can make a lot of

things look normal. But it can do absolutely nothing for the way the wind nymphs simply fade into nothing before me. And it can't disguise the way the wind catches Zosime, battering her back and forth to pull her up into the sky the way it did to me, Max, and Gigi on Mount Olympus.

The winds don't touch me, but they do drive the sirens back into the ocean, and I see in their faces a familiar fear. How similar must this be to the first time they fell, battered and betrayed by the breezes that carried them and forced into the oceans below? They give in now, as they must have done then, one after another. The Pacific queen, her face torn with grief and rage, is last to give in and give up.

Good. Riddance.

THIRTY-FOUR

A Loss

With the sirens gone from the beach, the world feels ordinary again. Beautiful, even, with the dawn and the sunlight and the fresh, sweet, salty wind. I've spent the last day mentally disapproving of what the sirens did—murder is wrong, everyone!—but right now I almost get it. Feeling the depths of the ocean for just a few hours—the mystery and cold and isolation—gives me a new appreciation for the world above.

Or maybe that's the exhaustion and delirium kicking in. Adrenaline, that foul-weather friend, is abandoning me. I stumble up the beach toward where Gigi leans against our same beat-up little car, her expression at once smug and proud.

"That went well," she says when I get close.

"I think so," I reply. "I think I can take planes again. I'd better stay away from the ocean, though."

I slide past her to the passenger-side door and try to make the choice between opening the door with my wrenched left arm or my burned right hand. Gigi saves me by opening it for me herself.

"I'll be right back," she says, her voice almost gentle. Well, as close to gentle as I think Gigi can get. She grabs my gill-soaking towel from the back seat and heads for the water to re-up. I'm grateful she doesn't suggest heading back to the Casino via crossroads. The people we rented this car from at the village deserve to have it returned, and I could use a little bit to regroup before talking to Faisal. He's probably come up with quite a few more questions by now.

Maybe even an answer, too.

I get situated and try to put my head back together. Everything is at once painfully bright and perfect and entirely too much. I don't try to get my seat belt on—Gigi's driving aside, I just can't stomach the thought of being hemmed in. But I do get the door closed and window open. It's electric. God bless electricity.

When Gigi returns, the beach towel is soaked and folded over.

"Arm up," she says, in a voice that brooks no disagreement.

I comply, and she moves my shirt and jacket out of the way, settling the towel back across my gills. I gasp in relief, and pull my right arm in over the towel, keeping it tight against my body. I'm lost in it as Gigi goes around to the driver's side and gets us on the road.

I cherish the feeling of the wind on my face through the window. To live in that wind—to be a part of it—and then to be sentenced to the depths… And, on top of that, to be allergic to change as a species, and have an outsider forcibly alter everything you are. Say what you will about wizards—and I do—but they aren't half bad at revenge and punishment.

Which is maybe not a great thing for me.

"So why can't you go back into the ocean?" Gigi asks

after a few minutes of reverie. "The sirens as a whole seemed pleased by the outcome. Only one of them lost. That's a decent result."

"It's not the sirens I'm worried about, though they'll probably be annoyed when they get back home and take stock of things. It's Poseidon who I *really* pissed off."

Gigi lets out a short, wry laugh. "Poseidon's—"

"Tell me he's dead, I dare you."

Gigi stares at me, and I give her a meaningful-but-futile look back at the road. "You think he's alive?"

"He sent the kraken after the trident," I say.

Gigi relaxes, looking back at the road again, to my relief. "So you didn't actually see him. Could just be the kraken wanted the trident. It lives in the ocean. The trident is a powerful artifact."

My face scrunches up, remembering the metallic ringing to the explosions at the Seven Spires. "Yeah, maybe. I didn't see him. I think he might have been there when the Seven Spires was destroyed, though."

Gigi sighs. "You destroyed the Seven Spires? That's a shame. Didn't you think they were worth preserving?"

The memory of the bones—so many bones—comes up to haunt me even here in the warmth and the wind. I give an involuntary shudder. "I thought they were... interesting. What about you?"

Gigi smiles the smile she uses when she wants to hint at something she's not going to tell me about. "I thought they were lucrative. I still have some of the things I took from there, you know. A few of them are in the Emporium. They remind me of someone..." She trails off, and I let her remembrance sit in the air. I don't call her back to the conversation until she returns of her own accord. "Is your mother all right?"

"I think she will be. The Atlantic king promised me she

would be all right if the Atlantic ocean was. The Atlantic ocean seems fine, and he struck me as a man who keeps his promises."

Gigi nods once and looks out at the road. She's still mostly gone somewhere. Why didn't I notice earlier that she had such a personal connection to all of this? Maybe I was too busy. Maybe she'll share it with me one day, but that day isn't today.

Checking on Mom is a thought, though. Probably too soon for confirmation anyhow, and I can't tell Olivia anything that will satisfy her. She's expecting an explanation from me to justify her trust. I don't know how I'll do that, but that's a problem for another time.

I pull my phone out of my pocket, and I'm greeted by a slew of missed calls, new voicemail messages, and dozens of text message notifications.

All but two of them are from Max.

I scroll through the text messages first. It's a repetitive and increasingly desperate medley of variations on the tune of "pick up your goddamn phone" and "call me." The time zone math is a little much for me to sort through right now, but it looks like he got back up and running with access to his phone around the same time I was sitting out in the water in my stolen boat, out of the reach of cell phone reception, waiting for the Atlantic king to feel brave enough to surface.

I call up my voicemail and listen to his first message.

"Beth, don't ask me how I know this, but I think you're outside Boston right now. I don't know why you went there, but I can guess, and it's a really, really bad idea. Beth, just... just call me back."

His voice is a little desperate, but he's clearly doing his best to hang onto his usual light tone. The next message, however, doesn't have nearly as much of that normality.

"Beth, you're in Atlantis. Just… stop. Don't. There's something I didn't tell you… I didn't think you were that fucking dumb. Beth! Pick up your phone!"

I hang up my voicemails. No sense in getting a play-by-play of Max's disapproval of my decision-making process. I don't want to relive it right now, and none of my missed calls are later than our conversation through the communication stone. I'll go through them later for any information he may have inadvertently given away.

But he does deserve some response. He should know the wind nymphs aren't about to bat his plane out of the air. I navigate to my speed dial and give him a call. After one ring, the call disconnects. Did he hang up on me?

I try to call again, but this time the call doesn't even attempt to initiate. Is this asshole seriously ignoring me? Just because I wasn't going to sacrifice my life for the possibility of finding the ritual of longevity?

I sigh. No, that's probably not it. I set down the phone so I can pull my glasses down over my eyes without using my left arm. Just as I thought, I'm black and white through the glasses. It's the coloring of someone affected by the curse that comes from not paying a troll for his services. And Wilbur's services were putting me in touch with Max.

Well, the curse should make it harder for me to contact Max, not impossible. I try a text. Maybe that'll give me a better chance.

Apocalypse averted. Grabbing Faisal from the Casino and going home. Mission accomplished. Stand down, team.

It takes two tries, but the text goes through. There are little typing dots. And then none. And then little typing dots again.

You left Faisal at the Casino??????? I get after a moment.

It's fine, I type in reply. *He's safe.*

It sends on the third try.

Typing dots. No typing dots. Typing dots. No typing dots. A knot forms in my stomach.

Isn't he? I type. On the fourth try, it sends.

Safe isn't the problem. Max replies, the barest second later.

My eyes snap to Gigi, driving down the road with all the care of a puppy after a tennis ball on hardwood floors.

"Gigi, do you think Faisal is okay?" I ask. I don't like the sharp, cruel grin that greets my words.

"Oh, I'm sure he's perfectly healthy. Aloysius said he wouldn't let any harm come to him, and I believe him."

Gigi can't lie, and I agree with her assessment of Aloysius's promise. But there's something mean under there. "What aren't you telling me?"

She doesn't look at me when she responds, and she keeps her face even, but her smile does her talking for her. "Time moves differently in the Casino. You know that. You experienced it last year. Didn't you notice the flag out front?"

I had, but I didn't know what she meant. She knew that. "And how is time running inside the Casino now?"

If Gigi feels any remorse for not telling me what it might cost when she suggested we stash Faisal at the Casino, she doesn't show it. "Right now, it's running very, very fast. I'm sure Faisal is fine. I just don't know how old he is by now. And I'm sure he's quite sick of the supernatural world. Such a pity."

Anger and despair well up in me in equal measure. Hot tears roll down my cheeks. I try to remember how he looked when I saw him through the fountain water. How old was he? I couldn't see him. No wonder his voice was so weirdly resigned. No wonder he'd had time to find out about the lights and the trident. "Why?" I ask. "Why would you do that? What did he ever do to you?"

Gigi's smile falters. Only a tiny amount. Not much.

"We discussed this earlier. He's a distraction for you. He'll hold you back. He'll keep you from what you can be. It's for the best. Well, the best for me."

A harsh laugh cuts its way out of my throat, fighting with a heavy sob. "Gigi," I get out, my voice rough and horrified, "I need him."

I should speak better. I should have a better way to tell her what he means to me and how much she fucked up. But it doesn't matter. My words—the brokenness of my voice, more likely—gets through to her. She fixes me with a long, evaluating stare, and for once I don't want her to look back at the road. When she speaks again, her voice is softer.

"I may have miscalculated," she says before turning her head forward, her grin conspicuously absent. "If he's worth keeping, he'll stay around. We'll be there in a few minutes."

That may be the closest I'll ever get to an apology from Gigi.

The rest of the trip back to the village goes by in a blur, though not a long one. The tears keep coming, but I can't talk anymore. I can't do this without him. I should have told him sooner. This is my fault. I should have known something like this would happen if I didn't protect him.

When we reach the village by the crossroads, I stumble toward the valley with the Casino in it, bringing the towel with me. Gigi doesn't come with me right away—she's got to turn the car in—but she doesn't object to my petty theft. Of course she wouldn't.

The forested hill is difficult to navigate, and I go slowly —both because it's hard and because I just don't have much left in me. No humans are being shepherded up the steps. When I'm at the base of them, Aloysius appears.

When he takes in the state of me, he moves down the

staircase with solid grace, pausing only long enough to throw some words in a language I don't speak to an attendant I can't see.

He reaches his arms around me when he's in range, and I find myself lifted, pulled up into Aloysius's embrace. He carries me up the steps and through the great doors, now open wide.

When we cross the threshold, Aloysius sets me down, and I slump against the massive doorframe. The door reminds me uncomfortably of the one that shut on me in the Seven Spires, but instead of the black of night outside, I see something almost as unsettling.

The crisp, pristine morning, with a slight breeze through the trees and rays of golden sun hitting branches all spread up a hill is frozen. *Almost* frozen. There's just enough movement in it to give me the sense that it's not a still image. Just enough that I can feel it, but not enough that I can consciously pick out anything that's actually changing as it does.

"He's all right," Aloysius says to me, leaning against the opposite doorframe, his pose a mirror to my own but relaxed and at ease rather than exhausted.

"And how long has he been all right?" I mean the words to bite at him, but I'm too tired to do it well.

"Only a year."

"*Only* a year," I say with as much spite as I can muster. I hate that I'm relieved. A year is too long, even if it's not as bad as I'd built it up to be in my head on the drive.

"Yes," Aloysius says, his voice rich and low. "Only a year. And if your goals are what I believe they are, and you succeed, a year of his lifespan will be proportionally small. And if you fail, he won't reach the end of his natural life in any case, and nothing has been lost."

The words are cold, but his voice is warm.

"Why?" I ask hoarsely.

"That wasn't the bargain. I said I would take him in, and we would have a conversation. You are so selectively courageous, my Elizabeth. So quick to jump at tigers, but even faster when you run away from words. Ask me the things you've wanted to know for a long time first, and I'll give you answers."

I open my mouth to protest, to find an excuse. This is a terrible time for this conversation. I'm in no fit state. But there's no *good* time for me to have a talk I don't want to. The man isn't wrong.

"Do they heal?" I ask. "When someone gambles their soul in your casino and loses some of it, does it grow back?"

Aloysius's eyebrows raise, and he gives me a delighted, appraising smile. "Yes. Slowly, to be sure. But eventually, they heal."

I breathe in, readjusting the towel tighter across my gills as they show the first signs of itching. It's going to be convenient to get rid of these things, but God, I wish I knew how Wilbur was going to take them from me so I could stop worrying.

"I don't think you'll like it. Trolls don't have much magic in that way. It's going to be knives and pain. I'm sorry for that."

My eyes go wide. "You can read my mind?" I don't know why I'm surprised.

"I can hear your prayers. It's part of you carrying my blessing. Some of my luck applies to you, and when you put a wish—or a hope—out into the world, it finds me."

My cheeks warm. Oh God, what kind of things have I been hoping for? I try to scan back over the last six months, hoping there's nothing too horrifying that I've unknowingly "prayed" for. And that, I realize too late, is a prayer in itself. One that I see hit Aloysius as he pulls himself up, closing the distance between us in three long strides.

"That's incredibly invasive," I mumble into the shrinking space between us. "I should have known that was happening."

He folds his arms across his chest, and I feel our already large difference in height keenly, leaning as I am and straight as he is. "I expected you to seek me out sooner. To come find me and ask. I didn't yet know the uneven edges of your courage."

I don't know what I'll say to Olivia. I don't know when I'll be able to say it. "I guess I could stand to do better at that."

Aloysius's crossed arms fall. He reaches out to touch his flower on my lapel, examining it closely as if he can see the blood I put on it in Atlantis, though it must have long since washed off in the ocean. "Most people could stand to do better at *something*. It is a close connection, and I can't answer your prayers directly. I'm not that kind of god. Your gambles are my worship, and to lend you more than the luck you rely on would be to taint that worship. But I can give you a safe haven when you need it. And I can pick up the pieces when you fail, as all eventually do. If that isn't enough, and you want to return my blessing, you can."

But would I survive it if he did? How many times has my use of his luck saved me just over the past day? And how many more times over the last six months? There's no reason to believe this is the first time Kristoff has set into motion an arbitration that might get me killed. He probably started smaller and scaled up until he got to apocalypse, and I've just been too goddamn lucky to notice.

It's all a part of the same decision—stay in this world

of wizards and danger or listen to Max and walk away. Humans don't survive here without accepting powerful help. Just ask Phoebe, if you can get her to focus long enough.

"No," I say. "I'll keep it."

Aloysius gives me a nod that manages to appear both solemn and affectionate, and I feel something seal between us.

"You asked why I kept Faisal here, knowing he would be here longer than intended and knowing that would anger you. I owe you an answer. You are the first priest I've had in a long time," he says, smoothing and consolidating my wild, half-wet hair. "He's important to you. You pray for him often. I thought I should know what sort of man he is. That doesn't happen in a conversation, or in an hour."

I try to form angry, hurt words to let him know he's overstepped, but I can't find them. "I'm your priest, am I?"

"Choose a different word, if you want to. It makes no difference to me. You are to me what you are to me. And you can be angry with me for my actions if you want, but I deem them fair. And it is my right to deem what is fair. Besides, you've had six months to get used to the world as it truly is. Faisal deserved some time to catch up."

I shake my head. "So you gave him twice as much time as I've had?"

Aloysius smiles. "You strike me as a fast learner. But Faisal has spent his time here well. We've had a lot of visitors. He'll be more useful to you now than he would have been before. You're welcome for that. It'll make it easier to keep him."

The anger that was starting to fade roars back to life. "Not all relationships are about what you can get from each other," I say, awash with bitterness.

Aloysius leans in close to me. "No," he says, the intent word and stare speaking to a thousand private thoughts I didn't know would be overheard, "they aren't. And you should remember that more often."

Aloysius grips both my shoulders for a moment with gentle hands before returning to his side of the doorframe. We lean across from each other again in silence for a moment. There are more things I could say—things I *should* say. But right now, words aren't coming easily. The lack of sleep, the physical exhaustion, the trauma of the last day—it's all catching up to me. It feels good just to be still. Just to look out over the almost-frozen forest, and search for sure signs of things that have moved. To breathe the smokey-sweet hookah air spilling out from the depths of the Casino. Eventually, Aloysius speaks again.

"If it matters to you—which it *should*—I approve of him."

It shouldn't, but it does.

"I believe he will suit your purposes well, Elizabeth."

I swallow and give him a smile and a half laugh that comes easier to me that I would have believed an hour ago. "Is that so? So are you going to steal him? Make *him* your priest?"

Aloysius's laugh has a warming quality to it, one stronger than I've encountered anywhere else. "No, certainly not. He suits *your* purposes. He wouldn't suit mine at all."

Aloysius beams at me, and I forgive him. You're not supposed to need to forgive your god. But of the two gods I've had any contact with, this one has done me much more good than harm.

"I think Poseidon is alive," I say.

Aloysius's eyes dart around, as though ensuring we aren't overheard. He nods once, almost imperceptibly.

"I think I angered him," I say, and Aloysius greets the words with a smile.

"That's not difficult to do. I'll give him a century or so to cool off, and then make our apologies."

A century. Such a different time scale. I'm not sure at first what makes me feel all warm and fuzzy about Aloysius saying those words. But then I put it together: *our apologies*. Of the people who know what my goals are, Aloysius is the only one who has ever said anything to make me think he believes I can do it. And survive.

"No way to speed up that process?" I ask. "I don't *want* to go swimming anytime soon, but most of the world is ocean. It could get inconvenient."

Aloysius tilts his head, and the morning light suits him. "I'll think on it." He looks out at the frozen world he's had so much more time to grow fond of. I see a love in his face I envy, though I can't tell what's behind it. The transparency in our relationship is remarkably asymmetrical. But then, our relationship as a whole is. Maybe that's okay. "And imagine," he continues, "all this trouble over nothing."

I sigh. "A dead nymph isn't nothing."

Aloysius's eyes glimmer. "A dead nymph isn't possible. Their bodies can be destroyed, sure, but they don't die. They only splinter into thought and light."

My eyes fly wide, and I swear Aloysius smirks as he sees the realization hit me. "In the ocean... those were the water nymphs?"

"Rebuilding themselves slowly, cell by scattered cell."

They weren't a single being. Or a swarm of millions. That's why they couldn't answer. They were a combination of different swarms, all mixed and thinking together. Multiple beings in millions of pieces but linking and thinking as one.

"Give it, oh, fourteen hundred years or so, and I'll see the Nymph of the North Wind again. She may not remember herself. None of them did last time. But it'll be her."

He's talking, but I'm staring dumbfounded out at the almost-frozen landscape.

"I don't agree with sirens on many things, but they get one thing almost right," Aloysius says, moving to me and putting a hand on my shoulder again. "They believe that worthwhile things don't change. In truth, worthwhile things don't give up, even if they have to change to keep going."

I look up at my god, tears brimming in my eyes, although I'm not sure exactly why. The whole day, maybe.

"Faisal has much to pack and many goodbyes to say. It'll be faster if you wait for him outside. You need to face what awaits you, and you need rest. You won't get that here. Not now."

He gives my shoulder a light squeeze, and I have the feeling of having been firmly—if affectionately—dismissed. I step forward across the threshold into the frozen world.

And then Faisal's voice—God help me, *Faisal's voice*—comes from the space beside me mere seconds later. "Beth," he says, simply.

I'm just about fall, but I catch myself, even as Faisal moves to catch me but can't with his arms full of luggage.

He looks good. I mean, I always think he looks good, but it's more than that. He looks healthy. Rested. Though I think I see something haunted in him that I'm hoping is my imagination. His normal folded garment bag is gone, replaced by a large red-and-gold duffel bag that looks well made, but isn't from any brand I recognize, and a few smaller pieces of luggage that match it looped over his shoulder and on his other arm. His clothes are pressed and gleam in the warm light of the morning. Silk pants and a silk shirt, embroidered with designs of jeweled flowers and onion domes. His hair is a little longer, and shaggy. He looks like he could have stepped out of the past—centuries ago.

And he's smiling. He's smiling warmly at me. Everything is going to be okay. He wraps his arms around me and pulls me close. I let the sodden beach towel that's been pressed against my gills fall away.

He holds me for a long time. I cry into him, though I'm not sure how I have tears left to give, even ones of joy. When he pulls back and looks at me, I see worry in his features, but he does me the favor of not asking about my many injuries and changes.

"I missed you," I say.

"I missed you longer," he says.

"I missed you more."

His smile breaks wider on his generous mouth, and he leans his forehead down to rest on mine. "Agree to disagree."

"If you're done trying to be adorable," Gigi's voice floats up from the bottom of the stairs, "I'm well ready to get out of Greece."

I nod and raise my head to look back into the Casino. But the great big wooden doors are closed to me, now, though I didn't see them shut.

"Thank God. Me, too."

THIRTY-FIVE

A Promise

Gigi agrees to bring Faisal through the crossroads this time without putting up a fuss. The journey is jarring to me, as it always is, even when I'm not such a mess. I keep an eye on Faisal, trying to tell if it's freaking him out. But he's unfazed. If anything, he looks relieved and interested to see the outside world. I guess after a year spent trapped in a casino, he's just glad for a change of scenery.

When we get to the familiar field that is the closest crossroads to Springfield, Gigi abandons us. Something about things to do while she's out. I don't ask further. She drops my hand and lets go of the crook of Faisal's arm and steps away into the crossroads, leaving us alone in the empty field.

Faisal closes his eyes and breathes deeply.

"I'm sorry," I say, reaching forward and taking his hand.

"You didn't mean to," comes his Zen reply.

I raise an eyebrow. "Yeah, but I should have known better. I was distracted."

Faisal accepts my hand and pulls me closer to him. "Given what was going on, if anything, *I* was the distraction."

"Yeah, but—"

Faisal laughs. "Beth, I was angry about it. I was *really* angry about it for a long time. But I got past it. We don't need to rehash right now."

He drops one of his bags, and I let him pull me against him again, wishing for home before realizing Aloysius must hear that longing. That's fine. I mean, it's weird as hell, but it's fine.

Times like this, it would be handy if there were a closer crossroads. An Uber is going to be pricey from here, if we can even get one to come. I start reaching for my phone, but Faisal squeezes my hand and motions with his head toward where the closest road is. As he does, I hear the sound of a closing car door.

I follow Faisal's gaze and see a heavyset man in a slightly-too-small suit standing next to a limousine. Wordlessly, Faisal and I walk toward him.

When we're within speaking distance, the driver asks, "Elizabeth Baker?"

I nod, and he opens the door for us.

"From Max?" I ask, trying to sound casual but hoping like hell it's Max rather than Kristoff. The driver nods, and then gets an awkward look on his face.

"I was told to say..." he trails off for a second, looking between Faisal and me. "He says 'sorry for the kiss.'"

Faisal gives me an inquisitive glance, and I roll my eyes.

"He thinks he's funny. I'll tell you later."

I expect we won't be able to speak freely until we get home, but I find the partition is already up when we slide into the back seat, and as we pull out on the road, I hear

loud, angry music thumping away up front. More instructions from Max, I suppose.

"So?" Faisal asks. I slide into him, accepting his arm
around my shoulders.

"A kiss was how Max took a couple hours of your
memory away yesterday."

"Yesterday," Faisal muses.

I give his hand a squeeze. "Yeah, yesterday."

He takes my hand, puts it on his left cheek, and shoots
me a questioning glance. I move our hands to his right
cheek, to where Max had kissed him. He nods once, and
then looks off into the far distance with a very clear *oh when
will my husband return from the war?* expression on his face. I
offer him the little laugh he's looking for, and he gives my
hand a quick kiss.

"Do you think he'll do it again?" he asks. And for the
first time since he appeared beside me, I detect an angry
edge in his voice.

"I yelled at him for it. He promised he wouldn't. So,
yeah. He probably will." My heart rate starts picking up. I
shouldn't do this now. I can't have this conversation now. I
need to wait. But I can't stop myself from saying the words
that come next. Maybe I've learned my lesson about
putting off necessary conversations. Or maybe I'm just
overcompensating. "If you're planning on sticking
around."

Faisal sighs, hurt in his eyes, and leans his head down
onto mine. "Of course I'm sticking around."

My cheeks flush. "This isn't what you signed up for."

Faisal lets that sit for a second. "I've had time to think.
Plenty of time. And even if I didn't love you, which you
seem determined to forget I do, it would be the right thing
to do."

The right thing to do? I'm not sure I follow entirely,

and Faisal must sense that because he continues without any prodding.

"When the Casino is running as fast as it was, there are a lot of things that like to come take advantage of the extra time. I met a lot of creatures over the past year. Some of them were amazing. Most of them were terrifying. And I don't think I met a single one that placed any inherent value on a human life."

A vision of the sirens' nests, and their great hulking Seven Spires of bones, flies up in my memory. And then so does Phoebe, scattered and full of fears she can't put a finger on.

"Wizards aren't much better," I add. "Or *any* better, even."

"Does that include Max?" Faisal asks.

I shake my head. "Not yet." I feel like there's something to add there, but I don't know what it is, so I continue on. "What about your experience with the monsters makes staying with me the right thing to do?" I think I get what he's saying, but I'm too tired right now to make the connections. I need him to spell it all out. The feeling of the movement of the car and the warmth of Faisal's arm around me is giving my last holdout of adrenaline the go-ahead to take the rest of the day off.

"Because what I hear about you, and how people *talk* about you, you have a chance to shake up the power structure. Give humans a place in it that we fight for and know about. Things *can't* stay as they are."

I close my eyes. "Shake things up, or die trying." It's half a joke. Sort of. But Faisal doesn't acknowledge any joke in it.

"Oh, I know. We're almost certainly going to die. But I can live in that *almost* with you. I can't be the man who wouldn't. It's worth trying. And if anyone has a chance, I believe it's you. I know I can't do magic. I get there are rules, and I don't have your exception, but I can help. I can be here. I can be someone you can trust. On one condition."

I open my eyes and shift around so I can see him a little better. I'm expecting his warm smile, and some kind of sweet rejoinder about his condition being a kiss, or—considering it's been a year since he's seen me—something considerably more when we get home and I've had a chance to clean up. But instead, I get a serious expression.

"What condition?" I ask.

He clenches his jaw and casts his eyes around the shiny leather interior of the car. "You know that scene in *Spider-Man*… or I guess there are scenes like it in all of those movies. But there's a busload of kids, and then there's his love interest. And he has to choose between the two. But he's Spider-Man, so he doesn't have to choose. He saves them both."

"Yeah," I say, not liking where this is going.

"I need you to promise me that if something like that comes up, you'll remember that you're not Spider-Man, and you'll make the right choice."

I blink a couple of times. A year to think, and he thinks of this? "I was kind of Aquaman earlier," I offer with a little smile, trying to pull one out of him. He only gives in a little.

"Different universe," he says. "Doesn't count." He holds my gaze for a long moment before he continues. "I'm serious, though. I need you to promise me. I can help, but I'm a weakness. I know that. And I wouldn't be strong enough to live with it, if you made the wrong choice for me."

I've been thinking a lot about lying lately.

"I promise," I say.

The warmth and generosity returns to his smile, and he kisses me deeply. I feel the desperation in him, the need for me that I would expect after so long apart. He pulls me in tighter. I *reeeaally* don't have the energy, but still. How long is this drive back into town? And how tinted are these windows?

I feel his hands on my hips, then on my waist. Then sliding higher on my abdomen.

He pulls back before it gets too heated. I shoot him a questioning look, and he glances between me and my gills. He's got a comically conflicted expression plastered on his face.

All the remaining energy, tension, and fear falls out of me in the uncontrolled laugh he's looking for.

"Sorry, you're into fish now," I say, collapsing into him. "I don't make the rules."

I bury my face in the strange, sweet, smokey scent that clings to him from the Casino. He says something back to me, some kind and funny words, but I don't hear them. I'm already lost to the safety of sleep and his arms.

THIRTY-SIX

A Price

____

When the limousine drops us home, Wilbur's car is in the driveway and the lights are on in the house. *Gills*, he'd circled on the paper. Now? He's going to take them *now*?

"What is it?" Faisal asks, his arm around me, supporting me as we walk toward the porch in what I hope is a non-obvious way.

"Remember I told you about Wilbur?"

Faisal thinks for a few seconds. I told him a year ago, from his perspective, I have to remind myself. "The troll?"

"Yup. I owe him for connecting me to Max to get me out of a jam. But I couldn't pay right away. I guess he's here to collect."

A shade of worry crosses Faisal's face. "Oh, you should get on that," he says. I don't know how long it's going to take me to get used to Faisal suddenly knowing more about some aspects of the supernatural than I do. It's not a flattering thing, my slight jealousy.

"Don't know why he couldn't wait until tomorrow," I mumble.

Faisal shakes his head. "It's not a choice he's making. It's cause and effect. It might set in by tomorrow."

The dropped calls. The failed texts. It's already starting. "Guess we'd better do it now, then." I give in, resigned. "But after I have a second to clean up."

Faisal helps me up the steps onto the porch. "Why?" he asks. "What did you promise him?"

Wilbur opens the door before I can answer. His expression is grim, which I'm glad about, to be honest. I watch his face and Faisal's face as I introduce them to each other. They both seem a little guarded but generally friendly. That's good, I guess. Better than the alternative.

Wilbur isn't warm and welcoming to me the way I've gotten used to over the last six months. Still mad, I guess.

Leaving a troll alone with my boyfriend isn't something I expected to be okay with, but he doesn't seem scared and it's Wilbur, so I let it ride. Wilbur lets me disappear away to the bathroom to clean the ocean off me, which I'm grateful for. And it'll probably help with avoiding infection, I'm guessing.

Or maybe not. Maybe Wilbur has some kind of magic way of taking what he's owed, whatever Aloysius may think. That would be nice, but I'm not hopeful. He seemed too grim for that. And he had something, I remember when I'm in the shower. On the table…

Knives. He had a set of knives in a leather carrying case. Wicked knives.

When I'm done in the shower, I put on pajama pants and my loosest shirt. Then I return to the bathroom and grab the shower curtain down off the hooks and bring it downstairs with me. There's going to be enough fallout from today. Don't need to add carpet cleaning to the list.

Faisal and Wilbur are sitting on the couch in the living room. I struggle to read the expression on either of their faces, but their body language isn't tense. Well, not until they see me. My eyes dart over to the table. Yup, knives. And a small torch, and a metal rod. I swallow hard and use the last of my energy to put on a brave face.

"Shower's free," I say to Faisal. I want to get a minute to talk to Wilbur alone and don't want Faisal to see what's about to happen more than I care if he actually showers. I stole the shower curtain, anyway, so it's a thin fiction. But Faisal picks up on it.

"I'll leave you to it," he says. And for a second, I think he's about to shake Wilbur's hand like a father would his daughter's prom date, but he doesn't.

Wilbur goes to the kitchen and rolls up his knives as I lay the shower curtain out on the floor. The pain from when my gills were made is too recent a memory not to eat at me, but I try not to dwell on it as I lie down.

Wilbur wanders back over with his knives in one hand and a cup of water in the other. He hands me the water, sets down the knives and fishes a pill from a pocket.

"It'll make it easier," he says. I sit up and accept his gift, swallowing it down and gulping the water in the glass with a thirst I didn't know I had. Wilbur gets the thick metal rod with a rubber handle out and starts heating it with a torch.

I wince in anticipation. Max'll fix it, and cauterizing the wound is a good way to keep me from bleeding out on my living room floor, I guess. But this isn't going to be pleasant. I'd be terrified if I had the energy, and if the familiarity of home weren't such a soothing balm. I hope whatever Wilbur just gave me is strong stuff. I have a feeling it will be.

"What are you going to use the gills for?" I ask, trying to break the ice and get us toward sorting out whatever his problem is.

"They're rare," he says without looking at me. It's not an answer, but I don't really care.

"Why are you mad at me?"

That gets a look, but no answer.

"Come *on*," I say. "It's been a long day, cut me a break. Why are you mad at me?"

Wilber shifts his gaze back to the metal he's heating, and I think I've failed. I cast around for something more convincing to say, but he eventually speaks before I come up with something.

"Everything has a price," he says. I wait, hoping he'll get a little more explicit. He does. "People have a price."

When was it exactly he got mad at me? I'd thought it was before we got into this whole siren mess, but maybe it wasn't. Maybe it was when I told him I was bringing in Gigi and Max. His face wasn't visible for that conversation, so it's harder to pinpoint.

WBBOM is written in ancient German, so I've had to get help translating some passages. I reached out for help with translating the entry on trolls, since I was so close to one and it seemed like a good idea to be better informed about them. The university professor who helped me translate it had a tendency to go all the way to casual, colloquial language with his translations, which struck me as a very intentional choice. He translated one sentence as follows: *Trolls, like all bullies, are essentially cowards.*

Coward is a pretty negative term. But then, I don't blame an ancient wizard for not having a very rosy view of trolls. Another word for cowardly is cautious.

"Sometimes the price is worth it," I say as Wilbur's eyes flick back to the metal rod.

"Sometimes," he answers, but he doesn't seem quite sure.

"I would have died if it weren't for Gigi and Max."

Wilbur grates his teeth. He was being metaphorical, and I went straight literal, and it's made him uncomfortable. I try to get back to his comfort zone.

"And what's my price?" I ask. "Isn't it pretty high?"

Wilbur considers, flicking his eyes in the direction Faisal has gone, although I wasn't thinking of Faisal when I said it. "Not all bridges lead to safe places," Wilbur says.

I try again to speak his language. "Some people are better at walking over dangerous bridges than others."

He looks my broken body up and down, and I stifle a laugh despite my growing nervousness about the heating metal rod, now changing color.

"Better is a relative term. As is *lucky*," I say meaningfully. I don't know if Wilbur understands Aloysius's true nature, but of all the people I know, he seems most likely to.

He doesn't answer right away. He seems to be considering something. My instinct is to blame him for not being more active—to point out that I wouldn't need to rely on those people he doesn't trust if he wouldn't just disappear so much of the time. But if there's one thing I've learned over the past day or so, it's that some people are more comfortable with changing who they are than others. And Wilbur will be as helpful as he can be to me. He's trying. The look on his face right now tells me that.

I take a big swing. "It's not the bridge's fault for leading to dangerous places, anyway."

The way Wilbur's eyes flick to me when I say that, and the haunted look on his face, tell me I guessed right. I reach out and give his arm a squeeze. And then a sudden wooziness hits me, and I blink as the world spins.

"Lie back," Wilbur says. "You're ready."

He gives me a wooden spoon from the kitchen—one Faisal and I bought from Walmart back in college and have hung onto through several moves—to bite down on. It makes me feel like an old-timey pirate, and I feel a laugh come out of somewhere that is both inside me and disconnected from me at the thought of Wilbur with an eyepatch and a peg leg.

I feel something sort of ticklish on my abdomen, and look down to see a strip of flesh—gills, some distant part of me recognizes—being lifted out of me and slid unceremoniously into the now-empty cup that the water had been in.

My eyes are still on the red flesh of the gill and the way the blood mingles with the vestiges of water in the cup, when white-hot pain shoots through me and a strangled cry makes its way around the wooden spoon in my mouth.

And then my head is raised up and laid on something soft. Faisal's face, upside down and kind, fills my view. I'm in his lap. He's saying words to me. Comforting words I catch in bits and pieces. I hold on to the sight and sound and smell of him, swimming above me, and push the pain away.

A long time later—was it a long time?—when the cup is full of gills and I'm less than I was, I feel myself lifted, and carried, and laid in something familiar.

"It's okay now," Faisal's voice comes to me from far away.

Finally, it's time to rest.

THIRTY-SEVEN

A Friend

I wake up thirsty and with a pounding headache in the bedroom I share with Faisal, the afternoon light pouring in through the window. I've got that backward feeling you sometimes get when you've gotten out of sync with the normal diurnal flow. But that's far from a worst-case scenario, so I can't say I really mind. Faisal isn't here with me, but I guess I don't know what his sleep schedule is. If I'm out of sync with the world, how much more is he?

My fingers trace to my abdomen, where I find bandages and pain. Taking stock, I find more pain, though not nearly as much as I should by rights. From top to bottom we have: headache, wrenched arms, cut hand, burned hand, excised and cauterized gills, boiled legs.

It's not ideal. My eyes shift to my nightstand where I usually plug my phone in, and I find it there. A quick check shows me what I'm hoping for: a text from Max.

Made it back. Tried to text you earlier, but it wouldn't go through. Troll? Come over when you're ready for these healing hands.

There's an emoji of hands in the praying gesture after

it. If I had the energy, I'd comment that it's thankfully not his hands that do the healing. Probably a good thing I don't have the energy to do that, since I'm getting a huge favor from him.

In fact, I should probably do something nice. Or helpful. Whatever. My jacket is lying on an armchair we keep in the bedroom because it makes us feel fancy, despite the fact that neither of us ever use it. I fish out the scroll from the Seven Spires covering Max's wizard ancestor's life. When Gigi glanced over it quickly before I fell asleep in the back of the car, she said it looked like bits and pieces—the significant deals he'd made with supernatural creatures, maybe. It does have a section with a drawing that *has* to be a spell, though. Gigi didn't bother translating it, and if it's from Max's wizard lineage, he probably already knows it or will learn it anyway. But it can't hurt. I unfold the paper and send Max a series of photos.

I wander out to look for Faisal. He's in our home office, which is, as always, a bit of a mess. He's working on the laptop he used in college that he upgraded away from as a graduation present. He must have lost the one he had during his year in the Casino.

"Trying to remember everything you used to know?" I say, and Faisal just about jumps out of his skin.

He didn't use to startle easily. What has the last year been for him? But he smiles when he sees it's me. "Something like that. How are you feeling?"

I put a melodramatic hand over my heart. "Like a hero. Unfortunately."

He smiles again. It warms me. "Is whatever Wilbur gave you still working?" he asks.

I shake my head. "Only partially. Gonna go take care of that, though. Max knows a healing spell."

Faisal goes to close his laptop. "I'll drive you."

"Oh, no, thank you. I'd feel better if you don't get anywhere near Max until we work out an amulet for you." I can't read what crosses Faisal's face when I say that. I used to be able to read everything there.

"But you'll be safe?" he asks.

My hand goes to my amulet. "Always." I smile at him. "Be back before you know it."

He stares at me for a long moment, another expression on his face I can't read. I'm not used to this. I resent the year of his that was taken from me. I resent the thousand ways it must have changed him that I haven't had long enough to find out yet.

"Olivia called to tell us your mom was found wandering around on the beach. She wants to know what happened in Boston. Hell, *I* want to know what happened in Boston."

Shit, Boston. I've been so busy being relieved I forgot the problem that started it all is still there, festering.

"I'll tell you later today. Catch you up on everything. Fill in every blank you can think of."

Faisal nods, but he isn't satisfied. "You should tell Olivia, too. I was looking at the trove earlier. You know she could help with it."

A spike of fear sticks in my chest, and I see Faisal read it plain as day. He still knows me. He didn't miss a year of my life. "I can put her off for a while, and I'll let that happen for now. But she's going to find out. You should make it sooner rather than later. One day you'll learn it's easier that way."

"It isn't safe," I say.

"Nothing is," Faisal replies. "She was your father's daughter, too. She has as much right to the trove as you do."

"I never said I had a right to it," I grumble.

Another expression I can't read crosses Faisal's face. With effort, he turns back to his laptop.

I put on a bra, stay in my pajama pants, and head out to the car. Just before I head out the door, I take a moment to peek out the front window, to see if Mr. Thompson, my neighbor, is there, so I can avoid him. In the wake of the emotional upset from the last few days, the feelings I have as I make the check stand out more starkly than they usually do.

There's fear, there, that I'll run into him. And a feeling of betrayal, and guilt over that feeling. I let out a harsh breath that triggers pain, even through Wilbur's drugs.

All this time, my fear that Faisal would leave when he found out seemed so justified. But it wasn't. And it's only just *now* occurring to me that my unfair assumption might have had nothing to do with Faisal.

Mr. Thompson—Henry—had been my ally six months ago. The lone human in-the-know with me. The victim, along with my mother, of my father's choices. And when given the choice, Henry had let Max take the memories of the supernatural from him. I can't blame him for that—he deserved peace. But the fact that he made that choice still cuts at me. Maybe I can let it go, now that I'm willing to look at the feeling of betrayal it for what it is. Maybe not. But it seems like it'll be easier now that I know for certain that Henry's choice isn't the one Faisal will make. It wasn't something I should have let color my perception. And it probably wouldn't have, if I'd been willing to look at it straight, instead of hiding behind excuses.

Excuses like the ones I'm making to avoid telling Olivia. Maybe Faisal's right—I should tell her sooner, rather than later. But I'm not telling her today.

I head out to the car and make my way over to Max's expertly restored Victorian cottage at Eighteen Mayflower

Way. He greets me at the door, doubtless warned by the wards he has around his house that compel him to go see what's happening and when someone approaches.

"You're looking well," he says with a shiny smile on his face. I return it as best I can, which isn't much.

"Did you get my message?" I ask, sliding by him into the house. Max doesn't have protective wards around his house to keep people who mean the owner harm from entering, the way I do. Even if he did, I would be able to enter them.

Most of the time. Probably. But he can never enter mine, so that's not worth quibbling over.

"Yeah," he says, closing the door. "I'll translate more of it later. But most of it just looked like a history of deals he'd made?"

I wander into the living room, and he follows behind. I just woke up, but I'm still exhausted. The sooner we get this done with, the better. I wander toward the table where he healed me last time. I don't want to stay long in the living room. Too many bad memories associated with it.

"It looks like there's spell in there, too. Don't know what it is, but hey, a spell for a spell. That's fair, no?"

Max hesitates, but then follows me. "I guess that's fair. Don't go assuming it's a precedent, though."

"Oh, you know me. I never assume."

Max laughs, but his enthusiasm fades as he looks over my body. "You're a mess," he breathes.

"It's been a shitty few days."

"I told you not to let my masters know who you are. I told you that six months ago."

He had. But I hadn't had much of a choice at the time. I don't dig that old wound open—I've got enough new ones to deal with at the moment. I shrug, instead. "I'm alive."

"Not everyone is."

I can't be held responsible for that. That's not my fault —not really. But I don't argue the point with him. The way he said it was soft, like it was more for him than it was for me. I get a feeling it's a long-running internal debate of his, and my presence when he said it was incidental.

"Do you think he'll try again?" I ask, and Max lets out a harsh little laugh.

"Oh, he'll try again. Kristoff always tries again. It'll be hard, though. Keeping it from Moira is tricky, and now that I know, he'll need to get rid of you in such a way that I won't have any evidence that he knew and kept it from her. As long as there's no evidence and it's my word against his, she'll take his. But he'll have to be sneaky with it. He's going to have to go through a lot of effort. I don't think he wanted me to know, but he'll still get rid of you even now that I do."

"Seems like he went through a lot of effort *this* time. He made a net that went all the way over the Seven Spires."

Max shrugs. "That's not too much effort. He probably just made a little piece and duplicated it a bunch of times."

"You can do that?"

Max smirks. "No, but he can."

"They're still teaching you things." I say it softly. I mean a lot behind it. I mean "that's how they keep you trapped." I mean "that's their trick." I mean "that's the hook they have in you." He hears it all.

"Yeah. That's how it works. About twenty-four to fifty-ish is considered wizard adolescence, in some ways. They give me a lot of rope. I'm expected to rebel a little, but I'm not free. Not really."

He puts on a weird, Nordic-sounding accent and says,

"But what is freedom if you don't use it?" He looks at me for a reaction, but I don't have one to give him.

"I didn't actually meet Kristoff," I explain. "He sent Phoebe."

Phoebe. Poor Phoebe. Max's eyebrows rise. "You met Phoebe?" He seems... pleased?

"Yeah, why?"

He shrugs. "She's lasted longer than most. Good for her."

So casual. I don't know what to say. At my stunned expression, Max looks unsure of himself—something novel in a day of novelties. "Kristoff and Moira aren't good at it."

"What?"

"Mind magic. They're bad at it. They're just... there's a natural inclination, and they don't have it."

"And you're good at it?"

The earnestness of Max's expression makes me uncomfortable. "I'm fantastic at it. I could never do to anyone what they did to Phoebe. Not unless I wanted to. And I wouldn't want to."

A long moment passes between us, in different worlds. I'm thinking of what Phoebe said—of the distance Max needs to have to survive and be accepted. The distance I'll take from him—the distance he deserves not to have to carry. It must read as doubt, because Max sinks into himself and goes somewhere else—somewhere I don't know about and can't follow.

"Do you want to start with your arm?" he asks eventually, his voice tight.

I shake my head and maneuver myself painfully up onto the table, grateful for whatever of Wilbur's pill is left in my system. "Let's start with the big one first. Get it out of the way."

I lift up my shirt to reveal the gauze taped across my abdomen, and Max's expression darkens. He goes to a drawer in the kitchen to retrieve some scissors and returns intent but worried. He cuts off the bandage and reveals what's left of my body—gills excised and burned. Jesus, it looks bad. It looks so much worse than in my snatches of memory.

Max is frozen, staring at the wounds with an eerie stillness.

"What did this?" he asks, carefully expressionless.

I'm on the defensive, and that's not fair. It's enough that I've suffered the injury—I shouldn't need to justify it. "I had gills for a bit. Wilbur required them as payment for getting me in touch with you when I was in the Seven Spires."

Max's gaze flicks up to meet mine, his eyes an intense green. "The troll did this?"

"The troll saved my life, and then he took the gills I had no way of dealing with. Could you have removed them?"

Max stares at me for longer than is comfortable, his face twisted in anger. With three great heaving breaths, it melts into pleading. "I can get you back under the treaty. If you let me, I can do it. I swear, I can."

The sense of betrayal is familiar, but exposed as I am, it's overwhelming. "The treaty doesn't protect humans."

"I promise it'll protect you."

"That isn't good enough." I look down at the burned mess. "Are you going to patch me up?"

I don't look up at Max's harsh voice to see the harsh expression that must match it. "I shouldn't," he says. "I should make you deal with the consequences of your actions. That's the only thing that's going to convince you. You won't learn if I don't let you."

When I do look up at him, the anger isn't there anymore. He looks resigned—almost as tired as I felt yesterday. "So should I leave, then?"

He motions with his head for me to lie down on the table, and I do. He heals my wounds, speaking magic words over them quietly so that I can't hear them. When he's done with my abdomen and moves on to the others, I tell him how I got each one, leaving nothing out. I speak quietly, like an apology. He calls me an idiot, warmly.

By the time he's finished, I just feel tired and a little achy. There are no remaining traces of the day's adventure on me. My only scars are from a time I fell off my bike, and from a wound I got six months ago that he didn't heal fully. Max, for his part, seems a little tired as well. Healing takes something out of him. Good to know.

He stands in the doorway as I head out onto the porch. I turn back when I'm down a few steps and see him leaning at an angle, long body off kilter with the lines of the house.

"I'm your first friend, aren't I? Your first real friend, who knows anything true about you?"

His face crumples up, and he searches for words. "What does that even mean?" he asks after a second.

"Yeah," I say. "I thought so." I turn and start moving toward the car again. "See you Monday? Nine a.m.?"

"You know, I've always thought ten was a much more reasonable time to start the day."

"Nine thirty, got it." I say over my shoulder, seeing that Max has taken a few steps out onto his porch.

"Nine forty-five, best I can do."

I drive back home and manage to put off checking the recording on my phone of our session until I'm sitting safely at the kitchen table, behind the wards and facing away from any windows. I don't think there's a new spy on me yet, but it's good to be cautious.

The recording is gobbledygook and static. Apparently the come-and-see wards aren't the only protections Max has in place around his house. I'll have to try to get him to heal me somewhere else next time to get a decent recording of the spell. I'll have to look for an excuse.

"What's wrong?" Faisal asks. He's standing a few feet away. He looks stronger than he did when he went into the Casino, I notice now that I'm not distracted by my own injuries.

"Nothing important," I say, smiling with one side of my mouth. "But do you want see something cool?"

A smile plays around the corners of his lips. "Sure."

I reach out and form a magical connection to grab my keys on the counter. Then I change my Right Mind and shift my gesture the way Max showed me in the Seven Spires. The keys come flying to my hand.

I start giggling wildly, relieved and amazed at how easy it is now, after so many thousands of failed attempts. Faisal's laughing, too. And then he's close to me, leaning down and kissing me.

"That's pretty cool," he says, heat in his voice.

I kiss him back. I kiss him back for the rest of the afternoon.

When Olivia decides that something should happen, it happens quickly and efficiently. Less than a week after Mom was returned to the beach the sirens took her from, Olivia, Peter, Faisal, and I are all down in Florida, emptying out Mom's condo and loading up a moving container, slated to be delivered to an apartment above the Emporium. An apartment which just so happened to be available for below the market rate. I don't know how Gigi managed to figure out that my mom would be moving up here or got the ad in front of Olivia. I'm choosing to believe it's a favor. I will choose to do so right up until I find out what the real reason is. I'll die of worry if I don't.

Partway through packing, Faisal calls me into the kitchen, where he's loading up the contents of the fridge and freezer into a cooler for us to bring back separate from the moving truck.

"What is it?" I ask, keeping my voice low in response to the look on his face. He's got a jam jar in his hand, something red and frozen inside of it. I walk forward and examine a label, written on that strange kelp-based paper and tied on with a string that looks to have been fashioned from seaweed.

For the Arbiter. What has been promised should be delivered.

"Siren blood," I whisper, remembering the Pacific queen's idle promise. I didn't know the Atlantic tribe knew she promised me that, but it must have been them.

"Why? What's it good for?" Faisal matches my whisper.

"No idea," I say. "Maybe keep it at the bottom of the cooler. We should hold on to it. Just until we figure it out."

It turns out in the end that Olivia's efficiency was, as it very often is, a godsend. A few days after we get Mom moved, a freak flash flood washes away her whole condo complex. Poseidon's idea of justice is harsher than mine. Three of my mother's former neighbors die. I try not to wear those deaths too heavily around my neck. I try to let them be overwritten with the lives that my actions likely saved. It doesn't work well. Lives don't balance out that way.

But the words only come closest to working when they come out of Faisal's mouth.

───

A few days after that, I get a package in the mail with a Boston postmark. I do *not* bring it inside the wards. Instead, I open it out in the middle of the yard, with only my amulet-bearing self in close proximity. It turns out to be a cheap USB drive, nothing else.

I bring it to Wilbur's bridge, and he informs me, once he's done a full analysis, that there are two files on the USB drive. One is a video, apparently from a security camera, of someone who looks very much like me stealing a very expensive boat from a marina in Boston. The other is a README file that has two words in it: *You're welcome.*

Wilbur confirms, through his own methods for which I compensate him promptly, that the security system that the footage was from has no trace of me on the date and time when I should appear. Kristoff. Has to be. He's trying to act like he's done me a favor, but I'm not always that naïve. Boston is his territory, and it's his job to keep it clear from any evidence of magic, and I used a magic key to steal the boat. This doesn't need a response, and I am not indebted to him, however relieved I may be that there's no evidence of the crime.

While I'm talking to Wilbur, he informs me that he's moved the trove to a different server. Apparently, the one he had it on had some logon attempts when I didn't have his pen in my hand.

"Max had his hands on my phone for a while," I admit, and he gives me a heavy sigh.

"I'm not angry, just disappointed," he says with a reassuring joviality. He's accepted that I'm going to do dangerous things with dangerous people. We're all right.

And then he throws my phone over the side of his bridge without a moment's hesitation, completely ruining the moment. "I'll give you a list of the easiest-to-secure phones. That one was old, anyway," he says.

I file that under *Unfortunate* and move on.

The next week, I'm doing dishes in the middle of a Saturday afternoon, when I hear a voice with a Greek accent.

"Arbiter," it says, and I barely catch myself before I dunk a plate into the side of the sink for rinsing, right through the face of Zosime that floats there, semi-transparent.

"Zosime," I say, not sure what else I *can* say. "It's you."

She gets a confused look on her face, and it occurs to me that I really shouldn't say statements that could be misconstrued as such very difficult questions.

"You're alive," I say, to get her to move on. "But how are you talking to me? I thought you were in the sky. The trident only works in the ocean."

Her eyes sparkle. "What is a cloud but an ocean misplaced?"

Soapy water drips from the plate in my hand, starting to form a little puddle on the linoleum, but I don't mind. I take in her joy—the brightness of her features. "Have they made you a wind nymph?"

Her smile may or may not actually glow—it's hard to be certain. "Wind *god*," she says. "My new sisters each fed me one of their arms. I'm so many in me now."

That's unnerving as fuck, but she looks happy. She didn't before. "Are their arms going to grow back?"

Zosime gives me a shrug, and I look for any signs her face has shifted to look more like the eerily similar faces of the other wind gods. I don't find any. She looks like she looked before, under the illusion, and my glasses are a room away. No way to tell what she might look like through them.

"None of us know, but they don't mind. We're whole. We're right in ourselves again. I'm here to thank you, and to tell you we owe you a favor for that."

I nod slowly, thinking of the Pacific queen. I should feel worse about taking her child from her and throwing her up in the sky. Maybe. I haven't been able to parse that out. I haven't tried as much as I should.

"What happened to Aleko's body? Have you returned it to his family?"

At that, the first thing resembling sadness crosses

Zosime's face. But it's not the disheartened, broken sadness I'd seen there before. It's more wistful—melancholy, maybe.

"I keep his bones with me," she says, "carried on the north wind. I was his trapped princess in a tower, as he saw it. He was my brave prince come to rescue me, as he saw it. I thought he was wrong. I thought he was stupid. I know better now. I've changed and I can feel what he felt. I believe it would bring him joy that I am the one to keep him and remember."

Her joy returns, tempered with the memory of missed opportunity, giving it depth.

"Four favors," I say.

"What?"

"There are four of you. You are together, but you are each your own. I am owed four favors by the winds."

I feel ridiculous in my bare feet, soap suds on my hands, bargaining with newly minted gods. But Zosime doesn't seem to see how small and absurd I am. She only narrows her eyes, looks at the people around her out of the frame of the sink, and then returns her gaze to me with a new respect.

"We owe you four favors," she says, and is gone.

I give it a solid minute before I start the dishes again, just in case. And in that time, I think of how sad it is that Aleko will never know what became of the girl he died for.

The nice thing about magic—or the terrible thing—is that there's a spell for everything. And my trove may only have a small fraction of them, but a small fraction of a near-infinity is still a hell of a lot.

I find the spell. I do my best with the power of the

internet to translate the spell. And about a month later, I'm ready to test it. I'm sitting up in the attic, hunched over an elaborate circle pattern traced in pig's blood. The circle itself is fully in the area of the attic that hangs out over the porch. It's in the house, sort of, but it's beyond the line of the wards since the porch isn't over the basement. I figure this means that I can do this privately, and where I can easily retreat to the safety of the wards if the ghost I'm attempting to summon turns out to be dangerous.

And even if I weren't a romantic at heart, just dying to facilitate a conversation between Aleko and Zosime, learning how to summon the dead seems like a good idea. Apparently, word has gotten around that the arbiter doesn't just make decisions—she also gets to the bottom of the situation in order to make her decisions. I've noticed a disturbing trend toward my arbitrations getting a little trickier and a little less straightforward lately. Usually, it isn't murder—supernatural creatures take the loss of immortal lives much more seriously than the loss of mortal lives, since they are bound to last much longer. But it seems like only a matter of time until being able to commune with a spirit is going to come in handy.

After all, how much better would it have been if I could have just gone to where it happened, summoned Aleko then, and asked him why he did it? I don't know for sure that it would have avoided me angering Poseidon the way I did, but the chance seems higher, and a higher chance of a positive outcome is all I can ask for.

Plus, if the summoner's desires have any effect on which spirit they call up, I might end up getting to talk to my dad here as my little test. And I wouldn't mind that. I have some questions to ask him, too.

The pig's blood had been awkward but easy to source. I told the local butcher that I was making blood sausage. I was pretty nervous about asking, but I think the only thing that creeped him out or made him suspicious was how weird I was being about it.

The stencil to make the circle had been easy enough to create, too. I programmed it into the Cricut cutter in segments, and then glued them together.

The trickiest part, by far, was the incantation. But the more I listened to the recording I'd made months ago of Max performing a long, death-related spell, the more possible it began to feel. And when I tried to transcribe it as phonetically as I could, I recognized that all of the phrases for summoning a departed spirit were thankfully also in Max's spell from the graveyard. I just had to pull them out, edit them together, get into Right Mind—a state of unassuming hope—and repeat the words exactly as he'd said them.

That's still a tall order, though, and I end up playing the stitched-together recording on my laptop, and attempting to repeat the words for hours. So when a huge, squealing mass of swine comes barreling toward me out of the circle after attempt number nine hundred and seventy-two, I don't have the reflexes to get all the way out of the way. I end up sprawled on the attic floor, unable to stop the pig running around the attic, squealing and screaming.

A physical form. I thought I was summoning a spirit, but apparently it brought a body with it. And that body is massive. And terrified. And in my house.

I have no weapons. Why would I keep a weapon on hand for summoning a spirit? But as the pig comes around and barrels back toward me, I do the only thing I can think of in the moment. I lick my finger, reach into the circle, and rub down hard on the mostly dried blood, trying to smudge it and hoping to God that it works.

Yes, Aloysius, I'm summoning ghosts. Don't judge. You're not that kind of a god.

My guess is correct. The life drains from the pig's eyes as soon as the circle is disturbed, and it tumbles under its own momentum, stopping a couple of feet away from me, dead as a doornail.

I stare, dumbfounded. Even the sound of Faisal scurrying up the attic ladder and coming to sit next to me doesn't pull my gaze. It's not until I see his outstretched hand in my peripheral vision that I come back into myself.

I pull out my wallet, take out a twenty-dollar bill, and set it in his hand. He pulls it taught and examines it with manufactured pride.

"Gotta be human blood," he says brightly.

"Gotta be human blood," I allow. I reach forward and poke the body of the pig. It hasn't disappeared or started fading. It's as real and solid as anything else in the room.

"Do you think we could eat it?" I ask, and Faisal's answering chuckle bounces off the walls.

"As long as we never tell my parents we personally slaughtered a pig." His chuckle fades. "Oh. You actually want to try."

I flash him what I really hope is a winning grin. I always want to try.

The End

About the Author

Amanda Creiglow lives in Rhode Island with her little Pitbull and too many projects. She enjoys writing music, playing video games, and building things she probably shouldn't.

Visit her website to sign up for her mailing list at www.author.amandacreiglow.com.

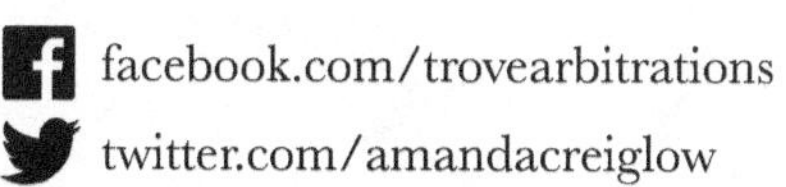

facebook.com/trovearbitrations

twitter.com/amandacreiglow

instagram.com/amandacreiglow